SUMMER NIGHT

ON

FRENCHMEN

STREET

CHRIS CLARKSON

Tu Books

An Imprint of LEE & LOW BOOKS, Inc.

New York

TU BOOKS, an imprint of LEE & LOW BOOKS Inc.,
95 Madison Avenue,
New York, NY 10016
leeandlow.com

Manufactured in the United States of America
Printed on paper from responsible sources

Edited by Stacy Whitman
Book design by Sheila Smallwood
Typesetting by ElfElm Publishing
Book production by The Kids at Our House
The text is set in Galliard MT Pro

10 9 8 7 6 5 4 3 2 1
First Edition

Library of Congress Cataloging-in-Publication Data

Names: Clarkson, Chris (Christopher Anthony), 1985- author.
Title: That summer night on Frenchmen Street / Chris Clarkson.
Description: First edition. | New York : Tu Books, an imprint of Lee & Low
Books Inc., [2022] | Audience: Ages 14 and up. | Audience: Grades 10-12.
| Summary: "Two teens from vastly different worlds discover that sharing
their strengths, including the love of their friends and family, may
just be the path to finding wholeness within themselves"—Provided by
publisher.
Identifiers: LCCN 2021056443 | ISBN 9781643795010 (hardcover) | ISBN
9781643795034 (ebk)
Subjects: CYAC: Dating (Social customs)—Fiction. | Friendship—Fiction. |
Twins—Fiction. | Brothers and sisters—Fiction. | African
Americans—Fiction. | Family life—Louisiana—Fiction. | New Orleans
(La.)—Fiction. | LCGFT: Novels.
Classification: LCC PZ7.1.C59435 Th 2022 | DDC [Fic]—dc23
LC record available at https://lccn.loc.gov/2021056443

For Kristen and Tyler Rose

1
JESSAMINE
2016

Solange's snakeskin pumps were abandoned by the door, one standing proud, and the other playing possum on its side. Beside her, crumpled in a heap of lavender and lace, was the dress we shopped for on Magazine Street last week. The dress that she had been so thrilled to find.

"Excuse me, ma'am. You sashayed in here serving body and hair teased to the gods. Why did you change? I demand an encore! Body. Dress. Wig. Grace." I pointed at the sad taupe button-down shirt she was wearing. "Put your high heels back on and act like you got some common sense."

Solange wiped at her tears. "Jess, I'm not in the mood to fool with you."

"Good, I'm not in the mood to fool with you either." I sank down on the floor beside her. She sniffled and wiped at her nose. "Why'd you change?"

"Why did you take down all the pictures of me on your wall?" she challenged, pointing to the collage of photos of my nearest and dearest on the wall. "I see you don't love me anymore either."

When she got to self-pitying, Solange had two modes: wallow for hours, or attack everyone who dared to get close. "Those pictures are five hundred years old. You've glowed up."

She had glowed up quite a bit. A year ago, she would've worn a taupe button-down shirt and tie to Commander's Palace for dinner to please everyone else.

Her stony expression cracked a little. She almost smiled.

"It's not that deep," she said. Solange adjusted the collar of the taupe button-down. "It's just a stupid birthday lunch. I'll donate this monstrosity after it's done."

"Solange"—I took her hand—"what happened to being unapologetic? Unapologetic was a big mood last week. This shirt isn't even your style. Don't leave the house like this. People will see you."

She pulled her hand back.

"S, you worked way too hard to feel comfortable in your skin. Those snakeskin pumps you got from the Thrift and Grab on Claiborne are cute. If you don't wear them today, when will you wear them?" I clapped my hands like a cheerleader. "Get dressed and let's go."

She sucked her teeth. "Ain't nobody get nothing from the Thrift and Grab." Solange's dark brown eyes stared straight through me. "It's not as easy as you're makin' it out to be. I know you got my back, cuz. You always do. I appreciate you for that, but there's a lot going on with my mama. This is *her* birthday lunch, and I don't know if we're going to be able to do this again next year. Ugh, I hate talking about this. Even when I'm trying to do me, she find a way to make it about her!" Solange bent her head and cradled it in her hands. "Her being sick changes everything. I don't know how long she's got."

"But . . ."

"But *nothing*," Solange snapped. The glitter around her eyes sparkled. She was still wearing the red lipstick we picked out at Sephora. I had bought the same shade because it paired well with dark skin with golden undertones.

She looked so pretty. Like me, Solange had inherited the best of the Blanchard genes. Large dark brown eyes, oval-shaped face, prominent cheekbones and a high forehead, and long legs and a long neck. She had always looked like royalty to me. I wished that she saw what I saw.

Solange asked me if I was ready for senior year. It came out of nowhere, a weak attempt at trying to change the subject. But I couldn't just sit back and stay silent. Yes, Auntie Myrtle was sick. But Solange had waited for *years* to live her truth. She walked on eggshells around her mama, shrinking back every time Auntie Myrtle threw a fit—and when it came to throwing a fit, Auntie Myrtle secured a spot in the *Guinness Book of World Records.*

Yes, she was sick. Yes, that was sad. But no, that did not mean Solange had to keep putting her life on hold. She was twenty-two years old and she deserved to live and be happy. And if that meant Auntie Myrtle didn't get her way? So. Be. It.

"Auntie Myrtle has to do the work, too," I said.

Solange rolled her eyes all the way back in her head. "I don't want to talk about this anymore. When she's gone, I'll be free. I won't have to worry about what she thinks. Cuz, I'm picking my battles. This is Grown-Ass Woman shit. Mess little girls don't understand."

When she didn't like what I had to say, I was a "little girl." When it came to dating and choosing a college, I was a "woman." Pick a lane!

"S, do you remember the first time you wore a wig outside?"

"I do," she said, nose turned up in the air. "It was a bad wig. That thing made my head itch."

I laughed.

Her eyes flashed like lightning in my direction. "You picked it out. You picked out the faux pas itchy wig."

I bit down on my lip to control my laughter. "I don't wear wigs. I didn't know better."

Solange leaned forward and sifted her fingers through my shoulder-length ebony curls. "I told you I was going to get you back by chopping off your hair while you were sleeping and making my own wig."

"You're so mean." I swatted her hand away.

She exhaled sharply. Her eyes drifted back toward my collage of photos. She seemed really sad about that, which was my fault. I had taken down the photos of her with a fresh fade and St. Aug sweater. And the photo of her with her ex-boyfriend Marcus, whom I really liked. She wasn't *Solange* in any of those photos. She was Darin. And Darin always had a little bit of sad in her eyes.

"What y'all doing in here sitting around?" Mama asked.

Solange looked just over my head, "Hey, Auntie Jo."

"Hey, baby, I love that shirt," Mama said, selling lies.

I rolled my eyes. Thankfully my back was facing her. "I don't like it."

"And no one asked for your opinion," she said. "Darin, we need to leave in about ten minutes. If Jessamine isn't ready, she can stay on home with her attitude."

Me and my attitude turned around to look at Mama. She was standing at the door, curlers in her hair and makeup almost done. She was wearing her favorite satin slip. *"Solange,"* I corrected.

Mama acted like I didn't speak. She looked down at her

phone and nodded. "I just got a text from JoJo. He's picked up Auntie Myrtle, and they're on their way to Commander's Palace. Ten minutes."

It frustrated me that Mama still called her Darin. Every time she did it I corrected her. But she still did it. My twin brother, the favored child, also corrected her. It was like she purposely ignored us.

"Darin, please be on your best behavior at brunch. I know that you and your mama have your differences. You're grown and I can't tell you what to do, but this is your mama's birthday brunch, and we don't know how many more she's got left. Show her some compassion."

Show Auntie Myrtle compassion? What was Mama smoking? Why couldn't Auntie Myrtle show *Solange* some compassion? How about we started there?

Once Mama was gone, I turned back to Solange and her sad button-down. That taupe disaster was not joining us for brunch. "This is the last thing that I'm going to say."

Solange sighed dramatically. "Now I know you're lying. You always got something to say. Talking about some *last.*"

My middle name was Grace for a reason. I could give grace when people needed it. I ignored her medium-rare dig. "We know that Auntie Myrtle is going to fuss anyways. Even if you wear *that,* she's going to fuss. So why not give her something to fuss about?"

⸺⧸⬦⧹⸺

When Auntie Myrtle saw Solange strut into Commander's Palace in her curves-waist-hips dress, snakeskin pumps, and lioness mane of big hair—she. howled. It was like a scene straight out of that old movie *The Exorcist.*

Mama shot me (the conspirator) and Solange (the co-conspirator) a salty look and rushed over to douse Auntie Myrtle in holy water. I tried not to burst out laughing. Auntie was cutting up so terrible, cursing and spitting, that all the white folks were looking at us. They were wide-eyed and clutching pearls. I think the fact that they were looking at "the Blacks" made both Auntie Myrtle and Solange act up more. Both were already natural-born performers.

The jazz band continued to play in the background. The musicians rocked to the tune of trombones and clarinets, and a piano player was bent over the keys, head bobbing along to the song coming from his piano. Every now and then he would look out at the audience and grin wide.

The people around us tapped their hands on the white table-cloths and their feet on the floor. Waiters moved from table to table to the rhythm of the music. Mixed in with the easy jazz was the scrape of knives and forks digging into biscuits and gravy.

"Myrtle!" Mama held out her arm. "Calm down. We came here to celebrate your birthday, not raise hell and act like we don't have common sense!"

"Take me home!" Auntie Myrtle screamed. "I don't want to celebrate a damn thing with *him* showing up here looking like a freak!"

The pronoun is her. I linked arms with Solange. Even if I wasn't getting in the middle of their fight, I wanted it to be clear that I supported my cousin. All day. Every day. Solange yanked her arm free, and she went in like her mama was a stranger off the street.

"What you mean calling me a freak?" Solange pointed a seafoam-green fingernail at Auntie Myrtle. "Look at that ugly cornucopia basket you got on your head and that doo-doo-brown suit you all stuffed into like a boudin sausage. Ain't nobody want to see that. *At least my shit fits.*"

Ooof. Auntie Myrtle's face crumpled up like a raisin. The sore spot was officially activated.

Joel, who'd been fading into the background like a pair of drapes, stood up and took the seat beside Auntie Myrtle. The seat that Solange was supposed to sit in. I was glad that Joel volunteered to take that seat. I didn't want third-degree burns from the steam coming out of Auntie's ears.

"Solange, Myrtle, *enough*!" Mama cried.

Mama just called her Solange. It didn't seem like anyone else noticed that except for me. Mama didn't even seem to notice because she was in crisis mode.

Auntie Myrtle sank down in her seat. Her wrinkled lips worked around a mint she was sucking with ferociousness. And Solange had the meanest look this side of the Mississippi on her face. The look was so mean, I was shocked that the fuchsia-colored wig she was wearing hadn't run off her head!

"Jessamine, Solange, sit." Mama motioned pleadingly to the chairs between her and Joel.

When Mama said *Solange* again, Auntie Myrtle started to work that mint even harder. It was for the best. That mint was taking the blows instead of our souls.

When our server came, Mama asked for more time. She looked around the table, her eyes darting from face to face. Mama was in full on peacemaker mode. *The odds are not in her favor.* Solange still looked mean. And Auntie Myrtle's fists were tight and shaking. I wouldn't bet against her in a boxing ring.

"Joel is applying to Harvard!" Mama randomly announced.

I reached for my water to take a salty sip. That was how she wanted to de-escalate a hostile situation? Joel and his favored status?

My twin looked up from his phone. It was suspiciously turned away from me and he had a privacy screen on. *That's new.* "Harvard is *one* of the many schools I'm applying to. And why are we always talking about my schools? Jess is also a rising senior."

Joel was wearing a green-and-pink short-sleeved seersucker button-down and khakis. That shirt was new. Pinned to his breast pocket was an enamel pin that I had created of the Gemini zodiac symbol. While we were not Geminis, the II symbol represented twins and two. Joel didn't believe in astrology, so he didn't make a big deal out of not getting a Capricorn goat.

"Myrtle." Mama lightly squeezed Auntie Myrtle's shoulders. "Joel is also applying to Yale. He has the grades. A four point oh GPA," she said.

I took another sip of water. My twin twitched his nose. To his credit, he never enjoyed when Mama gassed him up. Despite Mama talking up Joel like it was her job, Auntie Myrtle showed no interest. Her whole body was turned from the table. All I could see was her cornucopia hat and the jazz band behind her.

Solange wrapped an arm around Joel's shoulders. "Auntie Jo, I thought that JoJo wanted to stay in New Orleans to be a mentor. We need more Black men like JoJo in our community. Black men who know our neighborhoods and our culture."

Mama cleared her throat.

There was nowhere else for Mama to go. I *could* march in and cut the tension by telling them about the schools I was applying to and about the much-delayed personal essay I was working on. Speaking of mentors, my mentor, Ms. Nadia Guillory, was going to kill me. I'd been dodging her all summer.

I sank back in my chair and folded my napkin into vague origami shapes. The jazz band was bringing bass, drums, trombones, and my whole life . . . but this brunch felt sad. The Monets and Blanchards were sharing a table like we always had in the past. This time it felt different. Joel wasn't talking to me. Who was he texting? Solange was hurting and mad. Mama was focused on Joel, and Auntie Myrtle was dying.

There was a lot of change. It was just the beginning of the changes, too. Ugh. That made my chest feel tight.

And then . . .

"Reb, is that a man or a woman?" a man behind us asked.

Is that a man or a woman? Fight mode immediately kicked in. It always did when I heard a reckless comment like that.

I swiveled my whole seat around. I was not playing. Not today. Not ever. A white woman with blonde hair and a beige blouse glared at a red-faced man, who was smirking at Solange.

"What did you say?" I challenged.

Solange pinched my arm. It hurt because her nails were long.

I waved her away. Nope. This man was not going to insult my cousin.

"Jess, let it go. Remember what we do when they go low," Solange Obama said.

I remembered, but I was not in the mood to be a phoenix. Not today. If Solange wasn't going to fight her battles, then I would. I'd fight Auntie Myrtle and her hats and mints. I'd fight Mama and her inconsistency, and I'd fight this country, bruh! IDGAF!

Solange forcefully spun my chair around. She almost threw me to the ground in the process. I was turning eighteen in December. *I am not a child.* I tried to turn my chair around again, but Solange hooked her ankle around the back leg of my chair.

"You better not roll my ankle!" she said.

"Then move it."

She turned her head, eyeing me like she was daring me to disobey her. She wasn't my mama. I still had a fire burning inside of me. A fire that made me want to scream. How could she just take it? How could she let them make her feel small? How! And how did she expect that I stay silent?

She fought everyone's battles. Someone had to fight for her too. Especially when she was tired.

2
TENNESSEE

"REB, IS THAT A MAN OR A WOMAN?" Grinning, Dad leaned forward and swatted my knee.

"That's not funny!" Mom snapped.

Dad chuckled. "Jesus, Lauralee. It was a joke."

"Calling a human being *that* is a joke to you?"

It felt like the air in the restaurant was getting thinner. He was drunk. She was pissed. If we didn't leave now, something really bad was going to happen. The last time they got into a public fight, he got arrested. "Let's get the check," I said, trying not to sound panicky.

"No," Mom said, teeth bared, not even looking at me.

She set her snares back on Dad, fire burning in her eyes. He had moved on from his joke. Dad, ever the comedian, was dancing his index finger around in the air as if conducting the jazz band. It made me sick. How could he say that and just move on? Especially when the woman he'd called "that" was sitting at the table beside us. She heard him. Her whole family did.

Why didn't I speak up?

"Mom, he's drunk," I said.

"So?" She slapped her hand on the table. Her blue eyes were twin flames. "Silence is ignorance. I taught you better than that." She slapped her hand on the table again. "Speak up! I did not raise you to be a mediocre cis-het white man like your father."

Dad waved his hands and mimicked her, like he was a child. *They were both children*.

I buried my face in my hands. "Let's get the check," I repeated.

"The last time I checked, being a doctor trumps being a writer who only had one successful book!" Dad said. "If I didn't bankroll your dream, honey, you'd be out on the streets under that bridge."

This train was already off the rails. I couldn't stop this. If he kept digging, she was going to bury him. And he wouldn't stop.

"Richard. Apologize," Mom said.

I pulled the Commander's Palace birthday hat off my head. I should've went with my gut and told them not to reschedule my birthday dinner. It was weeks ago. I'd let them talk me into it. Mom had promised not to fight with Dad. He'd promised to lay off the drinks. And I'd reluctantly agreed.

"Richard. Apologize," she repeated sharply.

"For what, dear?" he asked, grinning wide.

"For being an asshole, *dear*," she snarled, not grinning. *Let's go, now!*

"Apologize to that lovely young woman!" Mom screamed.

People who had been discreetly looking in our direction were now openly staring. I couldn't hear the band. The jazz was drowned out by their voices—his smirks, her challenging glares, my silence, my fear, and my ignorance for not speaking up.

Everyone was staring. If I got them to leave, this fight could play out in the car. They could kill each other at home, not here.

I opened my mouth and prepared to speak. Not with a small voice. But a big voice. Louder than them.

It was too late. They were screaming. She was waving her hands around theatrically. And he was laughing, mimicking her actions and pointing at her.

The old restaurant started to spin. The large windows. The decorative wallpaper. The chandeliers. I gripped the table to keep from falling off the carousel.

They weren't my parents. They belonged to someone else.

I wasn't responsible for them. I was only responsible for myself.

My stomach lurched, acid bubbling up to my throat. I swallowed down the sick feeling. I had to wait until I got home.

They were still screaming.

At least no one knew me in New Orleans. It was so much bigger than Oxford, Mississippi. And if she smacked him or he called her the C-word and stormed off leaving us at a restaurant, my classmates wouldn't know.

"Apologize to that young woman!" Mom slammed her hand on the table, making plates and glasses rattle. But Mom knew that he wasn't going to apologize. She knew that.

I bowed my head and closed my eyes, trying to mentally escape to a place where they couldn't touch me. A place where it didn't matter what they did. I was just so . . . so tired. They started off the day so well. What happened?

"What woman?" Dad asked, narrowing his eyes at Mom and finishing off his drink.

"*Stop,*" I begged. My parents looked at me. Mom glared and Dad's eyes were red and glazed. He was still smirking. "This was supposed to be my birthday dinner." I spoke slowly, hoping that they heard every word. "Can we just have *one* day where everyone gets along?"

"Tennessee." Mom slammed the butter knife down. "We cannot all get along until your asshole father rights his wrongs."

"Mom . . . please . . ." *Please be the reasonable one.*

"Reb, it don't make no sense trying to talk her down. She's a woman. You know how women get when they need to be right."

I shot him a frustrated look. "Not helping."

Even though he was still digging his grave *and mine*, Dad kept on going. "Reb, when a woman is mad, you got to let her bitch. Let her bitch until she feels better. And with your mama being a bleeding-heart liberal, you got to give her extra time to bitch. The *Reverend Doctor Lauralee Luther King* is mad about everything." After he said that, Dad laughed so hard that his whole face turned purple.

Shut up, Dad. You're drunk. You're embarrassing us. The words were right there. Right there, but I couldn't say it. Why couldn't I just stand up to him?

"How. dare. you," she hissed. "You are a disgusting little man!"

"Disgusting little man," Dad mocked in a high-pitched voice.

"You are so intimidated by anyone different than you!"

More people turned around in their seats to stare. Some were pointing. Some were filming Mom and Dad's argument on their phones. The jazz band was quiet. The trombones had faded. There were no more drums. Just my parents raising hell and not caring who was there to witness it.

Please. Stop. My silent pleas were ignored.

"My God, how terrifying it must be to be a straight, cis white male in America! Anyone or anything different than what you believe in is a direct threat to you! Tell me this, *asshole,* what would you do if our son turned out to be gay? Would you disown him?"

I stared over Dad's head. His smile faded quicker than the bourbons he'd been consuming since we got there at eleven A.M. Dad's hazel bloodshot eyes fell on me. While her eyes burned with destructive heat, his were disapproving and cold. The laughter had officially stopped. The maybe-gay card had ruined his good time. And she knew it. She'd played her hand. She'd won.

I tapped my feet, hoping to control the involuntary spasms. I should be desensitized to their fights. They shouldn't bother me. They did, though. I hated how much their fights made me feel . . . small.

If I broke . . .

. . . would that be okay?

If I screamed . . .

. . . would that be okay?

If I said that I was tired of pretending that this shit didn't hurt . . .

. . . would that be okay?

If I showed too much . . . would they make me go back there? Would they punish me for feeling? Punish me for reacting, when that's all *they* did: react. It would be so much easier if I could disconnect from my feelings.

"You're a homophobic son of a bitch!" Mom yelled.

"Ma'am, please sit down. Are y'all ready for dessert?" I think this was our server. I couldn't see anymore. My eyes were closed. Sometimes that was the only way to escape.

"If I'm a homophobic son of a bitch, then you're just a *bitch*, aren't you, Lauralee?"

"Dad! Stop!" I yelled. It just came out. Enough was enough!

We were surrounded. An entire waitstaff of people surrounded us. They were all talking at once. Someone asked Mom to sit down. Someone said that if we didn't calm down, we would be asked to leave. *Yes, please.*

"Check!" I begged the server closest to me. I said it again, more desperate this time. "Please, can we have the check?" I didn't even know if they heard me. I felt so panicky. It was hard to focus.

Mom suddenly picked up her Bloody Mary. *No.* I knew what she was about to do. I tried to grab the glass, but she was too fast.

"Ma'am, please don't!" a server yelled.

The Bloody Mary flew through time and space toward Dad.

The glass barely had a chance to hit the floor before Dad jumped up. His temper was slow and legendary. It had always been. But when the wrong nerve was hit, we all had to pay for it. Yelling obscenities. Spit foaming from his mouth.

Dad roared and flipped the table.

He flipped the table.

Oh god. I placed my hands over my ears. *Oh god.*

"Look what you made me do!" he yelled at Mom.

Oh god. My eyes darted to the wait staff. More people were rushing toward us. Almost all the waiters were at our table. We were told to leave. A server said that they would get the check. People were standing and taking pictures and video.

Oh god. The last time they fought in public, the Oxford Police Department showed up. Mom and Dad were handcuffed and escorted out of City Grocery, but not booked with anything. If someone called the cops on them in New Orleans, what was I supposed to do? No one knew them here. No one would just let them go, free to terrorize another lunch or dinner at a time and location of their choosing.

My eyes were blurry. I didn't even care if I was crying. I just . . . I just couldn't hold back anymore. She had thrown a drink. Dad had flipped a table. We were getting kicked out. This was our first weekend in New Orleans. August was off to an excellent start.

Mom clapped her hands enthusiastically. "Ladies and gentlemen, please excuse my brute of a husband, Richard Williams. He is a Republican, a bigot, and a first-class asshole."

Mom clapped alone. No one joined her.

The check came. Dad whipped out his American Express and handed it to the closest server.

"We have to leave," Mom said, squeezing my shoulder.

I couldn't move. I couldn't pull my hands away from my ears. I couldn't walk. All I could do was sit and wait for the room to stop spinning.

"I'm so sorry," she told someone. "We will pay for everything. We will make this right." Mom squeezed my shoulder again. "Tennessee, baby. We have to go." She kissed me on the forehead. "I'm so sorry that your daddy ruined your birthday lunch. It wasn't supposed to be this way. I'll make it right, I promise."

I didn't believe her. She was lying. That's what they did.

I would never make the mistake of believing either one of them again.

3

JESSAMINE

"WHY DO YOU look like someone stole your puppy?" Solange asked as she sank onto the stoop beside me. She had been laying low for a few days, most likely to avoid talking about Commander's Palace.

"School is starting back up in two weeks. I'm not ready."

Solange laughed at my pain. "Girl, you are so dramatic. Here, take this huckabuck. It'll lift your spirits."

"Thanks, S." I tilted my head back and let the frozen delicious magic freeze my brain. I winced. "Oh, this hurts so good!"

"Don't it though?" She fanned herself with her hands. "It's too hot out here. Let's go inside."

I preferred battling the heat over Mama's bad attitude. She was in one of those moods where everything that I said was wrong. And I was already having a bad day!

The last thing I wanted to do was complain. The list of complaints were long. College apps. My best friend, Iz, was most likely moving to Arizona. My twin was MIA again. Woes. Woes. Woes.

I needed to reset ASAP or I was going to woe myself through the end of summer break. "Remember when that white man flipped the table at Commander's Palace last weekend?"

Solange giggled, thankfully taking my bait. "A mess, yeah?" She flipped her thick mane of blonde curls off her shoulders.

That wig looked hot! "Can you imagine if Black folk carried on like that?" She sucked her teeth. "Dude ruined the whole jazz brunch. I swanny!"

I snickered at her use of the word *swanny*. I only heard old people at church use it when they didn't want to swear. I tilted my head back and tapped the bottom of the cup. The magical-frozen nectar went straight to my brain. I was feeling better already. Problems be gone!

"Are you and Auntie Myrtle doing better?"

Solange belched. "Excuse me! I shoulda brought my champagne in my purse so I could fix me a proper drink. Can you believe that Ms. Hebert wouldn't put a little extra in my cup? The whole parish know she a drunk. Her tail shows up to church every Sunday smelling flammable!"

Solange had a master's in the art of dodging a question. I'd just check in with her next week to see how she was really doing.

She stood up. "I'm going inside with the AC. Come, join me, chile. Young people can get heat stroke, too." Resting her cup against her cheek, Solange sauntered inside.

I lingered on the stoop and stared out at the colorful shotgun houses on my block. Mr. Keith was sitting on his stoop listening to an old radio, and across the street, Ms. Rachel kept peeking through her blinds. That nosy old woman didn't even try to be discreet. What was she even spying on? I was just sitting on my stoop minding my own business!

The heat crept up on me. It warmed my scalp, making my hair, which was up in a bun, feel like a wool cap. New Orleans heat in August was a punishment. Showers were pointless because the second you stepped outside you were drenched in sweat and dirty again. And there was no point putting a brush through your hair because the humidity was its own beautician. My bun wouldn't save my hair from getting all frizzy.

I still wanted to tough it out a little longer. Mama was inside with the blessed AC and a ton of questions about college. I was too tired to lie convincingly.

Solange sauntered back out, snatched my huckabuck, and walked back inside. "Young people can get strokes too!" she repeated from the front room.

"Dang, you're so mean!" I called after her, pushing myself up.

Inside, the AC fanned against the cold sweat on my neck. I shivered.

Mama was sitting on the couch, her face set in stone. Her eyes were glued to a Tyler Perry show doing the most. She looked ready to pounce if I gave her anything less than "obedient daughter." Knowing Mama, she would probably stay mad until I gave her blood, a list of colleges and scholarships applied for, my firstborn, and the confirmation that I found a way to clone myself into Joel.

The longer I stayed in the den, the sterner her expression became. Thankfully, I didn't want to talk either. I headed toward my room, praying that I was off the hook.

"Nobody asked me if I wanted a huckabuck," she said.

I stopped dead in my tracks, back still facing her, front facing the freedom of my room. "Solange thought that you were sleeping," I lied. "You can have mine, Mama."

Because I was a good daughter, I found Solange, who was spread out on my bed like it was hers. She had set my huckabuck down on a Best Colleges book. I grabbed it and dutifully marched back into the den to extend my olive branch to the commander-in-chief.

Mama didn't waste a second with the olive branch. She said, "Jess, get me a spoon." Not "Jess, please get me a spoon." But, "Get me a spoon, wench!"

The. Disrespect.

"Yes, ma'am." I curtsied and grabbed Her Highness a spoon from the kitchen. When I returned, she took the spoon without a thank-you. "Iz is coming by tonight," I told her.

She adjusted her robe. "No problem. Did she eat already?"

"I think so." I took a step back. Right now, the mood was fine. If I lingered, it would turn. I took another step back. Thinking that I was in the clear, I turned my back and got ready to run to the freedom of my room.

"Ms. Nadia called me earlier. She said that you've been ignoring her calls and text messages."

I fought the urge to stomp my feet. Freedom had been so close. *Thanks, Ms. Nadia, for putting me on blast.* "I was going to call her back tomorrow."

"Come here," Mama said in the Tone. The Tone that enforced the "her house, her rules" law. I fixed my face and reluctantly turned back to Mama. She didn't just go off words. She read your face and analyzed your words. Maybe that was why she liked Joel more. His expression never changed. He always looked bored or tired, and when you paired that with his straight As, the boy could turn anything into gold.

Mama patted the spot on the couch beside her. I hated that couch. The Breath Couch. I called it that because it was so small. If two people were sharing it, they were basically sitting in each other's laps, breathing in the same air. I sank down beside her.

"Don't waste that woman's time."

"Mama, I'm not."

The couch creaked as she leaned in. Mama was literally staring into my soul. Her dark eyes, the shape of almonds, had the "don't play with me" look. She never gave Joel this look!

"You need to get serious about the opportunity you've been handed. Most kids your age would do anything to be in your shoes. You have one of the top Black attorneys in New Orleans mentoring you. She is taking time out of her busy schedule for *you*. Do not waste her time. Do not waste this opportunity."

Mama then started to list everything that I was not taking advantage of, one by one. "She has connections at Spelman, Tulane, Loyola, Howard, Cornell—the list goes on. She's offering to connect you with top tutors for the SAT and ACT with no charge to you."

I nodded. I heard everything that Mama said. She was right. I was lucky to be mentored by Boss Energy Nadia Guillory. She was everything that I wanted to be when I grew up: Intelligent. Savvy. Influential. "I'll call her tomorrow."

Mama pressed her lips together, clearly wanting to finish me off. "Are you looking for scholarships?"

"Yes, ma'am," I lied.

"You need to be proactive like your brother," Mama said, tapping on the couch with her pointer finger for emphasis. "If you need help, ask your brother."

I told her that I would ask Joel for help. She didn't comment. I guess she didn't believe me.

In my room, Solange was still laying on my bed. A Black hairstyles magazine was open in her hand. She rested her heavy head in my lap the second I sat down.

"I'm with your mama. You better call back Nadia Guillory. If you want to secure the bag, she's got the key."

I stared around my room, tired of being told what I needed to do. One side of my room still had the gray-and-pink flower-pattern wallpaper, the wallpaper that had been there when we moved to this shotgun years ago. The other side was painted a bright yellow color. Bright yellow for the sun. My whole room was supposed to be yellow. But Joel, Iz, and I got tired of tearing down the wallpaper and painting. To be fair, Iz and I got tired. Joel stubbornly refused to do all the work by himself.

"Scratch my scalp," Solange ordered.

Everyone was so bossy tonight. "Would you like a Coke with that, too?" I braided a piece of her blonde wig.

"Naw, I'm good on the drinks front. *Please*," she whined, sitting up. "I paid for that expensive ass lunch last week—is it too much to ask for a scalp to be scratched and greased? Dang! Y'all treat me like a troll living under the bridge begging for scraps!"

I cackled. She was the dramatic one. "Why are we talking about trolls?"

"It was on TV the other day and bae likes that mess." She flopped onto her stomach and kicked her feet up in the air, crossing her ankles.

Bae as in Creyshawn-bae? The illusive rapper from Atlanta that she told us about but never introduced us to? I patted my thigh. "I'll give you a five-minute head-scratch and that's it. Tell me about Creyshawn-bae."

"You need me to get the grease?" Solange took off her wig and rested it on the corner of my bed frame.

"Grease? What you need grease for? Girl, you are bald."

"You're bald!" she shot back.

That was a lazy comeback! I pulled my hair down from the

bun and shook out my thick and luscious curls. "Don't be a hater. Hating gets you nowhere in life!"

"Snip, snip," she said, making a cutting motion with her hands. "I told you I was using your hair to make my new wig, the Tatiana!"

She was so crazy. "Anyways, speaking of bae. How's Creyshawn?" I repeated.

Solange sat up. "My peanut head is doing just fine."

"Your peanut head!" I guess I didn't need the grease anymore. "Y'all are on nickname level? This is serious. Give me all the details!"

She held up her hands like she was about to dish some hot tea. My teacup was ready.

"Bae got me flowers the other day. And I'm talking about *real* flowers. Them flowers you got to order online and do the special delivery for. He had them delivered to my job, and you should have seen the bitter hos in that office hatin'!"

"At least he knows that you don't do flowers unless they're public flowers. He sounds like a keeper."

"I think . . ." She paused dramatically, bringing her hands to her face. "It's probably too early to say it, but I don't care, okurrr. He is the best thing that's happened to me in a while. And I'm already falling in deep love with him."

"You think you love him? Hasn't it only been a few weeks?"

Love to me was such a unicorn emotion. Like, not the love you shared for your family or best friends, but the love for people who didn't have to love you. I understood that love between people on TV or in books. The moments to be shipped. Stolen kisses. Holding hands.

But Solange never seemed to have that TV love. Hers was

more . . . car doors slamming in faces, clothes stuffed in garbage bags and thrown into canals, and two A.M. screaming matches about who ate the last cheese stick.

Solange looked me up and down. She was clearly waiting for me to say more.

I smiled. "I'm glad that y'all are connecting on that level."

"A few weeks is more than enough time to fall in love with someone. You're seventeen, you don't know nothing about grown-ass emotions. When you get to be twenty-two, you'll understand."

"Ohh, chile, she's defensive."

"When you meet him, you'll see why I'm defensive. He is fine. Like *so* fine. And he listens. Do you know how rare it is to find a man who checks every box? And, ooohhh." She raised her right hand like she was about to testify. "He's a Leo. In bed, I never have to ask for seconds. The first serving is plenty good."

She was really talking this one up. Maybe it was love? Not the two-A.M.-cheese-stick kind of love but the stay-up-late-and-talk-at-two-A.M. kind of love. "When will I meet Leo-bae, king of the first servings?"

"Tomorrow."

"Tomorrow?" I watched as she pulled her phone from her purse. She giggled. That was probably him. "Is he dropping by here?"

"What? No? I don't need your mama all in my business. I got Ms. Jeanette to give him a waiter position at Rue Margeaux."

Jesus,

    Mary,

        Joseph,

           . . . and the billy goat.

I pulled a hair tie from my wrist and tied my hair back up, hoping that would distract her from my face. I was gagged, couldn't even hide it.

"Why is your face like that?"

"My face is like nothing." I said.

"Uh-uh, don't 'nothing' me. Your face cracked. What was that look?"

I shook my head. There was no point trying to talk her out of it. She was stubborn.

"What you mean nothing?" Solange grabbed my arm, "Jessamine, you weigh two pounds sopping wet. I will sit on you unless you tell me what I want to know! Why did you give me that look?"

"S, c'mon. I'm tired." I tried to wiggle my arm free. No luck.

"*What?*" she repeated. "Do you think it's a mistake for him to work at Rue Margeaux with us?"

She wasn't going to let this go. Dang. "S, every time you get one of your boos a job, it always ends in explosions and tears. Kind of like that white family at CP. Flipping tables and getting kicked out of prestigious old dame restaurants."

"You lie. I don't flip no tables!"

"No, you don't flip tables. You smash them. Me Solange, me smash! Me mad!" For a pinch of dramatic flair, I jumped up and stomped around my room, punching the air.

"Lies," she said through her teeth.

As I stomped around impersonating Solange, my best friend Isobel (Iz) Santos stormed into my room talking a mile a minute in Spanish. I caught *punto* and *estupido* before her cell phone was flung across the room. She belly-flopped onto my bed beside Solange. Solange and I looked at each other with raised eyebrows. We already knew that this was dad drama. They were always butting heads.

"I cannot wait to move to Arizona!" she growled.

I joined her on my bed. "What did your dad do this time?"

Iz groaned. "Not even worth discussing. Can I stay here tonight?"

"Um, of course, BF."

"Yay!" Iz clapped her hands. "Are you staying, S? We can do mani-pedis and watch cooking show marathons. Please say yes!"

Solange moved her head from side to side. "While that sounds . . . fun, I gotta run by my mama's and make sure she doesn't need anything."

The thought of Solange and Auntie Myrtle getting into it again made me sick. "S, Iz and I could check on Auntie Myrtle. Why don't you stay here and rest?" I volunteered.

"Thanks, boo. But that mean ol' hag still belongs to me. You know how funny she gets about folks being in her house, even if the folks are kinfolks. I don't want her fussing y'all for doing me a favor."

I pouted. "We'll go with you then, offer support."

"Naw, baby doll. I better do this on my own." She stood up and walked over to me with her bag slung over her shoulder. Solange kissed me on the cheek, then circled back to my bed to kiss Iz on the cheek. "After I'm done with that mean ol' hag, I will be going home to Creyshawn. My peanut-head is going to satisfy me with a first serving. Love y'all."

"Love you!" I blew her kisses.

"Love you, mama," Iz purred. "That dress is fire."

"Really?" Solange kicked up her leg and whipped her head

to the side. "It's just a little somethin' somethin' I'm serving tonight."

"Out in these streets looking like a whole picnic!" I said.

Solange scooped up her wig. "Okay, y'all, for real for real, I'm out."

Once we were alone, Iz wrapped an arm around me. "She seems . . . good? Is she?"

I propped a pillow in front of Iz. She rested her chin on it and looked up at me.

"It's hard to tell," I said. "You know her. You ask her a question and she answers with more questions."

"Ha, that sounds about right. Maybe I can grab us a reservation at the Windsor for afternoon tea. Some girl time might make her feel comfortable enough to talk to us—if she wants to, of course." In total mom mode, Iz pulled out her phone. "How about next weekend?"

"I work all weekend."

"Boo!"

"And it's the last weekend of freedom." Saying that out loud made me feel heavy again. Senior year. Senior changes. Senior good-byes. Senior uncertainty.

She cuddled me, hugging me tightly. "How are you?"

"Swell!" I said, all chipper and fake.

Iz rolled her eyes. "Yeah, okay. You left me on read for three days. When I have to check on you through Joel, something up."

I made a whimpering sound. Emotions were gross. Senior year was coming. It didn't matter if I was ready for it. And I would have to deal with it soon enough. "Iz, can we just read and chill?"

Iz's perfect eyebrows arched and she nodded. Our friendship

ran deep. We'd been friends forever, so she could easily pick up on the things said and left unsaid. Sometimes it was a problem. But on exhausted days like today, when I just wanted to be a girl, a girl who didn't feel so much, I needed my best friend to pick up that "read and chill" was the ultimate I-don't-want-to-talk-about-it card.

Iz rolled off the bed. She plucked a book from our shared bookshelf. The Tiffany-blue bookshelf (painted by Joel a few years ago, when he was feeling nice), held about fifty books, books Iz and I had read together over the years.

She showed me the book and sat back down beside me. Our reading for the night was *How the García Girls Lost Their Accents*. That was a perfect vibe for tonight. Iz cleared her throat, turned to the first page, and started to read.

I rested my head on Iz's shoulder and closed my eyes. While she read, my mind started to wander back to the thorny places that I thought about too much or not at all.

Good-byes.

Finding the motivation to return Ms. Nadia's calls.

Contemplating where I belonged. Should I stay in New Orleans or catch a plane to the Big Apple and take my own bite? There were too many paths to take, and every path came with losing something.

I opened my eyes. The collage of pictures that still needed to be updated with Solange glared back at me. *Ouch.*

4
TENNESSEE

"Reb, unlock the door. This may be your room, but it's my house. Don't make me take it off the hinges."

Sighing, I closed my notebook. All I wanted was one day to myself. One day to prepare for school on Monday. I hid my notebook underneath the pillow. Dad didn't care about boundaries. He would read my entries and poems and judge.

"Open the door," he repeated.

I balled my fists. I wanted to scream. Afternoon sunlight streamed through my window. I could hear laughter coming from the streetcar stop, and somebody was playing a trombone. I wished that I was out there. Out there, Dad couldn't make me do what he wanted.

"Tennessee Rebel, don't make me ask again."

I dragged like a zombie to the door, unlocked it, and stepped back with crossed arms. Dad's dark brown hair was wet and he had a towel around his neck. For a few seconds, he stared at me wordlessly, hazel eyes digging holes. I didn't speak. There was nothing to say. After a while, he gave me a lopsided grin. "You're so serious, bud."

"What's up, Daddy?"

Dad frowned. "I'm making your birthday cake. Do you want chocolate or vanilla?"

"My birthday was July twelfth. It's August tenth. I think it's okay to skip the cake."

"That doesn't answer my question. Chocolate or vanilla?" He crossed his arms and squared his feet like he would stay there all day if I didn't answer him.

"Chocolate."

"Good, I don't like vanilla."

I started to close the door.

"Naw." He shouldered the door open and walked into my room. "I gave you space last week. I'm going back to Oxford tonight. Let's talk, man to man." Dad sat down on my bed. "What's going on?"

What kind of question was that? What did he mean "what's going on?" I wanted to laugh. Did I need to get a chalkboard and write out my long list of grievances starting with Oxford Friday Night Fights and ending with the Commander's Palace Table Smackdown?

I stared down at my feet. I had a lot to say, but talking with him got me nowhere. He didn't listen. It was like he went out of his way to not hear me. It had always been that way.

Dad patted the space beside him. "Sit."

"I've been sitting all day."

"*Sit,*" he repeated like I was a dog.

I glared at Dad. He glared back. Eventually, he looked away, setting his jaw, and crossing his arms. Dad didn't like me challenging his authority.

My legs were shaking and my heart wouldn't slow down. I could only challenge him for so long because he would sit there until I bent. He would find a way to win. He'd done it before. I dragged my feet to the bed and sank down beside him.

Dad messed up my already messy hair. "You know what's funny?"

Nothing. "What?"

"Up 'til you turned about eleven, everyone used to say you looked just like your mama. But now, you're the spitting image of me. I couldn't deny you even if I wanted to." Dad laughed, hugging me tightly, suffocating me. "The DNA test proves that's my boy!"

I stared at the minefield of boxes waiting to be unpacked. The boxes looked worse in the daylight. They made me feel like crap because I had no excuse. We'd been in the house for a week. For a week, I'd put off responsibility. I guess . . . I feared the boxes? Opening boxes meant unpacking things, and unpacking things meant unpacking feelings.

His hand went to my back, patting a few times. Hard thuds that I felt in my chest and in my soul. Each thud felt like: You're not good enough; I'm *not* proud of you, son; you look like me, but you aren't me.

"I know you're overwhelmed," Dad said.

I shrugged. Overwhelmed was a constant state for me, nothing new.

"Listen to me. Just 'cause your mama wants to be here to get her writing back on track doesn't mean you got to stay."

"Yeah, I do."

"No, you don't. Your mama is an adult and she's perfectly capable of taking care of herself."

That wasn't true. He knew that. For seventeen years, I had dealt with her "creative" episodes, and Dad had dealt with them for much longer. She was unpredictable when creating. She scared me when she was creating. She lost all touch with reality in the name of art. When she went creative-berserk, she got worse than him. I understood the danger of escaping into creativity and creating a world that felt safe. I coped most of my life that way—until the coping mechanism stopped working.

"Come back to Oxford. Finish out high school at Lafayette with your friends. I'd feel a lot better if you were with me. Kids need structure, and you won't get that here, not with her."

"I want to be here, Daddy."

"Rebel, are you even listening to me? I'm concerned about you."

"Don't be concerned about me. I'm going to be eighteen next year. And believe it or not, I *want* to be here," I repeated, staring directly into his eyes. Dad had this detached look in his eyes that I'd seen before. I didn't understand it. I would never understand how he could remove himself emotionally from Mom—and from me. She was his wife, even if they fought all the time. Didn't they *choose* to be together?

He moved his hand up to my neck, his fingers gripping loosely. "Why would you *want* to be in this dirty city with its high crime rate and ridiculous flooding? Yesterday, it rained for thirty minutes and the city was underwater!"

That's called climate change.

"Rebel?" His fingers tightened uncomfortably.

I shrugged. What else did he want me to say?

"Stop shrugging. I can't have a conversation with a shrug."

My shoulders stiffened. Dad dropped his hand from my neck. It used to trigger me when he got that look in his eyes. When I was a kid, that look made me want to run into the woods and never return. *I disappoint you.* "I've lived in Oxford all my life. Change doesn't have to be a bad thing."

He rolled his eyes and snorted.

"This is a fresh start for me. Nobody knows me here. Living

in Oxford was suffocating because everyone knew you and
Mama. When she does start writing again, she's going to need
someone here. Writing stresses her out."

"She's an adult. She can take care of herself, or hell, get a
support dog. I'm going to say it one last time: Taking care of
her is not your responsibility. You are a seventeen-year-old kid
who needs to focus on your senior year. It's ludicrous for you
to move to a new city your last year of high school. That is just
laying the ground for failure."

"I hear you, but when she's writing, she doesn't eat or sleep.
Someone needs to make sure she takes care of herself."

"Support. Dog." He doubled down.

Dad's eyes landed on each box in my room. Watching him
made me feel worse. Watching him kept me on edge, waiting for
the shoe to drop. He made me so anxious. I hated that.

Dad covered his mouth with his hand. "Rebel, speakin' of
last week. Your mama brought up something at the table."

Dad turned toward me. I already knew what he was going
to say. What he was going to ask. Why did I have to constantly
confirm that I was straight? *Why?* Mom knew that the thought
of having a gay son made Dad spiral. She knew that. But she
pushed that button every time she needed to win.

She knew that I wasn't gay. Mom asked me last year and
assured me that she would still accept me and love me if I was.
When I told her that I wasn't, she seemed disappointed, but she
seemed to accept it. Yet, here we were.

"She says that it's because you never show much interest in
girls . . ." Dad's voice trailed off. He watched me closely, like I
was an equation to figure out. "You aren't gay, are you, son?"

I hated that question so much. I didn't hate it because

I thought there was something wrong with being gay. *Dad* thought that, which meant every time he asked me to confirm that I was straight, he was really asking me to confirm that I was all right. That I was the son he'd prayed for.

I had never been that son. The boy he wanted.

I wrote stories, like Mom. I felt a little too loudly sometimes. I hated hunting. Guns made me uneasy. Fishing bored me to death. The only thing we agreed on was college football.

"Why are you asking me that again?"

"It's a simple yes or no question." He clenched his jaw. His eyes were like screws digging into me.

I swallowed, pausing. "Would it matter if I was?" My voice was shaky and small. I hated that a part of me wanted my dad to love me for me.

"Yes, it would and it does matter. Homosexuality is a sin. It's not natural for another man to lay with a man."

The way he makes me feel is not natural. Small. Forced into a corner. If I ever had kids, I would never make them feel like this, forced to prove that they were worthy of my love.

If I was gay, would that be easier? Dad would just hate me outright so I would always know where I stood.

"Do we have candles for the cake?" I asked, changing the subject.

Dad made some distance on the bed between us. "We do."

I pretended not to notice the distance. That distance had been between us for a while.

He stood and walked to the door, then paused and looked over his shoulder at me, disappointment written all over his face.

5
TENNESSEE

LATER, I STARED DOWN at the words on the notebook page, written in small letters, not my usual large and neat handwriting. Handwriting that I perfected when I was a kid because I thought it would be cool to sign books like Mom.

My words felt heavy. Too real. Reading the poem I just wrote over made me want to crumple up the page and throw it in the trash. I saw myself in the words. I felt my skin itching and the desire to find somewhere that felt safe.

Dad was gone, but I could still feel his presence in my room. Taking up so much space. Asking me questions. He was waiting for me to join him in the kitchen. That's the last thing I wanted to do.

I closed my notebook and walked over to my temporary hiding place, a top shelf in my closet. I pushed the notebook all the way to the back. I had to hide it, just in case Dad decided to search my room. If he found it, he would question me about my writing for sure. I didn't want to deal with his prying questions.

I also didn't want to be in the house anymore. For the last week, I'd pretty much been a hermit. I occupied my room during the day, wrestling with the idea of unpacking boxes and attempting to catch up on my summer reading. My new school, Magnolia Prep, had an extensive reading list that made me feel like I was way behind.

Maybe some fresh air would do me some good? Fresh air would also get me out of torture-baking with Dad. He'd act like the conversation we'd just had never happened. I couldn't do that right now. I felt raw for some reason. Maybe it was being in a new house, a new city, and them acting like their fight at Commander's Palace never happened.

There was one positive thing about being in this house. My new room had a lively view. Living on St. Charles Avenue, a super busy street in New Orleans, meant that I saw a lot of comings and goings: what appeared to be bachelorette parties stumbling off the green streetcar and Tulane or Loyola college students running along the streetcar tracks. And there was a musician who played the blues near the streetcar stop. He was there often, at daylight strumming his guitar and playing his harmonica, at twilight singing a song about his baby who did him right and who he did wrong, and at night he just played the harmonica.

Those people out there—the bachelorettes, the runners, and the musician—kept me company. It was like we were all creating art together. I wanted to be like them. Out there on the street-car, walking in the French Quarter where the buildings were old and a little crooked and painted Laffy Taffy colors.

Thinking about the people out there made me want to be one of them.

I remembered our waitress at Commander's Palace telling us that the best events happened in August. She'd said that this weekend was Dirty Linen Night, the sequel to White Linen Night, which happened a week before. She'd explained that White Linen Night was a day where folks wore their white linen and drank alcohol and checked out art in the Central Business

District on Julia Street. On Dirty Linen Night, folks did the same thing as they did the week before. The main difference was that their white linens from last week were technically dirty, and the local art was viewed in the French Quarter on Royal versus in the Central Business District.

Since we just moved to New Orleans and all my linen was packed away in boxes, I had to be creative. I grabbed a linen sheet from the closet and consulted Google on how to make a toga. My attempt ended up looking like a dress with one sleeve—but hey, it was still linen. I paired my linen toga with seersucker shorts.

Even though Dad said that we were going to bake a cake, I heard him in the living room watching the game. That was probably what he wanted to do all along. Bond with me over sports.

I snuck out through the French doors in the kitchen. I crept along the side of the mansion, careful of the large windows in the living room. If Dad saw me, he'd force me to watch the game with him.

Sneaking around the side of the mansion made me realize how lavish this house was. Out of all the houses in New Orleans, why did Mom select this one? Why did she need a Greek Revival mansion built in the 1800s to cure her writer's block?

The square footage was insane. Six rooms. Floor to ceiling windows in almost all of them. Each room was eclectic, too. One room had a bayou scene as wallpaper, another had a nautical theme, and one room was just birds and flowers. I could see her creatively being drawn to the versatile themes. But did that justify the decadence? Especially with Dad staying in Mississippi.

Dad had just cut the grass. It was already ridiculously hot, and the palms and banana trees in this side yard offered no shade.

I opened the gate and peered over my shoulder at the front porch to make sure that Mom wasn't out there writing. Thankfully, the rocking chairs were empty.

I crossed the street to the streetcar stop, which was directly across from my house, then waited for two minutes in the hot sun. Under the bright sunlight, the linen toga felt heavy. My legs were already starting to sweat. I should've brought water with me.

When the streetcar came, I immediately regretted my decision. It was *packed*. People were standing and sitting so it was impossible to move in any direction. Bodies were hot. The stench of perfume and cologne and armpits lacking deodorant hung in the air. A woman directly across from me swatted at the heat with her fan. Hopefully, that fan was giving her cool air, because it was hitting me with the flames of hell.

I took the streetcar to Canal Street, one of the main streets in New Orleans. It separated the French Quarter, which was downriver, from the upriver Central Business District. Towering palm trees lined Canal Street like skyscrapers. Canal Street was like the middle ground between where people worked and played. On weekdays it was usual to see tourists with beads and maps mixed in with men in seersucker suits and bowties.

Despite the heat, Canal Street was packed. Tourists crowded the sidewalks, waiting for lights to turn green. I avoided them, crossing the streetcar tracks to Bourbon Street.

There was so much going on. I moved through the sea of linen. It was so hot. Between the sun and the people bumping into me and dancing in the middle of the street, I felt claustrophobic. Police sat on horses parked underneath balconies, watching the lights and the people. On the galleries, frat boys congregated with ropes of beads on their arms.

Wow. I'd never seen anything like this before. Oxford life was . . . different.

Music was blasting from open purple-painted shutters and indigo-blue doors. Pop. Country. Rap. Zydeco. Whatever music someone could want was playing.

I reached for the pen tucked behind my ear and remembered that it wasn't there. I left my notebook at home. *Good*. Back in Oxford, I used to take my notebook with me everywhere. It kept me company, but it also held me back. If I didn't want to interact with people, I interacted with words. But being on Bourbon Street on this ridiculously hot day was living. There was so much to see. *Maybe I'll write about this when I go home?*

The sun was hot on my shoulders, burning me up. I forgot to put on sunblock. I'd pay for that later.

I walked all the way down Bourbon. There was a party of girls dressed in big cotillion dresses. Across the street from them, a homeless woman held up a sign asking for five cents. The revelers passed her by. I, unfortunately, didn't have any change.

As the late evening settled in, lush balcony gardens got their nightly bath. The sight of water dripping from hanging ferns made me realize that I was thirsty. That was probably why I was feeling dizzy. I stepped into a pink Creole cottage with green shutters, a place called Rue Margeaux. It had good music. Louisiana blues. Zydeco. Jazz.

The decor of Rue Margeaux was stereotypically Louisiana: alligators on the walls, mason jars of beads on the tables, and a bronze life-size statue of Louis Armstrong standing by the swinging doors leading to the back.

This was so different from Oxford.

In Oxford, a typical Saturday night for me started and ended with finding a corner in Square Books to read. Sometimes I wrote, too. My alter ego—the perspective I wrote from sometimes, Tennessee David—would love a place like this. He would talk to everyone and play something cool on the jukebox. It had been a few years since I rewrote my life experiences through the lens of Tennessee David, a fake version of me who was secure and had plenty of friends.

But this was me, Tennessee Rebel, choosing adventure. Choosing to dream a little, dream a lot, off the page.

I took a seat at the only empty table.

"Anything catch your eye on that menu, hon?" my server asked.

I did a double take. Her hair was different, rainbow-colored dreadlocks, but her face was the same. She was the woman Dad had insulted at Commander's Palace. This was my opportunity to apologize.

"Do you need more time, hon?"

"I'm sorry," I said shakily, "it's been a long night."

"A long night? It's not even eight yet! This is basically the afternoon on Bourbon."

I chuckled. Thankfully, she didn't seem to recognize me. I should still apologize though. Would that be awkward? "Do you got any recommendations?" I asked.

"If you're in the mood for savory, try the gumbo. It's not the best gumbo in the city, but if you're a tourist who doesn't know better, it'll do the trick."

"Who has the best gumbo in the city?" I asked.

She flipped her rainbow dreads off her shoulder. "If you

want real gumbo, you gotta go to someone's granny's house to get that or to a hole in the wall that looks like the health department should've shut it down ages ago. Since this ain't nobody's granny's—we got etouffee, fried chicken, chargrilled oysters . . . I wouldn't order those, they put barbeque in them. *But* the tourists about swallow the half-shell when they come out. So, maybe you'll like them?"

"I'll try the—"

She held up her hand and craned her neck toward Bourbon Street. I followed her attention to a guy talking to a group of women in tank tops and shorts. "I'm sorry, hon, would you mind holdin' on one second. I got to straighten a fool out real quick."

I nodded. "Yes, ma'am."

"How disrespectful!" she hollered. She picked up the rolled silverware on my table and threw it in the guy's direction.

My eyes widened. Ummm . . .

"Yes, Creyshawn Miller. I'm talking to your ass." She grabbed for another rolled-silver and aimed it in Creyshawn's direction. But she didn't throw it. "After I went out of my way to get you a job, you have the *audacity* to flirt with thots right in front of my face. Boy, you got me all the way messed up!"

Creyshawn stepped back inside. The group of women he was talking to quickly left.

"Ain't nobody flirting with nobody!" he protested.

"Mhmm. *Mhmm.*" She slammed her hand down on my table, making it shake. "What did you slip the high yellow one with no bra then?"

"The Wi-Fi password!" Creyshawn exclaimed.

"Boy, your ass is going to need to come up with a better

excuse than that. We don't got Wi-Fi here!" She punched at the air. "You know what. We're done. I'm over your raggedy-Drake-wanna-be-lookin' ass. You're canceled!" She made a motion that looked like turning the channel with a remote.

A few people had taken out their cell phones, shamelessly taking videos. The back of my neck got hot. They grinned and pointed at them. The attention that the waitress was getting took me back to Commander's Palace. Flipped tables. Molotov Bloody Marys. Trauma.

"Baby, c'mon, we're at work. Let's talk about this at home," Creyshawn begged.

"What home are you talking about? You don't pay rent or make groceries. All you do is raise up my Entergy bill and darken my couch with your skinny lazy ass. By eight I want all your shit outta my house."

"My shift don't end until nine, baby!" Creyshawn cried.

"Sounds like you better turn into the Flash and race yo ass over to Treme," she said with a shrug.

The chair beside me dragged across the floor. A girl sat down.

I turned to look at her—and the world kind of stopped.

She watched me with big brown eyes. The same big brown eyes that glared at me when Dad caused a scene. *Whoa* . . .

For what felt like a small eternity, she didn't speak. I didn't speak either. I was distracted with apologies and this thought that was totally inappropriate: *She's kind of pretty*. No, that wasn't right. *She's really*, really *pretty*.

The waitress was still hollering at Creyshawn, but it was background noise.

My heart was racing so loud. So loud that I couldn't hear anything else.

6

JESSAMINE

Two hours before the Creyshawn vs. Solange Smackdown

I WAS DOING THIS JUST TO SAY THAT I DID IT. Once I met with Ms. Nadia, Mama could check that off her long list of things I needed to do to be a productive high school senior.

I was nervous because I hadn't done the assignment Ms. Nadia had tasked me with. She loved action items. I loathed them. Who wanted homework in the summer?

"Are you nervous?" Joel asked, steering the car carefully to avoid a pothole the size of Montana.

My twin brother's voice rising above Jhené Aiko took me out of my head and back to the present. We were almost there—the high-rise where Ms. Nadia's law firm Guidry and Guillory LLP was located. It was like a futuristic castle looming over the rest of the Central Business District.

"Are you nervous, big head?" Joel asked again.

I reached in my purse for a piece of gum and took my time unwrapping it. "No, stubborn-as-a-mule-head, I'm not nervous."

Joel snorted. "That doesn't make sense."

"Your face doesn't make sense!" I popped the gum in my mouth. I was content with my insult. That was all that mattered.

Joel turned on his right blinker and pulled over near the sidewalk.

This is me. I clutched my purse close to my chest. My nerves felt like livewire, giving electric jolts to my mind, telling me to do reckless things like run or stop worrying about the future. Because the future was coming fast and it was scary.

Joel leaned against the wheel, propping his arms up. His dark skin was glowing radiant, a telltale sign that he was using my expensive facial wash and cream. I needed to hide it better. "Jess, are you going to get out of my car?"

"Eventually."

"How soon is eventually?" he asked.

I watched as a woman in a super authoritative business suit crossed the street. She was like Ms. Nadia—a boss who climbed to the top. A Black woman who had it all. Career. Ambition. Brains. Courage.

Joel was watching me like I was a goldfish in a bowl.

"What?" I said.

"I love you, but I need you out of my car."

"I love you, but this is *our* car."

Joel snorted. "It became mostly *my* car after you hit your fifth curb and sixth pole. Mama's insurance is through the roof because of your driving."

I stuck out my tongue.

"Let me know when you're finished here. I'll try to swing by and grab you."

"I won't," I said, opening the door to the eighth gate of hell, also known as New Orleans in August.

"Iz picking you up?"

"No, I'm heading to work after this. I'll just walk to the Quarter and catch a ride with Solange."

Joel made a cross with his hands. "Lord help us. S is the only person on the Gulf Coast who drives worse than you."

I have had enough of his mouth! "Bye, Joel! Go home and shave your beard. It looks terrible."

"Hater," he said, smiling big.

"Loser."

"Love you!" the mean twin added.

I grabbed my gym bag that contained my uniform and tennis shoes to change into for work.

"That's mine. I was wondering where my favorite gym bag went," he said.

I shut the door in his face. Mean twins did not get *I love you*s back. When was the last time Joel even used this gym bag! He was so contrary!

I took a moment to smooth down my smart seventeen-year-old-does-business outfit. I was styled in a black pencil skirt, a black blazer with a gardenia pin on the lapel. I loved to accessorize. My outfit was completed by a vintage pair of high heels that used to belong to Mama.

This look was too good not to document. I took a quick picture for social media and uploaded it. The five minutes it took to get the photo just right left me a sweaty mess. Oh, the things I did to . . . to lie.

I made my way into the building. It was ice-cold and full of white men and white women in power suits. They were on their phones or engaged in bone-dry conversations about settlements and court dates.

Ms. Sherry at the front desk gave me a big grin when she saw me. She always made me smile because she reminded me so much of Mama. A nicer Mama.

"How you doin', baby? I haven't seen you in a while."

"I know!" I reached in my purse and gave Ms. Sherry a

unicorn enamel pin. "That's for your cute sweater. Their name is Sparkle."

"Aww, what did I tell you about getting me gifts, cher?"

I waved my hand. "You asked me not to buy you gifts. I made that." I pointed to my gardenia. "I make all of these."

Ms. Sherry fixed Sparkle to her sweater beside a star pin I'd given her earlier in the year. It made me happy to see that she was still wearing the other pin I'd given her since I started visiting Ms. Nadia at her law office. "It looks perfect."

"You look perfect, baby. I'll let Ms. Nadia know that you're on your way up."

"Thank you!" I said with pep-and-lie. I said good-bye to Ms. Sherry and made the trek to my doom. Ms. Nadia was going to get me for being so unprepared.

My high-heels clicked loudly on the marble floor. *Doom. Doom. Doom!*

I pressed the elevator button and stepped aside for more white people in suits and power exiting. They mostly ignored me, but I got one quick smile from a white woman. I stepped onto the elevator alone. I pressed the button for the fifteenth floor.

My reflection stared back at me, split in two by the closed elevator doors. I had put my hair up into a bun. It was a bun of power. Volume, baby. And the baby hairs were laid and slayed. Nobody could tell me nothing, except for the little voice in my head that said, *Run.*

The elevator doors opened. *Too late.*

The fifteenth floor looked like a greenhouse. There were plants everywhere. Plants and windows. The fifteenth floor felt like the top of the world. From here, I could see the skyscrapers of the Central Business District, the spires of St. Louis Cathedral in the Quarter, and the winding Mississippi River full of barges and tugboats.

No matter how many times I was on the fifteenth floor, I never got tired of the view. This view was for the rich, the people who ate caviar for breakfast. Being on the fifteenth floor made me feel like a caviar girl. Even if I was only a caviar girl on borrowed time.

"Jessamine, come in, please," Ms. Nadia called from her office.

Ms. Nadia always spoke to me with a Black-mama tone. She made my nerves bad with all her expectations! When I was playing games and delaying things that I needed to get done, she immediately called me out.

I fixed a smile anyway. Sweet as tea. Sunny as a lemon squeezed inside for extra flavor.

Her office was huge. Steak-every-day-washed-down-with-expensive-wine huge. She walked over to her desk, big boss energy. When Ms. Nadia walked, she glided. Her shoulders were set in confidence. Her neck was long and her chin was always tilted up. She was like a cloud walker. No one on the ground could touch her. And even if they climbed up to the clouds, they probably still couldn't touch her.

"Did you complete the assignment I gave you last time we met"—she paused, making a show of checking her calendar— "in June?"

I kept a big smile on my face. She let the "in June" linger in the air.

Ms. Nadia looked down to stack some papers, then she held out her hand. "Your assignment on fifteen career tracks that you have considered since you were a kid, please."

I shuffled from left to right. *Sorry, Ms. Nadia. Waited last minute. Totally panicked. And forgot to send it. Please accept these notes on my phone. Completed last minute. But, hey, at least I did it.*

The stall was clearly too long for her, because she looked up. "My assignment, Jessamine."

Ugh. She made me so nervous. I wanted to be her *one* day. Just not *right now*. "Sorry, Ms. Nadia." I handed my phone over.

She pulled her hand back. "I need the assignment printed out. In college, your professors will not accept your phone." She stood and pulled out her swivel chair. "Sit here and complete your assignment. I promised my wife that we would go out to dinner tonight with her chaotic best friends, but—"

"Oh no, Ms. Nadia. Please don't let me—"

She held up her hand to silence me. "I was looking for a reason to get out of that anyway. I cannot deal with the drama. And my face won't be able to hide how much I don't want to be there. So, your lack of preparation will keep me at the office late." Ms. Nadia reached for her cell phone. She typed and spoke her response out loud. "Sorry, babe. I'm going to need to spend extra time with one of my mentees. Please bring home an extra gulf shrimp pasta. I won't miss the next dinner with Chaos I and Chaos II. Love you."

I gulped. Excuses didn't work on Ms. Nadia. I sat up straight practicing my best version of finishing school posture. "I'm working tonight. I can't stay that late."

"What time do you have to be at work?"

"At seven, ma'am."

Ms. Nadia walked around her desk. She pointed at her chair. "Get started, and if it gets too late, I'll drive you."

I felt like pouting. I was so tired. Between work and studying for the ACT and SAT, my brain couldn't take on anything
else. Even something as simple as creating a list of what I wanted
to do.

I sank down in the chair. Ms. Nadia's wallpaper on her computer was of her and her wife on their wedding day. Ms. Nadia
had honey-colored braids in that photo. They looked so happy.
So in love. What did that kind of love feel like? Was it the "ship-
ping" love that I saw on TV and read about in books?

Ms. Nadia opened a Word doc. "I want you to take this
assignment seriously. You don't have to know for sure what you
want to major in in college, but it helps. And thinking about
what you might want to do in the future opens you up to the
possibilities."

Possibilities.

The word was simple yet loaded. Possibilities. College.
Careers. Now my head hurt.

Ms. Nadia straightened an award plaque on her desk. "Why
the defeated look?"

"I don't have a defeated look!" I exclaimed, positioning my
fingers over the keyboard.

"Mmm," she said with a nod. "I've seen that look on your
face before. It's almost like you don't believe in your power."

"I *do* believe in my power."

I said it. But I wasn't sure that I meant it. What did she
mean by *power*?

I typed the first career that came to my head: artist. Daddy
had been a part-time artist. I smiled thinking about how he used
to take me and Joel to City Park. While Joel and I ran around,
he would paint.

"You're so brave, Jessamine. But I don't think you believe that." She pointed to the computer. "Make sure to dream big on that list. You can have the world, remember that."

……∺ℂℂ……

My mentoring session with Ms. Nadia left me feeling happy and sad. By the end of it, I had a list that included being an astronaut and a Supreme Court justice. But I still was drawn to the artist life.

I walked to Rue Margeaux in my comfy tennis shoes and uniform. It felt great being out of the Jessamine-does-Wall-Street outfit. I bumped shoulders with tourists living their best lives in string bikinis. Tourists always did a lot.

When I stepped into Rue Margeaux, my soul deflated. It was packed. Not only was it packed, but it was full of the worst kinds of tourists—the tourists who howled at the moon. The demanding ones who snapped their fingers and expected you to jump.

I did a quick scan on the restaurant, counting how many servers were working tonight. My count turned up three unfortunate souls.

In the packed dining area, one person stuck out. He was sitting by himself, wearing a white bedsheet. I guess that was his linen. *Ha!* How original. Instead of wearing his dirty linens he wore his *actual* linens.

He was looking around and nodding along to some Cajun song heavy on the accordions. It was a song I heard every shift, but I still didn't know the name of it. Linen boy looked in my direction. He looked familiar. Where did I see those saddish eyes, lanky body, and floppy brown hair before?

Why did I know that face?

I could count the white boys I knew on one hand.

Did he dine here before?

I stared at him, the puzzle in white linen, trying to sort through the scattered shifts I'd taken over the summer.

Then it hit me. I knew exactly who he was!

He was the boy that was sitting at the table with the blonde woman and crazy man who'd flipped the table at Commander's Palace. I had assumed that they were his parents by the hostage look on his face that day. Hopefully tonight he was alone. I couldn't handle someone flipping tables tonight.

I walked briskly to the back. Instead of tending to the full dining area, Solange was making out with a skinny guy near the kitchen. They were kissing each other like someone was going off to war. Mouths were all open and tongues were all wagging.

"I didn't realize that the Discovery Channel was looking for local talent," I said.

Solange reclaimed her tongue from skinny guy's mouth. "Boo, ignore this little girl and her rude mouth."

Creyshawn, aka Leo-bae, aka Boo, flashed me a gold-toothed smile. He was at least a little cuter than her last boyfriend. It didn't take much. He held out his hand. "You must be Langie's little cuz, Jessamine."

Langie? I was horrified that that nickname existed and that she allowed him to call her that. What was a Langie? It sounded like a lozenge. I blinked at Solange, aka *Langie*. Langie giggled and swatted Creyshawn's forehead with the palm of her hand.

I shook his hand. "Nice to meet you. Not to be rude or anything but can y'all get it on off the clock? It looks like a plane skipped MSY, landed on the roof, and dropped all the tourists off here."

Creyshawn laughed a little too enthusiastically. "Langie, your lil cuz is funny. I see where you get it from."

I maneuvered around them to clock in, resting Joel's gym bag on the chair beside Solange's Bendi-not-a-Fendi purse.

"She gets her humor from me," Solange argued.

Creyshawn kissed her. The kiss was wet and yuck. Public displays of affection were stomach churning, especially on bad days.

"S." I tapped her shoulder.

She ignored me.

"Langie, I'm taking table thirty-five."

She broke her kiss with Creyshawn, "Who's at table thirty-five? Is one of your little high school friends at that table?"

"Yes," I lied.

Solange waved her hand. "Nah, you can't have that table. I love you, but I don't love you more than my tips." Solange kissed Creyshawn one last time. "Let's get back out there before this child shakes me down for my tips."

"Whatever you say, Langie." He kissed her one last time, and they went out into the chaos hand in hand.

⸻⸻❦⸻⸻

Before stepping out into the busy night, I shook out my shoulders. They felt so tense. Next to the swinging doors leading out into the dining area was a bowl of nametags. Some people took theirs home with them. I never did because I knew that I would lose it. I dipped my fingers in the bowl and picked out a nametag at random.

"What home are you talking about? You don't pay rent or make groceries. All you do is raise up my Entergy bill and darken my couch with your skinny lazy ass. By eight I want all your shit outta my house!" Solange screamed.

I peered out into the dining room. Dang. Already?

"My shift don't end until nine, baby!" Creyshawn whined.

I couldn't help but laugh. I guess Leo-bae is Leaving-bae. Solange was standing at table thirty-five. Creyshawn was near the door, looking like he wanted to make a run for it. Every step Solange took forward, Creyshawn took a step back. He was scared!

I calmly walked toward table thirty-five. After the day I had, I would carpe diem and be a tourist. I'd give myself a five-minute breather to watch Solange versus Creyshawn, king of the zero servings.

And I'd talk to strangers. I pulled out the chair beside him and sat down.

7
TENNESSEE

SHE WAS SMILING AT ME LIKE SHE KNEW ME. Her eyes were big and bright and they sparkled with gold dust.

"You okay?" she asked.

I was staring. "Yes, sorry, long day." *Long day?* That was such a sorry excuse.

She folded her arms on the table. "Believe it or not, they were just making out with each other." She nodded at the waitress and the boyfriend she'd just kicked out.

"Really?"

"Yep! The yelling one is my cousin, Solange. You can't take her anywhere. And the one fighting for his life is Creyshawn."

"Does her . . . yelling . . . hurt business?" I asked.

She leaned forward and laughed. "Does it look like business is hurting? This is dinner and a free movie, and in New Orleans you get a lot of free movies. At least this one doesn't make you an unwilling participant."

I giggled. *Why am I so nervous?* "Business does look like it's booming."

Solange suddenly ran from the back. I didn't even realize that she had left. The girl sitting beside me watched her cousin, shaking her head. "Oh, here she go with that rolling pin again."

Rolling pin . . . again?

Solange ran at a full sprint after Creyshawn, rolling pin raised over her head.

"This is why I told her not to hire her boyfriends. Solange is too jealous. She can't even handle her boyfriend giving more attention to a hush puppy than her!"

She was talking to me, but her eyes wandered around the restaurant. I watched her.

"Aren't you concerned about him?" I asked.

"About who?" She looked at me now.

"Creyshawn. He doesn't have a rolling pin."

She smiled with her eyes closed. It was like she was tired or dreaming about something. "That boy can protect himself. He's managed to survive this long dating her. 'This long' as in three weeks."

"Your cousin looked really mad, though?"

"That's just her face. She was born mad. Seriously, if you look at her baby pictures that baby looks mean, just like her mama."

For some reason that made me laugh out loud. It felt strange and wonderful to laugh. Almost like I forgot how to do it. She rested her hand on my shoulder and she laughed, too. Her laughter was loud. She threw her head back, nearly falling out of the chair, and her whole body rocked. Her shoulders. Her earrings. At one point, her laughter was so animated that I thought she might fall out of her chair. That led me to sling my arm around her waist to catch her if she fell. The second I did it, I felt super embarrassed.

If she realized, she didn't say anything. She kept laughing. Which gave me time to remove my inappropriately concerned hands.

She touched me, too, though. Her hand was still on my shoulder, and she was sitting really close. So close that her leg was brushing mine. I tried to stop noticing the little things that were commanding a lot of attention and stole a quick glance at her nametag. Jasmine.

She smelled good, too. A little sweet. Citrus maybe. Floral, too. Jasmine? I didn't know for sure what the scent was. But I did notice that it smelled good.

"Solo tonight?" she asked.

I nodded along to the zydeco on the jukebox. "Yeah."

"Parents grounded?"

My gaze darted to her. She smiled knowingly. *She does remember me.* That was embarrassing. I winced. "I was hoping that you forgot."

She pouted. "How could I forget? The whole jazz band was all thrown off because of flying Bloody Marys and flipped tables."

I squeezed my eyes shut. No matter how hard I tried, the Commander's Palace smackdown always played in the back of my mind. "I'm really, really, really sorry about my parents. What my dad said about your cousin—"

She waved her hand in the air. "The apology is better coming from your drunk dad."

I still felt sorry. I should've said something. Mom was right about silence being ignorance. I cleared my throat, searching for a topic to change the conversation. "Do you think she'll come back?"

"Solange?" she asked.

"Yeah."

"No idea." She pushed her chair back and stood. "Okay, I better tend to the tables. The vultures are swarming, and they look like they have a taste for chicken legs." She did a little dance that wobbled her long legs.

That dance made me giggle. She threw her head back and laughed again. Her laughter was louder that the music.

"I'm really sorry about what my dad said." So much for changing the subject.

She waved her hand dismissively again. "Oldheads are set in their ways. You don't have to apologize for your dad. As long as *you* color outside the lines."

Color outside the lines? What did that mean? I stared at her, waiting for her to elaborate. She did not.

"I should get back to work." She slid her left foot back, then her right. She danced her hands in the air and did a spin.

"Jasmine—that's a pretty name."

She looked over her shoulder at me. "Who?"

"Your nametag. Your name is Jasmine, right?"

She spun back around to face me. "My boss has a graveyard of old nametags in the back. Sometimes I feel like being Jasmine or Summer, and when I'm feeling really wild, Gertrude is where it's at."

"You don't look like a Gertrude." I draped my arm over the back of my chair.

"What does a Gertrude look like?"

"Definitely . . . not like you."

She stared at me for a while, her eyes observant, her lips smiling. I felt the urge to look down or away. There was something about her—something about her smile, something about her eyes—that made me feel . . . a lot.

"Jasmine," she said, extending her hand.

I smirked. "But you just said that wasn't your name?"

"Today it is." She snapped her fingers. "Who do I have the pleasure of speaking with today?"

Her question left room for imagination. I could give her an exciting response. Who *did* she have the pleasure of speaking with? What if tonight I wanted to be more than the writer boy from Oxford, Mississippi? What if I wanted to be confident and bold tonight? A boy who wasn't ruled by nerves, but instead by courage and confidence. "My name is Tennessee."

"Go big or go home, huh?"

"No seriously, that's my name."

She closed her left eye and tilted her head. "Yeah, okay!"

"Seriously."

"*Seriously*? Where are you from?"

"Mississippi."

"Ah." She snapped her fingers. "A boy from Mississippi *would* be named Tennessee. How'd your parents come up with that?" She leaned in curiously, her arms folded behind her back.

I licked my lips. Fact or fiction? I'd give her fact. "My mom named me after Tennessee Williams, the writer. And my dad named me after the state. He didn't realize they weren't on the same page until she brought it up ten days after I was named, or so I'm told. And the funny thing is that I am kind of a writer."

"What do you write?"

"I used to write fiction. Now I write . . ." I almost said *feelings*. "Stream of consciousness."

She nodded. "Interesting. Seems like your parents fight about everything?"

"They do."

She stared at me, brown eyes contemplative. I stared back. Fighting the urge to look down or open my mouth and stick my foot in it.

"Well, boy-who-is-actually-named-Tennessee, I have iced tea to refill and receipts to print."

I nodded slowly, feeling weird because I wanted to keep her at my table, talk to her a little longer. "Can I order something with you after you refill iced teas and print receipts?"

"My cousin didn't take your order?"

"No, Creyshawn started flirting with those girls before she could."

"What can I get ya, babe?" She slid closer to me and leaned against the table.

Babe.

Ignore that. It wasn't for you. She was just being nice. Stop acting like you've never spoken to a girl before.

I grinned stupidly. "What do you recommend?" Solange had given me a whole rundown of the menu, but I wanted to hear it from her. When she spoke, I listened. She had that New Orleans accent that was Southern but mixed with something else. Listening to her was like floating down a lazy pool at the end of summer when the weather was starting to cool.

"If I was you, I would order the jambalaya. It's the most okay thing on the menu."

"The most okay thing? That doesn't sound like a glowing endorsement." That was me trying to make a joke. Hopefully it landed.

"Bruh, this is a tourist trap on Bourbon. The best you'll get is okay." She drummed her hands on my table. "But don't go leaving reviews telling nobody that Jessamine told you that."

Jessamine? I pretended like I didn't hear the slip. Jessamine was a pretty name. "I won't. My lips are sealed."

"What do you want for dessert?"

"What are my options?"

"Bananas Foster, pralines, and Ponchatoula strawberry cheesecake." She tapped her pointer finger on the table while listing each option.

"What is the most okay dessert?"

She leaned in a little more. *She's so, so cute.* Her brown eyes were probably the prettiest brown eyes that I'd ever seen. "The most okay thing is the Bananas Foster, and that's because it comes with vanilla ice cream. You can never go wrong when ice cream is thrown into the mix."

"Bananas Foster it is."

"Sweet, I'll put in that order for you."

"Hey, one more thing." Courage. Courage. Courage.

She had already started to walk away. She paused. "Tennessee-named-after-the-writer, I really need to get to work, or these people are going to Julius Caesar me."

"Can you stay my server?" It was a bold ask. An ask that I couldn't believe I was voicing.

Across the restaurant, a woman banged her cup down on the table. "Little girl, my water glass has been empty for the last fifteen minutes! What kind of establishment is this? The crawfish is hot and my mouth is spicy! I need some water with ice, now!"

I winced. She slid back over to me, practically bouncing on the balls of her feet. "Don't you need to get that? She said her mouth is hot and spicy. The crawfish did it."

Jessamine snorted. "Her mouth can stay spicy for a little longer. Calling me little girl won't make me get over there any faster." She fixed her bun. "That chick is not even my table. You're my first, which means I got to make sure you're good before I make sure she's good, you know what I mean?"

"I know what you mean." I stole a glance at the hot and spicy woman. She was popping more crawfish into her mouth and cursing under her breath. Her mouth couldn't be that spicy. "Umm . . . aren't you supposed to suck the head when eating crawfish?"

She nodded. "Yes?"

"That woman isn't doing that," I whispered.

She asked me quietly out of the corner of her mouth, "What is she doing?"

I attempted to be discreet with a casual glance in the woman's direction. The woman with the hot and spicy mouth had her head tilted back and she was dangling the crawfish above her mouth, then she dropped it in. "She's putting the whole crawfish in her mouth and spitting out the shell."

"No she's not!" Jessamine nudged me with her elbow.

"Look," I whispered, nudging her back.

"Stop! Before you get me in trouble," she said. Jessamine turned to look at Ms. Hot and Spicy Crawfish, who was still going to town on her platter. The next thing I knew, Jessamine was doubled over herself giggling, hand on my shoulder as if my shoulder was holding her up. This time I was extra careful not to slip my arm around her waist.

--------·ço·--------

Jessamine had to leave because Solange and Creyshawn never returned. She bounced among tables juggling glasses of iced tea and plates filled with seafood. She returned to my table once to bring me my jambalaya and water.

I tried to focus on the jambalaya instead of her. The rice with andouille and shrimp was a little spicy. It tasted better than okay to me, which made me eager to try great jambalaya at someone's granny's house.

I gazed outside through the open shutter doors. Bourbon Street was still like a conveyer belt of people. Conveyor belts going in all directions. People disappearing into bars with plastic containers shaped like hand grenades. One conveyor was stuck. People on that one were laughing and hugging. On another conveyor belt, people were ogling a man with a big snake around his neck.

"Happy Redux Birthday!" Jessamine said, setting down the Bananas Foster in front of me. A single lit candle was sticking out of a scoop of vanilla ice cream. "It's just okay Bananas Foster. Is there anything else that I can get you?"

"No, this is good. Great, actually."

"Perfect." She turned, seemingly dancing every time she moved.

I still had some nerve left in me. Some nerve that could guide me in being bold. Coloring outside of the lines. Doing something that fictional Tennessee would do. Soon I'd have to go home, to my room and my boxes. And it was too late for the jazz musician and his blues songs to keep me company on St. Charles. I would just have the rattling streetcars and carpe diem tourists.

"Coffee?" I spat out.

She stopped and turned to face me again

Louis Armstrong and Ella Fitzgerald's "Summertime" was playing on the jukebox. I couldn't help but notice the little details. The song. The look on her face that I couldn't read. My heart—which was beating so fast, so fast that it felt like I could pass out. And she was wearing this pin on her purple polo—it was a flower.

She placed her hands on her hips. Hopefully, she didn't realize how much I had been watching her. "What kinda coffee do you want? We got chicory, café au lait, cold brew, and iced."

Cold sweat dripped from my armpits. "I meant . . ." I licked my lips and raked my hands through my damp hair. "I meant coffee with you."

"Huh?"

I opened my mouth. Closed it. And thought of what I was trying to say. "What I'm meaning and failing at saying is, um . . . words." I dropped my hand down to the table. Why were the words not coming to me? *Brain, work.* "I would love to take you out for coffee sometime?"

She smiled without opening her mouth.

I held my breath. A smile was good, right?

"A girl is busy and booked."

That was a no. At least I tried.

"But . . ." she continued.

Oh, *but.* I raised my chin.

"Is that toga you're wearing for Dirty Linen Night?"

I nodded. She stared at me for what felt like years. "Have you checked out the galleries yet?"

"Not yet." Another bold statement fell out of my mouth. If not coffee, why not art? "Did you want to join me?"

She pressed her lips together.

I can wait until after your shift is finished. I almost said it. Nerves kicked in, stopping me.

Without answering, she turned and bounced to another table. I watched her even though I tried not to. She refilled glasses of water, juggled plates, printed receipts, pulled paper straws from her front pockets . . . and when I thought she forgot about me—she returned.

She set down a receipt with a zero total.

"There's no total on here?"

She snatched up the receipt, pulled a pen from her front pocket, and wrote down something. She slid the receipt back over to me. Jessamine had written:

Free okay meal. Happy birthday on us. I get off at nine.

I pulled out my wallet. "You don't have to do that."

"Nine work for you?" she asked, ignoring my wallet.

When I tried to take out my debit card, she took the wallet from my hand and placed it down on the table. Our hands touched for a second and there was a spark. A spark that made me pull back.

"Yes, nine is perfect."

Next thing I knew, she was gone. Did that really just happen? Did I really asked a girl to hang out with me? And did she really just say yes? I grinned wide. I couldn't help it.

For a week I had been all over the place. Starting a new school had me nervous. And the unexpected made me question everything. But at that moment, sitting at a table with a bowl of melted ice cream and a blown-out candle, I felt just fine.

8
JESSAMINE

SOLANGE STORMED INTO the break room after her shift had ended. She grabbed a handful of napkins and wiped at her face. "Do not say a word."

"Wasn't planning on it." I sure wasn't. The only words I planned on saying were *I'm keeping all of your tips!* but the rolling pin couldn't be accounted for. "Is he still alive?"

"For now." She threw the napkins onto the counter. "His skinny ass is fast and this bitch don't run in no heat. All I know is he betta be out of my house by the time I get home."

It was funny—just last night she had been raving about him. I guess his peanut-head status had been revoked. Leo-bae of the zero servings. "Are y'all done done?"

Solange sucked her teeth. "All men are garbage. 1-800-TRASH!"

I kicked out the stool next to me. "You look like you're about to pass out. Sit."

She stuck up both her middle fingers. "There are more rolling pins in here—keep messing with me." Solange sat down and her shoulders slumped. She rarely slumped. Her posture was usually finishing school perfect, unlike mine. "You saw him flirting with those out-of-town-floozies, didn't you? I know I wasn't going crazy and making it up. You saw it, right?"

Out-of-town-floozies. That was a new one. If I lied and said yes, that wouldn't make things better. And I couldn't confirm or deny. I met Creyshawn for a second. And in that second, she was all up on him performing surgery on his lips with hers.

At the end of the day, the real tea was that Solange was insecure. Beating someone up wasn't going to make them stay. It also wasn't going to stop them from looking at out-of-town-floozies. "Maybe you should talk to him?"

"ABOUT?"

"Just trying to be helpful."

"I don't wanna talk about it anymore." Solange laid down on her crossed arms. "I'm tired and I got another shift after this to try and make that damn Treme rent for this month. It ain't going to pay itself."

"You need me to raid my piggy bank?"

Solange frowned up at me. I frowned right back at her.

"Jess, I need more than some pennies. I need a prayer, a winning lottery ticket, and if I can't get none of that, I need a rich man who will marry me for my winning personality alone."

"Lawd. That rich man better hide his rolling pins! 1-800-Ask-Creyshawn!"

"Girl, bye." She held up her hand inches from my face. "Oh yeah, there's a white boy out there in a sheet. He about scared me to death lurking in a corner. I almost put him in a chokehold 'cause I thought he was trying to steal something."

Oh! Yes. I completely forgot about him. "S, you can't just go around putting people in chokeholds because you're mad."

"I wasn't mad. I said I was scared."

"Is he still alive?"

"Yes. He spoke fast and told me that he was waiting for you." She scowled. "When you'd start dating white boys?"

"*Dating* is a strong word. I don't know him. He asked me to meander through art galleries on Royal and I said yes because I'm bored."

"Mhmm," Solange snorted as she sat up. "Then why'd you ask me if you could take his table?"

"I did not."

"Look here," Solange pointed a nail at me. "When I introduced you to that trash-bag Creyshawn you asked to take that boy's table. You never do that. Don't act like you got amnesia."

"If you say so. I got college apps to pay for, just like you got Treme rent."

"You still lying. Go on out there and take Isidore Newman out on Royal so I can close up and go about my life."

"He looks more like a Magnolia Prep guy to me."

Solange stuck her pointer finger in her mouth and made a gagging sound. Everyone knew that Solange only dated St. Aug boys. That was where she went to school—a hundred years ago. "What happened tonight?" I asked her.

"With . . . "

"With Creyshawn?" I said.

Solange looked down at her nails. "He showed me who he was. Your mama always says that when someone shows you who they are, believe them. I'm believing that Creyshawn is a low-down-dirty, ugly-possum-looking, raggedy-ass . . ."

"You done?"

"No, rotten-egg-breath-having . . ."

"S, with the way I saw you kissing him when I walked in, his breath seemed minty fresh!" I laughed. She did not laugh with me. I let the laughter fade. "Anyway, if he loves you like you said you love him . . ."

"What you talkin' about? I didn't say a dayum thing about loving his muskrat-lookin' self."

I smirked. Did he look like a muskrat or a possum? Couldn't be both. "You did say that you loved him. The receipt shows that you said you *loved* him at eight thirty last night."

"I didn't say that. That don't even sound like me." She dragged her purse closer and started rummaging through it.

"Look who's got amnesia now! Maybe in the morning he'll want to talk?"

"No, he won't. Where is my phone?" She kept searching her purse. Maybe she was trying to see if he called? Solange cared about everything more than she let on. "I told him that I hated him and didn't want to see him again."

"Why'd you say that?"

"Iyanla Vanzant if you don't leave me alone!"

I rested my chin on her shoulder. Solange meanly shrugged her shoulder away. "Your head is big and your chin is heavy. Leave me alone," she said.

Stubbornly, I placed my heavy chin and big head right back on her shoulder. This time she didn't shrug me off. Her phone was resting on the counter right behind her. I walked my fingers to it, groaning as I stretched. "Here you go, babe."

She grabbed her phone and pressed down repeatedly on the screen. Creyshawn was her wallpaper, wearing a sideways baseball cap and a big grin, making the heart sign with his hands. I shifted my attention back to her. She looked . . . sad.

This was why I liked fiction. In fiction, you always knew the ending. And if you didn't like it, you could create a new one. I nudged her a few times with my elbow. She didn't fuss, a telltale sign that she was elbow deep in her feels.

"You saw him flirting though, right? He looked like he would run off with one of those little thotlings if they winked at him. I hope he falls into a pothole and drowns!"

It got silent. The AC hummed through the vents. It sounded like a whistle or a scream. I chewed on my lip and waited for it to pass. An unpleasant image popped into my head. Dumplings. Starfish. The sun gently rolling over brown water. I placed my hand to my gardenia pin and gripped onto it, tight.

Say something. Anything. Cheer Solange up!

Missions and distractions were good for me. I nudged her again. "How about I tell the writer boy to float away? And we can go to Hot Tin and drink French seventy-fives and talk about vacations to Disneyland."

Solange's shoulders rose and fell as she took a deep breath. "I know you think you're grown, but you're still a child. I'm not bringing your ass to Hot Tin." She dived into her Nada Prada bag again and pulled out a whole bottle of champagne.

She was a magician. How did that big thing fit in there? "You can't drink that whole bottle by yourself."

"Watch me."

"Don't you have another shift after this?"

Solange waved her hand nonchalantly. "That shift is best done with some feel-good in my tank. Leave me alone, Jess. If you're hanging out with that boy, make sure your location tracking is on. When I call, you better pick up on the first ring."

"Yeah, yeah." I eyed Solange and the bottle of champagne. "You sure you don't want me to stay?"

"Yes, I'm sure. My new bae rosé champagne knows how to treat a girl right, no cap."

9
JESSAMINE

I LOVED RANDOM ADVENTURES. Getting in a car with no destination in mind and ending up in a new place, or befriending boys with sad eyes and shy smiles. Boys who wore linen togas and spoke real slow. There was a SAT word that perfectly described the way Tennessee spoke: He drawled.

We walked together on Royal. Slowly, because it was hot and miserable. Tennessee kept stopping to listen to tour guides explain the hauntings and macabre history of New Orleans to wide-eyed tourists. I drank him in like a buzzing bee consuming nectar.

When a tour guide spoke of pirates, his long neck turned to the group. When a tour guide spoke about red-light districts, he practically joined the group. And when a tour guide mentioned the great New Orleans fire of 1788, I swear he almost pulled up a chair to sit beside the guide.

"Writer boy, very nice to meet you." I held out my hand.

He stared at me with starry eyes. He went with the flow, though. "Nice to meet you . . . again."

"Thanks so much for joining me on this tour." I held out my hand toward a yellow Creole cottage with blue shutters. A lantern was flickering at the door. "This house here, haunted."

"Really?" he asked, sounding like a child.

"Yes. Walk with me, writer boy." I signaled for him to

follow and took Tennessee down Royal Street, pointing out hidden courtyards with water fountains and lush greenery. "Haunted courtyard," I explained. "A pirate named Lafitte Smalls haunts this alley. Every fourth of August he bellows a haunted song.".

Tennessee craned his neck, peering into the dark alley that smelled like humidity, piss, and vomit. I held my breath. Oh, the smells of New Orleans!

"Why the fourth of August?" He asked.

"Because that is when Lafitte Smalls lost his lover Blackbird Tchoupitoulas in a battle to the death! We stan a queer swash-buckling love story."

Tennessee nodded in agreement. "We stan."

That right there, major points. Homophobic straight boys were so boring. Wait. *Maybe he's gay?* I smiled back at him, appreciating his starry eyes and open mind.

"What song does Lafitte Smalls sing?" starry-eyed Tennessee asked.

I tried not to giggle. He believed me. C'mon, writer boy. Does Lafitte Smalls sound like a pirate to you? And Blackbeard Tchoupitoulas! Bruhhhhhh. "The pirate sings—" I paused for theatrics. Tennessee hung on. A willing participant in this web of swashbuckling lies. "The pirate sings 'Baby, All I Want Is Some Gumbo.'"

"Gumbo? Why does he sing about gumbo? Why not about his lost love? I have so many questions."

I giggled. "Tennessee Williams, you are a word that starts with *G.*"

His eyes widened a little. It was barely noticeable. But I noticed it.

"*Gullible.* Our gay pirate romance does not exist. It is false. Maybe you could write it?" I started to walk again. It was too hot to stay still. Sweat was literally coming out of every pore.

Tennessee jogged to catch up with me. A quick look to the right turned up a boy who wasn't as gangly as originally thought. He had some muscle, just a little bit.

"I need a costume change," I said.

He nodded, his head bobbing up and down with less enthusiasm than he started the night with. *Did I offend him when I called him gullible? Probably not.* He walked beside me, his footsteps keeping rhythm with mine. My right foot. His right foot. My left foot. His left foot. Even when I picked up the pace, he matched me.

Tell me about the stream of consciousness you write? The question begged to be asked. An exploration of who Tennessee Williams was. I held back on the question. This was a swashbuckling adventure. A book that would be returned to the library. Why beg for reality when I could treasure fiction? "Want to be Others tonight?" I asked.

He looked at me, staring for a while and thinking unknown things. He'd just stare. When I stared back, he often looked away. It was like he didn't realize that he was staring.

"Others?"

"Yeah, Others are fake people in the real world," I explained.

The expression on his face got more confused.

"I'll show you!" I dragged him into a shop on Toulouse. I perused the aisles, snatching up likes and tossing the likes in Tennessee's direction. He didn't ask any questions or make any objections. He just followed me with starry eyes and a permanent triple-strawberry tint to his face. He blushed a lot, too.

"What do you like the most?" I asked him.

He looked down at the armful of clothes. "Outta all this?"

"Yep."

He tried to analyze the likes one by one, by using his other hand to navigate the hangers. "Um—this one is sparkly. I guess I like the sequins on this one? Um . . ."

I giggled.

"What?" he asked, open-mouthed.

"You are such a boy."

"I *am* a boy?"

"I'm never taking you shopping again."

"Wait, I'll do better." He set the clothes down on a round couch and crouched down on his knees. I watched as he meticulously looked from each item to me. Every now and again he'd nod or shake his head. Finally, he picked three, then jumped up and handed me the items. "I like these."

"What do you like about them?"

"How they look."

I stared at him, wanting to smile but trying not to, because . . . just because. I took his selections: A tennis dress—a very short tennis dress (surprising). A romper. And a pantsuit. They were all cute, but very different.

"I'm going with the romper!"

Next, we went on a mission to accessorize. I gave Tennessee twenty dollars and told him to pick out a piece of jewelry to match my romper. That game didn't last long. He came out of a shop with earrings that couldn't have been less than fifty . . . and he had change! *Twenty dollars' worth*. Bruh. "This is my Other outfit for the night. Now you gotta pick out yours."

He still seemed confused about the Other game, a game

that I created with Iz so we had an excuse to be anyone but ourselves. Others was the best excuse to let go and let fiction.

I posed a few times in my blush-pink romper, hand on my hip. Then both hands on my waist, then a little spin, because I loved to be extra-extra-read-all-about-it. "The game of Others means embracing everything you are and everything you're not. You add to who you are. And you sprinkle on who you're not. There are no rules in Others—except embracing freedom and saying yes to fun."

"That sounds like a lot of fun," he drawled.

Good. It seemed like he was loosening up a bit. "What are *you* wearing tonight? What will be on the menu, dah-ling?" I snapped my fingers in a circular motion.

He looked down at his toga. "I guess I'll start by retiring the toga."

"Lead the way to your Other outfit!" I turned to the right and then to the left.

Tennessee started walking back the way he came. There were so many people on Royal, drinking and dancing. They were bumping into me. I latched onto his toga. He looked down at me. The boy with the triple-strawberry cheeks and the starry eyes—he smiled. It was a soft smile. A smile that I rarely saw from boys. That smile made me pull back.

Fifteen minutes later, Tennessee was officially an Other. He picked a swanky floral button-down. It was black with red roses and white lilies. His paired his floral print with jeans. Jeans were a choice in this heat!

"We gotta take a pic to document these lewks we're serving." I whipped out my phone, leaned against him, and blew a kiss to the camera. Tennessee did this thing where he tried to smile, tried to look serious, and then appeared to go through an existential crisis about what to do with his hands.

"Flex," I said.

"That's such a bro thing to do."

Even though he complained, he did what I said. He threw up his arms, flexed, and grinned wide at my camera. Once the picture was taken, I did a quick edit and sent it to Iz. I couldn't post this borrowed library book on social media.

Iz responded right away: *WHO IS HE?*

I left her on read.

He patiently waited for me through edits and texts. He'd been doing that all night. Tennessee was nice. Maybe too nice? Which made me feel like I should leave him early.

"Now that we have our Other costumes should we go see art?" he asked.

"Are you a writer and an art connoisseur?"

Tennessee looked confused.

I giggled. "Forget it. Let's go see art."

"Follow me." He shoved his hands in his khakis.

He said to follow him, but did he know where he was going? I was the native. He was the Mississippian. I let him lead, though, curious to see if the fish could find his way swimming upstream.

The tourists were out of control. Too many people not moving in wilted linen, damp with perspiration. I latched onto the back of his floral button-down, risking touching him again. "Keep swimming!" I ordered.

Tennessee swam. Because he was so tall, everyone got out of his way.

He swam to an art gallery with wide-open spaces. There were

brightly colored paintings on the walls. Paintings of the French Quarter at dusk, and little kids dancing in front of buildings.

Glorious AC pumped from the vents. I held up my arms, letting the AC hit me where it counted! During the summer, I had two rules for surviving. I hugged buildings closely, sticking to the shade, and I paid note of the shops that gave good AC, the kind of AC that grabbed at you when walking past and lured you inside to spend all your money. "Heat relief therapy AC" is what I called it.

"You need a drink?" he asked.

"Do *you* need a drink?" I threw the question back at him.

Tennessee appeared to think about it. Funny that he couldn't tell if he was thirsty.

"I'll get us drinks," I volunteered.

"No, I can."

"I'm already gone!" I said, rushing to the water pitcher. It was full of lemon and orange slices, but it still tasted like tap water. I weaved through the crowd back toward the skyscraper with the swimmer's build and handed him a paper cup. "Served fresh from the tap. It tastes briny."

"Briny?"

I giggled and raised my paper cup to him. My smile fell a little when I saw what he was looking at. Tennessee was standing in front of a painting of a Black ballerina dancing in a sea of darkness. The only colors in the painting were brown, black, and pink. Her skin was brown. Her child-sized brown shoulders drowned in a sea of inky blackness. There was no light around her. The Black girl in the leotard with the pink bow in her hair was the only light in the painting. All that darkness had to feel so heavy on her small shoulders.

"Do you like this?" he asked.

I looked away from the ballerina, pushing down the feelings it stirred inside of me. Tennessee was watching too closely. I could feel his eyes. I didn't want him to see. What I was feeling wasn't meant for library books to read.

That Black ballerina painting looked like it was painted by Daddy. I shivered, not sure if it was because of the AC or the memory that was swimming up to the surface, struggling to break free. I pushed the memory back down, holding my breath. Go away, sad girl. Not today.

Tennessee was still watching me.

"My twin brother is an artist. He has an art show coming up." I started to walk. Standing next to the ballerina painting was too heavy.

I gravitated toward something lighter, a painting of people dancing on Frenchmen Street. The colors were blue-and-black swirls, and the people were shadows with bright red dresses and purple suits. "What do you see?" I asked him.

Tennessee inched closer. "Life."

His response made me pause and take another look at the dancers. The painting looked chaotic to me. Too many colors were swirled together. Too many dancers. Too much going on.

"What do *you* see?" he asked, stroking his jaw.

I could feel the Black ballerina pulling me back. The painting said, *Come swim with me. Don't leave me alone in this inky-black sea*. I risked a glance just beyond Tennessee's shoulder. Her arms were raised above her head and her right leg pointed out to the darkness. She carried so much grace in her small, statuesque body. Her lifeless eyes stared off into the endless black distance. Her eyes were so small compared to the rest of her face. I sighed, releasing the heavy weight that was sitting on my chest. Why did the Black ballerina look so sad? What had she seen? What had the painter seen?

Women in white dresses were pointing at the Black girl in the painting. They were all white women. Did they think the ballerina looked sad, too? Or did they just see the bright pink bow and think childhood innocence and rainbows? I frowned down at my blush-pink romper. I didn't like this Other outfit anymore.

Tennessee inched closer to the painting of the dancers on Frenchmen Street. His arm brushed against mine. I didn't want to be here anymore. It was too . . . suffocating. "How about we change venues? This one is getting full."

Tennessee leaned against the wall. He rested his head near the frame of the Frenchmen painting. "Are you okay?"

I laughed. It was a reactive laugh, nervous. Why was this boy that I barely knew asking if I was okay?

His lips pulled up slightly.

"Are you ready for magic?" I walked briskly away from him, needing to run run run.

Tennessee kept up with me. When I walked fast, he also walked fast. My legs were long and so were his. Our strides were in sync.

Things got way too serious in the art shop. This wasn't supposed to be a serious night. I didn't check out the library book to feel sad. Escape! I demanded escape! Fantasy or bust!

I stopped underneath the Fischer-Gambino sign and gestured toward the door. Tennessee cupped his hands to the window and peered inside. From the window, you could see that she was expensive. Fischer-Gambino was for footballers, doctors, and reality housewives with deep pocketbooks.

"In here, my friend, we have grandeur. If you're looking for the perfect chandelier to hang over your luxury piano, this is your place!" I reached for the door. Tennessee nearly knocked me down to open the door for me. It was hilarious. We had encountered eight doors tonight, and he'd opened every one. I was not used to that.

"Thank you," I said, stepping into the AC and splendor.

Tennessee followed me to a lamp that looked like it was made of gold. He examined the price tag and his eyes widened, then he backed away from the lamp like it was a rattlesnake. Curiously, I checked the price. *Ohh, yes. I don't want that on my tab either.*

He wandered over to a couch that had a floral pattern similar to his shirt, only red with green-and-white flowers. He sat down.

A writer boy dressed in flowers, sitting on a chair of flowers, called for documentation. I eased my phone out of my bag and took a quick photo. At that moment, he looked up.

"Did you take a photo of me?" he asked.

I nodded.

"Can I see?" he asked.

I sank down beside him on the couch, crossing my legs. Tennessee scooted closer. He was so close that I could feel the hairs on his arms on mine. *He's too close.* I opened my camera roll and showed Tennessee his photo.

"Wow. I kinda look cool there!" He touched my phone and then immediately pulled back. "Sorry!"

"No, it's okay." I handed him my phone.

Tennessee stared down at the phone with wide and starry eyes. He ogled the photo for a while, his eyes unblinking and his mouth open.

"Who are you, Tennessee Williams?"

"Who am I?" he asked slowly.

I nodded. Tennessee handed me back my phone. I almost

asked him for his number so I could send the picture to him. I stopped myself. If the library book gave me his number, I would have to give him mine. And we would no longer be Others. We would be familiars, unless I changed my number.

"What do you mean by '*Who am I?*'"

"Who are you? The Cliffs Notes version."

Tennessee shifted in the couch. "I'm a student."

"Where?"

"Magnolia Prep." He said.

I knew it! "What else do I need to know about writer boys from Mississippi?"

Tennessee ran his hands through his floppy brown hair. It was starting to curl at his ears. "Hmm, I dunno. What do you like about this place?"

"You don't like it?"

"Naw, not saying that. It's cool. Really expensive though."

I giggled. "That's the point. I can't afford anything in here, but I can dream about one day affording something. This trillion-dollar couch could be mine."

Tennessee clasped his hands and smiled down at the floor.

"My best friend and I used to come here when we were having a terrible day. We would pretend like we had bags full of money. We left empty-handed, but it always cheered us up. The pretending."

Tennessee tilted his head and looked at me. "So this is fantasy?"

"Yes. It's a secret world." I took out my phone and pulled up his picture again. "Tennessee in Wonderland."

Tennessee's lips pulled up at the edges. "I have a random question."

"What's your random question?"

"If you could be anything, what would you be?"

My response was easy. "A bird."

"Why a bird?"

I flapped my arms in the air, careful not to knock anything off nearby tables. "So I can fly. I want to see the world and I don't want to pay for a plane ticket every time I want to get up and go. What about you? What would you be?"

Tennessee thought about it for a while. "Hmm, if I had to pick something I don't think that it would be an animal. I'd probably be a train or something."

"A *train*?"

Tennessee nodded and tapped his feet on the carpet. "Trains, airplanes, and cars function the same. They all get you from Point A to Point B. But planes travel in the clouds where you can't always see the world underneath. Cars are prone to getting stuck in traffic. On trains, you can see the world and keep going until you run out of track."

Tennessee's response was unexpected. A train. "What happens when the train runs out of track?"

Tennessee tilted his head up toward the ceiling. "I would walk or swim to the next train tracks."

Are you a runner like me? A pessimistic avoidant like me? I winced at the sharpness of my thoughts. This library book was not the escapist literature I was looking for. Maybe it was time to return him and check out a new book.

"I love this," Tennessee said, dragging me out of my thoughts. He pointed to my gardenia pin. "Where did you get this from?"

"I made this."

"How?"

"I don't actually make them. I go to this place in the Marigny that does it. But I do make the artwork for each enamel pin."

"Do you draw the artwork by hand or do you do it on the computer?" He seemed interested.

"By hand, and then I scan it into the computer and bring it to the shop." *If you are interested, I can show you.* I looked away. Why did I keep trying to share my world with this boy who I wouldn't know come tomorrow? "I think my fake credit card is all maxed out. Let's go to Frenchmen and compare art to life?

10
TENNESSEE

JESSAMINE SAID THAT Frenchmen Street was where the locals went to have fun, and that Bourbon Street was for the tourists. We walked up Bourbon, once again taking in all the sights. Heat did not bother these people. The combination of extreme heat and alcohol looked dangerous to me, but it didn't seem to be stopping anyone's good time.

Jessamine complained a few times about the heat. I ducked into a tourist shop selling rosary beads, voodoo dolls, and T-shirts and bought us both water.

"Tennessee, that water was probably five dollars!"

"It was six," I teased.

"If I knew you were buying fifteen-dollar tap water, we would've gone to the CVS."

"It was four dollars," I said, handing her the water.

Jessamine thanked me, twisted off the cap, and took a little sip. She started to walk again, weaving through the crowds of wide-eyed people. On the corner of St. Ann and Bourbon there were two gay bars. It was dark in both. EDM and pop music converged on the street. I could see people inside, sitting close together in bars. Fans were going. A couple was making out right outside Oz.

Frenchmen Street was crowded, but not as crowded as Bourbon. It was dark now. There were bars with live entertainment playing inside, people sitting at tables and having animated conversations. People were spilling out of the bars, and people were walking in the middle of the street, their arms linked.

"Does the floral print dance?" she asked.

"Do what now?"

Jessamine pointed ahead of us. There were two dueling bands ahead of us. The dueling song was a heady mix of trombones, drums, guitars and trumpets. It was the kind of song that made someone like me, who couldn't dance, want to tap my feet and try to dance like everyone else.

Jessamine raised her hands over her head and swiveled her hips. "Do you dance?"

Jessamine kept dancing. She made me smile a lot. "I wouldn't call myself a dancer."

She grabbed my hands and tugged me down Frenchmen, closer to the dueling bands. When she touched me, my nerves ticked up. The heat cranked up. I felt like my neck was on fire—my face, too. I tried not to focus on the feeling of her hand in mine. The little shocks. The tingles because I wasn't used to a pretty girl taking my hand.

The colorful old buildings swirled around me in a rainbow of colors. Jessamine stopped on the fringes of the crowd. "Make a face," she said.

"A face?"

"Yes, an I-don't-care-what-anyone-thinks face. Like this." Jessamine pulled her hair down. Curls fell around her shoulders and framed her oval-shaped face. While I stared on, stuck and stumbling on words, completely lost in her, she grabbed me by the shoulders.

"Do it!"

"Do what?" I said quietly, a whisper over the dueling bands and the joyous cheer from locals and tourists living their lives.

"Let go, have fun. Make a face." She narrowed her eyes at me and stuck out her tongue. *"Do it!"*

We were surrounded by people walking the streets, dancing to live music inside dimly lit bars—and some had stopped to watch us. I had always shied away from attention. I liked flying under the radar. Making quiet moves.

But standing with her in this crowd of people was not a quiet move. It was loud and bold. If I kept thinking, I would find reasons to overanalyze everything. I was tired of doing that. Tired of thinking too much and being quiet.

I breathed out, attempting to tap back into the courage I felt earlier. I had asked her to coffee, and that was why we were here.

My hands fell just underneath her elbows. Jessamine was still making that face; her eyes were big and wide and her nose was wrinkled. With each second that passed, her face got more crazy. The revelers were closing in on us. Laughing people. People swiveling their hips and clapping their hands. Singing people.

I followed her lead. My eyes crossed, my lips curled up, and I puffed out my cheeks.

Jessamine giggled, throwing her head back and shaking out her hair. Then she grabbed my hands again and started to spin me. The world was suddenly on fire. Everything was a colorful blur. The music started to clash. The dueling bands. The music from the bars. Someone was singing karaoke somewhere.

There was chaos. And there was us.

Our hands were slippery. I almost lost her a few times. Her eyes widened. She would hold onto me tighter. We were spinning and spinning. Two strangers on a carousel. Her hair was in her face. Sometimes I couldn't see her face. She was falling back. I held on tighter. This moment was kind of magical.

It felt so nice to randomly spin on a street, lose myself with this girl I just met. Be courageous and not think about what I should say or do next. This spinning felt nice. After we stopped, the world was still shaky and bright around us.

"Dizzy?" she asked.

Jessamine's hand was flat against my chest, a little too close to my heart. I struggled to catch my breath. I was winded from all the spinning in the heat.

I nodded to her "dizzy" question. I already wanted to see her again. It was too soon to ask. I didn't want to look clingy.

Jessamine rocked her shoulders back and forth, moving away from me. Her feet were light like a ballerina's. She spun and rocked and swiveled her hips. It wasn't just her body that moved, but also her hair. When Jessamine danced, people noticed. There was something about her. Something that just made people stop and stare.

This night wasn't going to last forever. At some point, I would have to go home and she would have to go home. This night was a one-off. A once-upon-a-time-in-New-Orleans kind of thing. What did she call me besides Floral Print? Oh, yeah, Tennessee in Wonderland.

She made me sound so cool. I wanted to lean into that, the feeling that this stunning girl who laughed louder than the music found me worthy of spending a night with—in a totally G-rated way, of course.

· Jessamine was lost to the crowd. I couldn't see her. All I could see was people with their brightly colored drinks and their contagious smiles. I should dance, too. I should live, too. Just this once, right?

That's what my fictional alter ego would do. Tennessee David would dance. He would talk to strangers. He wouldn't care about looking stupid or having the worst coordination when he danced. He would just dance.

I tried working my way up to it. Awkwardly rocking my shoulders. Awkwardly doing some foot shuffle movement away from the crowd. I was the worst dancer. What was I supposed to do with my arms and legs when I danced? Jessamine emerged from the crowd.

She grabbed me by the hands again and dragged me back into the fray. Inside the crowd, it was hotter than ever. So hot that I couldn't breathe. I'd lost my water somewhere. Maybe I set it down when we started to spin? Jessamine was doing her ballerina footwork again and punching at the air. At one point, she held her hair back with her hands and looked up to the sky with her eyes closed.

This had to be a dream.

·····ogo·····

After we danced, we wandered around some more. It was getting late. I didn't want to say good-night to her, even though I could feel my eyelids getting heavy. Jessamine languidly strolled through dark alleyways that led to lush green courtyards and uneven streets frequented by mule-drawn carriages.

We ended our late-night wander in front of St. Louis Cathedral, a church that had been burned down three times. Jessamine was silent now. She stood with her arms crossed, and her eyes zeroed in on a tarot card reader. I was greedy to get more time with her, so I asked if she wanted to get her cards read. Jessamine immediately turned that down and told me that it was time to say good-night.

At that moment, thunder rumbled, and a light rain dripped down from the blue and black sky.

"Do we have to say good-night?" I dared to say out loud.

"Yeah, I need to go to sleep. School is on Monday." Jessamine wrinkled her nose up at the moon.

"Is it okay if I give you my number?" I asked.

She hesitated. It was a short hesitation, but long enough for me to notice the uncomfortable silence. Was I was being too pushy or clingy or both?

"Sure." Jessamine grabbed her phone from her purse and unlocked it. "What's your number?"

"662-555-1988."

"Cool. I'm saving your number under Writer Boy." Jessamine tossed her phone back in her purse. She waved to me and started walking away. "Get home safe, okay?"

I opened my mouth, wanting to say something more. She stopped and turned back to me.

"Tennessee!" she yelled across the courtyard.

"Yeah!" I called back.

"Have you read *A Streetcar Named Desire* by your name-sake?"

"Not yet."

"When I call your name, I want you to scream, 'Stella!'"
Stella? Who is Stella?

"Can you do that?" she asked.

Jessamine was standing underneath a lamppost, bathed in

bright yellow light. The old buildings around her (probably haunted) added to the moment. It felt like we were somewhere else. Europe, maybe? "I can do it."

"Tennesseeeeeeeeeeeee!" she screamed.

I felt a rush. A rush of feeling alive. "Steeellllllaaaaaaaaaa!"

As I finished yelling, a man in a seersucker suit exited the alley between the Cathedral and the Cabildo and also yelled, "Steeeeelllllaaaaa!"

The man held a cane, which he pointed at me. "You're either too early or too late for the New Orleans Literary Festival." He chuckled. "But when in New Orleans, what is time? New Orleans is not concerned with following the rules." He patted me on the back and yelled, "Steelllllaaaaa!" again as he walked away.

I looked to the place where Jessamine had been standing. My heart sank. She was gone.

11
TENNESSEE

"You're up early?" Mom said through a yawn.

I looked up from my LSU Tigers mug of coffee. Mysteriously, my University of Mississippi mugs had disappeared overnight and been replaced. "I couldn't sleep, and I gotta make sure you eat." I tried to smile and be cheerful.

To be honest, I couldn't sleep. Jessamine and her legs were doing laps in my mind. And the memory of her smile was like the sun burning behind my eyelids. I ended up giving into my old sleepless night habit: I got up and wrote. Unfortunately, writing started at five A.M.

Mom waltzed around the kitchen. "You were out late Saturday night and into Sunday morning." She took the plate I set out for her and helped herself to the spread of fresh fruit, eggs, bacon, and biscuits. She plopped down in the seat beside me and smiled warmly. "Your dad didn't notice, but I did. Did you have fun?"

There was no way I was telling Mom about Jessamine. "Yeah."

"What did you do?" she sang.

"I explored and wrote." I diverted my attention to the various plants that had popped up around the kitchen. There was a huge fern propped by the French doors leading to the backyard. More plants that would be dead by next week, unless taken under my care, were on the kitchen island. I turned around a baby cactus on the table between us. It was in a bright blue pot that read SUNNIER DAYS AHOY!

"I see that you are declining to answer."

"I was thinking about school," I lied.

She popped a strawberry into her mouth. "Your uniform looks good on you. I love the blue blazer paired with the white shirt, and blue-and-red striped tie." She brushed imaginary dust off my blazer. "Are you nervous?"

"I think so. I don't know what to expect. I'm not sure if I'll fit in." It was all negative self-talk. Dad got on me a lot about that. But he wasn't here.

Mom nodded. "I get that. Starting over is hard. But we're together. Remember that."

I nodded. She was right. We were together. But for how long? When Mom started creating, she went into this state where she didn't eat or sleep—all she did was create. And when she was frustrated with whatever she was creating, she took it out on whoever dared to get in her way. Dad used to call her Tornado Lauralee when she got like that. I guess in New Orleans he would call her Hurricane Lauralee.

"I loved Magnolia Prep while I was there. I think you will, too."

Magnolia Preparatory School was her alma mater. She grew up in New Orleans and went to school with the same people and built friendships. Mom was also very social when she wanted to be. At Magnolia Prep she had been a *cheerleader*. My mom, a cheerleader. She also did speech and debate. And she was homecoming queen. I would be none of those things.

"You're in your head. Get out of there. Thinking leads to spinning, and spinning leads to nowhere."

I took a sip of my coffee; it immediately made my stomach feel worse.

Mom scooted her chair closer to mine. "Babe, I'm trying to be sensitive to the newness of all of this. In fact, I've cleared my schedule for the week. I'm not editing. I am going to be spending time with you. Pick your adventure next weekend. Whatever you want to do, we'll do it."

I nodded. This was terrible. But I did not believe her. Work always came first with her. If she had an idea that she needed to get out, that was priority. "That sounds great, Mom. I'll think of something." I saw a bill sitting next to the baby cactus for Magnolia Preparatory Academy. Mom and Dad were paying $20,000 a year for me to attend that school. We could get a car for that much.

I had mentioned going to one of the few public schools, and they both turned down the idea. Surprisingly, they were on the same page about me going to a private school in New Orleans. They argued that Magnolia Prep would look good on my transcript. Mom also argued that the charter schools in New Orleans were not the best. Dad jumped in on that argument and threw in a handful of casually racist comments to support Mom's argument, and that started a huge fight. He left New Orleans without saying good-bye to either of us.

"Just remember, if you strike out, you will still have tomorrow to start over again," she said.

That wasn't true. If I struck out and did something completely embarrassing, I would be known for that thing forever. It was like the time Jefferson Price ate too much fiber in eighth grade and shit his pants, and literally up until I left Oxford he was known as Shit Boy. Reminder, no fiber for me.

I smiled at Mom. It was another tight smile. Decent practice for getting through the day.

I'd bring my journal with me. If I found myself feeling anxious, I would write something. An alternate first day, maybe? Or I'd pretend that Jessamine wanted to see me again and write our next adventure. Maybe that was too pathetic. Wait. No. I wasn't supposed to write alternate realities and alter egos anymore. Dreaming of what could be made me freefall when I came to terms with what was.

"What are you going to do while I'm gone?" I asked Mom.

"I don't know." She shrugged. "I reached a good place in my manuscript."

"Good."

"And now that your daddy is in Oxford and you're starting school—I may take in the air. It's been a while since I've gone to City Park. I might drive out there and sit underneath the shade of ancient live oaks draped with Spanish moss and contemplate how I can be a better mother to my son."

It was dumb how badly I wanted to believe her. It would be awesome to tell her about Saturday and ask for her advice. *Mom, what should I do? Does it sound like Jessamine likes me? Am I jumping to conclusions? Yes, it was just one night. But that one night was great.*

"How about I drop you off to school? And I'll pick you up?" She straightened my tie. "Sound good?"

"Maybe tomorrow."

Mom was watching me, looking worried. I didn't want her to worry about me.

"I—I'm going now," I stammered, grabbing my bookbag and slinging it over my shoulder. "Wish me luck."

"All the luck!" Mom pulled me into a quick hug and kissed my cheek.

⚬⚬⚬

Magnolia Prep had a senior class of one hundred students at the most. My peers were mostly white. The second I stepped into school, they knew I was the new guy. Heads turned, and some girls whispered by their lockers. I got a few smiles that I wouldn't call genuine, but they were polite. People were friendly enough.

The hardest parts of Day One was the introducing game, PE, and lunch.

The introducing game was in AP English. I took my seat in the back and hoped and prayed that the teacher wouldn't single out the fresh blood. But Ms. Morris did that and more. She made me introduce myself and tell everyone where I came from. Someone said, "That's why he sounds like that" in response, and then I had to share an exciting fact about me.

My go-to exciting fact was that I was a writer, but I didn't say that out of fear of someone asking me what I wrote about. *Pure wish fulfillment!* Instead, I let my interesting fact be that my mom was a published writer and that she was from New Orleans.

I didn't tell them *what* she published because *View from the Mississippi* was a porno for bored housewives. It was technically classified as a paranormal romance, but there was a lot of sex in it. I was still traumatized by the time one of my classmates brought the book to school in eighth grade and everyone took turns reading it. All I could do was cover my ears and wait for the teacher to realize what was happening. When I mentioned that Mom was a writer, a few students whipped out their cell phones, and an okay day turned to shit.

By PE, word got around that Mom wrote time-travel erotica. For the rest of the first day my classmates teasingly referred to me as Reginald, the character in *View from the Mississippi* who traveled back in time to decide if he wanted to marry his first cousin or his adopted sister. I had no idea what Mom was thinking when she wrote that.

I ate lunch in the library, hiding with the dead poets.

Mom texted me. I checked my phone, expecting to see a text asking about my day. Nope. The text said that she was at City Park and that she needed my urgent input on a storyline.

The rest of the week went like that. Mom texted me during class for *urgent input* on her story and I remained the topic of discussion. Some guys in Anatomy and Physiology laughed at me when I was called on to ask a question. And a girl in English class told me that she heard I was bi, and she wanted to know if it was true.

I was used to being the topic of discussion in Oxford because of my parents' antics. But this was new and weird—people taking interest in *me*.

∞

An unexpected miracle happened on Friday. There was a note in my locker. A note that read:

Dear New Guy,

Welcome to Magnolia Preparatory Academy! I apologize that I was not there to welcome you personally. I was vacationing with B and J (Beyoncé and Jay-Z) in Turks and Caicos. Meet me for lunch in Lafayette Square.

Warm regards,
SOB

LOL. I just realized my initials spell "son of a bitch." Consider yourself a lucky bitch! See you soon.

Saint Olivier Baptiste

⋯⋯⋙⋘⋯⋯

Saint Olivier Baptiste was sitting on what appeared to be a gold throne underneath a white tent. He was wearing a light blue suit with a gold metallic pattern, shiny black shoes with gold buckles, and he kept looking down at his watch. The watch appeared to cost more than the tuition at Magnolia Prep.

And that wasn't the most bizarre part of it. He sat at the head of a table. The table was set up with eight chairs and there was *wait staff*. I watched with wide eyes as they stirred golden pans of food. Whatever they were stirring smelled delicious.

"Saint?" I asked.

He didn't hear me. He was on his phone, typing something with urgency.

"Why do boys have to be so difficult? For the life of me, I don't understand why he won't just take the Mercedes Benz off my hands. It's just sitting there in the driveway. And what's he driving? A moving bomb, that's what!"

Uh, okay? I rested my hands on the back of the chair and leaned forward. "You're Saint Baptiste, right?"

"Are you asking?" he said, placing down his phone with an exasperated sigh.

"I, um . . . reckon?"

He dropped his shades, his dark eyes studying me. "Are you telling me that you've been at this school for four whole days and you don't know who I am? I mean, there is only one other Black person at this school."

I licked my lips. Should I know him? This was my first time seeing him. I mean, I overheard my classmates saying his name and talking about his lavish "Gatsby" parties, but this was my first time putting a face to the name. "Umm . . ." I glanced at his outfit and the huge tent in the middle of the park. "When I opened your invitation, confetti and glitter came out of it. I'm still trying to get the glitter out of my eyes. You got to be Saint if I'm going by all of this." I gestured at the tent and catered table. I wondered how come he could have a special lunch out here while everyone else had to eat in the cafeteria.

Saint reclined back, keeping me on ice.

Two people walking in workout clothes approached the tent. Someone came out of the blue, a security guard maybe, to tell them to not walk so close. I looked back at Saint, surprised. Was he an actor?

"How do you know who I am?" I asked.

"Sit." He flicked his wrist and pointed to the seat across from him.

I pulled out the seat and sat down. Even though it was humid and unforgiving outside, the tent felt nice and cool. There were multiple fans set up and a cool mist was being sprayed in what appeared to be five second intervals.

Saint clasped his hands. "How do I *not* know who you are? You got an accent that is too country to be from here, you're tall, and you're fresh blood in an inbred pool of New Orleanian socialites. You're the fresh catch of the day, darling. Don't worry, the socialites will get bored with you eventually and it'll be like you don't exist. To quote my friend Heidi Klum, 'One day you're in, and the next you're out.'"

I rubbed the back of my neck.

Saint placed his shades on the table. "You may be asking yourself, why does the fabulous and handsome Saint Olivier Baptiste invite you to lunch? A handsome but ordinary country boy from the backwoods of Mississippi like yourself."

Backwoods of Mississippi? Is that what people were also saying about me? I had two options, let my classmates' words tear me up or lean into it. I decided to lean in. "A country boy who is also inbred and can't decide if he wants to marry his first cousin or adopted sister?"

Saint's eyes widened and he pointed a gold-painted nail at me. "You have humor! That's key. All these Magnolia Preppers including myself, the Grand Dame of Magnolia Preppers, have gone to school together since we were toddlers. We date our own. Hang out with our own. Most of us will even marry our own. Fortunately for you, Backwoods, I like a little swirl."

Oh? Swirl like vanilla and chocolate? White and black? Did

he think I was gay? I smiled down at the table, feeling like I should correct him, but worrying that correcting him might come off wrong.

"You, backwoods boy, are new and shiny. Because of your sparkle, you get an automatic invite to my masquerade ball."

"Masquerade ball?"

"Yes. At Gallier Hall in November. I am only inviting a select few. Think of it as a lottery. The who's who of New Orleans will be there rubbing elbows. The who's who and you." He spoke a lot with his hands, and his voice often drifted into song. Saint was interesting for sure.

"Thanks for the invite." November felt so far away.

Saint sighed. "Okay, confession. This lunch was not for you. I invited this guy I've been seeing. He should be sitting where you are. But he is stubborn and turns up his nose at extravagance where others gladly indulge. Because he didn't show, I needed a reason to have this production! I can't just sit out here looking fabulous in this Versace suit, eating lunch alone. Saint Olivier Baptiste does not eat alone unless he chooses to do so!"

How many times had Saint referred to himself in the third person? I'd never met someone who actually did that in real life.

"Maybe he'll still show?" I said.

Saint waved his hands. "He won't. He claims that he wants *privacy*."

"Well, if that's what he wants, this isn't private—like, at all."

Saint hooked his hand underneath his chin. "Are you gay?" he asked.

"No . . ." I said, and quickly added, "But I don't care that you are."

"How do you know I'm gay?" He reclined back in his throne and crossed his legs.

"Well, you were just talkin' to me about a dude. And your style. I'm not an expert on fashion but your outfit reads kinda gay to me. No offense."

He snapped his fingers three times in the air. "Yaaaaas. Read for truth. Periodt." Saint chuckled. "At least she's honest. I think I might keep you around. It's a delicious development. Friend the outsider. Share my insider secrets." He turned to a white woman standing closest to him. "Serve him a little of everything. And when we're finished eating, box up the rest and distribute it around the city. New Orleans' homeless population isn't getting any better."

I looked over his non-uniform again. "How come you don't have to wear this?" I asked, pointing to my own school uniform of blue blazer, white shirt, and blue-and-red-striped tie.

"My parents donate beaucoup money to this school. They are not going to tell me nothing if they want to keep receiving the Baptiste checks, okay!"

As I watched the server prepare a plate for me, I went out on a limb. When I hung out with Jessamine over the weekend, I focused on tapping into courage. I should do the same with Saint. "What's your guy's name?"

"Joel," Saint said dreamily. "He's tall, dark, handsome, and has this luscious beard."

A luscious beard, huh? I bit my cheek to keep from chuckling. "If he likes privacy, how about you do something private for him? It can be extravagant, but not in the wide-open like this."

"Booboo, Saint does not hide."

"What if *he* hides, though?" I thanked the server as they set down a plate in front of me.

Saint rested his hand against his cheek. "How do I focus on what he needs?"

I waited for Saint to crack a smile. He did not. Oh. Damn. That was a serious question? "Um . . . have you ever had a boyfriend?" Ironic that I, the boy who never had a girlfriend off the page, was asking that question.

"A boyfriend? Like a leash with legs. No, ma'am," he said.

I reached for a fork but did not start digging in because Saint wasn't eating.

"Teach me how." Saint waved away the plate the server brought him. "I'm not hungry."

"Teach you how?"

"Show me how to care. Or tell me what caring people do. Help me be better. What are you doing next weekend?" Saint pulled out his phone. "Swap numbers with me. I'll set up a date for us to hang off campus."

I pulled my phone from my pocket. There were fifteen messages from Mom. The last one said, *HELLO? Did you see my previous text messages?*

12
JESSAMINE

I SURVIVED THE FIRST WEEK OF SCHOOL!

It was fraught (ACT word of the day) with trials. Low motivation. Meetings with career counselors and Ms. Nadia about the path I wanted to take post high school. And exhaustion at every turn.

My nearest and dearest had a tradition on the first Friday of the school year: We celebrated getting through the first week with a gathering. Usually we hung out at Solange's house and watched movies and cooked our favorite foods. When I say we cooked, I meant that *they* cooked. This Friday, we were celebrating at Chicory and Grind, a coffee shop where Solange and Joel worked.

Iz was across from me, working too diligently on homework. Didn't she get the memo? This was a no homework zone!

"Iz, you're being boring. Homework is for Sundays."

She looked up from her computer. "Five more minutes, chica. I got to finish this personal essay so Mr. Johnson can proof it."

I tapped my nails on the table. *It's August.* There was still plenty of time to complete personal essays. But Iz and Joel wouldn't stop talking about theirs. I stared out the window. A little Black girl was walking down the street with her mom and dad. They were swinging her between them. She was grinning and kicking out her legs, seemingly thrilled that her feet weren't touching the ground.

Seeing that family made me think about Daddy.

Joel joined us. He slid into the booth beside me. Like a good twin, he graced us with coffee-bean-espresso magic. "Iz, a treat for all your hard work."

She blew him a kiss. He blew her back a kiss.

"And, Jess, because you're my twin."

Rude. I work hard, too! I took a sip of the brewed delight. Joel knew how to make a good cup of coffee. He was so good at it that at home I refused to make my own. Luckily, he also enjoyed a good brew, so he'd make me coffee whenever fixing some for himself. Everything in Joel's coffee was balanced. The right amount of sugar, milk, and coffee. "What about my hard work?" I voiced while tapping my coffee cup on the table.

He snorted. "I walked past your class the other day and I saw you sleeping."

"*What*? I was not sleeping in class!" I defended.

Joel ran his hands over his neatly trimmed wavy hair, faded low on the sides. "You were. But that's *your* GPA, not mine. If you keep it up, you're going to end up at Bayou State University."

Iz took a sip of her coffee. She was wearing this super cute University of Arizona sweater that hung off her shoulders. *We get the point, Iz. You're leaving!* "Is Bayou State University in Louisiana?" she asked.

I hadn't heard of Bayou State University either. Mama sure didn't mention it. Ms. Nadia didn't mention it either. I studied Joel curiously.

"Bayou State University does not exist. What I'm saying is, the only college that will want Jess if she sleeps through her senior year is no college." A text message pinged on Joel's phone. One text message turned to eight. The contact was cryptically saved as Trouble.

"Who is Trouble?" I asked. I shot a look at Iz.

Iz's brown eyes lit up. We'd been BFs long enough for me to recognize that her interest was also piqued (another ACT word).

Joel immediately turned his phone over, proving that he had something to hide!

Iz closed her computer. "Is this a girlfriend?" she asked.

This was why I loved her. When I went in on Joel, she went in. Unless Solange was around to defend him (which she always did), Joel was at our mercy. *Cue the wicked laughter.*

"Y'all need to chill out," he said. "Trouble is just this guy I'm tutoring."

"Are you tutoring him in French?" I asked in a purr.

"I don't take French, silly."

"French kissing!" I said, blowing him kisses.

Joel rolled his eyes so far back in his head. "You're so immature. How are we even the same age?" He snatched my coffee, acting just like Solange. *Mean!* "I only make coffee for nice people."

We sat in silence for a bit after that. The musical vibe in Chicory and Grind that Friday was nineties music. Solange liked to play nineties music. She said that it was a vibe. The song that was playing now made me think about someone that I didn't want to think about. He was a returned library book. A boy who came to life in the floral print. Maybe I only remembered him because of his name. How can you forget a boy named Tennessee Williams?

Solange walked out of the back, putting on her hoop earrings. Solange was dressed up, honey! Her makeup was flawless. Eyeshadow had her bright eyes looking bigger than usual. And the bold red shade of lipstick she was wearing brought all of the drama.

"Yes!" Iz clapped. "I *love* this!" Iz was such a hype girl. That's why she was fam.

Solange danced with her hands in the air. She ended her dance with a twerk. "This lewk is called classy and ratchet. I'm going on a date." She sank into the booth beside Iz.

I glanced at Joel. He glanced back at me, looking worried.

"Where are y'all going?" Iz asked trying to be all supportive.

Solange starred at me and Joel. "I don't know. He said that he's going to surprise me. What are y'all telekinetically talking about?"

"*Telepathically.*" Joel corrected. "Telekinesis is moving things with your mind. Telepathy is communicating with your mind."

I sighed. Blerd alert. Blerd alert.

Solange didn't come for Joel. *If I'd said that . . . ha!* She just kept on talking about her date. This guy was Dominican and he was a banker. He had a good head on his shoulders, and he was going somewhere in life, unlike "the failure"—her words—that was Creyshawn.

"That sounds exciting," Iz the diplomat offered.

"I think so. It'll be good to go out. All I've been doing is working to pay that Treme rent and taking care of Mama. I deserve some fun." She flipped her dark blonde wig off her shoulders.

"S," Joel said, sliding my coffee back to me. "Do you think

that you should take some time to focus on you? I mean you *just* broke up with this Creyshawn guy."

Joel's cell pinged again. A few times. Ohh. Now Trouble was calling.

Solange sighed.

Joel turned over his phone again. He was definitely lying about who Trouble was. People you were tutoring weren't that needy!

Solange placed her hand over Joel's. "I know y'all are worried about me. Yeah, I'm dating again, but I'm not looking for Creyshawn's replacement. I just need a distraction from everything that is going on up here." She tapped the side of her head. "I got a lot going on, y'all . . . and I just need a little break. This break just happens to come in the form of a very fine man who wears a suit like it's another layer of skin, okay?"

Iz rested her head on Solange's shoulder. "I wouldn't trust a boy to distract you. Boys come with unwanted complications."

"Amen," I said.

Solange's eyes narrowed at me. "What happened to the white boy who was waiting for you the other day?"

"I don't know any white boys," I lied.

Joel turned in the booth so his whole body was facing me.

Iz leaned in, too, all eyes on me. *C'mon, BFF. Don't join in on this attack.* Unfortunately, my *telepathy* did not work on her. "Yeah! Who was that cute boy in the picture? You sent me a pic and then ghosted."

I shrugged, still playing clueless.

"Yeah, who is this guy?" Joel said, forgetting that I was three whole minutes older than him. Which made him technically my baby brother, and I deserved the right to interrogate him, not the other way around.

"Who is Trouble?" I shot back.

My comment made Joel set his lips tight.

"What's his real name, JoJo?"

We were twins, but he treated me like a stranger on the street. Who knew about his robust love life or lack thereof? If someone did know about it, I wished that they would share with me! Older sisters wanted to know.

"Leave me alone, Jessamine."

Solange wiped her hands together. "Y'all got a lot of secrets, and y'all are making my nerves bad. I'm leaving." She reached in her purse and pulled out a twenty-dollar bill. "Y'all put that toward something good to eat." She started to get up, paused, and slapped another ten dollars down.

Solange had several of the enamel pins I made for her stuck to her purse: a pair of scissors, a unicorn, and a heart. Iz was also wearing one of the many enamel pins I made for her, a pin of two girls hugging. That one had taken a long time to draw. And Joel was wearing the You + Me pin I made for him. I loved when my nearest and dearest wore my art. It made me feel all fuzzy inside.

⚬⚭⚬

Later that night, I took a long shower, scrubbing off the first week of school. I also washed my hair, which meant that I'd be up late. I tied my hair with a towel and walked into my room. Iz was laying on her stomach watching something on my computer, and Joel was sitting at my desk painting something.

"How is your art show coming along?" I asked him, flopping

on the bed beside Iz.

"It's coming," Joel said with a nod. "There's still time for you to get involved."

"I'll pass."

Joel snorted. "We'll see about that."

"We sure will," I challenged right back. It wasn't that I didn't want to participate in Joel's art show. I did want to. It was for a great cause, giving back. But these days, anything extra was too much. Maybe I should talk to Ms. Nadia about that? Ask her how to navigate low motivation. I think that was what I had. Ugh. I needed to change the subject.

"How is your love life, Iz? Since Joel won't talk to us about Trouble." Joel immediately started to pack up his sketchbook and watercolors. He was so sensitive! "Why are you leaving?"

On his way out the door, he waved. He was definitely hiding something.

"Meh. The boy I'm kind of seeing in Gentilly asked me to be his girlfriend."

I smiled sleepily. Guys were always trying to lock down Isobel Santos. She was like a unicorn because she didn't want to be anyone's girl and guys didn't understand that. "You said no?"

"Of course. Boys only have one purpose. A purpose that they can be outsourced for when they don't act right."

I giggled at her use of *outsource*. My BF was a mess.

She poked me.

"Why am I getting poked?"

Iz poked me again. "Who was the guy in the picture? It's just me now. Tell meeeee."

Ugh, we were on the topic of Tennessee again. "A boy that

came into Rue Margeaux."

"Did you have fun?" she asked.

I closed my eyes, shutting out my room. I didn't want to talk about Tennessee. He wasn't real. He was just a stranger on a train. Our paths would never cross again. And if they did, I'd pretend not to see him. The memories of the night were already starting to fade.

Faded moments and memories. I wondered if he still thought about me.

Soon, being here with Iz like this would also be a faded.

Ugh. I didn't want to think about that either. Why did my mind keep doing this when we had a whole year left?

For years, my room had been the space where we read together, danced until we were dizzy and out of breath, and cried together. I admit that it's hard for me to let people see me—I don't know why. But Iz saw me. And now, she was about to go to Arizona and I was about to go . . . somewhere, someplace—alone.

I turned over on my side to face Iz. We were both lying on our stomachs, facing each other. Iz smiled. Dust fairies floated down from the ceiling and tangled in her hair. I raised my hand to catch them. Iz also raised her hand, flattening hers against mine.

"What's going on with you, Jess?"

My nose twitched. "What's going on with me?"

She nodded a few times.

My lips trembled. I closed my eyes and tried not to think so hard. I didn't want to think. Not at all. All I wanted to do was watch TV and stop the clock counting down. I opened my eyes again and saw that Iz's eyes were wet.

"You feel like really far away. Are you okay?"

Iz was worried about me. That sent me into panic mode. I was okay. Seriously. I was just tired. "I'm fine. I promise. Life is just moving really, really fast. I feel like I'm running to catch up with it."

"Are you sure you're running?" Iz asked.

I scowled. "What does that mean?"

She shrugged. "It doesn't seem like you're running to me. It seems like you're stopping. And the Jessamine I've known all my life is a fighter. Why aren't you fighting?"

Before I could respond, we heard what sounded like fireworks.

I froze.

We looked at each other, confirming. Waiting. The next thing I knew, there were more fireworks.

And then there was screeching tires and the unmistakable wail of someone screaming.

13
JESSAMINE

I USED TO wake up in the middle of the night screaming. Usually, it was a side effect of a bad dream, a monster chasing me. Sometimes it wasn't a monster. But sometimes it was fireworks. An endless explosion of fireworks and screams.

It used to happen once a year, but now it seemed like the fireworks happened every other month. It didn't matter if the sun was out and burning bright. It didn't matter if kids were out playing on the lawn or drinking cold drinks on stoops. It didn't matter if you were having a crawfish boil with loved ones. It did not matter. The fireworks could still find you and kill you.

Because the world kept going, sometimes I forgot about nightmares and the fireworks that kept me up in the night, the black screens that the cops set up to hide death. Temporary shields for Black boys with black eyes and open mouths.

Once I heard the screeching tires, I jumped up. Someone was screaming. They'd been shot. It sounded like they had been shot at least ten times. *"Joel!"* I screamed.

In my nightmares, the boogeyman was a shadow. It was a faceless towering entity that took with clawed hands. I crashed into Joel's room. His bed was neat. His watercolor painting was on the floor. He wasn't in there. "Joel!"

I ran to the kitchen, pushing past Iz. She tried to grab for me, but I pushed away from her.

He wasn't in the living room either, which meant that he was outside.

The front door was open. My stomach dropped.

Why did he go outside? Why didn't he stay in my room?

JoJo.

I took a step toward the door. The heat rushed in, choking me. Making it hard to breathe. I couldn't see anything through my tears. I was so sure that something happened to my twin.

I sprinted toward a crowd of people standing in the middle of the street. The dim glow of flickering streetlamps and porch lights revealed the grim sadness on my neighbors' faces. The kind of grim silence that echoed how many times they'd seen this.

It was silent.

I sucked a raspy breath into my lungs. I exhaled sharply. The blood on the street, black in the darkness, did not belong to Joel. The blood belonged to Ronnie Jackson.

"No, no, no! My baby!" his mama screamed. "Noooooooooo!"

The moon was full and violent. Its aggressive light shone into Ronnie's eyes. There was no sparkle there. No life. He was gone. Ronnie Jackson was gone.

I sunk down to the ground, unable to stand any longer. Ms. Darla was on her knees. Her son Ronnie's body was limp in her arms. Screaming and sobbing, Ms. Darla kept his head pressed to her, as if her screams would resuscitate him.

When I used to have nightmares, Mama would pick me up in her arms and bring me to her room. She would make me tea and put on my favorite cartoons. I was too old for that now. But sometimes I wished that it was okay for me to still go to her and say, "Mama, I'm scared, can I sleep with you?"

I searched for Joel in the crowd of people. I found him crouched down on the ground hugging crying kids from the neighborhood. Soon they would be old enough to understand. Maybe they understood already. Youth doesn't promise life.

Sirens echoed through the night, death chariots racing to the scene of the crime. Another dead body. Wrong place. Wrong time. Guilty of a crime. Guilty of daring to live. It didn't matter. Death chariots always came to collect.

The cops came. The paramedics came. The black screens came, popping up like tents to hide wide eyes, open mouths, and blood-dyed streets.

Ronnie was dead. I could still see him. When I closed my eyes, I saw Ronnie lying on the hot asphalt. I didn't want to see his lifeless body anymore. I was safe in my room now. Safe, but not really, because I kept seeing Ronnie. His legs were wrong, bent at unnatural angles. His eyes were white and still. Ms. Darla had cried and held him in her arms, praying to God to not take her baby. Her baby was already gone. His head rolled back, his arms limp, his mouth open like he was singing a song to birds and angels.

I knew Ronnie. Joel did, too. We used to giggle together in church when Mr. Charles ate too many beans and passed gas. (Not just any gas. Stink-bomb gas that burned your nostrils and made you choke.) We rode our bikes together on the levees. Went to second lines together. And Ronnie Jackson had been Joel's first kiss. It was a dare that I made them do, but Joel seemed eager to do it.

They'd kissed only once. At least once that I was aware of. Hopefully, he wasn't Trouble.

My tired eyes fell on Joel. He was sitting far away from me and Iz, working on his watercolors again. That's what he did when he didn't want to talk. He talked by making art. I should make art, too. Watercolors always made me feel better.

"I can't believe he's gone." Iz broke the silence.

I nodded. It was all I could bring myself to do.

"Can I get anyone anything?" Iz asked.

I shook my head and smiled at her. It didn't seem real. How could he be dead?

Two days ago, I saw Ronnie riding his bike. Solange and I were coming back from somewhere. I had rolled down the window and yelled his name. He'd turned to look at me, tilted his chin up and said, "'Sup."

I don't know why he was killed. Maybe he got into something? Got caught up with the wrong crowd? Maybe it was just an accident. A bullet meant for someone else. In the end, it didn't matter. He wasn't alive anymore.

A shiver crept up my spine. It was so sharp and sudden that it reminded me that I needed to pee. I needed to pee three hours ago. But I didn't want to get up. My legs wouldn't do what my brain was telling them to do. And I guess a part of me was still processing. It happened. People got shot. Kids got shot. All the time. It could've been me or Joel or Iz or Solange. It wasn't, though, and for that I was thankful.

Joel set down his sketchpad and stood.

"Where are you going?" I asked.

"The bathroom." Joel glanced over his shoulder at me. "I'll be right back, okay?"

I nodded. Not sure why I was acting like Mama. So jumpy.

Iz rested her chin on my shoulder. "I called Solange and asked her to come over."

"You shouldn't have. She has a date tonight." I licked my lips. They tasted cracked and bloody.

Joel came back into the room, and Mama followed right behind him. She sat down on the edge of my bed and for a while didn't say anything. She just looked between the three of us. Who called her? She was working tonight.

"This city is only getting worse. All this killing needs to stop," she said.

That didn't make me feel better.

"JoJo." Mama turned to him. I already knew what was coming next.

"Yes, Mama?" he asked.

"You could've been out there with Ronnie."

"We haven't been close in a minute, Mama," Joel said.

I guess Ronnie wasn't Trouble. Knowing that didn't make me feel better.

"It doesn't matter if you haven't talked to him in five years. That *still* could've been you. These children are out here killing just because they can. A seventeen-year-old boy is dead. And for what?" She shook her head violently. "I do not want you staying in this city." Mama pointed at Joel. "There have been too many close calls. I know that you want to be a mentor to these kids, but your life means too much to me. You have a chance to get out of this city. You got to take that chance. I've worked hard for both of you to have a chance to go to whatever school y'all want."

"Do we have to talk about this now?" I mumbled. "Joel's okay. He's still alive."

She flashed her wide eyes to me. "We do have to talk about this now."

I hated how she did that. Why did everything have to turn into evidence for why Joel couldn't stay in New Orleans. If he wanted to apply to Xavier, then damn! Let him.

"I hear you, Mama." He spoke slowly, choosing his words carefully. Joel always did that with Mama, like he didn't want to disappoint her.

I focused on the sound of the fan whooshing around our heads. I could still hear the sirens. The death chariots screaming. Cars sped by, blasting loud music. They probably had no idea that the streets had just been covered in blood. I let all the sounds bleed together until there was silence.

Ouch. My brain hurt. My heart hurt. What was I supposed to do with this pain, this fear?

I closed my eyes and went back to the night I chose fantasy over reality.

Lying was easier. That girl I showed to the writer, that girl I sometimes showed to my friends . . . that girl didn't exist. She helped, though. When hard days ran up on me, knocking me off my feet, those Sunday feeling days, I reached for her.

The liar who made stank faces when she danced. The liar who sometimes pretended that she had stepped off a plane from Los Angeles or Manhattan. The liar who wore her pearls and Mardi Gras tiaras over her scars.

Because scars were ugly. They were real.

If only the writer boy knew that I was a fake girl in the real world. A girl who lied to be okay.

14
TENNESSEE

"SWEETHEART, ARE YOU SLEEPING?" Mom asked.

Even though my eyes were closed. I'd been awake for a minute. It was the weekend, which meant that I finally got the chance to sleep in. Also, I had stayed up late being the sound-board for Mom's ideas last night. I volunteered because that was the only way I got to tell her about my first two weeks at school.

Mom sat down on the edge of my bed. "Tenn, it's ten A.M. You don't usually sleep this late." When I didn't respond she squeezed my shoulder. "Are you mad at me?"

Why would I be mad at her? I rolled over to face Mom, nuzzling my head underneath the sheet. "I'm not mad. Just a little tired."

Mom's eyes looked bloodshot. Did she sleep at all last night? Her skin was super pale, too. The kind of pale that shouldn't happen in New Orleans unless you were a vampire. I got a sun-burn just from stepping outside to go to school. In Oxford I could get away with skipping the sunblock—not here.

Mom ruffled my bangs. "I have a question for you, sweetie."

I guess I could sleep when I went to college. Mom had opened the curtains and window in my room. The sheer cur-tains hung still in the stifling humidity. I could hear the streetcar and a discord of music from cars passing by on St. Charles.

"Tenn?"

"Sorry Mom. Still waking up. Of course, you can ask me more questions."

"You say *more* like it's a burden. I'm not trying to burden you." Mom stood up and placed her hand on her hips.

I tried my best to keep my face emotionless. When she got like this, picking apart my enthusiasm or lack thereof for discussing her craft, it was easy to get on her bad side. I didn't feel like getting the cold shoulder for days. One-word responses and heavy sighs every time I tried to talk to her.

"Sorry?" I apologized, even though I didn't think I did anything wrong.

Eventually, she sat back down. "Don't turn into your daddy. Stay my sweet boy."

I couldn't look at her. That wasn't fair.

Mom looked around my room. It seemed like she was observing the lack of unpacking. But I didn't think so. She was probably taking a beat after the veiled you're-just-like-your-daddy comment before launching into story talk. "I'm sorry, Tenn."

"That's okay." The words were automatic and conflict avoidant. I still couldn't look at her.

"You're not like your father. I don't know why I said that."

"It's okay, Mom. What about your story did you want to talk about?"

Mom leaned back on the bed. "Do you want to get breakfast at this cute place in the Seventh Ward? I've been wanting to try it ever since we moved back here. It has the best biscuits and the absolute best shrimp and grits that you've ever tasted."

I had never tasted shrimp and grits before. "Bet."

Mom's nose twitched. "Bet? What does that mean?"

"It means like deal."

"Ah." She giggled. "I see. You're already making new friends."

That was a perfect opportunity for Mom to ask about my friends. Last night we spoke about Magnolia Prep. She had been interested in finding out if any of the teachers that had taught while she was there were still at the school.

"So, my story."

Story talk turned into an hour conversation about a romantic quadrangle, alternate dimensions, and the best way to resurrect a character. During Mom's hour-long monologue, Saint texted me at least ten times. When I reached for my phone, Mom told me not to be rude and took it.

At the conclusion of story talk, she forgot about breakfast in the Seventh Ward and hurried off to go write.

I took a moment before texting Saint back. He wanted to study together for the Anatomy and Physiology quiz next week. While studying on a Saturday didn't sound like fun, hanging out with Saint outside of Magnolia Prep sounded awesome. And it would get me out of the house. I asked him when and where we should meet. Saint said now and dropped a pin of his location. He told me to dress casually.

—————⚬ℛⵔ⚬—————

There was nothing casual about the way Saint was dressed. Casual for Saint was a gold flowy silk robe. It kind of looked like a boxing robe, embroidered with a complex floral pattern. Underneath the robe was a black shirt and pants. I couldn't tell if the fabric for the black shirt was also silk or something more expensive. Saint's shoes were turquoise colored, and they curled at the toes. They looked like elf shoes!

"I know I said casual, but . . ." Saint came in for a hug, then leaned away, holding me by the arms, and observing my outfit with a tsk, tsk, tsk expression.

I chuckled awkwardly. "You said casual. Casual for me is jeans and a white T-shirt."

"I see. Sometimes I forget that the straights need a little more direction."

"Aren't we just doing homework?"

"Just doing homework?" Saint threw his head back and guffawed. "When does Saint Baptiste *just* do anything? It's the weekend, and the weekend is for joie de vivre." He linked his arm in mine. "Come in. Welcome to Casa Baptiste." Saint gestured around.

His house was bigger than mine. He led me through French doors into a room with a grand piano. There was a Persian rug situated underneath the piano, which he said was named Dorothy. That room had a library of bound books. I wanted to spend more time in that room. I had this thing about seeing what books people read. What was on someone's shelf said a lot about them.

Saint whisked me from room to room, through pocket doors that led to wide open spaces and to a super green courtyard that smelled like olive tree blooms. My favorite room in his house was the Harlem Renaissance room. It was full of paintings on oil canvases of Langston Hughes, Dizzy Gillespie, Countee Cullen, and other famous artists from the Harlem Renaissance.

"My mom painted these," Saint said, casually touching the golden frame of an African American woman wearing a flapper dress and singing.

"No way."

"Yep, when she has free time, she paints. Mona channels her inner Lois Marilou Jones."

I'd never heard of Lois Marilou Jones. I'd have to Google her when I got home. "Your mom is so talented."

Next, Saint whisked me through a sculpture room. "The Centre Pompidou has displayed some of her work."

"Did she make this sculpture, too?" I asked, totally in awe of the bust of a man in front of me.

"No, my dad made that." Saint took my hand. "I'm thinking about bringing Joel here. He's into art. What do you think?"

"I think that sounds like a great idea. He should feel comfortable to be himself in your house."

Saint squeezed my hand. "That is what I was thinking." He led me to a room that looked like a greenhouse. There were several people tending to giant bowls of leafy plants. Classical music was playing. And there was a fountain in the middle.

"This is very bucolic, don't you think?"

"For sure. What do you do in this room?"

Saint let go of my hand. He walked into the bucolic room, switching his hips from side to side. "This is the inspiration room. If my parents are in town, this is where they sculpt and create. And this is where I host most of the events held at home. The energy is good here, you know?"

"The energy is mellow in a good way." I had this weird urge to tell Saint about my mom. I had driven to his house feeling a little anxious, worried that I wouldn't be able to shake it. But being at his house was helping.

"Let's take afternoon tea over here." Saint strutted over to two white chairs that looked like they had never been used. He sat down in one, crossing his legs, and gestured for me to take the other. I sat down, scooting to the very edge.

"Have you ever had afternoon tea before?"

I didn't want to live up to his Backwoods nickname. "No, sir."

Saint squinted. "Interesting." He reached for a tiny gold bell and rang it a few times. The sound carried over the classical music and water fountain. He set the bell down. "When's your birthday?"

"Oh, you believe in zodiac stuff, too?"

"I do, but I'm asking because my friend's birthdays are holidays to me." Saint pulled out his phone. "When?"

"July twelfth. When is yours?"

Saint snapped his fingers. "Too bad it passed. We'll have to celebrate next weekend or something."

I bit my lip to keep from smiling. There was no way he really cared about my birthday. I mean, we just met. "When is yours?" I repeated.

Saint shrugged. "I don't tell people. One time I got this guy a PS4 for his birthday and he felt so pressured to match my gift that he broke up with me!" Saint flicked his wrist. "Boys and their egos. Thank god you're not led by ego."

A man wearing a crisp white button-down and black slacks walked over. "Mr. Baptiste, are you and Mr. Williams ready for afternoon tea?"

Saint clasped his hands. "We are. Please have Mr. Julius bring out all the courses at once. There has been a change of plans. My good friend needs a *Pretty Woman* moment, don't you agree?"

A *Pretty Woman* moment?

The older man gave me a once-over, scanning my T-shirt and jeans.

"Absolutely," he said.

I awkwardly crossed my arms, not sure what else to do.

"We'll take what we want from the courses. The rest you can have the staff box up and deliver around the city. Also, please bring out a tea menu. I can't decide if I want Darjeeling or that delicious rooibos tea."

"Of course, Mr. Baptiste. I'll let Julius know that you are ready for all the courses, and I'll bring out a tea menu to you."

"Thank you, Mr. Dean."

When Mr. Dean left, I asked, "What is a *Pretty Woman* moment?"

Saint explained that *Pretty Woman* was an old Julia Roberts movie. In the movie, she played a *lady of the night* (Saint's words). That made me laugh uncontrollably for some reason. In said movie, the male lead gave Julia Robert's character his credit card to get some new clothes, and somewhere along the way they fell in love.

"So . . . my *Pretty Woman* moment is transforming from a lady of the night to a classy-designer-label broad that you fall in love with?"

Saint screamed. "Nashville has jokes! I am gagged and loving it! C'mon now, Mr. Comedian."

"I wasn't even trying to be funny."

······⊗······

After tea, we went to Canal Place. As promised, Saint gave me the *Pretty Woman* experience. I tried on Other clothes that I would probably never wear anywhere.

Saint gave me a thumbs-up or thumbs-down on outfit

selections. Sometimes he wasn't even paying attention to me. On my final Other costume change, plaid corduroy pants and a five-hundred-dollar blazer, I sat down beside him.

"Nashville, you're out in these streets looking like somebody's daddy."

I laughed. "No thanks."

He smacked his lips together and took a picture of him blowing a kiss. "Speaking of daddies, sending this to Zaddy."

"Zaddy Joel."

Saint snickered, "Nashville, do me a favor and never say *zaddy* again."

"How about we both retire it?"

Saint turned his phone over and rested it on his knee. "Deal."

⁙

After returning from the mall empty-handed, Saint and I went back to his house to watch *Pretty Woman*.

We mostly talked through it. Saint talked about Joel. I almost talked about Jessamine. We spoke about the colleges he planned on applying to.

Mom texted me.

I didn't bother checking. I already knew what she wanted. And right then, my anxiety was gone. Spending the day with Saint had me feeling so high.

15
TENNESSEE

A COUPLE WEEKS LATER, Dad threw a curveball. He randomly decided to come to New Orleans. Usually, his visits came with at least two weeks' notice.

To make the random appearance worse, he wanted to spend every moment with me. I couldn't even chill in my room without Dad yelling, "Tennessee Rebel, where are you?"

In the morning, we went to Café du Monde. Our table was near a musician singing everything from country to alternative songs. The fans were going above us, but they were just pushing around the stifling air. Oxford in October was comfortable, but New Orleans in October, still felt like summer.

Dad munched on a beignet. A snowfall of powdered sugar fell from his mouth. "How has school been, Reb?"

I took a sip of water. A bold pigeon walked toward the powdered sugar near Dad's brown dress shoes. I watched it pick at the sugar, fleck by fleck. Dad took another huge bite, raining down more sugar on the blissed-out pigeon.

Because I didn't answer him right away, he glared at me, eyebrows lowered. "You hear me talking to you, son?"

"Yes, Daddy." I hated calling him Daddy. I used to call him that when I was a kid, but now that I was older I wanted to call him Dad. I tried it once and he got mad, calling me disrespectful. I could not wait to go to college and get away from him. "School is cool."

"Cool?" He laughed. "How is your generation going to acclimate into the work force using *cool* and *uh-huh* to respond to every situation?" Dad shook his head. "I expect more from a twenty-thousand-dollar-plus education. I want straight As. Focus on your studies."

"Yes, sir."

Dad flicked his hands, throwing more powdered sugar onto the ground. More pigeons flocked over to the feast. Dad looked down at the pigeons and wrinkled his nose. "This whole city is full of beggars."

⸺◦❧◦⸺

I didn't want to go straight home with Dad. I lied and told him that I had to do some shopping before going home. He told me that I had to be back by five P.M. since tomorrow was a school day.

There was one place that I wanted to go to, a place that I knew that I shouldn't. She didn't text me for a reason. I'd given her my number, but she hadn't given me hers. That was really all the information that I needed. The tennis ball was in her court.

That didn't stop me from walking down to Bourbon. Even in the daylight, it was still packed. There were more families with strollers in the morning, fewer people standing outside with signs inviting people inside dark rooms. Some beads were still being thrown from balconies, but the vibe was much tamer.

When I got down to Rue Margeaux, I was saddened to see that it was closed. A sign on the door said, "Laissez les bon temps rouler: Closed on Sundays."

Still not ready to go home, I wandered around the French

Quarter. I didn't make it back to Frenchmen, but I did walk down Royal Street. I peered into art galleries and looked for ghosts in courtyards with fountains and blooming flowers.

I then made my way down to the Central Business District. I figured that if I had to go back, I would just walk. Walking would take longer, especially in the heat. I would take the heat over my too-big house that strangely felt too small when my parents were both home.

Near Julia Row, I stopped into a coffee shop called Chicory and Grind, where a sign outside the door caught my eye, advertising an open position. A job would give me an excuse to get out of the house, and a chance to make my own money.

Mellow R&B was playing. The walls were full of photos and art from New Orleans's three hundred years' worth of history. Throwback Mardis Gras parades. People dancing at Congo Square. Mardi Gras Indians. Louisiana musicians also showed up on the walls—legends like Louis Armstrong, Fats Domino, and Irma Thomas.

"Can I help you?"

I glanced at the register and almost died. *Seriously?* Her hair was different—short and blonde. But her brown eyes were familiar. She was slightly taller than me. "Solange?"

She studied me, confused. "Do I know you?"

I laughed a little. *You're Jessamine's cousin.* My heart skipped a beat. What were the chances of running into Solange again? Was New Orleans that small? "Yes . . . you, um . . . threatened to call the police a few weeks ago on me at Rue Margeaux?" She tilted her head. That probably wasn't the best lead. "I was with Jessamine."

"*Oh* shit!" Solange leaned across the counter. "You right, linen sheet dude! Are you looking for her?"

"No!" I said quickly, probably too quickly.

Solange was giving me the side-eye and a smile. "Are you here for coffee?" she asked.

"No, are y'all hiring?" I pointed to the board outside.

"How old are you?" she asked.

"Seventeen, ma'am."

She smiled. "What do you know about coffee?"

"I know that I drink it every morning."

"Can you make iced coffee?"

It couldn't be that hard, right? Make hot coffee and dump ice in it? "No, ma'am. But I'm a quick learner."

Solange tapped her fingernails on the counter. "Do you have customer service experience?"

Eh, no. I had no work experience. "Not really. But I guess a lot of customer service is treating everyone with respect and being professional at all times, which I can do."

Tapping her fingernails on the counter again, Solange looked unconvinced. "This coffee shop is LGBTQ friendly. All kinds of folks come in here, and when I say all kinds of folks, I mean *all kinds*; this is a safe space. Are you comfortable working in a space like that?"

"Absolutely."

Solange observed me for a while longer. I felt a little uneasy. It was low-key impostor syndrome. I had zero work experience. Heck, I barely had people experience outside of my parents and Saint. Why would she hire me? Especially when she just referred to me as "linen sheet dude." *Unfortunate.*

"You're seventeen, so you'll need to fill out some additional paperwork to work here."

My ears perked up. "Really?" I shouldn't have said that out loud.

Solange kept her smile, which put me at ease. "Let me go get that paperwork started for you, and you can drop it by here sometime next week."

The bell above the door jingled again.

"Speak of the devil," Solange said. "Cousin, your friend is applying for a job!"

I turned around, not expecting to see her. But there she was, the girl who had been running through my head since August. Jessamine. She was dressed like she was going to an interview, in a gray blazer and this professional-looking skirt.

I suddenly felt so self-conscious. Yes, I looked for her at Rue Margeaux. But I had worked up to that. This, I didn't have a chance to work up to.

"Hey!" I said way too enthusiastically.

She blinked, seemingly taken aback. "Writer boy? What are you doing here?"

"Um, manners!" Solange clapped her hands. "Tennessee just filled out an application for a job."

Jessamine stared back at me like she didn't know me, like we didn't spend a night together dancing and looking at art. That was all the confirmation I needed—that was why she didn't call me. She didn't like me like that.

Jessamine walked over to the counter. I wasn't sure if I should look at her or if I should look at the floor. Maybe it would be best if I didn't apply for this job.

"Could you get me some water, cuz?" she asked.

"Only if you act right," Solange said.

Jessamine took the spot beside me and leaned against the counter. "Out of all the coffee shops you could pick. Ironic that you picked the one where my cousin and twin brother work at." She thought about something. "That is irony, right?"

More of a coincidence.

"Here, y'all, stay hydrated. People out there having heat strokes left and right." Solange placed glasses of water in front of us. "And here you go, Tennessee. Fill this out and get it back to me." She handed me a folder and then stepped from behind the counter, staring at her phone. "Jess, where is your brother? He has a shift in ten minutes, and he is always here early. I need to get to the skating rink."

Jessamine giggled.

Solange passed her a warning look. Jessamine raised both her hands. "I think he's with Trouble," she said.

"Who?" Solange asked loudly.

"The person who is tickling his fancy. Tickling his funny bone. Tickling his desire," Jessamine said breathily, tickling the air.

I listened to their conversation but tried to act like I was busy with my cellphone. I had ten texts from Mom. The first text said *Quick question* and the rest were paragraphs about her characters and plots that required paragraph responses.

Solange pointed to me and said, "Run."

Huh? I looked up from my phone, confused.

"That's what Creyshawn did," Jessamine muttered under her breath. It was so quiet that only I could hear it.

Solange stepped outside with her phone to her ear.

Jessamine turned to me. "My twin brother is bossy and so is she. If you do get hired here, which you will, you need to speak up."

It seemed like Jessamine had a lot of ideas about who I was from our first meeting. I thought that I showed her the most outgoing version of myself. Apparently, I was wrong. "I can handle it. I'm used to dealing with personalities. My parents gave me plenty of off-the-clock training." I didn't mean to be self-deprecating. It just kind of came out.

Jessamine pulled her braid onto her shoulder. She stroked it for a few moments. Her eyes were fixed on Solange outside. "I'm getting Vietnamese iced coffee. That's the only coffee that I want, and they don't serve it here. Do you want to come with me?"

"I'd love to." The words fell out of my mouth too quickly.

Jessamine laughed and clapped her hands. "I'll take that as a yes!"

16
JESSAMINE

WHY DID I INVITE HIM TO COFFEE?

Tennessee set down two Vietnamese iced coffees. He took the seat across from me, his knee pressing against mine. I felt the urge to pull back. I ignored it—I didn't want him to notice.

"Did you just come from Café du Monde?" I asked.

Tennessee's eyes popped wide like a fish. His expression read, "How did you know?"

Writer boy has no poker face! I pointed to his blue-and-white-striped short-sleeve button-down. "The powdered sugar gave you away."

"Oh no!" He dramatically checked his shirt, pulling at the edges and checking his collar. "I can't believe I just applied for a job with beignet sugar all over me."

A little bit of beignet sugar never hurt anyone. "It's not a problem. My cousin chases men with rolling pins on the clock. If she is the hiring person, I'm sure she'll let your little sugar habit slide."

He exhaled, blowing up strands of his brown hair.

It was weird that I ran into him at Chicory and Grind. I honestly had no plans on seeing him again. Strangers on trains and all. "Thanks for the VIC."

"VIC?" he asked.

"The Vietnamese iced coffee. Yum." I raised the delicious coffee brew to Tennessee. "Cheers to you getting the job."

He hesitantly raised his VIC. "I didn't get the job yet."

"You'll get it," I said with a wink. We clinked plastic VIC cups. I removed the lid and took my first sip of magic. Sweet. Creamy. Coffee beans. Yes. Yum. *This girl is happy now.*

Tennessee stared down at the VIC, his eyes real concentrated on the cup.

"What's wrong?" I asked.

He smiled and shook his head.

"You don't like it?" I asked.

"No, I do . . ." He smiled again. "It just tastes different from the coffee I've had."

"Y'all just have regular coffee beans in Mississippi?"

He pushed away his VIC and leaned against the small table. "They have all kinds of brews in Oxford—where I'm from."

I had no idea where Oxford was. I didn't care to ask either. Which reminded me: What was I doing? Why was I here? Why did I invite the writer boy to coffee? I did that. Not him!

My cell buzzed. I turned it face up. My lock screen was a picture of me and Iz at school last year. We were in the library surrounded by torture reading (required reading), and she was hugging me. *My BFF was leaving me.*

There was no time to be sad. I pressed down on Mama's message.

Mama: *Where is Joel.*

I texted back: *With Trouble.*

I turned my phone facedown before she could ask any more questions. Tennessee was staring around the coffee shop. I watched him for a while, wondering how long it would take for him to notice me watching him. It took him about ten seconds. Once our eyes connected, he blushed triple strawberry.

His triple-strawberry blush took me back to that night. *Red*. Ronnie on the street. Red on his shirt. Ms. Darla holding Ronnie. Red on her shirt. The street. Red everywhere. In the potholes. Big potholes full of red. Even the moon was red. My hands, too. Red. Blood everywhere.

"Jessamine?"

At first, his voice sounded like it was in a tunnel. Then I saw his worried eyes. Music slowly flooded my ears. "Yes?" My voice sounded distorted and twisted. Tennessee still had worried eyes. I forced a laugh, needing to throw him off. "What's wrong? Why are you looking at me like that?"

He still looked worried. Too worried. I looked away because I couldn't take the worried eyes from a boy I barely knew. I could barely take the worried eyes from the people I knew.

"Are you okay?" he asked. Tennessee was looking at me like I was fragile or something.

The too-deep concern in his eyes made me want to run. That would be way too obvious though. Instead of running, I cupped my VIC and took a sip. "I'm fine. I skipped breakfast this morning and lunch this afternoon. This VIC is throwing my body into overdrive." I added a fraudulent giggle as an extra layer of throw-the-boy-off-the-trail. He still didn't seem convinced.

"Did you want to grab something to eat after this?"

I took another sip of VIC. His concerned expression had changed to care. He had on this nice-guy smile and there was a softness in his brown eyes. His smile seemed sincere. It was time for a change of subject. "I bet your friends back home are missing you."

Tennessee looked away, his face dropping a little.

"I guess the real question is, are you missing your friends?"

Tennessee shrugged. "I guess they miss me."

You guess? What kind of friends did he have at home? Tennessee didn't bother elaborating. "Have you made any friends since you moved here?"

He laughed, shaky. "I just moved here. I'm, um . . . still in the process of making friends."

"Are you shy?" I asked.

Tennessee rested his cheek against his fist. "Sometimes, not all the time."

"You seem shy to me."

"I'm just nervous," he said.

Tennessee glanced from the spot he had been staring at on the black-and-white-checkered floor to me. Usually, I would've asked what made him nervous, but for some reason, I didn't want to touch that. There was something about him. Something about the way he spoke. Something about the way he stared. Something about the way he moved so quietly. He was a different species of boy.

I took another sip of VIC. Ronnie was still on my mind. Even with Tennessee sitting across from me, all I could feel was this rawness in my stomach and throat, the rawness that made me feel like crying. Death wasn't something I could ignore, no matter how hard I tried.

Ouch. Ouch. Ouch.

I pushed the VIC aside and cradled my face in my hands. "What do you write?"

Tennessee's cheeks slowly turned a darker shade of triple strawberry. "Um . . ."

I giggled. "It's not a trick question!"

He giggled, too. Tennessee leaned away from me, slouching back in his chair and crossing his arms. There was a bright neon light directly behind his mop of brown hair. The multi-colored light read READY, SET, COFFEE, GO!

"I write about a world that I want to live in."

"Fantasy?"

He nodded. "I guess you could say that."

"Do you have a favorite quote from one of your fantasy novels?"

He appeared to think about it. He'd nod and then shake his head as if dismissing the quote. Eventually, I told him that he had five seconds to pick one.

"Fine. This is the only quote that I have memorized: 'You are all my fears in human form.'"

I took a moment to process that. "Deep."

Tennessee shrugged and fumbled around for his VIC. He took a sip and stuck out his tongue. *He is definitely not a fan.* Mississippi boys clearly didn't know a thing about good coffee!

"Question," I said, holding up a hand like I was in class.

"Sure."

"If your fears are in human form, does that make them easier to defeat?"

Tennessee looked down at the table. "I actually don't know. What do you think?"

"I don't know either!" I said, giggling.

The multicolored neon lights behind Tennessee's head changed to all neon red. Now it read: READY, SET, COFFEE, BLOOD, GO!

I blinked. The multicolored neon lights changed back to READY, SET, COFFEE, GO!

17
TENNESSEE

"IF YOUR FEARS are in human form, does that make them easier to defeat?"

That was one of the last things that she said to me.

Two weeks ago.

It played over and over in my head. The quote that probably was the reason she ghosted me. I thought about it too much. When I was at school, when I was at work. When I was having a conversation with Mom, on those off days that she felt like talking.

I kept wondering why I said that to her. It was too much to give her that quote. I should've said something else. Anything else. But that was what I went for. A quote about fear and humans. That was why it had been a month since we last spoke.

"What you got going on tonight?" Joel asked. He was standing at the register, phone in hand.

I turned to him. "Just homework."

"Urgent homework?" he asked as he put down his phone.

"I don't think so. I have a paper on *Death of a Salesman* due tomorrow. But I already started that."

"Cool." Joel stroked his beard. The way he said *cool* dragged out like there was something more he wanted to add.

How is your sister? That was the question that I wanted to ask, but I was too chicken.

"Since you don't got a lot going on tonight, wanna hang out?"

I stared at Joel for a few seconds, sure that I had heard him wrong. He didn't repeat himself. "You want to hang out?" I clarified.

Joel chuckled. "Yeah, only if you do."

"I do." I felt a weird giddiness. I'd been working with Joel for a month. He was nice, but he mostly kept to himself. If I had a work-related question, he was super thorough in his response. In the past, if I asked him anything that was not work related, he kind of clammed up. "What do you want to do?"

"Food?"

"Sounds great." I could hear the overeagerness in my voice. "Do you have a place in mind or should I Google?"

Joel waved his hand. "Naw, bruh. The Fried Chicken Festival is going on right now."

I laughed. "Another festival?"

"I told you, Tennessee!" Joel pointed at me. "All these tourists come in here asking about the festivals. I've lived here all my life so I know the festivals by heart, but you need a little cheat sheet."

Solange rushed from the back room. She looked . . . worried.

"How are my boys?" she asked.

"Good, cuz." Joel turned his phone over again. "You good?"

Solange nodded. "I gotta head over to my mama's. Let's close up early."

"Naw." Joel waved his hand. "You go on to Auntie Myrtle's. Take care of whatever you got to. Tenn and I got this."

Solange placed her hands on her hips. She looked between

me and Joel. There was something different about Solange tonight. Ever since I'd known her, she always had a full face of makeup on. She also wore brightly colored wigs and blouses, instead of the black Chicory and Grind polo. Tonight, she was wearing a Southern University sweater and jeans. There was no makeup and no wig.

So many times, I wanted to ask her if she was okay. I always stopped myself because Joel was her cousin. He was her family. It didn't seem like my place to ask.

Solange reached in her purse for some cash. She handed it to Joel. "Y'all get something nice to eat. Close down the coffee shop early. The Fried Chicken Festival isn't going to be open all night."

"Solange, we don't need this." Joel walked around the counter with the cash out. "It's free to attend."

"Admission is free. The chicken ain't." Solange hurried toward the door. When Joel tried to stick the cash back in her purse, she held up a hand karate-style. "Don't make me knock you back to first grade. I will do it!"

Joel sighed loudly. "You always talking about Treme rent and your fifteen thousand jobs, but you out here giving out money every day like it's Christmas."

"That's how I show love. Money. Let me just do me, okay? Dang." Solange waved at me.

I waved back.

"Close early, Tennessee. Don't let Joel try to keep this shop open for clients who aren't coming. They all down in the Quarter burning their tongues on fried chicken!" She threw her head back and laughed. It was subdued compared to the usual way she laughed. There had been times that I stepped outside to take out the trash and I heard her out there. Her laugh was kind of like Jessamine's—warm, safe, full of life.

Joel locked the door behind Solange and turned the sign from OPEN to CLOSED. "I'm not going to argue with her. Let's get out of here."

᠊᠊᠊᠊᠙᠊᠊᠊᠊

The Fried Chicken Festival was held in Woldenberg Riverfront Park. There was a ton of people. So many people packed together on the grass in front of a large stage and on the Moonwalk, which was a walkway along the river.

As Joel and I navigated the crowds, we stopped by various stands to try the variety of fried chicken. It was weird and cool at the same time. Weird because we weren't really talking. Joel wasn't a small talk kind of guy. He didn't ask questions just to ask them. He asked questions that he wanted to know the answer to.

"I've had enough of people for today." He laughed. "Do you want to hang out here longer?"

"I feel like I've seen enough. This was fun. But so many people."

"Do you need to get home?" Joel asked.

I did have homework to finish, but I did not want to go home. There was something about going home when there was still daylight outside that made me sad. Daylight in New Orleans felt like it should be embraced with carpe diem.

Joel was looking at me with pensive dark eyes. His eyes were so much like Jessamine's. Their eyes were big and even though they were dark brown, there was a lot of brightness there. I looked away, because staring at Joel while thinking about Jessamine probably wouldn't translate well on my face.

"Bro, you don't have to."

"No, I'd love to."

Joel nodded. "Cool."

We walked along the Moonwalk through the crowd of running children and somewhat sober adults. Joel stared straight ahead, saying nothing. His silence often made me uncomfortable. It made me want to spin in my head and ask him tons of questions. But I practiced chilling out, focusing on what was going on around me and not Joel's silence.

There was music lingering in the air. The bands performing on the big stage and the Steamboat Natchez were also adding a whistle-like melody to the overall song. I looked to the river, where a huge barge was making a turn at the place where the river bent.

Joel veered off toward the concrete steps that led down to the river. There was a couple making out on the top step and a child throwing pieces of bread to swarming seagulls. I followed Joel down to the last step. The river was choppy, swirling with white foam and planks of wood and various other bits of debris.

"This is art," he said.

I tried to take in the art that Joel saw: The river. The Crescent City Connection, which was a pair of bridges that lit up at night and took traffic from the Eastbank, where most of New Orleans was located, to the Westbank on the other side of the Mississippi. A few people were jogging along the path on the Westbank. They were so close, but so far away.

"Jessamine said that you're a writer," he said.

My cheeks got warm. *She talks about me to you?* "Yeah, I write. It's not great or anything, but . . ."

"Tennessee, stop that." Joel shook his head.

"Stop, what?"

"Tearing down your art and yourself. Everything you create has value. Even the pieces that might not be your favorite."

His words sat with me. They percolated in my head. He was right. I was a writer, but I never felt like I was a *good* writer. It was just something that I did to help with escape. "What made you get into drawing and painting?" I asked him.

Joel pulled his phone out of his pocket. He looked down at the screen and sighed. "My dad used to take me and Jessamine around the city and he'd paint for hours and get us into it, too. That was how he relaxed after a long week. Now, it's how I relax."

"You're an awesome artist. I've seen some of your sketches." I said.

Joel smiled modestly, his attention focused on the seagulls, which were still swarming and multiplying. "Thanks, Tenn. Have you seen any of Jessamine's art?"

I tilted my head toward him. "No?"

"Aww, man. You should ask her one day to see it. She might show you."

I laughed. "I don't know about that."

"She talks about you sometimes, which means that she likes you. If she likes you that means she might be in the mood to share, especially because you're a writer and all. An exchange of art." He grinned wide. His grin lingered for a second or two and then his eyes got clouded. "Speaking of art, I have this community art show coming up later this month. I'd love if you could come out, bro."

"I'm there." It came out easy. Joel was opening up a little. And I was obviously in the market for friends. It also didn't hurt that he was Jessamine's twin.

Joel looked down at his shoes. "When you write, do you try to make sense of the world around you?"

That was another personal question. Did personal questions mean that we were growing? "Kinda. But mostly I write to escape chaos." The chaos in my mind and the chaos outside. "Does art help you make sense of the world around you?"

Joel chuckled. "Art helps me understand *why*. It also helps me deal with hard things, like . . . a friend of mine died."

"I'm so sorry, Joel."

He shook his head quickly. "Life happens. No one's time is promised here on Earth. If I didn't have art, I'm not sure how I would get through the bad days. That's what I was saying about art having value." Joel touched an enamel pin on his pocket sleeve, a pin of a heart with stiches down the middle. "You know another great thing about art?"

"What?" I asked.

"I'm not good with words like you writers. It's not self-deprecation, it's just fact. There is this, um . . . this guy I'm talking to." He looked at me quickly, like expecting me to have a reaction. I fought the urge to enthusiastically confirm that I was an ally. "He's a words kind of guy. He is direct and tells me exactly how he feels, like *all* the time. And . . . that . . . makes me nervous. I feel things. I feel a lot for him, but I don't know how to say it. So I paint him sunsets and he gives me words. But I think my painted sunsets are not enough."

Joel shrugged. The shrug said that he didn't care, but his words said something else. Before I could respond, though, Joel said, "I actually have some homework of my own to finish. I think we should call it a night."

I nodded in understanding, even though home was the last place I wanted to be. "Are you sure you don't want to talk about it some more? I'm a good listener."

A dark cloud passed over the sun, and over Joel's eyes as he watched the river crash against the steps, just inches from his feet. He took a step back.

"Let's go," he said.

18
JESSAMINE

"Jess!"

I waded through the murky brown water. The stink burned my nostrils. It was so quiet. Except when it wasn't. Even though I couldn't see them, I could hear them. The barking dog, the whimpering baby, the dying person.

They were dying.

The water was so high.

I knew how to swim 'cause Daddy taught me, but most Black people didn't. At least all the Black people I knew didn't. Mama was scared of water, and so was Joel.

This water wasn't chlorine. It stunk and was full of rotting things and rotting people.

Everything was gone. Our house. My dolls. My friends. They were gone. All gone!

I swam past the faceless people. I poked a leg. Dead. I pulled hair from black eyes. Dead. I saw a baby. Dead.

Someone had to be alive. Someone, somewhere . . . everyone couldn't be dead.

I'm coming. *I'm coming!*

I treaded the brown murky water, keeping my mouth shut. There were so many starfish in the water with me, their bodies spread out like angels. Fat arms. Fat legs. Floating, as if waiting to ascend to heaven. Dumplings in stew set to boil.

I saw someone I knew.

Someone I used to know.

We used to play basketball together.

My teacher was there, too, facedown, black hair floating like ink around her.

And Ronnie was also there, a bullet hole still smoking in his chest.

My body was so tired. Every muscle ached, but I couldn't stop—I wouldn't stop. I doggy-paddled to keep up my energy before I turned out like them, dead in the water.

You got it, Jessamine.

You got it, baby.

Daddy's voice cut through the stinking blackness like a trombone.

A whistle. A wish. A song. A whisper. A scream.

I kept doggy-paddling past the places I used to know.

My home! The corner shop! The candy lady!

Gone.

The rotten brown water punched at my throat and clawed at my arms. The heat rolled off the waves, cooking me. Choking me. Killing Me.

There was death in the water.

And on dry land—there was death. We were all dumplings set to boil in the pot.

In attics. In the Superdome. In hotels. On the streets.

Help was not coming.

SOS.

O

S

⸻⸻

"Jess, wake up!"

Hands were on my shoulders, dragging me underneath the water. No. Please. Don't. Please! I balled my fists and struck out at the air. I didn't want to die. No. Please . . . No.

"Jessamine!" Mama's voice cut through the horror. She was holding me, her fist balled against my back. Her other hand cradled the back of my head. "Baby, wake up. It's just a bad dream. Just a bad dream."

I peeled open my eyes to see Mama. She had taken out her rollers and was wearing her work clothes. She wiped at my tears. "I'm sorry, Mama. I didn't mean to wake you."

"Just a dream," she repeated, rocking me back and forth.

We were in my room. Where there was no water. Or starfish. Or dumplings.

Just dry land.

I closed my eyes. It had been so long since I had one of those dreams. I balled the fabric of Mama's cotton shirt in my hands. *What would I do if she ever died?* Tears filled my eyes again. I tried my best not to fall apart, but I couldn't help it.

Mama kissed my eyelids closed. "Baby, I have to go to work. I wish I didn't," she said. I looked at the clock—only ten P.M. How long had I been sleeping? I couldn't even remember crashing into my bed. Was it in the morning? In the afternoon? Why didn't anyone wake me up?

"I asked Darin to stay with y'all tonight."

Through my blurry eyes, I saw Solange and Joel standing behind Mama, watching me like I was a baby duckling that just fell out of a tree. I straightened up and wiped away the rest of my tears. I didn't want them to see me as weak.

Mama kissed me one last time. "Hopefully, I'll be back before you and JoJo head to school in the morning."

When Mama left, Solange took her place on the bed beside me.

"S, you need to correct her when she calls you the wrong name," I said.

"Girl, I'm not worried about that right now." Solange crossed her legs. "I'm worried about you. What's going on with you?" She placed her cool palm against my cheek. "You don't have to act all tough for me. I know about Ronnie. I heard Ms. Wilson talking about it at the corner store."

Enough time had passed for me to get used to the fact that Ronnie was gone. We weren't that close. People died. Life wasn't promised. Death happened all the time. I knew all that. I knew it.

But still, seeing Ronnie dead in the street like that, it made me think about how life was like paper. Paper could be ripped, cut, balled up, shredded, and disposed of, so easily.

Solange stared through me, her eyes and lips set in disbelief. She turned to look at Joel. He had moved to a beanbag next to my bookshelf. "How are you feeling, JoJo?"

"I'm aight," he said.

She nodded. "Y'all are tough. That's just how us Blanchards are built. We don't need nobody. At least, that's what we tell ourselves. It's okay to ask for help. Y'all knuckleheads understand?"

"Yes, we gotcha," Joel said.

"Jess?" she asked, whipping her head toward me.

I nodded. My head felt heavy and way too full of sadness.

Joel deserted the beanbag for the bed. "How is Auntie Myrtle? She doing okay?"

Solange looped an around Joel, her charm bracelets jingling with every movement. "She's fine."

Solange was lying. *Why can't she take her own advice?*

"You can talk to us, too," I said, snuggling closer to her. Solange wrapped an arm around me. I snuggled in deeper. Her shirt smelled like comfort, baby powder and the slightest spritz of Coco Mademoiselle, our favorite perfume.

"I know," Solange said with a sigh. "My mama is dying. There isn't much more to say than that. We still fight every night and by dinnertime we've done made up and we're watching her soaps. There's not much more to say." Solange shook her head and stared down at the floor in a trance.

Then Solange changed the subject abruptly "JoJo, your mama is on a mission. When I got here, Auntie Josephine was telling me that I needed to talk you out of staying here."

"Of course she was." Joel sighed and leaned back against the wall. "She won't leave me alone about that. Every time she hears about someone dying, she comes after me about how I need to leave."

I spoke up. "That's how she shows that she cares about you."

"She doesn't try and run *you* off," Joel said.

He was right. She didn't. I guess in her mind I wasn't in as much danger as Joel was. Mama worried about him a lot.

Solange pulled Joel down over to lay beside me. The three of us were now laying side by side like soldiers staring up at a starry night. Which reminded me—I turned off the lamp beside my bed.

The ceiling was illuminated with glow-in-the-dark stars. It was a simple magic trick that Joel, Solange, Iz, and I had worked on years ago. The stars, which you could only see in the dark, were always a welcome light when life felt hardest.

Life felt pretty hard right now. I could admit that.

"I'll make us some sustenance," Joel said, sitting up.

"What that mean?" Solange asked.

I giggled.

Joel sighed. "Sustenance. S-U-S . . ."

"Boy!" Solange swatted in Joel's direction.

He laughed and jumped up. "It means 'nourishment.' Some food to fill us up."

I turned over on my side. I didn't want to see the stars anymore. Joel flipped on the hallway light once he left my room.

That little bit of hallway light made my face visible to Solange. "Have you spoke to Creyshawn?"

"We haven't spoken since August. I've gone on a few dates just to distract myself. But going on dates only makes me feel worse. I'm done with men for a bit. I'm gonna focus on securing the bag and figuring out what the hell I want."

"That sounds very . . . adult."

She folded her arms across her chest and held onto her shoulders. "I'm tired. If it ain't replenishing me, it needs to go."

"I hear that."

"Talking about replenishing. What is replenishing you these days?" she asked.

I giggled. "Am I a plant?" The giggle hurt deep in my chest.

"I thought my use of *replenishing* was clever. Don't at me."

I raised my hands in surrender. That was a great question— that I was not going to answer. What was replenishing me?

Solange rolled her eyes. "That's why you be having those nightmares. You don't deal with emotions."

"You're one to talk! Thank you for telling me about myself, Solange Giselle VanZant."

Solange clucked her tongue. "Leave me alone, *beloved*."

Something delicious-smelling wafted from the kitchen. Joel had been in there for like two minutes and already magic was happening. I sighed, letting out some of the heaviness that I'd been holding in.

"Oh, PS your little boyfriend is cool."

"My little boyfriend?" I asked, playing with one of her charm bracelets.

"Yeah, girl. My employee Tennessee Williams. I wasn't sure about him when he came into Rue Margeaux wearing that sheet. But he's grown on me."

I smirked. "I'm surprised that he lasted this long working with you and Joel."

"Drop by and see that boy."

"Eww, why would I do that?"

"Eww?" She pinched me.

"Oww! You're so mean."

Solange sat up. I nearly asked her to stay, but I caught myself.

"Don't go breaking that boy's heart. He's a nice boy," she said.

"You just met him. You don't know him. Your loyalty should be to me."

Solange cackled. "Why? You used to always rat me out to my mama when I did something I outta not be doing. Joel was the only loyal one."

"I was eight."

"An eight-year-old snitch!" she said. "Tennessee doesn't look like the type to snitch. So I'm aligning with him and leaving you and your snitching self in the cold!"

"How many jobs do you have?" I asked, not so subtly changing the subject. She always seemed to be working somewhere new.

"Nunya." Her eyes glazed over. "Tennessee calls me ma'am."

"That shouldn't give him extra points. You are ma'am."

Solange looked down. "I get sir'd all the time. Even if I'm looking extra cute—cheetah-print-bodied-dress-and-heels cute—these little boys still be sirring me."

"*Who?* I'll beat them up."

"You know I can handle my own." She stood. "I'm going to preemptively help myself to whatever magic JoJo is making in the kitchen. Let me know when you feel like taking advantage of my superior listening skills. I can do more than look pretty, I'm also a listener." Solange winked and left me alone in my room.

------ঙ৯------

It had been a while since I went into the closet.

I turned on the light.

The dim yellow glow fell on button-down shirts, slacks, and three pairs of polished size eleven dress shoes. I stood there for a while, feeling like a lost child. My fingers itched to reach for one of the shirts. My favorite was the canary-yellow button-down that had a peacock feather still pinned to it.

I reached out, stopped, and pulled my hand back.

I couldn't.

Not tonight.

Solange's laughter drifted from the kitchen, pulling me away from the box of memories.

19
TENNESSEE

EARLY OCTOBER FLEW BY. I spent a lot of days after school with Saint. We watched old movies that I never heard of, and I ironically gave him boy advice. He'd use my suggestions on Joel and return with the results. It was hilarious because Joel was like a science experiment. Saint and I put our heads together and closely analyzed what worked, what didn't, and where new approaches needed to be made.

On the St. Charles mansion front, Mom remained in a good place creatively. She still texted me at school, but she wasn't as demanding.

And October brought paychecks. When I wasn't hanging out with Saint, doing homework, or thinking about Jessamine—I was working. There was so much freedom in buying what I wanted without asking for an allowance from Mom and Dad.

⚬⚬⚬

Solange was sitting at the break table surrounded by Halloween decorations. Her hand was resting against her cheek, and she was busily writing down something. She seemed distracted and sad again.

"You need help with those decorations? I love decorating for the holidays!"

I hit her way with way more enthusiasm than I meant to.

"Oh, hey, love." Solange wiped at her eyes. "I completely forgot that you worked today." She set down her pen. "I'm glad you love decorating because I was going to ask the whole crew to pitch in."

The whole crew?

"FYI, during the holiday season—basically October through Mardi Gras—my little elves turn whatever place I'm working at into a festive sanctuary. Usually, I pitch in, but I have less time these days. What do you say to hocus pocusing this place?"

"I'd love to," I said, working up the nerve to ask if she was okay. "Who is the crew?" There was a faraway look in her eyes—a look that told me she wasn't really into this conversation. When I was down, talking to people sometimes got me out of my funk.

"Joel, Iz, and Jessamine," she said. "I'm sure you'll be glad to see her."

I focused on not doing two things: smiling and nodding. Jessamine seemed to come and go like a rainstorm. I didn't want to seem needy or make her feel like she had to avoid me because I was always wanting more of her time, when I was lucky enough to get a second.

Solange picked up a medium-size pumpkin with glitter all over it. She stared down at it for a while. "This is a happy pumpkin. I think we should make it a centerpiece."

⸻⸙⸻

It was a slow night. Joel and I started setting up the Halloween decorations. I strung up orange lights shaped like candy corn around the coffee shop. Joel hung up some streamers and set glittery pumpkins on all the tables. Even the usually retro Chicory and Grind playlist was switched out for songs that fit the Halloween vibe. Joel and I made sure to leave some decorations for Iz and Jessamine to help with.

My cell phone pinged on the counter. I picked it up. It was Saint.

SAINT: Why didn't you tell me?
SAINT: You work with Joel!
SAINT: He told me about his work friend Tennessee.
SAINT: There is no one else named Tennessee. It has to
      be you.
SAINT: Where do you work?

The texts kept coming. I couldn't respond fast enough. The next thing I knew Saint was *facetiming* me. I ignored the call and started to text him back, but he attempted to FaceTime me again. *Dude, working.*

The bell above the door jingled. Our first customer in the last hour.

Saint was calling me now. I picked up, planning on telling him that I'd call him back after work, but he launched into a conversation.

"He blocked me."

"Huh?" I said because I couldn't exactly talk with Joel right there. "What happened?"

"I said what happened: He blocked me like I was just another."

Maybe it's not meant to be? It's what I was thinking. I mean,

I gave Jessamine my number and she wasn't calling so . . . I just got a job working for her cousin and with her brother.

The optics of that weren't good.

"Where do you work? He owes me a reason for cutting off our two-month fling."

It did not seem like a good idea to tell Saint where I worked if Joel blocked him. If they had issues, I didn't want to get in the middle of that.

"Backwoods, are you still there?"

"Yes, and you got to give me a better nickname than Backwoods."

"Fine, *Nashville*. Where do you work?"

I looked at Joel. My tongue felt thick in my mouth. We had a decent thing going and I didn't want to complicate it by getting involved in his relationship. I looked from Joel to the two customers standing in line—and dropped my phone.

Jessamine stood close to Joel. She was wearing her school uniform, a plaid skirt that showed off her long legs with a white dress shirt tucked in. Her hair was down. She wasn't wearing any makeup, but she did have on red-framed glasses. I bit down hard on my cheek to keep myself from running over to her, hugging her, and asking her to hang out again.

"Nashville!" Saint yelled.

Oh yeah, shit! I dived down to get my phone. "Hey, Saint, sorry, sorry."

Next thing I knew Jessamine's friend was walking over. She extended her hand, "Hi, I'm Iz."

I shook her hand with my free one. "Saint, can I call you back?"

Iz's eyes widened. "Are you talking to *Saint Baptiste*?"

Joel also turned to me.

I nodded, feeling a bit overwhelmed. Iz screamed and jumped like five feet into the air. Jessamine was watching Iz curiously, but she hadn't looked at me. Did she even see me? Was she ignoring me? She was so hard to read.

"Nashville!" Saint yelled again. "Turn on your location, I'll find you."

"Saint"—I raked my hands through my hair—"lemme call you back, 'kay?" I hung up before he could tell me not to. Iz was still beside me. She looked excited and I was sure it had something to do with Saint.

"Jess, come!" Iz waved her over.

Jessamine turned her back to Iz and snatched up something from the counter.

"Jessamine, give me that back!" Joel snapped.

She jogged to the front of the coffee house cackling. Joel hopped over the counter. She screamed, still cackling, and ran over to Iz. She was carrying Joel's sketchbook, which he'd been working in before Solange tasked us with decorating. Jessamine thrust the sketchbook into Iz's hands.

"I thought this sketchbook would be full of love letters!" she exclaimed, still not looking at me.

I looked down at my tennis shoes. My cell phone was buzzing again. I already knew it was Saint.

"Ugh, you're so aggravating, always playing." Joel held his hand out to Iz, who gave him back the sketchbook that Jessamine had stolen.

Joel tapped my shoulder with his phone. "Tennessee, could you watch the register for a second? I have to make a quick call."

"Yeah, of course. I got it."

Jessamine fanned herself and looked around the coffee shop. I tried to keep eye contact, but she seemed to be avoiding that. I guess—damn, I guess, that night we shared meant more to me than her. And that Vietnamese coffee date also meant nothing. I swallowed down the lump in my throat.

Iz looked between me and Jessamine like she was trying to figure out something. "He knows Saint Baptiste."

Jessamine stopped fanning herself. "You do?"

I nodded slowly. "He goes to my school."

"Oh yeah, I completely forgot that you go to Magnolia Prep." Jessamine turned to Iz. "He looks like a Magnolia Prep *prep*, doesn't he?"

"He does, but Saint brings cred to that school." Iz focused back on me. "Is he as fashionable in real life as he is on the Gram?"

"I guess?"

"Writer boy doesn't know anything about fashion," Jessamine spoke up. Now she was looking at me and keeping eye contact. "How'd y'all link up? I bet he isn't just friends with anyone. Are y'all dating?"

Wow. So, she thought I was bi. Our connection was one hundred percent in my head. I was just going to go home, get underneath my bed, and stay there until next fall.

"We're not dating." I balled my fist and braced it against the counter. "He's dating Joel."

The second I said it, I regretted it. Joel was in the break room and couldn't hear me. What if he wasn't even out to his sister? Did I just out him? How could I take it back?

Iz and Jessamine both had wide eyes. "Wait, what?" Jessamine said.

"Nothing."

She shook her head. "No take-backs! You said that Saint Baptiste is dating *my* brother."

I fumbled for a lie. "Um . . . no, I didn't."

It was too late. They were already conspiring. And my cell phone was vibrating again. I could not believe I just did that. Joel was probably going to hate me now.

"Iz! Saint is Trouble! Answer that," Jessamine said, pointing to my pocket. "If that's Saint, tell him that we're going rollerblading with Joel and he's invited."

"And you're invited, too, Tennessee!" Iz added.

Jessamine gave her a look—another look that I couldn't read. Whatever that look meant, I knew what I needed to know. She didn't like me. At least not in the way I liked her. I'd made it up.

With shaking hands, I pulled my phone out of my pocket. I didn't feel like talking to Saint—I didn't feel like talking to anyone—so I texted him.

ME: You're invited to go rollerblading with Joel.

"Where?" I asked Iz.

Iz told me the location and I texted it to Saint.

I wasn't going. I had already done enough damage for today.

"Are you okay?" Iz asked.

I wasn't aware that my face was doing things. "Oh, yeah."

Joel returned from the breakroom. He set his phone down on the counter and leaned against a shelf stacked with Chicory and Grind and New Orleans themed mugs. "We good?" he asked.

Joel was looking at Jessamine when he asked that. She was smirking at her twin brother. The kind of smirk that came with receipts. I was sweating now. There was only one thing to do. The right thing. "I told them about Saint."

Joel's eyes flashed in my direction. His expression gave nothing away. Seriously, if there was an entry for stone-faced in the dictionary, Joel's picture would be there. "And?" he asked, his voice getting softer.

"How'd you secure that bag?" Jessamine asked.

"Same way you secured that one," Joel said, pointing at me. "Anyway, y'all gossip some more. I got homework to finish." He grabbed his phone and went back to the breakroom.

20
JESSAMINE

IT HAD BEEN A TERRIBLE DAY. I was trying my best to be peppy and nice, but all my attempts were backfiring. Clearly, I'd said something to offend Tennessee because he was looking at me with this wounded expression.

He looked different. His hair was shorter, shaved low on the sides and longer on top. His shoulders didn't slump as much as they used to. And his eyes didn't remind me so much of a puppy dog anymore. They seemed a little wiser?

Why does he still like me?

He hadn't verbally expressed like. But, bruh, the way he looked at me. His lingering looks made me want to run, fast. I hadn't planned on gaslighting him. The plan was to friend-zone him. Introduce him to Iz. Invite him out to rollerblade with us. Ignore his glittering eyes when they got extra glittery, and keep Iz between us at all times. That was the plan.

I did miss our scattered conversations. That was annoying because how could I miss scattered conversations with a boy I barely knew? A boy who was so different from me? *A boy who goes to Magnolia Prep!*

I knew I messed up because he wasn't talking to me anymore. He spoke to Iz and he spoke to Joel (until Joel stormed off in a bad mood). Even when I tried to catch his eye, which he had been trying to do with me earlier, he ignored me. I decided to leave him with Iz and went back to check on Solange and Joel.

My cousin had her faux-alligator skin "notta-gator" purse slung over her shoulder. She stopped and scowled. "Why are you looking deranged?"

"Deranged?"

"You were looking deranged!" she said, pointing at my face. "If you were wearing that face when I walked past you, I'd cross the street. Shifty-ass expression!"

Oh, she was so mean.

Solange pulled a wig cap from her purse and fitted it on her head. The cerulean blue wig came out next. She fit it on and shook it out. "I got a second or two before I got to get to the next job—y'all going rollerblading, right?"

"Bet."

She nodded. "What did y'all hooligans say to Joel?"

"What do you mean, y'all hooligans? There is one hooligan: Tennessee. He's the one . . ." I pursed my lips together. I almost said that he was the one that told us about Saint being Trouble. I knew that he didn't mean to say it, poor thing. His whole face turned a shade darker than triple-strawberry.

Solange curled her lip. "Are you going to finish that sentence sometime this millennia?"

"Where did Joel go?"

"He went outside," Solange pointed to the back door. "You gotta quit pickin' on your twin. You got to know when to cut him some slack."

Why was Solange making me out to be the bully? I didn't do anything! "I can't help it that Joel is sensitive."

"Have you looked in the mirror?"

I dodged the question in true Solange Blanchard fashion.

Solange waved her hand. "I gotta go."

"Give me a mini-update on how you're doing. You don't ever come around anymore." I said.

"I was just over Auntie Jo's, don't lie on me like that." She stood up and grabbed her purse.

"You were over there eating, not talking."

Solange leaned forward to hug me and gave me a kiss on the cheek. "Go outside and talk to your brother."

After Solange left, I took a deep breath before heading out to talk to Joel. I found him leaning against the building with his arms crossed. I stole the spot beside him and mimicked his stance.

"Are you mad at me?" I asked.

"No."

"You're lying. I have a bachelor's degree in reading all the things you say and don't say."

Joel took a step to the left. There was a wider space between us now. "Maybe if you applied the same effort you put into my dating life into school, you'd have a better GPA."

That stung, but I wasn't going to feed into it. Whatever. "Thanks, Mama."

He chuckled. It was a little strained. "I'm not mad at you. It's Tennessee. I guess I thought that I could tell him stuff without him running to tell you."

"It was an accident."

"Are you defending him?" Joel said accusatorily.

"No, I'm not."

Joel kicked at a rock with his boots. "Saint told me that Tennessee really likes you. They're friends, so I can tell you his stuff, too."

I frowned.

"But I'm not going to do that." Joel walked over to the door leading back into Chicory and Grind. "I'm over talking about this."

I wanted to resolve this. But that clearly wasn't happening now. Joel held the door open for me. I thanked him and gave him space. I went back out to the coffee shop area. Iz was alone, dancing to "Monster Mash" with a string of papier mâché pumpkins.

"Where's the writer?"

Iz did a twirl and wrapped the pumpkins around her head like a shawl. "He left, boo."

My eyes widened. "Why? We still need to decorate!" I gestured around at the half-decorated coffee shop. There was so much left to do. And okay, we didn't need Tennessee's help for that, but still!

"The three of us can handle Halloween decorations," Joel said, joining us again.

But I needed to apologize to Tennessee. I ran out of Chicory and Grind. I looked right toward Camp and left toward St. Charles. I spotted him walking briskly toward St. Charles. The sky was cotton-candy pink and bubble-gum blue behind him.

"Tennessee!" I yelled.

He stopped. He didn't turn.

I didn't know why I was doing this. I should let him think I was a jerk and end this. End this, whatever it was.

Tennessee turned.

I jogged over to him. Jogging was not a thing I did. Yet I was doing it for him?

"Where are you going, writer boy?"

"Home?" he said, like it was a question, not a for-sure destination.

"Why?"

"Because—"

"I invited you to hang," I reminded him, struggling to catch my breath.

Tennessee looked down at his shoes. I also looked down at his shoes. His shoelaces were untied. He bent down, but I beat him to it.

"Jess—" He paused, as if realizing he called me Jess. "Jessamine, please, I can tie my own shoelaces."

"Naw, bruh, you can't. Every time I see you, your shoelaces are untied. It's a hazard. And you're giraffe-tall. If you fall, it's all over with."

He flushed triple strawberry, which made me feel some relief. I untied his laces all the way.

"People are looking at us," he said, crouching down.

I smiled. "So? I don't want you to fall and break your neck."

"I can tie my shoelaces. I promise you, I'm a big boy."

I kept going, tying the most secure double knot I could. He tried to stop me but I said, "Ah!" like Mama used to do when me and Joel cut up as kids. Tennessee pulled back.

"Thank you," he said when I was finished, running his hand through his hair.

I stood up. "You know how you can repay me?"

"How?" he asked.

"Go rollerblading with us. What are you doing, anyway?"

"Tonight?"

I nodded. "Yes."

"I doubt Joel wants me there," he said.

I searched his eyes. "You work with him. What are you going to do, avoid him every shift? C'mon, live a little. The oldheads say that the best time to live is seventeen."

He licked his lips. "I never heard that before."

I wrinkled my nose. "Fine, I made it up. But isn't seventeen like a rite of passage or something? Be young and free with us for a night. Say yes, Tennessee. Say yes."

I thought about apologizing again. The urge was fleeting.

"Are you sure you want me to come?"

"I'm sure," I confirmed.

He looked at me like he did the first night at Rue Margeaux, starry-eyed. His eyebrows were slightly raised, his lips parted, his eyes stuck like he was watching Fourth of July fireworks. That look made me feel all warm, and it also made me want to run again.

Cancel him. Ghost him. Run far away from him!

Kiss him.

Kiss him hard.

I looked away from his glittering puppy dog eyes. "So, Saint's coming, right?"

That question made Tennessee wince.

······❦······

At the rollerblading rink, Iz and Joel were having the time of their lives. Joel was laughing so loud that I could hear him over the music. It was good to hear him laugh. He was always so serious and focused. A glance over my shoulder turned up Iz and Joel flying by, arm in arm. I would be out there with them, tearing up the whole floor, but I had a beginner on my hands.

Tennessee was wearing knee-pads, elbow pads, and a helmet. The rollerblades were to the side. He nervously eyed them like they might bite him at any moment. Every now and again he looked from the rollerblades to the rink. I would've pushed him to skate, because adventure, but I was okay sitting.

"I can't believe you've never rollerbladed before," I mused.

He tapped his fingers on his thighs, a sheen of sweat on his face. Without thinking, I used my hand to wipe away the sweat on his cheek. I thought it would be gross, but I wasn't grossed out. He looked at me and gave me a small boyish smile. "I haven't. It's ridiculous how nervous I am. I mean, it's just roller-blading. Not giving a speech in front of three hundred people."

"It's not ridiculous."

"It is," he insisted. Tennessee raised his shaking hands. "Look at my hands. I'm a mess."

I watched as his hands involuntarily shook. Jumping to the rescue, I grabbed his hand and held it tightly in mine. "So what if you fall? You got protective gear. You got this, Tennessee."

He took in a deep breath and then exhaled. I wondered if he was nervous about something else.

"We should just do this thing, right, get it over with?" he said.

Tennessee stopped trembling and he reached in his pocket, telling me, "One sec." I watched as he opened a music app on his phone, then pressed a button and held it up.

"What are you doing?" I asked.

"I like this song," he said with a little grin. He took a screen-shot of the song playing.

"What do you like about this song?" I asked. I had no idea what kind of music he liked. We never discussed that.

"Do you want a truth or a lie?"

"I like both." I crossed my legs toward him.

"So a lie. Um . . . I'm making a soundtrack for my story."

"And the truth, since the lie was so . . . dry?"

He looked at me with an open-mouthed smile.

"You create fiction," I teased, "and that's the best lie you can come up with? *Truth!*"

"Okay, okay." Tennessee stroked his jaw. "The truth is that sometimes a good song comes on when we're together and I, um, want to remember that song. I guess it reminds me of you?"

I held my breath. *Run. Cancel. Ghost.* What songs were we talking about? What song had been playing when I danced with him on Frenchmen? What song had been playing when he almost spat out his VIC? How many songs had occupied the spaces between the floral print and this rollerblading rink?

"That's the truth." Tennessee turned away.

What do you like about me? The question popped into my head, but I didn't ask it.

"Hey, Jess. Can I ask you a random question?"

"Depends on how random the question is, and if I want to answer it."

His wiped his hands on his jeans. What was he nervous about?

"Are you ever going to ask me this random question?" I asked, leaning in.

"Yeah, just working up to it," he said with a little laugh. "Do you think you're going to stay here for, um . . . for college?"

I looked down. That wasn't fair. He wasn't supposed to ask me about college and the future. That was only something Mama and Ms. Nadia were supposed to bug me about. We were not discussing college. Deadass. That was where I drew the line.

I looked back up. He was watching me. Waiting. "Where are you applying?"

"I asked you first," he said.

"I asked you second," I said right back to him.

He pouted.

I shrugged. Still not budging on this one.

Tennessee listed off the schools on his hand. "I'm applying to Stanford, NYU, the University of Maryland, UC Berkeley, and Yale."

None of those schools were in Louisiana. Not like it mattered or anything. I smiled at him. "Have you always known what schools you wanted to apply to?" I asked him.

Tennessee was still watching me in that way he watched people, staring you dead in your face unless he was nervous. And then he awkwardly stared everywhere but at you. Why did I pay so much attention to his mannerisms? I didn't want a bachelor's degree in Tennessee. This book needed to be returned. Take that L, Jessamine. Take that L.

He thought about my question, tapping his hand against his cheek. "Not really. All I knew is that I wanted to be far away from my parents. What about you?"

Should I answer? Should I keep my schools to myself? If I didn't answer, it might make things awkward. More awkward than they already were. "Top schools are University of Arizona, LSU, Southern, flirting with the University of Texas, and I guess Dartmouth, because that's where Shonda Rhimes went."

He looked at me, confused. "Shonda Rhimes?"

"Tennessee Williams, how the hell do you not know who Shonda Rhimes is? Do you live under a rock? *Grey's Anatomy* has only been on for, like, five hundred years. My mom was like a baby when that show started, and it's still on. Shonda's got a whole production company, Shondaland."

The song playing now was "I Put a Spell on You."

He giggled down at his knees, which were jumping a lot less. "I only watch a little bit of TV . . . Would it be weird if I also applied to LSU?"

That threw me for a loop, because I thought that he wanted to get away from his parents. "LSU is not Yale," I spat out.

"Yeah, but Saint's applying to LSU, and so are you."

"I haven't applied to anything yet. And I might change my mind on LSU."

Tennessee sighed.

"Okay," I said. "So say I apply to LSU and you apply to LSU and we both get in. It's not like we're going to be BFs and hang out every day. This is real life, you know?"

Also in real life, I would choose Iz over him, always.

The lights from the skating rink bounced off his hair and the side of his face. I looked down at his hands on his knees. Why did Tennessee want to apply to LSU because of me? We only met a handful of times. How could he make life decisions based off a few meetings? This library book needed to be banned!

If I was honest for a minute, just a minute, there were quite a few things about Tennessee that I liked.

I liked that he was kind.

I liked that he was patient.

I liked that he always seemed to see the best in me, even when I was being a complete jerk to him.

I liked that he wanted to sneak in an LSU college app in because he wanted to be where his friends were.

And I loved how he made me feel. Like a normal girl in a normal world.

As my mind raced, Saint Baptiste sauntered into the skating rink like a boss. He wore a navy blouse, which was tied in a knot in front, slim denim jeans, and fresh white kicks. The second he walked into the rink, everyone noticed. People started whispering and snapping pics, but no one approached him.

Saint looked around the skating rink. He watched someone for a few moments, probably Joel. People took out their phone to take pictures of Saint. I heard someone compliment his outfit. He engaged with them, but only minimally. It was like the people around him were small satellites. But he was caught in someone else's orbit. I followed his attention to the skating rink. Literally everyone had stopped rollerblading. Everyone but Joel. Joel was living his best-life, tearing up the rink like he was going for Olympic gold.

Saint floated over to Tennessee. He did not just walk, he glided.

"Nashville, I need to talk to you." Saint smiled at me. "I'll just take him for a few minutes, I swear. I'm pretty, but not as pretty as you."

Tennessee laughed, sounding nervous again. "Saint, cut it out."

"He has a big crush on you!" Saint whispered loudly.

I laughed it off even though Joel had already spilled the beans. "He shouldn't. I'll break his heart."

The second it came out of my mouth I regretted it. What. Why. Ugh.

Tennessee slowly stood. For some reason, I felt like grabbing his hand and saying that I was just joking! It was a joke!

Don't take it so seriously! But I didn't say anything. I just let him leave with Saint.

Saint linked his arm in Tennessee's and glanced over his shoulder at the rink a few times. Tennessee was walking fast; he sometimes did that when nervous. I saw Saint tug on his arm and say something to him. Whatever he said made Tennessee slow down. Saint glanced over his shoulder again.

Curiously, I turned back to the rink. Joel was holding Iz's hand, and they were making a lap together. Joel was treating Saint like he didn't even exist. I bet that hurt.

21
TENNESSEE

SAINT ROLLED DOWN the windows of his silver Lexus. "First he blocked me and now he's ignoring me." Saint tapped his fingers impatiently on the steering wheel. "I'm looking like a thicc snack out in these streets and he's *ignoring* me!"

When Saint went on rants about Joel, which was often, my main job was to listen. He didn't need me to offer solutions anymore. In fact, when I did offer solutions, he often treated it as if I didn't say anything at all. For ten minutes, Saint told me how cute and thicc "with two c's" he was, and pointed out that he could have any boy he wanted.

What I wanted was to go back and talk to Jessamine. She said that she would break my heart? And that made me spin. It made me wonder if I was being foolish. It also made me wonder if I was still seeing what I wanted to see.

"What would you do?" he asked.

"Um." I needed to stop thinking about Jessamine and focus on Saint. *What would I do?* I knew what I wouldn't do. I wouldn't show up looking "thicc" and like a "snack" because I didn't have the confidence for all that. I sighed, getting rid of all the nervous questions and energy. "What do you know about Joel? What's something you know that I don't?"

"How does that help me right now, Nashville?"

I leaned back against the leather seat. This might take a

minute. "I don't have much experience being where you are, but I'm guessing that it helps to know Joel. It might give you a little insight into why he's blocking and ignoring you?"

Saint groaned, "Fine. I'll play." His phone vibrated in the cup holder. The person calling was saved in his phone as Monet "Boo" Artist. Saint promptly hit ignore. "He's a Capricorn. He reads Baldwin and Morrison . . . for fun. And he always treats me like an option. Also, he has a really big eggplant emoji."

I almost choked, taken off guard. "What *else* do you know about him?"

Monet "Boo" Artist called again. This time Saint let it ring.

"Do you need to get that, Saint?"

"I'm tired of always chasing him. Baptistes don't chase. We attract. Should I know more than that?" he asked.

"What does he do on weekends? What's his favorite SEC team, if he has one? Are you his first boyfriend? Does his mom know he's gay?" I felt a twinge of guilt again thinking about the conversation at Chicory and Grind.

Saint chuckled. "No wonder you're single. Who wants to answer all of those questions?"

That comment stung a little. I was just trying to be help-ful. I didn't want to show how sensitive I could be, so I kept it moving. "I think you can only understand why someone acts a certain way by getting to know them. That's what I'm trying to do with his sister."

Saint chewed on his fingernail. He looked down at his nails and then at me like I caught him doing something embarrass-ing. "Don't tell anyone I do that."

"I won't. I bite my nails, too."

"Eww."

"Why don't you ask him what he likes? Maybe not today, since he's ignoring you. But when he comes around, if you're still feeling like talking to him, ask him about himself. Go fishin'. It's like tennis." I mimicked serving a tennis ball over a net. "Think of it like that. You serve. He serves back. And keep going back and forth until you find a subject he's comfortable talking about."

"Let's try." Saint swatted my thigh. "Ball is in your court."

"No, it's yours. I served first. Hit me with a question. Ask me something that you want to ask Joel."

"Are you a top or a bottom?" Saint said with this mischievous grin.

I tilted my head to the side. "Is that sexual?"

Saint snickered. "I hope he's a bottom or vers kind of guy."

"Everything can't be about sex. You gotta get to know him for more than his body. Take him out on a Halloween themed date, I dunno. Or . . . because he's private, invite him over, cook him dinner, watch a movie. *Get to know him.*"

"What's wrong with leading with sex?" Saint asked.

It was as if I hadn't said a word.

"I have to be aggressive with him. If I don't, we'll just sit there and look at each other."

"Serve the ball back to me," I said, turning in my seat toward him.

He mimicked hitting a tennis ball back at me.

"How'd y'all meet?" I asked.

"We met at Second Line Sunday. He was the only person there who didn't know who I was. Have you ever been to Second Line Sunday?"

"Naw, what's that?" There was so much to do in New

Orleans. Maybe one day I'd figure out all the events and festivals.

"Aww, man, you need to go. It's music everywhere. People dancing in the streets, on top of roofs, on tractors . . . it doesn't matter where. It's a good time. One day when I go, I'll take you with me."

"That'd be cool."

"Serving the ball back to you," he said.

"Okay. What do you got?"

"Not really a question. I'm thinking of inviting his sister to my November masquerade ball. Maybe y'all can go together. It seems like she is into you."

"You think so? I can't read her."

"It seemed like you were reading her just fine when I showed up," Saint pointed out as he adjusted the air vents.

"Really?"

He nodded slowly. "*Yes!* I'd wife Joel today if he looked at me the way she looks at you."

I rubbed behind my neck. It was hard to believe that Jessamine was into me. She was always hot and cold, which didn't make me feel the most confident around her.

The back passenger door opened. Joel slid into the backseat. That was my cue to leave. "I'll just . . ." I reached for the door handle.

Saint locked the doors.

I reluctantly pulled back. *Okay, Saint?*

"I'm too cute to be waiting around for a *boy* who doesn't know what he wants," Saint said loudly.

Joel said, "Hey, Tenn, can I talk to Saint for a second, alone?"

"Sure—"

Saint cut me off. "All I know is somebody better not call me no more talking about some 'What are you doing?' I'm not a McDonald's drive-thru. This sweet tea is expensive and knows its worth!" Saint turned around to glare into the back seat.

Good for him for standing up for himself. I reached for the car door, but Saint promptly locked the doors again. The doors were already locked! *Um, can I leave?*

"Tennessee, stay. We were having a conversation. If Joel wants to talk, he could answer the phone when I call him. He could be available when I'm available. He could drop one of his many responsibilities to make time for me. Joel Monet, you are not the only senior who is busy!"

It was getting hot in this car. *Saint, please unlock the door.*

"Yo, it's not like that," Joel said.

"Oh, you could've fooled me." Saint crossed his arms.

Joel sighed like the weight of the world was on his shoulders.

"What's it like? If it's not like that," Saint challenged.

This was not a game of tennis or fishing. This was more like jousting. "Why don't y'all work this out amongst yourselves. I'm going to, um . . ."

"I still needed to ask you about that thing, Nashville," Saint said, placing his hand over mine. "I won't be long with this boy."

Joel crossed his arms. "What do you want from me, Saint?"

"I want consistency."

"I'm giving you consistency. I'm me. I've always been me."

"I need more than just the version of you you're giving me," Saint said.

I turned to the back seat to look at Joel. He scowled at me. He didn't want me there, but Saint did. *Shit.*

Joel balled his fist and raised it in the air like he wanted to hit something. He brought the same fist to his mouth. For a while, he didn't say anything. His dark brown eyes went to Saint's back. "I told you when we started that this is hard for me."

"I know," Saint said, his voice getting quiet.

"Do you?" Joel said with a quiet frustration. It sounded like all the words were through his teeth. "I'm not like you. I can't just do what I want. Wear what I want. Act like—"

"Act like what? A queer? A faggot?" Saint asked.

I chewed on my lip as Joel cringed at the words *queer* and *faggot* like they got under his skin. From where I sat, the passenger, watching Joel and Saint, it felt obvious that Joel was not yet in a space where he was comfortable expressing his sexuality through the lens of others. His sexuality was part of his identity. Not a shared identity with Saint, even if they were together. I think Saint saw that as well, but he was coming from a place of hurt.

"Joel, it doesn't matter how masc you present. At the end of the day, you like boys. For the last week you've been chilling with me in my California King, *mine*. You like boys. Who cares?"

Joel shook his head. "You simplify things. You simplify everything because you can."

"It's not simplifying, boo. It's a fact. You waste too much energy living for everyone else."

I cleared my throat, hoping that Saint would stop serving so many jousts. I'd suggested tennis and fishing for a reason. The point of tennis and fishing was to let the other person reciprocate.

"Do you even want to do this anymore?" Saint asked.

"Do what?" Joel questioned.

"*This.* I don't got to be your boyfriend, but I got to be something."

That was good.

"I can have anyone I want, Joel." Saint raised his voice. "There are people out there waiting in line to be with me."

That was *not* good.

Joel raised his chin. "Then go have everyone out there! You don't need me then."

"Um, Joel," I spoke up.

He looked at me angrily, kind of like I was some person off the street. Someone who he didn't work with, hadn't started opening up to. "Why are you still here, Tennessee? I don't want something else getting back to my sister."

"Sorry," I apologized. "I know it's not my place, but y'all are both my friends—"

"It is your place, you're my BF and I trust your opinion," Saint said without blinking.

BF? We'd known each other for two months. I cleared my throat, "Joel, uh—do you like spending time with Saint?"

He still stared at me with hard eyes, reinforcing that this was none of my business. I didn't want to make an enemy out of him. "I mean before you just end it, can't y'all meet in the middle somewhere, like find a place where y'all feel comfortable and talk about what you need?"

Joel closed his eyes.

"What do I do now?" Saint mouthed to me.

I gestured at Joel. "I dunno—hold his hand?" I mouthed back.

Saint reached in the back and took Joel's hand. "I like you."

Joel didn't answer right away.

It's time for me to leave. I was confident that Saint had it from here.

Joel said, "I need you to go slow. And I need you to be patient with me. I struggle with this, and it's not your fault. It's mine."

"Okay," Saint said, nodding, "we can try. I just need you to be more consistent. Half the time I feel like I'm doing this by myself. I don't want to be lonelier in a relationship than out of one. I'm fabulous, love. Lonely doesn't wear well with Ivy Park."

"I'm sorry," Joel apologized.

"There is only one way for you to say sorry." Saint puckered out his lips.

Joel leaned forward and kissed Saint. He kissed him softly at first. And then there were sound effects and Saint grabbed onto Joel's shirt and suddenly Joel's shirt was off. It was *definitely* time to leave.

Saint reached over to the driver's door and unlocked the doors, silently saying that he also wanted me out. He didn't have to tell me twice.

⸱⸱⸱⸱⸱᰾⸱⸱⸱⸱⸱

When I stepped back into the rollerblading rink, I searched for Jessamine, but she was already gone.

22
JESSAMINE

A FEW DAYS had passed since I last spoke to Tennessee at the rollerblading rink. I was hoping that distance would make him lose interest.

The Saints game was muted in the background. Mama was sitting at the table with a stern expression going through mail. The mood appeared bad. I'd have to test the waters first.

"How do I look?" I stepped into the kitchen, serving LBD and legs. Mama side-eyed me like I stole something. *We have a bad mood on aisle five.* "Mama?" I twirled around. "I'm giving you Black princess fantasy realness." I ruffled the lace of the skirt.

Ms. Bad Mood snorted. "Black-princess-fantasy realness, it's too short. Go change into something age appropriate."

"What?" I tugged on the hem of the skirt. "This is past my thighs!"

"Too much leg."

"I can't help that I am ninety-five percent legs."

"I don't like it." She waved me away with an envelope.

"If I came out here in a potato sack, you wouldn't like that either."

"Sure wouldn't."

I joined Mama and her bad attitude at the table. *I am wearing this.* "I hope you plan on coming to Joel's community art show."

"I'm working tonight," she said.

"Mama, the show will be over by lunch, so you'll have plenty of time to run errands. JoJo has been working on this for months. . . . Can you at least make an appearance?"

"Do you have a full-time job?" The whites of her eyes flashed at me and there was a tone.

"No, ma'am."

"You got two children going off to college?"

"No, ma'am, but—"

"I don't want to hear it, then."

I stared at Ms. Attitude-in-Chief. Ever since Auntie Myrtle got sick, Mama's patience had been thin. It was how she grieved, I guess? I tried not to make her nerves worse than they already were, but this community art show meant everything to Joel. "Mama . . ."

"Yes!"

Dang. "JoJo's been working on this community art show since school started back up. You know how he gets when it comes to his art. He'll tell us we don't have to go, but he gets all in his feelings when we don't show."

"I've seen it," she said. "Those kids have been in and out of my house with canvases, watercolors, papers, and pens. I know it'll be good. Whatever JoJo sets out to do, he excels at it."

"Come, then, Mommy."

"I have to go to work. If I didn't, I would be there."

"You can come before work," I reasoned.

"You're an artist, too. Will those people see your work?"

Mom had completely dodged my question. She knew that I hadn't been making much art lately. The only thing I occasionally did was make sketches for my enamel pins. She was wearing one by the way. An enamel pin I made her last Mother's Day. It was a bouquet of roses.

"Mommy, pleaseeeeeee."

"Jessamine, I can't. You're going, Iz is going, Sol—" She paused. "Solange might even show up."

My ears rang with joy. Mama just called Solange by her name again! She'd been doing that more lately. Even if it was inconsistent, I still considered it a win. "Joel wants *you* there, though."

Instead of responding to my third invite, Mama said, "There's leftover red beans and rice in the fridge. You'll have to make something to go with it."

She was so stubborn. I knew the real reason why she didn't want to go to Joel's show. She didn't want to "encourage" him. The art show focused on Black youth in New Orleans. And the main message was that Black youth needed mentors. Mentors from here. People who knew the neighborhoods. People like Joel, who wanted to stay. The show was called "Rise Up," and the art told the story and made the case for why Joel didn't want to go anywhere.

I had seen some of the pieces myself before the show. Black youth navigating violence. *Ronnie.* Black youth navigating school. Black youth raising themselves. That was the story for a few of my classmates.

I sighed and let the heavy thoughts float away. They made me feel tired. The kind of tired that was worse than a Sunday tired. It was unidentifiable. Twelve hours in bed. Thirteen hours at school. A-weekend-spent-writing-an-English-paper kind of tired.

"This could be JoJo's last year here if he goes off to one of those Ivy Leagues you want him to," I said at last.

Mama looked at me, her eyes giving away nothing. I couldn't

tell if she was mad at me for pushing the community art show so hard, or if it was something else, like Joel going up North? Maybe she was just sad. College was also a good-bye game for her. And we had always been together.

Mama turned away. Suddenly, it felt like we were in different rooms. She was so distant. What was I supposed to do about that? Try to cheer her up? Ask her if she wanted to talk about Auntie Myrtle—because she never talked about her. Mom was like Solange in that way. They suffered in silence.

"Where are you with your college applications? Ms. Nadia said that you were doing the bare minimum." She looked at me with warning eyes.

I didn't want to talk about that. Why did every conversation have to go there? College applications and the real world were no fun. "Mama, come to the art show."

"I'm more interested in talking about your future." She dropped her eyebrows. "Half the time you live in la-la land, only dealing with things when you have to. Jessamine, you're going to be eighteen soon, and you won't have me or Ms. Nadia to look after you. You got things to do. What would've happened if I didn't remind you to register for the ACT? Why you didn't register when JoJo and Iz did is a mystery to me."

"A girl nearly misses ACT registration once and gets a reputation."

"This is about more than that. I have to be on you about scholarships, I have to be on you about colleges, I have to be on you about making time for your mentor—who is taking time out of her busy schedule to make sure that you're successful! It's time to grow up. Time to be more responsible like your brother."

Ouch. I smiled anyway, a smile so big it would make the sun jealous. "Think about coming, okay?" I stood up, ready to run from her spotlight.

Mama sat back in her chair. "If you need help, you got to tell me. I can't read your mind."

"I don't need help. I'm fine. I am."

Mama stared at me with tired, bloodshot eyes. She looked older. That made me sad. "Sometimes when I talk to you, baby, it's like you're not even on the same planet with me."

"I am! I'm right here. My feet are on the ground." I bounced up and down on the balls of my feet to prove the point. *I am fine. I am okay.* "Here, present."

Mama said, "Sit back down. I'm not done talking to you yet."

"I'm gonna be late," I whined.

"The show is an hour and a half, isn't it?"

"Yes, ma'am."

"Then you won't be late. Sit."

Reluctantly, I sat.

Mama ran her hands through my hair, twirling curls around her fingers. "You used to speak to me about things."

"I still speak to you about things."

"You don't," she said with a small sad smile. "You used to have a calendar where you wrote in the things we would do every week. Sometimes we read books, sometimes we watched movies, sometimes we painted our nails and watched the Saints. That calendar used to be full of our time. In October, we used to go to the pumpkin patch. I know I'm hard on you, but it's because you're my daughter. And I want what's best for you."

Mama had gray in her hair. Bags underneath her eyes. She looked so tired, like she needed to sleep. I don't know why I thought it, but I thought that one day she was going to die. What if I went away to Arizona with Iz and something happened to her while I was gone?

The Sunday feeling was sinking in again. "Mama, I'm sorry if you feel like we haven't been spending any time together."

Mama's lips turned down at the edges. "To be fair, I can't let you take all that blame. This year has been rough. Everything going on with Darin, I mean Solange, and your auntie dying." Her lips trembled. "I feel so tired, and I'm trying my best—"

"I know. I'll get a new calendar and fill it up. How about next weekend we watch movies and paint our nails?"

"I would love that." Mama's eyes got cloudy.

I reached for her hand and squeezed.

"I'm serious about you talking to me," she said. "No matter what's going on with me. If you need help, I'm here, and I'll always be here, you understand?"

That wasn't true.

She couldn't promise me that.

She couldn't promise forever. He couldn't. An image of his closet popped into my head. I tried to shake it. But I saw it too clearly. His clothes, moved into this house even though he never lived here. I swore that some of his clothes still smelled like his cologne. Daddy smelled like the sea, like the beach. I used to tell myself when I missed him that that was where he was at, sitting on the beach in the sun and building sandcastles.

I eyed her gray hair again, the strands mixed in with ebony. Would I have to imagine her at the beach with him someday? Thinking about that made me want to cry.

"Is Mama coming?" Joel asked.

"She said that she's going to try," I reported.

He nodded, eyes looking around as if looking would make her appear. "I hope so, Jess. Hey, I want to show you something." Joel led me to a painting.

My body tensed. The painting was a blast from the past. It was so old that I had forgotten about it. Joel stopped walking. I watched the back of his head. The room felt like it was spinning. *Why is that painting here?*

"Jess?" he said.

My heart was pounding. It was going so fast that I felt like I needed to sit.

The painting was on a canvas. It was the distorted face of a brown-skinned girl around five or six years old. Her facial features were made up of the sharp edges of geometric shapes. Sharp lines for sharp edges and sharper hurt. She almost looked like the ballerina in the art gallery.

My eyes drifted to the bottom of the canvas where *Jessamine Grace Monet* was scribbled in the right corner. The title of the piece, *Refugee*, was written underneath my name. I vaguely remembered completing that piece in fifth grade.

I tore my eyes away. That girl with wide and displaced eyes was a reminder of the months we lived in Shreveport after Katrina. Behind the sharp edges and geometric shapes was a memory. Fragments of a chaotic and water-logged past I didn't want to remember. Seconds, days, and months that Joel didn't seem to remember. It was like I made them up, watery dreams that only existed in my head. But still, I saw, heard, tasted, felt, and cried memories.

Where's our house? the girl asked in the painting.

Gone.

Where are our clothes? the girl asked.

Gone.

Where is Mama's job? the girl asked.

Gone. They fired all the teachers.

Where did Joel find this painting? I thought I'd thrown it away. It stirred up negative emotions in me. Heavy feelings that brought me back to how awful it felt to be in Shreveport. A strange place, where the music was different, and we were in a house crowded with Mama's side of the family, the Blanchards. There was also no Daddy. Shreveport was the first place I had to live without him. I couldn't dream up beaches and sandcastles up there.

"Jess, I hope you don't mind me putting it up," Joel said. His voice was a sharp pinch, shaking me awake.

"No, I don't mind!" I lied, tearing my eyes away from the watercolors and hard shapes. The girl with the curly black hair, black eyes, and long ostrich neck was not me anymore. That was a different Jessamine Grace Monet. She had been left in Shreveport. A part of her had also died in Shreveport.

"I'm not selling it. It's just for display. But if you do want to sell it, let me know." Joel hugged me. He looked at the door again, looking for Mama . . . or maybe Saint?

Why didn't he ask me to put this painting up? What if someone saw? What if Tennessee saw? What lie could I come up with to deny that this painting was mine, and that girl was me?

Joel hugged me tighter. "I'm going to go make some rounds and make sure everything is good."

"Go make your rounds, JoJo." I latched onto his T-shirt. "Did you invite Trouble?"

He tightened his lips. "No, not to this. I couldn't."

I nodded, leaving it alone, then scanned the crowd of people. I locked eyes with Tennessee. He was standing with Iz by the door. *Damn.* Iz also locked eyes with me. I thought she would walk over to me with Tennessee, but she didn't. She pushed him in my direction, and she went in another. *Traitor!*

It was too late to back away from the painting. I watched Tennessee set his attention on it. His always-observant eyes seemed to take in every bit of color, every line, every emotion, and every piece of me that he wasn't supposed to see. For some reason, it made me mad. *This isn't for you, Tennessee!*

"You painted this?" Tennessee asked pointing to my name.

"Nope," I said.

He quirked an eyebrow. "Your name is on it, though?"

I entered a staring contest with him, childishly trying to get him to back down. He didn't. Instead, he turned back to the painting. "The writer and the artist."

I snorted. "One painting does not make an artist."

"So, this *is* you," he clarified.

I opened my mouth, ready to deny, deny, deny again.

He smiled down at his boots. "This is kind of a weird thing to say, but I think we're both drawn to sad things."

I crossed my arms. "No clue what you're talking about, writer boy." My walls were up. So high up that he couldn't scale them. "I got more rounds to make, so I guess I'll see you around."

"I'm about to head out," he said.

You just got here? I masked my surprise with a carefree grin. Showing interest was dangerous. Admitting that I wanted him to stay was . . . acknowledging something that I wasn't ready to.

……ᕽ……

The kids at the community center showed out. One kid was painting as people watched. In another corner, five kids were dancing to bounce. The "bidders," mostly older white people wearing suits tried to break it down like Big Freedia.

Iz and I walked around the community center, tipping the kids—mere pennies, no doubt, next to the *checks* that the rich white people were writing for their art and to put toward their college funds. I made sure to steer clear of Tennessee.

I lingered behind the check-writing capitalists and listened as they oohed and ahhed the talent . . . the talent that included me. "This painting is exceptional," a woman said about *Refugee*.

"You shouldn't sell it," Iz said, appearing beside me. How convenient that she was beside me now that Tennessee was not lurking near.

"Why not?" Joel said he wasn't selling it, anyway, but I wanted to know.

"Because I want to buy it."

"Why would you want to do that?"

"Because *you* made it. And because I want to support a local artist and my best friend."

"I'd probably get more money from them," I said, scanning the crowd against my will for Tennessee. I couldn't find him. Did he leave?

"Sure, but I'm asking nicely." Iz bumped into me, bringing me back down to earth.

"Sold—to the lowest bidder!"

"Wooo!" She threw up her hands and did her own bounce

move, which was all hips and butt. Rude gal. *I can't take this girl anywhere*. This was why I loved her.

An hour into the community center art showing, Solange showed up. She made a beeline for Joel.

"How is she holding up?" Iz asked.

I didn't know. Solange spent so much time with Auntie Myrtle when she wasn't working her five hundred jobs that she never wanted to talk about it when we were together. "Let's go say hi." I linked my arm in Iz's and led her to Solange.

"Joel, where y'at? Get in here!" Solange hugged Joel and picked him up in the air, then set him back down on the ground. "I've been out here asking every tourist and local with a checkbook and cash to come out here to support y'all. Little cuz, you're doing big things and I am so proud of you!"

"Hello, Ms. Solange." I tapped her on the shoulder.

"Ms. Jessamine," she said, popping a Zapp's Voodoo chip into her mouth. "And Iz." She hugged Iz.

"Love your heels!" Iz pointed down at Solange's highlighter-yellow pumps.

"Thanks, girl—five sizes too small. They try damn hard to discriminate against a bitch with big feet. I need Big Bird size." She was obviously exaggerating, but the shoes did look like every toe had to fight for its life. Talk about a snug fit!

Solange fluffed her mane of honey blonde hair and dramatically turned away. Then she looked back at us over her shoulder. "Pardon me, ladies. I'm gonna go and cut it up with those kids." She raised her arms over her head and danced away from us, singing, "Heeeey, heeey, heeeey!"

Someone touched my arm. I spun around and about fell out

at the sight of Mama. I screamed and hugged her neck. "Mama, you came!"

"I did," she said, looking around. "Is that your piece over there, baby?"

"Yep, Joel put it up."

Mama stared at the painting for a while. As she stared at it, she slipped her arm around my waist and said, "You got something in the mail from the University of Arizona." She reached in her purse and handed it to me, watching me closely. "I thought you were only looking at schools near New Orleans?"

Iz gasped. "What? When? How? Chica, you didn't tell me!"

So much for that being a secret. Iz launched herself into my arms.

Mama took a step back and it looked she wanted to cry. "I didn't know you were applying to schools in Arizona. I thought you were staying in Louisiana with—" Mama stopped.

With me. Even though she didn't finish, I heard it.

"I'm gonna apply to Southern and LSU, too, Mama. It's just one school in Arizona." I didn't feel like getting into a drawn-out conversation about this. Talking and thinking about college exhausted me. If someone could just do the apps and personal statements and take the ACT and SAT (for the schools that required that) I'd gladly pay them. I'd donate all my time and sanity to babysitting bad kids and take up extra shifts at Rue Margeaux to pay them. But alas, I had no volunteers.

And, even worse, I couldn't pay anyone to make those Cs I got last year disappear. It should be illegal how easy it was for a few Cs to tank a GPA.

She opened her mouth, inhaled, and looked away. "Arizona is far."

"It's just one school," I repeated.

She nodded. "Okay, let me go let JoJo know I dropped by." Mama hugged me one more time. "Be good, and y'all better be in the house by eight. Tomorrow is a school day and nothing good is happening in this city after dark." She also hugged Iz and walked over to Joel.

23
JESSAMINE

AFTER THE ART SHOW, Iz had to go to Mid-City to have dinner with her dad. I had planned on walking home or taking the bus, but Joel insisted on driving me home. I was lowkey still mad at him for using my artwork without telling me. A warning would've been nice.

"All right, we're here." Joel parked the car in front of a Garden District mansion. It was two stories with white columns, blue shutters, and yellow paint. The flower garden in front appeared to be managed by a team of ten. Bright bursts of sunny and happy flowers smiled back at me.

I arched an eyebrow at the house. "Where is here? This doesn't look like home to me."

When he didn't respond, I looked from the second-floor balcony to him. Joel had a guilty expression on his face.

"Saint invited us to a kickback at his house." Joel killed the engine and sat back in his seat. He scrubbed at his eyes with his hands and dropped them down to his mouth.

"Trouble invited *us* to a kickback?"

"Yeahhhh," he said. "I guess he invited you because Tennessee will be there. And stop calling him Trouble."

I was still mad at him . . . but how often did he talk about Trouble? Never. I had to choose my words wisely. One wrong word, and Joel would ice me out. "You don't ever go to kick-backs. What made you decide to go to this one?"

Joel stroked his beard. I could tell that he was nervous. That was huge. People didn't make Joel nervous.

"It's not a big deal," he said, looking at the house like it might jump into the air and get him.

"It is a big deal. You're nervous, but you're seeing him anyways. Pushing through the nerves. That's brave, especially because we all know how cautious you are."

"I'm cautious because he's so different from me. Saint doesn't care what people think. I do."

Why do you care? I chewed on my lip. What I wanted to do was whip out my pom-poms and launch into a cheer. *Do you! Be you! Screw anyone who tries to tell you who to be! Love who you want. Be with who you want. Love you so hard that other's people's hate is muted!!* It's what I wanted to say, but I practiced listening. Tennessee taught me that.

Listen. Learn. Be still.

"You don't have anything to say, Jess?" Joel looked at me warily.

"I always have something to say." *Why did you hang that canvas?*

"I know, which is why it's weird that you're being silent."

I unclicked my seatbelt. Joel also unclicked his. "You care a lot about what Mama thinks. You always have," I said.

He looked down.

"When she says jump, you do it. When she tells *me* to jump, I take a nap and then a detour to the jump. And most of the time I don't end up jumping anyway." I giggled and Joel smiled with me. "She was terrible when Solange came out and worse when Solange started wearing whatever she wanted to. For a people pleaser, I can't imagine how hard it is to be you when you aren't what the person you love the most wants."

"Dang, Jess, that's deep."

"Sometimes I can be deep."

Joel brought his hands to the wheel. He gripped it like he wanted to drive the getaway car far away from Second Street.

"You like him a lot?" I asked.

"I do."

"What do you like about him?" I asked, testing the waters to see how much Joel would tell me. I couldn't remember the last time Joel trusted me enough to let his guard down and just let me geek out and be his twin sister.

Joel exhaled. "I like the way he makes me feel." He scrunched up his face. "I'm so tightly wound all the time. I'm always trying to manage how I act, what I say, who likes me, and if they don't, how can I get them to like me. It's not like that with him."

My heart was fluttering. *Be still.* Look at JoJo all glowed up! Hearts in his eyes. And in love with a BOSS. "Secure that bag. You'll never have to work a day in your life if you snatch up a Baptiste."

Joel laughed, "I'm not about that life. And I done told you, look who's talking. Tennessee lives on St. Charles. I dropped him off once at his house after work. It's huge."

I smiled. "Do you remember his parents? Yeah, no thanks!"

"I like Tennessee. He's cool people," Joel said.

"Ohhh . . ." I waggled my eyebrows. "You're getting greedy, JoJo! You want a Tennessee-Saint sandwich? You wanna be in the middle?"

His eyes glazed over. "You need to stop doing that, bruh.

You like him, too. You're not fooling nobody, especially not me."

Instead of allowing Joel to trap me into telling the truth, I opened the door. "I believe this is our stop." I walked up to the door and rang the doorbell.

I expected Saint to answer in his glitter, glamor, and fabulousness, but instead, Tennessee answered. He was wearing the same T-shirt, flannel, and jeans that he wore to the art show. Of course he wouldn't change for a Saint Baptiste soiree. If Joel told me where we were going, I would've brought a change of clothes for sure.

Tennessee gave me his Tennessee smile—bright eyes, a dimple, and the triple-strawberry blush. It was almost like my treatment of him at the art show didn't happen. Why did he let me get away with treating him like I didn't care?

"Sorry that I didn't get to tell you how awesome your art show was," Tennessee said.

"You're good bro, I'm just glad that you could make it."

Joel raised his right hand. Tennessee clapped his hand against Joel's and gave him the man half-hug. Boys were such bizarre creatures.

Tennessee then gave me a hug, like we didn't just see each other at the art show. He hugged me like I hadn't been distant. His hug felt nice. He smelled nice, too. The smell of citrus and sandalwood were tangled up in his flannel shirt. Was that his cologne? His shower gel?

I pulled away before I smelled his neck or hair. "Hey to you again, writer boy."

He untangled his long arms from around me. "I'm glad you came. Y'all come on in."

I stepped in after Joel, who went straight up the stairs like he knew the house. Shoot, he probably did. Tennessee closed the door behind me.

"He's got a pool," he said.

I'm sorry for being mean. "We love a pool," I said instead.

He was already doing the thing where he stood too close to me and didn't break eye contact. This boy made it hard for a girl to hide. I walked around him. "I'm not trying to get my hair wet though. So no pool for me."

Saint's house was huge. The foyer alone was probably the size of my house. I wandered around the foyer with its paintings of Black aristocrats, larger than life. The paintings, all framed in gold, seemed to tell a story: A Black aristocrat coronation. A Black aristocrat wedding. A Black king and queen sitting on thrones.

Every room had a theme! I was in love.

In the kitchen, wonders were being prepared. A full staff catered a meal of lobster, steak, corn maque choux, crawfish hushpuppies, boudin, mac and cheese, and more. There was dessert, too! Petit fours, macaroons, and turtle cheesecake.

I was drooling and in the way, so I carried myself outside into the backyard. I wandered to a porch swing hanging from the limb of a live oak. For a while, I sat, appreciating the garden, the silence, and the slight coolness in the air. Late October and November were my favorite months.

Tennessee hadn't followed me. *What is he doing?* I took out my phone, hesitated, and texted him. I told him to join me outside on the porch swing.

When I texted, he came.

Tennessee sat down beside me, and I stretched my leg over his, like we were old friends. He looked down at my cute olive-green fall boots and told me he liked them, which made me smile. It would help if he didn't say nice things.

"And I like this, too." He touched my dress, almost my leg, but not quite.

"Me too. It has pockets."

"Ahh, functionality," Tennessee said.

I giggled. It was a fake giggle. Fake girls gave fake giggles when they needed to hide real feelings. *No. I need to distract.* "What do you think our boys are doing upstairs?"

"Don't know, but Saint said to send Joel right up to his room."

I shook my head and grinned. "Hopefully they're being safe! I'm not trying to be an auntie yet."

Tennessee settled into the porch swing, draping his flannelled arm around the back. He started to massage my ankles with his free hand. I don't think he realized he was doing that. It felt really good, so I didn't say anything.

"How's Magnolia Prep?"

"A blur. There's not really time to make friends . . . but I guess that's okay. I got Saint."

"Yeah, you do. I'd say you're doing pretty great in the friend department."

"How's school going for you?" he asked. The massaging of my ankles stopped, and he turned his body more to me.

As long as we didn't start talking about college again, talking about school was okay. "I always get my best daydreaming in at school, so I'd say it's going all right."

His eyes lingered on mine. He was saying things to me without speaking. It was the kind of wordless things that boys said when they were interested. He smiled at all my words and tilted his head to the side when I spoke. His eyes were sometimes shy and sometimes they wanted.

I think . . .

That I liked him. No matter how much I liked to run.

He gave me that Friday feeling. Late October days. Cozy sweaters. Cute boots. Cinnamon-and-pumpkin-flavored tea. Saints season.

This was too much thinking about Tennessee. Redirect.

"Oh!" I looked to the right. "A satsuma tree!" That was the perfect opportunity to take my leave. I jumped up and went over to the tree. I stood on my tippy toes and picked two satsumas. Satsumas were so cute. Iz and I used to call them clementine juniors. I tossed one into Tennessee's lap and sank back down into the swing.

"Baby oranges," he said.

"Satsumas."

Smiling, Tennessee peeled off the skin. Once the satsuma was de-skinned, he popped the whole thing into his mouth.

I pointed at him and cackled. "You're supposed to peel it apart!"

"But I can fit it all in my mouth?" he said around the satsuma.

"You know what that reminds me of?"

"What?" he asked, still talking around the satsuma.

"Your mouth is full!" I kicked his boots with my fall boots. He sheepishly apologized. "It reminds me of the time that woman ate the whole crawfish. Remember that?"

"Yes! Her mouth was hot and spicy. And she was mean."

He was so close again. Giving me that Saturday, we're-good-friends smile again. I kept laughing anyway despite the slight ache in my side. "She was so mean, and she looked mean, too! Like she'd beat you up for making eye contact!"

Tennessee's eyes squeezed shut as he laughed, shooting satsuma all over the place.

I wrinkled my nose. "You're gross."

"I guess it's better being gross than taking five years to peel a satsuma. By the time you're eating that I'll be a sophomore in college."

"Then do it for me, since you're so fast and all." I held my satsuma out to Tennessee.

Instead of being a normal person and taking the satsuma with his hand, he used his mouth. Tennessee bit into my satsuma, and once the flesh was exposed, he peeled off the skin with his fingers. "Ta-da!"

"I can't eat that," I said, turning my body away from him on the swing.

"Why not?" he asked inching closer to me with the Tennessee-germ satsuma held out.

"Because of your germs!" I waved him away. "Get that thing away from me."

"We shared germs before."

"Have not." Since he was still trying to give me the contaminated satsuma, I crossed my arms. This was a nonnegotiable. I didn't want that satsuma.

"You totally shared a Vietnamese iced coffee with me on day one. You got my germs, Jessamine. I'm sorry, don't know what to tell you."

I narrowed my eyes at him, and he beamed down at the freshly cut grass like he knew my secret. I liked him 25 percent.

I snatched my satsuma back and took a bite.

"Does the baby orange taste good?" he asked.

Okay. I liked him more than 25 percent.

Tennessee Williams was a solid 30 percent on the like scale.

·······ჶჲ·······

After dinner, Saint invited us to the den for a game. Four giant pillows were set out on the expensive-looking rug. I took the pillow beside Tennessee.

"Friends, we're playing twenty questions," Saint announced, still standing. "Here are the rules: I ask y'all questions and y'all answer."

Joel scowled at his boo. "I don't think that's how this game works."

"That's how my version of this game works." Saint switched around the room. His nighttime attire was fabulous. He dramatically flipped his floral-print silk nightgown. He was so unapologetic. I loved it! Serving lewks left to right. Yaaass, honey. "Tenn, you're first, my straight-challenged friend," Saint said.

Tennessee, sitting next to me, straightened his back.

I glanced at Tennessee. He was tracing circles on the blue-and-white-checkered rug we were sitting on. He lifted his head, his eyes kind of wide. "Um, okay. What's my . . . err . . . question?" he asked Saint.

Saint tucked his hand underneath his chin. He sauntered, hips hips hips, over to Joel and sank onto the pillow beside him. Saint propped his elbow up on Joel's shoulders and ran his hands through Joel's waves. I expected Joel to jerk his head back, because he was hella serious about people touching his hair, but he didn't. Weird and wow.

"Kiss her," Saint said.

Wait. What?

"That's not a question," Joel said quickly.

Tennessee's mouth dropped.

Before Joel could start bellyaching again, I took over. I scooted closer to Tennessee, cupped his chin, and turned his face to me. They were all watching.

Closing my eyes, I brought my face closer to Tennessee's.

Thirty percent like meant kissing him wasn't a thing. It was just lips and not at all sexy because we had an audience. I inched closer to him. I touched his face. His eyelids closed partially. He licked his lips. He smelled like citrus, sandalwood, and spearmint. One kiss wasn't a big deal. In fact, one kiss would prove that I didn't actually like him . . . and I would be free!

I pressed my lips against his. His lips were soft and full.

When he kissed me, his mouth opened all the way.

I felt his tongue and his nose pressed against mine.

Tennessee's thumb was now tracing sketches against my cheekbones. Give the boy an inch and . . .

I breathed and pulled away from his greedy hands and his spearmint-flavored lips. "Satisfied?" I asked Saint, smirking as if my whole body wasn't tingling.

The worst thing about that kiss, the absolute worst thing, was damn percentages. Tennessee was at a solid 30 percent. Eating satsumas whole and being a weirdo by massaging ankles got him there. But that spearmint-flavored kiss bumped him up to 50 percent.

I was in 50 percent like with Tennessee Williams, and that was horrendous.

24
TENNESSEE

LATER THAT NIGHT, Jessamine walked beside me. Her hands were tucked into the pockets of her black dress and she was looking down at her boots. I'd been talking to her, but she wasn't hearing me, because her eyes were on the ground. I watched her, trying to catch her eye for a second. And that was when I realized what she was doing.

She was trying to walk in a straight line. She'd take one step, cross her right foot over her left. Take another step. Cross her left foot over her right. And then she'd repeat.

Jessamine giggled whenever she wobbled. One time she almost fell, but I caught her.

"What are you doing?" I asked her.

She wrapped an arm around my waist. That caught me by surprise. Anytime she touched me, I was caught by surprise. Then she squeezed my side, still giggling. "I'm sober, I swear!" She threw her head back and laughed into the night.

For the first time since moving to New Orleans, the night was cool. The sound of her laughter echoing off the candy-colored stucco and brick mansions made me feel warm inside.

I didn't want to say good-bye to her tonight. I never wanted to say good-bye to her. Because good-bye came with too much waiting in between. And waiting came with questions.

It was like every time she left, it took time for her to get to know me again. Now, we were friends. Tomorrow, we might be strangers again.

"Hey," I said.

"Hey yourself, satsuma boy." Jessamine kept walking, right foot over left, left foot over right.

I wanted to ask her again about her painting. Who knew that she was also an artist? I mean, I knew about her designing pins, but I didn't know she could paint, too. There was so much about her that I didn't know. Would she ever let me know her?

She was significantly ahead of me. I jogged up to her and linked my arm in hers. This made her stop and look at me. She was still smiling, looking so happy. *So* happy. I tried not to stare, but it was hard. The way that the light from the lampposts was hitting her. All these little details, lighting up her eyes.

The way she moved, like she was always floating on clouds.

The way she laughed, so effervescent. Her laughter was like shaking a Coke and then taking a sip. The fizz went straight to your nose and it burned. It burned because it was impossible not to react to Jessamine's laughter. I felt it when I was near her. And I heard it, all the days between the August day we met and this cool October night.

Hey, I like you.

It was what I felt. I knew it because Jessamine was always on my mind. The feeling I got when she was close to me couldn't be described. It was a flying feeling. A lightness that crept up when I heard a song that made me think about her. She also made me dance. In the morning before school, in the evening before a shift, on the days when I knew I wouldn't see her.

She was that girl. Her heart was huge. And I just couldn't *not* fall in love with her.

"What?" she asked.

I searched for the right words. "You kissed me."

Jessamine folded her arms behind her back and did a spin. She was in the light one minute and then back in the shadows. Somehow, she kept leaving me behind. Now she was near this oak tree that had to be at least one hundred years old. Its roots were pushing up the sidewalk, like so many sidewalks in New Orleans.

I jogged up to her again and wrapped my arm around Jessamine's waist. She pushed me away, but then pulled me back to her. Then she hugged me tightly with one arm. *I like you, Jessamine.*

"Bruh, it was a dare," she said, talking about the kiss again.

"You liked kissing me." I didn't know why I said it. I was feeling bold, I guess.

"Tenn, let me go."

She said "let me go," but she was the one holding me. When I tried to let her go, she spun me around. More like a her-arm-whacked-me-in-the-forehead half-spin. "Oww!"

"Sorry, you're so tall!" She knocked on my head gently. "Your head is hard."

"My head is hard?"

Jessamine narrowed her eyes at me, her mouth was smiling and frowning. *Cute.* "How about *you* liked kissing *me*. I felt your tongue trying to sneak its way into my mouth! Radioactive boy!" Jessamine whirled away from me and continued walking toward St. Charles, where the streetcar line picked you up to go upriver (Audubon Park) or downriver (French Quarter).

"Hey, I just had to share more of my gross germs with you. I can drive you home since you're leaving the car with Joel." I pointed behind us. "My car is back that way, closer to Magazine Street."

"Aww, thanks, but I can manage. I'm not a damsel in distress."

"I got a whole car, Jess."

"I got a whole RTA app on my phone," she said, pulling her phone from her purse and waving it at me.

I should leave her alone, let her go. Too much of me probably wasn't a good thing for her. But I didn't want to give up yet. I walked in front of her with my back facing St. Charles and the streetcar line, and my front facing her.

"You're going to trip," she warned.

I shrugged. "It'll be worth it."

"I see your shoelaces are still tied." Jessamine gave me a double thumbs-up.

"Thanks to your indestructible double-knot."

"During Saint's game, you said that you danced? I didn't know you danced."

"Yes, you do. I danced with you on Frenchmen." Jessamine pushed me out of the way and started walking briskly again. She was almost running. Thankfully, it felt nice outside, so even if I had to sprint after her, I wouldn't be a sweaty mess.

"When's the last time you danced?" I got in front of her again and resumed walking backward, facing her.

"I dunno, like yesterday in my room."

I smiled. She did that, too. "Show me?"

"Boy, are you crazy?"

"Yes." *Crazy about you.* And bold!

Jessamine narrowed her eyes. Finally, she threw her head back and said, "Fine! Will you leave me alone after that?"

"Most likely." That was definitely a lie.

Jessamine slipped her purse off her shoulders and handed it to me. She also gave me her phone. She switched her hips left to right and fluttered her hands in the air like a butterfly.

The glow of streetlights and porch lights from Garden District mansions fell upon Jessamine as she jumped into the air and landed squarely on her right foot. She stretched her left leg behind her and pointed at me. She did a spin, twirling, twirling, and raising her hands above her head.

It was like watching a ballerina. Was she a ballerina *and* an artist?

I don't know how long she danced because I couldn't take my eyes off her.

Jessamine stopped spinning. "Now you dance!" She walked back over to me and retrieved her belongings. "Dance, Tennessee. Let's go back to Wonderland. Floral shirts and floral couches, remember?"

I took off my bookbag and placed it on the street.

"Eww, the street is dirty!" She snatched up my bookbag and slung it over her right shoulder.

I had two options. Play it safe. Do the Frenchmen Street move that I had perfected. Or, wildcard. Switch it up. Channel the Floral Print. Be bold. Be brave. Live.

I flapped my arms like I was about to fly away. Jessamine immediately started to fall all over herself with laughter. The more she laughed, the more I got into my "dance." I spun around and did a karate kick, almost rolling my ankle in the process. That made her scream and slap her hands on her knees.

"Tennessee, I can't breathe! Stop! Stop!"

Because she was still laughing, it felt like livewire was rushing through my body. I couldn't stop. I wouldn't stop. I did a jumping jack. And tried to be light like a ballerina like she was. I did a sloppy pirouette. I only knew what that was because Mom used to take me to ballet recitals.

"Bravo!" She clapped her hands. "We love to see it. Tennessee Williams, the teenage writer of the ages having fun and living his best country-fried life. Yas. Yas. Yasssss."

"My dancing has improved?" I asked, choking on the coolish air as I struggled to catch my breath.

"Hmm," she placed my bookbag back on my shoulder. "You could still use some work, Williams. But the effort is there. You may join the world of fun kids after all." She inched closer.

I tried not to breathe so hard. But it was impossible with her so close.

Jessamine rested the tips of her flats against my shoes. She peered up at me, the moon reflected in her eyes. "The world of fun kids comes with endless satsumas, no school days, and no stress."

"I want to be a fun kid."

Jessamine giggled. "Keep dancing and you'll get there." She gently held onto my arm with one hand, standing on her tippy toes to kiss me on the cheek. "Before I forget, this is for you." Jessamine reached in her purse and pulled out a little plastic bag. "Wear with care! ¡Adiós!"

She was already walking (almost running) toward St. Charles again. I looked down at the small bag in my palm. In it was one of her enamel pins that I often saw on Joel and Iz. This one was a book, and on the cover it said TELL ME A STORY.

That was the first time I fell in love with her.

25
TENNESSEE

FOR HALLOWEEN, the Williams family had a tradition. If Dad was there, we got dressed up, passed out candy to the few kids that made the trek out of Oxford proper into the county where we lived, and we watched wholesome Halloween movies. If Dad was not involved, Mom and I got dressed up, we did not pass out candy, and we watched *The Rocky Horror Picture Show*.

This Halloween, I dressed up as a mummy. It wasn't the most original idea, but I waited till the last minute—the last minute being an hour ago. So, I got low-key inventive and used up a whole six-pack of toilet paper.

I knocked on Mom's door. When she didn't respond, I knocked again.

She'd been holed up in her room for a few days working on her novel, but it was *Halloween*. Even when she was way off, she came back to herself for at least a few hours. Halloween was her favorite holiday. Instead of knocking a third time, I let myself in. "Hey, didn't you hear me knocking?"

She was sitting on the floor hunched over her computer, balled up pages and fast-food bags surrounding her. There was no costume in sight. I couldn't help but feel a way about the lack of costume. This was our thing. We were at least five hours away from Dad. And she didn't want to celebrate our tradition?

"Okay, well," I said when she didn't answer me. "I just wanted to let you know that I come with costume and candy. *The Rocky Horror Picture Show* is ready to stream."

"That's great, honey," she said in a tone that was like a verbal shrug. She started typing.

Her room smelled sour—*is that her?* I crouched down on the floor beside her. "How about we both be mummies? There's more toilet paper."

"Uh-huh." She shook her head.

"I'm sure your characters need a break, too. Maybe they want to go to their own haunted Halloween bash?"

"If I don't finish this scene, I won't ever finish it."

When Dad was around, he didn't take no for an answer. When she was bad, he made her walk. He made her eat. At least, when they were getting along, that was what he did.

"C'mon, let's do a quick block around the McGehee School."

Mom kept typing as if I didn't speak. Did she even hear me? Did she even see me?

I didn't want to be an asshole. But this was our thing. One thing we did together. One time that she pretended to care. I had barely asked for anything since school started.

I stood up and pulled open the curtains. I also opened the windows to let in some fresh air. It was cooler outside tonight, and St. Charles smelled way better than her writer's bunker. The trombone player was outside again. His blues notes drifted up to Mom's open window.

The people standing by the streetcar line were dressed for Halloween. One woman was wearing a cat bodysuit with a long tail, and one guy was dressed like . . . a lamb?

"I don't want to hear all that!" She waved her arms at the window. *"Close it!"*

"It stinks in here."

"If *my* room is offending you, then you can leave."

I couldn't back down. I wouldn't. "It's Halloween. You've been working nonstop for four weeks. Take a break. Get dressed up." I unraveled some of the toilet paper around my waist and teasingly held it out to her. "This costume took all of fifteen minutes to put together." I was wearing a ratty University of Mississippi T-shirt underneath and an equally ratty pair of mesh shorts underneath all the toilet paper.

Mom glared at me with a look that could kill. A look that made me feel like I was the bad guy. What was my crime? Caring too much? Wanting to spend our favorite holiday together?

She jumped up and rushed to the window. I fought the urge to flinch. Usually when she came at Dad, he got hit. Mom elbowed me out of the way and slammed the window shut, jerking the curtains closed so violently that they fell.

I could feel my heart thumping in my chest. Mom stared down at the curtain rod and the curtains, and then she turned to me.

I had no words for her. Forget Halloween. Why did I even bother? All I wanted to do was make sure that she took a break and enjoyed her favorite holiday.

"I'm sorry, honey."

"It's okay," I said quietly.

The urge to run snuck up. If I put on my running shoes and sprinted as fast as I could, maybe I'd be free? She could stay here in this sour room with her stories. With her characters. "It's okay," I said again. "It didn't take long to make this mummy costume." I started to tear it off.

Mom grabbed my hand. "No, Tenn. It's not okay. You're right. You're right."

She buried her face in her hands. "My writing has been shit . . . *pure shit* . . . and with everything that's on my plate, I'm struggling to figure out the best way to get it done. I do care about what's going on in your life. I do. I want to hear about Magnolia Prep and your friends. I love that you've been hanging out with friends. I love that you're not here because you have a life. It should be that way your senior year!"

What was on her plate? I cooked dinner. I used her debit cards to pay the bills. I put gas in the car. I mowed the lawn. I cleaned the house. I watered her plants. What. Was. On. Her. Plate?

"Can you take a break with me?" I asked.

"I desperately need one," she said, grunting.

"If you don't want to do Halloween, we can do something else."

"Tenn." She shook her head. "I hear you, love. I do. Writing isn't just a hobby for me like it is for you. It's my life."

"What about me? Aren't I part of your life?"

Mom stared back at me blankly. Her expression read that she didn't care. I wanted to believe that I was reading her wrong, but I'd seen that look before. The look of indifference. The look that proved that she really didn't care.

Mom drifted back toward her computer.

"Choose me, Mom." I pointed both thumbs at my chest and gave her a cheesy grin. She stared back at me without cracking a smile. "Your fictional characters will be right here waiting for you when you get back."

"I can't leave," she said. "With your daddy in Oxford, I don't have to worry about being pulled in different directions. I get to focus on writing the best story that I can. You know how much my creativity takes from me. I do want to be here for you. I do want to hear all about your friends and school and Jasmine. I want my life back."

Jessamine. I didn't bother correcting her.

"Once I get this story to my agent, I will be free. After five flops, I know this will be the one to get my career back on track." Mom didn't even bother turning around to talk to me.

"When do you think you'll get it over to her?" I asked.

"Hopefully before Christmas," she said. "But I can't give you a timeline."

Before Christmas! We weren't going to spend any time together until Christmas? *I am going off to college next year.* I stared at the wall. "If you're getting the story over to her by Christmas, then why can't we watch one movie tonight? You don't even have to get dressed up."

"Because I can't."

"What can you do?" I asked, trying to monitor my tone.

"Why are you being so pushy?"

"We live in the same house, but I feel like I live by myself."

"I'm sorry about that, baby," she said to the computer.

"Don't be sorry, just give me an hour of your time. Forget the movie. We can make dinner. Eating is mandatory." *Spending time with me is not.*

She scowled at her computer.

"Please? We can make a pizza? Since you can't cook, I'll let you roll the dough and cut up the veggies and stuff. Please, Mom."

She tilted her head up toward the ceiling, sighed, and said, "I'm also pretty good opening up a jar of tomato sauce."

Good. She made a joke. "Keep it up and I'll have to knight you co-chef."

"Let's plan on dinner, but if I'm in a place in my story that I can't leave . . . let's aim for tomorrow, okay?"

It sounded like she was canceling on me already. Seriously? I had canceled costumes. I canceled the movie. I even cut down the time she had to spend with me.

"Your characters aren't real."

"Pardon?"

"Your characters, they aren't real. I'm real. I'm asking you to spend time with me."

"I know that, dear. And I told you that we will spend time together tomorrow once this scene is finished."

"What if I'm busy tomorrow?"

She rolled her eyes and groaned. "What is this? Tit for tat? I told you . . ." Mom paused. "You know what, Tennessee? What else do you need to get off your chest? Please do it now, so I can finish what I'm working on and have time to eat dinner with you. Going back and forth like this is only wasting time. Time that I don't have. What else do you need to say, Tenn? What else do you have to get off your chest, huh?"

When she was done with a conversation, that's what she did. She got a tone and made me feel like I was wasting her time. Her characters were always first. I didn't want to be jealous of her characters. They weren't real people.

But . . . it's hard not to be jealous of them.

I was jealous of the way she agonized over them.

Jealous that they got all her time and left me with seconds, scraps.

Even my seconds were about her characters. At school, when I was hanging out with Saint, even when I was studying for the ACT and SAT, she'd ask me to read this scene and tell her what I thought. And then she'd be gone.

What did I have to do to get her attention?

Get in a car accident?

Die?

Bleed . . . again?

That was really dark.

I meant it, though. *What do I have to do for some attention?*

When was it my turn to get a word or a sentence in the novel that consumed her life?

--------❧--------

Mom came down to dinner—not in a good place. I had since changed out of my mummy costume. It was clearly for the best, because she hadn't bothered to change her clothes.

She took the jar of tomato sauce, uncapped it, and dumped it on the pizza dough.

I wasn't ready for the sauce yet, but okay. She had a frustrated look on her face. It was almost like she felt forced to spend time with me. Maybe I should just tell her to go back upstairs and let me finish dinner. "I can take it from here. You can go back to your characters."

"I'm sorry that I made you move to New Orleans," she said.

Her response surprised me. "Why would you be sorry about that? I like it here."

Mom walked over to the trash can and dumped the unrinsed tomato sauce bottle into the bin. That's how out of it she was. Not recycling in her house was a violation. "I didn't ask you if you wanted to live in New Orleans. I just decided for you. And you let me."

"You didn't decide for me. I could've said no if I wanted to. Anyways, we still have our house in Oxford and Dad is still there. I chose to come here." I don't know why I felt the urge to defend my decision.

Mom closed her eyes like I'd said something wrong.

"Did you hear what I said?" I couldn't stop talking and defending even though I was tired. "I chose to come to New Orleans."

"If you moved down here because you were worried about me, that isn't a choice. That's what your daddy told me. You were worried. Is that right?"

How was I supposed to answer that?

"You should've stayed in Mississippi. We moved down here so I could finish my goddamn book, and I'm no closer to finished than when we left Oxford." She threw her head back and screamed.

"Mom, it's going to be okay. Just breathe." My voice was shaking. I was nervous and I hated that. "Just breathe, okay? It will all work out." I approached her slowly and touched her shoulder.

"Don't patronize me!" she cried, violently jerking away. *"I cannot breathe.* You don't understand! You don't understand what it used to be like. I used to be someone. My books were on all the bestseller lists. People wanted to talk to me. They recognized me on the street. I was the darling of the publishing industry. After hundreds of rejections, *my story* became a bestseller! And now, all I am is a washed-up has-been who can't make a bestseller list to save her life."

"That's not true."

"It is true. Everything I write is shit! And my books don't sell. They haven't sold since *View from the Mississippi*."

I breathed in and out, focusing on trying to keep my cool.

"I need to get out of this space. I need a change of scenery."

"Huh?"

Mom stormed out of the kitchen. I followed her up the stairs.

"What do you mean a change of scenery? We just moved here!"

Mom grabbed her suitcase from underneath her bed. "I'll be gone just a few days. You won't even notice I'm gone. Just a few . . . Excuse me." She pushed past me and went to her closet.

Wow. She was serious. "You're leaving me?"

Mom grabbed a jacket from her closet. "I promise that I won't be gone for long. It'll be a short break to inspire me. A change of scenery to get the ideas flowing."

Moving *here* was the change of scenery. Moving here was supposed to get the ideas flowing. "How long will you be gone?" a voice I didn't recognize asked.

"I don't know." She slammed her hands on her suitcase. "I just need to get away. I don't know!"

"From me? I'll leave you alone. I can ask my friend if I can stay at his house so you can have more space."

She zipped up her bag. "It's not you. You're not the problem. It's me. I can't focus here. Once I'm focused and I get my edits done, I can enjoy my life again and spend time with you." Mom pulled her suitcase off the bed and wheeled it toward the stairs. She was moving so fast. Too fast.

I jogged after her, *"Mom!"*

"What, Tenn?"

"Wait!"

"I can't. Let me go. I just need a second where I'm not a wife or a mother." She grabbed her keys.

What did she mean that she needed a second when she was

not a wife or mother? Dad was in Oxford and I was here, taking care of myself. *What did she mean?*

She was walking so fast, almost like she was racing to get away from me.

Stop for a second . . .

. . . I'm just asking you to stop.

For one second.

I reached for her arm. "Mom, please, stop. Please, just . . . *stop.*"

She jerked her arm free of my grip. "I can't."

"Why not?"

She turned her head away like she was done with this conversation. Done pretending to explain to me.

"When are you coming back?" asked that same small voice I didn't recognize.

"Soon."

How soon? I swallowed the question down. I didn't ask because I didn't think she would care.

"I'll go with you?" I said, even though I knew it wasn't what she wanted.

"You can't."

"I can." What was I supposed to do in this big house by myself? I wasn't Saint. What was I supposed to do? "Why can't I come? I can't stay in this house by myself."

"Yes, you can." She touched my cheek. "You're a big boy. And this is your home."

This home felt more like a museum. A place people stopped to gawk at on Garden District tours. It wasn't my home. I didn't know this place.

Mom backed away from me slowly. "Just give me a little

space, honey. I'll write something great. Really great. When I come back it's going to be all about you. Okay?"

I looked down. *Yeah . . . sure.*

⁓⁓

It was dark in the house.

I couldn't bring myself to turn on the lights.

I should call Dad and tell him what happened. That was the *responsible* thing to do. I didn't feel like being responsible, though. He would ask me questions that I couldn't answer. And he would make me go back to Oxford to live with him. No thanks. He was worse than her. And I was seventeen. Next July, I'd be eighteen. Not old enough to drink legally, but I'd be an adult in the state of Louisiana.

Another reason I didn't want to call Dad was because I couldn't stop crying.

Men weren't supposed to cry, because it didn't solve anything. Men were supposed to pick themselves up by the bootstraps and keep going. Only weak men cried. That's what he made me believe. I had to act with him. Be on guard with him.

I didn't want guards.

I didn't want Dad.

I just wanted to feel sad, okay?

Because that was how I felt.

26
TENNESSEE

NOVEMBER 1

I DIDN'T GO TO SCHOOL.

I stayed in bed.

It rained a lot. Bright flashes of blue lightning. From my window, I saw that St. Charles was flooding.

The jazz musician was playing his trombone by the streetcar stop. This was a sad song. A song that fit the endless downpour of rain. I didn't even know why I was sad.

This was what Mom did. She left. And my senior year hadn't been about her. Even when she was home, she was locked up in her room working. Sometimes I didn't see her at all.

I texted Jessamine because I hadn't heard from her since the art show. I didn't want to go back to being a stranger until we ran into each other again.

She didn't respond.

NOVEMBER 2

My heart felt like it was trying to kill me. It had turned into a ticking bomb. Every beat took a second off my life. I knew I was being dramatic and self-pitying, but I didn't know how to stop. Everything just hurt so much.

It was storming again. Bright blue flashes blinking repeatedly.

White lightning shooting in zigzags across the sky. At one point, the wind and rain was so bad that I had to get up to latch the window shutters closed.

I had a calculus test on Friday. Which meant that I needed to get out of bed and go to school. In the afternoon, I tried. I told myself that I would go for a walk. Walk the streetcar tracks up to Louisiana Avenue and circle back. Pretend to be a tourist. Smile at strangers. Pretend that my heart wasn't ticking me to a slow, excruciating demise. I made it to the black gate right outside our house, the gate that separated our too-big-for-one-person mansion from the street and neutral ground (the traffic divider and streetcar tracks). I turned around and went back to my bed.

Around five, I got a text message. I grabbed my phone, hoping that it was her. The message was from Solange.

SOLANGE: Hey, hon. You were on the schedule for today. Text me back and let me know that you're okay.

I attempted several apologies for missing my shift. I deleted those and started to explain what had happened with Mom. Those texts got deleted as well.

I went back to sleep.

················

I woke up at ten P.M. to my phone ringing. Groggily, I reached for it. "Hello?"

"Hey, it's Joel. I'm in your neighborhood. Can you talk?"

I rubbed tiredly at my eyes. "Joel?"

"Yep, can you talk?"

"Yeah, man, sure?" I ended the call feeling like I was in a dream. Joel was the last person I expected to hear from. Saint hadn't even called. That stung a little. I wish it didn't.

I swung my legs over the side of the bed. For a bit, I sat there. My room was pitch-black. Clothes were everywhere, and unpacked boxes were still in the middle of the floor. The boxes made me feel shame. *It was November.* We moved to New Orleans the first week of August. For three months, I'd accomplished nothing. What was wrong with me?

I picked myself up and put on mesh shorts and a T-shirt, then walked down the stairs. At the bottom of the steps, I paused and took a moment to get myself together. For a moment, I allowed myself to just stand there at the bottom of the steps. My museum was fit for royalty. Marble floors, high ceilings, pocket doors leading to extravagant libraries, elaborate wallpaper patterns of jungles and exotic animals in the dining room. This museum should be a happy place. A place filled with people and love. But it felt like a cage.

My lip trembled. *No.* I couldn't cry. Not when Joel was somewhere close by. Thinking about Joel set off my grenade heart. I was glad to see Joel, but seeing him made me wish that it was Jessamine or Saint.

I unstuck myself and went to the door. I stepped outside into the cool night. St. Charles was quiet tonight. A group of people on colorful bicycles zoomed past. The streetcar rattled by. A child was blowing bubbles from the open streetcar window. I sat down in one of the four rocking chairs on the huge porch.

Joel pulled up about five minutes later. "You like Big Shots?" he asked as he came through the gate.

"What's a Big Shot?"

"A New Orleans tradition. Peach or strawberry?"

"Strawberry."

Joel handed me the glass bottle. He had just come from Chicory and Grind because he was wearing the uniform, which reminded me that my irresponsible behavior meant that Joel or Solange probably had to work longer hours.

"Thanks, Joel."

"You got it." He sank down in the rocking chair beside me.

I twisted off the cap and took a sip. The fizz tickled my throat. "It's good."

"Good." Joel stared off toward the streetcar going in the opposite direction. "You know why I'm here, right?"

"No, I don't?"

Joel turned toward me, "I got both Solange and Saint in my ear about you. Solange is worried because you don't ever miss work. And Saint won't say he's worried, but he keeps telling me when you miss school. What's up with you?"

"I'm fine." The lie was unconvincing.

He nodded slowly. "Tennessee, we've been working together for a few months. I hate to tell you, but I've seen you lie. And dude, you're the worst liar I've ever seen."

I looked down, not knowing how to respond to that. "I guess I am a terrible liar, huh?"

Joel nodded and playfully tapped my shoulder with his fist. "I'm not the best liar either. The other day my mama asked me if I have a girlfriend."

My eyes widened. "What'd you say?"

"I told her that I did. I panicked."

I nodded sympathetically. I understood what it was like

to panic. When my parents used to make me pick sides, I would panic. I would dissociate. That only made them get louder and more demanding. The only solution was to come back down to earth and pick a side.

After I picked a side just to be left alone, I'd worry that the side I didn't choose hated me. I used to always pick Mom's side. She was scarier when mad.

Joel sighed and folded his arm behind his head. "Now she's asking to meet this imaginary girlfriend and trying to figure out who she is. My mama's worried that it's a white girl." He laughed.

I laughed, too. "She's not a white girl. No danger there."

He laughed some more and so did I. Did he and Saint talk about these things? I hoped that they did.

"What are you going to do, Joel?"

"I dunno? Light some sage, say a prayer, and move to a different neighborhood."

I nodded, thinking about it. "At least Jessamine's got your back. It's not just you against your mama."

"I don't want to get Jess involved. This is my problem, not hers." Joel sunk down in the rocking chair and crossed his arms.

"Would you tell your mom the truth?"

"I'm scared," Joel said honestly. He took a sip of his Big Shot. "I'm not like Solange and Jessamine and Saint. They're braver than me." He snorted. "Now it's your turn. I get bored listening to myself complain. What's going on with you?"

"You can 'complain' all you want."

Joel's phone went off. He pulled it out of his pocket and sighed. "Mama summons."

"You need to get that?"

"No, not right now. What's up with you? Why aren't you going to school and work?"

Mom and Dad had been my problem forever. My embarrassing problem that sometimes bled into public. At least this time it didn't. Where did I even start to describe this? "You saw my parents at Commander's Palace?"

"There was a lot going on that day. But I remember them fighting. Are they always like that? Not to be rude or anything."

"They *are* always like that," I confirmed.

Joel wrinkled his nose. "How do you handle that?"

Not well. "I'm still learning!" I said, laughing. The laugh sounded forced.

Joel was silent for a bit, which made me scared that I said too much. I looked at him and he said, "If you ever need to vent about them, I'm here to listen."

"I appreciate that, Joel." I would probably never take him up on the offer.

"How about I hang with you for a bit? Just in case you feel like talking some more?"

"I'd like that. You can talk, too, if you feel like it."

Joel's phone lit up again. He looked down. "It's a text from Saint. He's asking if you're still alive. I'm going to tell him to come over and see."

⁓

"You're alive!" Saint waltzed into the courtyard wearing what appeared to be his autumn best, including this oversize orange sweater with a crown on the front. He gave me a life-squeezing hug. And then he handed me a bouquet of sunflowers.

"Saint?" I laughed, confused. "I miss school for a few days and you thought I died?"

Saint gripped my arms tightly. "You don't ever miss school!"

That was true.

Saint looked at Joel, who was still sitting in the rocking chair staring off toward the streetcar line. "He acts like he doesn't know how to say hi."

I also glanced at Joel, who was now picking off imaginary lint from his shorts. This seemed like another conversation that I didn't need to be a part of, kind of like that time in Saint's car. "Thanks so much, Saint. I'll go put these in some water."

Saint kicked Joel's shoes with his green flats.

"Don't scuff my shoes, yo," Joel said.

"I bought you those shoes, yo," Saint snapped right back.

"You want them back?" Joel asked, staring at Saint now.

I wrapped an arm loosely around Saint's shoulder. It was clear that Saint and Joel had feelings for each other. They spent a lot of time talking about each other. But for whatever reason, they always argued when they were together. It made me sad. "Why don't you help me find a vase for these beautiful sunflowers?"

Saint surprisingly didn't put up a fight. He circled his arm around my waist. Once we stepped inside he said, "You smell like Cool Ranch Doritos."

"What? I do?" I sniffed my shirt.

"Yeah, the heavily seasoned ones."

"Do they smell worse than the rest?"

Saint shrugged.

Embarrassed, I tried to pull away from Saint, but he held me tighter. We stepped into the kitchen. Saint loosened his grip on me and walked straight to the fridge. He opened it and peered inside. "That's what I thought. I'll have my people bring you over some meals."

I walked over to the kitchen sink, grabbing a yellow vase from the cabinet underneath, then filled it with water. Saint pulled out a chair at the table. I didn't have to cut the sunflower stems, so I placed them in the water and walked the vase over to Saint.

"Let's play tennis," I said.

Saint mimicked serving me the ball. "You serve first. Where have you been?"

"I've been here," I said, sinking down into the chair across from him.

Saint shook his head. "I mean where have you been, up here?" He tapped his head.

I blinked a few times. Saint rarely asked personal questions. First Joel and now Saint. I stammered my way through an explanation. "I, um . . . My mom left. . . . She was struggling with her book. . . . I was feeling sad. . . . I, um . . ."

And just like that, there were tears.

It was so embarrassing. I didn't mean to cry in front of Saint. I didn't want to cry in front of anyone. Why was I even crying? *What's wrong with me?*

Saint stood up and he walked over to me. I tried to wave him away. I told him that the tears would be over soon and that I would be okay. Saint crouched down and he touched my knee.

"It's okay to cry, Tennessee."

I shook my head. No.

"Yes. My dad once told me that the strongest people cry— and they don't just cry, but they cry in front of others because they're not afraid to be seen. There is strength in vulnerability."

I didn't realize that I was covering my face until Saint pulled down my hands. He was smiling at me. He wasn't alone. Joel was beside him, standing.

"Y'all, I'm sorry," I apologized.

"Apologize one more time and I'll make you buy me a Cartier watch, boo." Saint pulled back the sleeve of his sweater to flash what I assumed to be a Cartier watch.

Joel sank down in the seat that Saint had been sitting in. "It's more like if you apologize again, he will buy *you* a Cartier watch."

"I never bought you drip," Saint said, turning to look at Joel. "Tennessee is my friend and I love him. I just *sometimes* like you."

Joel laughed. "Good to know. Does that mean you'll stop blowing up my phone and start blowing up his?"

Saint tugged on my hand. "Let's go back outside. This kitchen is getting a little warm with all the hot air he is blowing out." He stood up and tugged on my hand again.

Before I could get up, Joel also stood. He circled his arms around Saint and hugged him tightly.

Saint held on tighter to my hand, squeezing so hard that it almost hurt. Joel pulled one arm free from Saint's waist and grabbed Saint's arm, tugging a few times, until Saint let go of my hand.

Joel linked his fingers inside Saint's and nuzzled his nose against Saint's cheek. This also felt like a private moment. A moment that I shouldn't be a part of.

"You're always mad at me." Joel kissed Saint's cheek and then his ear. "Why are you always mad at me?"

Saint closed his eyes. "Because you are inconsistent."

"You always say that."

"Because it's true. The ice-cream machine at late night spots are more consistent than you." Saint tried to squirm away from Joel, but Joel hugged him tighter.

"C'mon," Joel begged. "Don't you see me trying?"

I tried not to watch them. It was not hard. They had already forgotten me. Saint attempted to break free. Joel kept him close, begging him to stay, to be patient, to see that he was trying. Eventually, Saint stopped struggling and he started smiling.

When Saint smiled, so did Joel.

"I hate you," Saint said.

"I heart you," Joel replied.

27
JESSAMINE

SOMEONE ELSE DIED YESTERDAY.

Her name was Claudia.

She didn't go to my school, but we grew up together.

I heard that she was home when the fireworks went off. She was sitting at the table, probably doing her homework or watching TV when a stray firework found her.

Claudia was just there. It was the wrong time. The wrong place. Her home. And now she was dead.

This time I didn't have to speak to grief counselors, because Claudia didn't go to my school. She was just another—another person dead, another statistic for Mama to throw at Joel.

It made me sad.

So . . . so . . . so . . . sad.

Worse than the Sunday feeling kind of sad.

I did everything I could to get the sad taste out of my mouth. I shopped. I ran, even though my legs burned and itched. I rode streetcars all night and all day. I watched movies with Iz at Solange's Treme apartment. I did homework. I tried to sleep. I tried everything. Everything only made it worse, especially sleeping.

When I closed my eyes, I saw Claudia.

I saw her sitting at the kitchen table. She looked like me, her skin dark like mine, her eyes brown like mine. She also looked like Joel, then she looked like Iz, then she looked like Mama, then she looked like Solange.

After staying up for days and nights, I went to City Park. I got one of the blue bikes and rode as far and as fast as I could go. My legs pumped. I closed my eyes and I was gone. I raced through the live oaks decorated with thick swathes of Spanish moss. I flew, up in the air, pedaling faster and faster past happy people, their grinning faces. Where did these happy people live?

I was going.

Gone, gone, gone!

Nothing could get me. Nothing could touch me. Not fireworks. Not death. Not love!

I kept going, pumping my legs until they hurt. Finally, I got to the place where no one existed. The wooded space where there was a clearing for me to sit and disappear. I let my blue bike fall to the ground. I walked out into the field, stretching out my arms and letting the coolish breeze sift through my fingertips like flour.

I sank down into the grass and hugged my knees to my chest. I was afraid. I had been afraid since—since senior year started. Senior year, the year of responsibilities and good-byes.

Taking a deep breath, I focused on being still, being quiet, and focusing on the small things. Like the sun tickling my skin. The sound of birds chirping. The rustling of the Spanish moss in the trees. The slight sting of the cool breeze.

I saw Claudia again. The fireworks left blood dried on her face, blood dried on her hand, blood on the floor, blood in her eyes, blood in her mouth. . . . Then I saw Ronnie and the bloodred moon.

Someone was whistling. I could hear water, too. The water was coming.

My cell phone vibrated.

Tears filled my eyes when I realized that I didn't just have one text, but four. One from Iz. One from Joel. One from Tennessee. And one from Mama.

I opened Mama's text first.

It was one emoji.

A heart.

⟋๛

"Y'all started the movie without me." I crawled onto Mama's bed.

"We can start it over?" she offered.

"Naw, we can't do all that," Joel said, passing the popcorn bowl over to me.

Scowling across Mama at him, I took the popcorn bowl. I grabbed a handful and popped it into my mouth.

"Don't be greedy and eat it all," he said.

To be extra greedy I grabbed two handfuls. If he noticed, Joel acted like he didn't. He fluffed his pillow and laid back down. My heart did flip-flops as I watched the TV colors fall against Joel's face. Blue on his nose. Red on his lips. Yellow on his white teeth when he grinned. He was okay. We were okay. We were all okay.

Mama wrapped an arm around me, "How did your meeting with Ms. Nadia go today? Did you get some feedback on your personal essay and narrow down the scholarships you're applying for?"

These loaded questions were not making me feel relaxed.

When she didn't say anything else, I followed the blue lights from the TV to her eyes. She stared at me. Her attention not wavering.

"It's November, Jessamine. You are behind."

"Y'all." Joel sat up. "How can we watch a movie with a whole side conversation going on?"

Mama sighed heavy and focused back on the TV. I smiled across Mama at Joel. He caught my eye and he also smiled. *Thanks for saving me, twin.*

......⁊ₒ......

Joel walked into my room. He took a seat on the edge of my bed and looked right at me, all in my face.

"What are you doing?"

"Keeping watch." He crossed his arms.

"Keeping watch of what?"

"Keeping watch of you."

I dropped my eyebrows at him.

"You've been having those nightmares again," Joel said.

I sighed. "They'll go away on their own."

"I know they will, but I'm gonna sit up with you for a bit."

"Like that's not weird or nothing."

"Do you want me to go?" he asked, pretending like he was about to get up and leave.

"No." I fixed my glasses. "How are you, JoJo?"

"Sad about Claudia, but other than that, I'm okay . . . I guess."

I smiled weakly. Poor Claudia. Her poor family. What would they do tonight? It's not like they could watch a movie with her or sit up to ask about her day. I opened *The Great Gatsby* and started reading for my homework assignment. I'd read the book several times and could quote it verbatim, like Joel could quote the movie we just watched.

"Did you want to read to me?" I asked him.

Joel looked up from his sketchbook I thought he was going to laugh and say no. But he didn't. Joel took *The Great Gatsby* from me.

He started to read, and for the first time in days, I slept, clinging to my twin brother.

28
TENNESSEE

It was November 15. Mom had been gone for just over two weeks. Since she left, she called once and sent a picture of a beach in Key West. She said that the best writers escaped to the Keys including Ernest Hemingway and my namesake Tennessee Williams. I guess that was supposed to make me feel better.

Saint's big masquerade party was coming up. He had mentioned it a few times at school. He said, "You're going to be there, right? You're one of the *many* guests of honor."

I still wasn't feeling 100 percent. Everything took more energy than it should. Showering. Brushing my teeth. Studying for tests. And the SAT was coming up. At the moment, I didn't feel confident in my test-taking skills. But the show had to go on, right?

⁕

The invitation to Saint's party was clutched in my hand. I stood frozen at the stairs leading up to Gallier Hall, working up the nerve to go inside. There was a ton of people. They were all dressed up: suits, dresses, and extravagant masquerade masks. And then there was me: no suit jacket, a bow tie, and wrinkled pants. Saint would have something to say about my "costume," and it didn't help that my mask was a two-dollar grab from a tourist trap in the French Quarter.

I made my way up the stairs. The massive front doors were open, and two people were standing outside collecting tickets, a man in an all-white suit with a black checkered mask and a woman in a shimmering ball gown with peacock feathers in her hair. They looked fancy. Maybe I should've tried a little more.

"Ticket," the man said.

I handed him the golden ticket. He took it and told me to enter.

"Sir, pick up your crown, map, event schedule, and gift bag in the entryway. Don't forget to take a picture in the room to the right, so you can be entered into the Saint-of-the-Ball masquerade contest. The winner gets a thousand dollars in cash and three thousand dollars donated to a local charity of their choice."

A thousand dollars in cash AND three thousand dollars to a local charity!

Inside Gallier, there were people wall to wall. I saw a few classmates from Magnolia Prep. We exchanged quick nods and smiles and kept it moving.

Everyone else was much older. For some reason, I expected to see more people our age.

Servers offered trays of colorful drinks called the Tchoupitoulas, the Bywater, and the Nine Muses. The food— plates of shrimp and cocktail sauce, Bananas Foster, and bite-sized bowls of jambalaya—was served by buff dudes in shiny boxer briefs and jerseys with *Saint* on the back. Black-and-gold Saint, not *the Saints*.

Speaking of Saint, where was he?

I wandered around the large space, giving awkward smiles

and even more awkward head nods. There were choreographed dancers in one room. A light show in another that made the room look like it was underwater, and in another, a second line parade was starting up. I'd seen a few second line parades since moving to New Orleans. The first line was the brass band—including trombones, tubas, trumpets, other brass instruments, and a drumline—and sometimes a wedding party or family. The second line was made up of guests and other people joining in.

"Excuse me?" Someone tapped me on the shoulder.

I turned around. A tall African American woman beamed back at me. I recognized her immediately—she looked just like Saint. They even dressed the same. "Mrs. Baptiste?" I asked, even though I knew.

"Tennessee." She didn't ask; she knew. She leaned in to give me a one-armed hug and a kiss on the cheek. "Please call me Mona. It's a pleasure to finally meet you."

"Finally" meet me. Did Saint talk about me to his mama?

I smiled and tried my best to be chill about it. I don't know why, but it made me happy. If he spoke about me to his mom, that meant our friendship was real, even if he didn't always text me back when I texted him or call me back when I called him.

"Where's your cold drink? Where's your food? This is a party!"

"I was looking for Saint."

"You're wasting your time, baby. He's not here."

"He's not here? But . . . this is *his* party. He's been talking about this party since we met."

Mrs. Baptiste flagged down a Saint server with colorful drinks. She picked up two, then handed me a yellow one and kept the pink one for herself.

"The Felicity is for minors. The Claiborne is basically a French seventy-five with lagniappe, so not for minors." She took a sip and guided me toward a room that was not themed or filled with people. "If you don't mind, I'd love to get to know the friend my son is always raving about."

Raving. I refused to believe that he raved about me.

Mrs. Baptiste sat down at a piano. I sat down beside her and took a sip of the Felicity. It tasted like expensive Kool-Aid.

"Every year Saint invites fewer of his peers to these events, so his dad and I always end up filling the space. I tried suggesting a smaller venue, but Saint won't have it. Just like his father, he is all about the optics. I do not believe that he will be making an appearance tonight."

"I wish he told me that he wasn't coming."

"I think it was a last-minute decision. The boy that he's dating didn't want to come to the ball. And because Saint has always been all-in or nothing at all, he chose the boy over the ball." She shrugged and took another sip of her drink. "I wish he would've chosen the ball. He's too young to be so consumed with romance. It's fleeting at seventeen. I try to tell him that, but this Gen Z generation thinks they know everything."

I chewed on my lip. I didn't want to believe that romance was fleeting at seventeen. I wanted to believe that it could last. "I wish he would've come, too. Maybe I could call him and Joel and talk them into making an appearance?"

Mrs. Baptiste flicked her wrist elegantly. "Don't waste your time. If he planned on attending, he would've already made his grand entrance. He's not coming. Anyway, enough about young enamored love. Saint tells me that you're from Mississippi?"

"Yes, ma'am."

"Oxford, right?"

"Yes, ma'am."

"And your mama's a writer and your daddy is a doctor?"

My mouth dropped. How did he remember all that? "Yes, I told him that a while ago."

"He remembers what he wants to remember."

And apparently, he also listened? I smiled, thinking of all the times I thought I was talking to air. The times I stopped talking because I thought he wasn't listening. The times I was talking about Anatomy and Physiology (because we were in the same class) and he switched the conversation to Joel.

"Tennessee, it was great meeting you. Thank you for giving me an excuse to stop smiling in everyone's faces! My face hurts from all that smiling!" She leaned in and gave me a hug, a tight hug. That felt nice.

"It was great meeting you, too, Mrs. Baptiste. I love your artwork, by the way."

"Thank you, mon cher. *Mona*," she corrected with a wink. "Please let Saint know when you and your folks are free for dinner. We'd love to have y'all over." She gave me one last tight hug, made a cross in the air, and headed back out into the crowd of people with a smile.

I couldn't imagine bringing my parents to the Baptiste house. Saint was my friend, and I wanted to keep it that way. Who knew what offensive thing would come out of Mom or Dad's mouth?

The second line had moved out into the hallway. White handkerchiefs swayed back and forth and people were dancing. Since I was here, I should go out and join the second line. I should dance and wave around the handkerchief and do the things that people did at parties. I should, because all that waited for me at home was a whole lot of silence.

I was tired of the silence.

"I found you."

Jessamine.

She sat down beside me. Jessamine was wearing this long black dress with this light fabric. It was almost see-through, but not quite. The dress showed off her legs, her super long legs, and she had an umbrella over her head. Black looked good on her. Whenever she wore black she also wore bright red lipstick. It's what she would call a look. I guess this look was her trademark? Black dress. Red lipstick.

"Isn't it bad luck to have an umbrella inside?" I asked.

"Satsuma boy, this is not an umbrella, it's a parasol." She bumped me with her shoulder. "Why are you hiding in the piano room, when there's a party going on out there?"

"I'm not hiding." I gazed around noticing for the first time that I was alone in the room. When did the other people leave? Outside, people were engaged in lively conversation.

"Bruh."

My cheeks warmed.

"I've been stopping by Chicory and Grind expecting an iced vanilla latte with a hint of cinnamon, and you haven't been there to make it for me."

I couldn't help but to wonder how much Joel told her. "I've been sick."

Jessamine tilted her head to the side. "Are you feeling better?"

Her eyebrows were kind of pinched. Joel probably told her. "I think so."

She touched my cheek and then turned her hand over to feel my forehead. "Iz makes a mean chicken noodle soup. It'll burn the sick right out of you." I smirked and looked down at her lips. My eyes found hers again. She looked down at my lips, and I held my breath. Being this close made me think about that time at Saint's house, when we had been playing twenty questions and he dared me to kiss her. She had kissed me. It was quick, but still, thinking about that kiss got me.

How she smelled.

How soft her hair was when I ran my hands through it. How her hair smelled like roses sometimes. Sometimes it was tangerines.

Her skin always smelled like cocoa butter.

She placed her hand to my chest.

I closed my eyes and leaned in. I expected Jessamine to stop me. She didn't. Her lips were soft and still against mine. I breathed her in. I opened my mouth. I closed it. I brought my hand up to her face. She opened her mouth and her tongue slid inside my mouth. A shiver shot up from my leg. Jessamine wrapped an arm around my shoulder. I scooted closer to her on the bench. At one point, my tongue was more in her mouth than mine.

Then Jessamine pulled away. She slid across the piano bench. There was enough space now for someone to sit down between us.

I forced air into my lungs. Thankfully, the music was still so loud or else she'd hear me breathing like I'd just ran a triathlon.

"You're radioactive now," I said, attempting to make a joke.

"I need my satsuma tree." She pouted.

"Why do you need that?" I asked, covering the piano keys so I could rest my arms on the cover.

"So I can ward off demons with glittering eyes."

"Am I the demon with glittering eyes?" I asked, giggling.

Jessamine turned away from me and crossed her arms. "I don't appreciate you putting this hex on me! I don't want your germs. I don't want your radioactive juju."

"I want yours, though."

"I'm not radioactive," Jessamine said, pushing lightly on my shoulder.

This was a bold thing to do, but I did it anyway: I scooted on the bench closer to her. I leaned forward and wrapped my arms around her waist and rested my head against hers. In the past, she might have pushed me away. This time, she didn't. "I missed you," I said.

"Why'd you miss me? I'm miserable company." She also leaned against the piano cover, staring straight ahead. Occasionally her eyes would drift over to me, and then she'd promptly look away.

"Naw, you're the best company," I said.

Jessamine peeked at me from the corner of her eye. I nuzzled into her curls, smelling her hair.

"Are you depressed?" she asked.

I stopped. "Why?"

"Joel told me you were depressed."

I swallowed. Suspicions confirmed. Joel ratted me out. *Why?*

She rested her hand against my cheek, curling her fingers. "Do you need me to play you something? I can DJ without music, you know that."

"It was just a tough week, that's all. I'm okay." I smiled really big to convince her.

Jessamine stared at me seriously without blinking. She wasn't buying it. "It seems like the sad flu is going around. We got to stay vigilant against it," she said.

"How?"

Jessamine placed her hands over my eyes. "You're the writer, right?"

"I am the writer that hasn't been doing much writing lately."

"Okay, writer boy. When things get hard for me, I go to the world of fiction. Pick your poison."

"A poisoned apple," I threw out.

Jessamine giggled. "A poisoned apple is not one of the options. The options are wreaking havoc at the Shoppes on Canal Place or fireworks at the top of the world. Two options. Two seconds to choose. Choose wisely, or else I will choose for you."

I reached for her hands and attempted to pull them from my eyes.

"Ticktock!" she said.

"Okay! Fireworks at the top of the world."

Jessamine pulled down her hands. I opened my eyes. There she was. Right there. Her big bright eyes. The only eyes that I had wanted to see after Mom left. I exhaled, letting out all the air that I had been holding in.

"Are you ready to take a rocket to the moon, Tennessee Williams?"

"Absolutely, let's go!"

⁓⊙℘⊙⁓

Jessamine took me to the top of a skyscraper in the Central Business District. She knew the lady that worked at the front desk. We took the elevator to the rooftop, where the city lights were so bright. The rooftop had a barricade around the ledges. A concrete wall that was high enough to maintain safety, but not too tall that it took away from the view. I'd never seen New Orleans like this before!

I held out my arms and let the wind howl around me. Being up here made me feel like I could fly. Over the winding river. Over the skyscrapers. Over all the old buildings that once were banks and now were hotels or businesses.

"You have to close your eyes," she said.

"How will I walk?" I asked.

"I won't let you fall." Jessamine crossed her arms. "Do you trust me?"

I nodded slowly.

"Cool, now close your eyes."

I did as I was told, bringing my hands over my eyes. Jessamine circled her hand around my wrist and led me forward. At the top of the world, the wind howled. The breeze was cold, stinging my cheeks and making my teeth chatter.

"Okay, stop."

I stopped moving.

"Simon says, open your eyes!"

Jessamine sounded so excited. Her excitement battled the cold breeze. I opened my eyes. Once again, she was the first thing I saw. Her hair was whipping around in the wind, her curls flying freely across her high forehead. She was beaming, brighter than the city of lights that was New Orleans from this altitude. So, this was what fireworks at the top of the world looked like?

"Don't look at me, writer boy! The fireworks are out there!" Jessamine gestured toward the Crescent City Connection, which rose over the Mississippi River like a gigantic floating bridge lit up by a thousand bulbs.

Jessamine said that the magic was out there, but to be honest, all the lights in New Orleans did not measure up to her. I don't know why I did it, but I boldly took a step toward her. When I took that step, she stopped gesturing to the city.

I took Jessamine's hand.

"What are you doing?" she asked.

"I don't know," I said, shrugging.

Jessamine's eyes darted back and forth, searching mine. The funny thing was, I didn't know what I was going to do, until I did it.

In the romantic comedies that Mom and Dad watched (when she made him pay penance for something), the place to kiss the person you really liked was on a rooftop with a view or in the rain. This felt like the right place. City lights, check. Cold weather, check. The girl I liked, check. Nothing and everything to lose? Checking that box twice.

I leaned in, eyes open, ready to pull back the second it became clear that she didn't want me to kiss her. I got *so* close. So close. And then Jessamine reached up and she pinched my nose, stopping me.

"Tennessee, radioactive germs are magnified at the top of the world."

"Really, I didn't know," I said, giggling.

Jessamine nodded slowly, a smile tugging at her lips. "Enjoy the view."

"I am enjoying the view," I said, giggling again at how distorted my voice sounded in my ears.

The wind whipped around us, howling and whistling. We

probably couldn't stay at the top of the world for long, because it was that cold. Jessamine let go of my nose, and she backed away. "No more radioactive kisses, Tennessee Williams! If you attempt that again, I will be forced to put you in time out!"

I raised my hands in surrender.

Jessamine reached in her purse and pulled out four glow sticks. "I wanted sparklers, but Ms. Sherry said that they're a fire hazard and she would get in trouble for letting me have those up here. So our poison is diluted, but it's still poison." Jessamine handed me two glow sticks.

I couldn't remember the last time that I played with glow sticks. *How fun.*

"Now, you go stand over there, writer boy." She waved me down to the other side of the building like an airplane marshaller.

I pointed my pink glow stick in the direction I was walking.

It wasn't lost on me that Jessamine already had the glow sticks before coming to Saint's party. This was premeditated. Was it because Joel told her that I was sad? Was she doing this to cheer me up?

The wind whipped again, and I turned my face away from the whooshing sound.

"Keep going, Williams!" Jessamine said, waving me farther.

I started to run. The wind slowed me down, coming off the river. And pushing me to the right. "Keep going?" I yelled.

"Yes!" she screamed over the wind.

I kept going until she yelled for me to stop. I turned around and looked at Jessamine. She was so far away. "Now, you have to do what I say!"

"Okay!"

Jessamine dropped her arms. "This is called the helicopter."

She raised her arms over head. "Watch what I do." Jessamine waved the glow sticks in the air, moving her arms around in a circular motion. She did a spin, jumped in the air, stomped her feet, and then threw her arms out and screamed, "We're young. We're free. We control our destiny!"

There was something poignant about her words. Especially the way they carried over the harsh whistle of the wind. Even Mother Nature couldn't silence Jessamine. I mimicked her, putting an extra dose of passion into my spin, jump, stomp and scream.

Who knew what tomorrow would bring? Tomorrow she might go back to ghosting me for weeks, but at least tonight we were making fireworks on top of the tallest skyscraper in New Orleans.

Youth and freedom felt so sweet.

29
TENNESSEE

I COULDN'T SLEEP.

I got up at six A.M. that Sunday morning after the ball. The plan was to do something other than lay in bed all day thinking about Jessamine. The plan was to check on Saint and see how last night went for him—once it was an appropriate time to do so. I'd study for the ACT. I'd clean up this house, which would probably take the rest of the day with the state it was in.

I cleaned the part of the house that I lived in and finally worked up the nerve to go into Mom's room. It was exactly as she left it, crumpled up pages on the floor and old food.

I started picking up the trash. It felt okay being in there. I didn't feel mad or sad, which was good. It meant that I was moving on, right?

I came across a creative board. It was the closest thing she had to pictures in her room. The creative boards were filled with words and magazine cut-outs of actors who were stand-ins for her characters. Even when she wasn't with me, her characters were still there, letting their presence be known.

The longer I stared at the creative board, the worse I felt. Going back to school and forcing myself to do social things like attend Saint's ball made me feel better. But I still felt this ache in my chest. *Abandoned* felt like too strong of a word to use. But if I was honest, I did feel abandoned by her. She told me to call her if I needed money and that she was monitoring my bank account to make sure that I had everything I needed. That didn't make her any less gone. We were coming up on three weeks of MIA now.

I left Mom's room, shutting the door behind me. An urge to check my phone snuck up. *Nope. Not doing that.* On the list of busy activities was ACT and SAT prep, and I had a paper on *As I Lay Dying* that I'd been putting off. What the hell was going on in that book anyway?

What is Jessamine doing now?

"No," I said out loud.

I jogged downstairs to the kitchen. I had no idea why I was running. A shower would be a good idea, and so would brushing my teeth. I didn't want to be like Mom when she got too obsessed with one thing. Why did I feel so scattered? Thinking about it made it worse.

I turned on the TV to quiet the silence and started up a fresh pot of coffee.

It didn't matter what I did. Jog. Clean. Watch TV. Create lists. I kept going back to last night when we danced on top of the world. When the wind whipped around us and we screamed about being young, free, and in control of our destiny. And then after that, when she held me and I held her for, like, twenty minutes.

I went back upstairs to my room. I sank down on the bed and picked up my phone. She hadn't texted me, but . . . there was something better, or maybe worse? Jessamine had followed me on IG.

I hadn't used IG in years. What did she find on that page?

I took a few deep breaths before opening Pandora's box.

It was bad.

Camouflage appeared to be the only style of clothing that I owned. There were random shots of nature. And every picture of me had one thing in common: my eyes. They were dead in every picture.

I couldn't look at that page anymore. It was making my lungs feel tight. And it was making me feel like I was sinking into a small, dark space. A space that was silent and cold.

I swallowed. There was something so scary about her seeing me as the boy from Mississippi. The boy who didn't have any friends on IG. The boy before her.

I didn't want to remember who I used to be.

I went to Jessamine's page. She had a lot of friends. I scrolled through her feed of bright pictures, full of people she loved. Pictures that were full of life—unlike mine. There was a picture of her dancing at a second line, and there was another one of her singing into a corn on the cob at a crawfish boil, while Solange gave her a "Solange look," and there was a picture of . . . me.

I leaned forward, lungs working overtime, because I couldn't stop breathing hard. I clicked on the picture, careful not to like it. The picture was a collage of four pictures, two from when we danced on Frenchmen. When did she have time to take those pictures? And there was the floral print. She had labeled the collage of photos: "On Sundays, we make new friends."

Friends. For some reason that word overrode everything. Did she think of me as a friend? Is that why she distanced herself from me sometimes?

"Tennessee? Honey!"

Mom?

I looked up at her wide-mouthed. How long had she been standing there?

"I was screaming loud enough for the Quarter to hear me!" Grinning wide, she pulled me into a hug. A hug that was way too tight.

My mind was stuck. I couldn't turn the gears fast enough. Mom was home. She was tanned. She was hugging me like everything was okay. And then, Mom was grabbing my phone.

"I love this picture of you, Tenn!"

I was too slow. My hands clumsily fumbled for my phone. Mom whirled away from me like it was a game. "Mom! Give me my phone back."

"Who took this picture of you? I want it. Send it to me. Never mind." She took a screenshot and started typing something. "Never mind, I just sent it to myself."

"Can I *please* have my phone back?"

"Is this your girlfriend? She's gorgeous! I love her hair!"

I turned away from her excited eyes. It felt like she punched me in the stomach. Seeing her now, after her almost three-week absence, hurt. She didn't even lead with a *sorry* or ask how I was doing?

"Why don't you invite her over?"

I shook my head at her and consciously chose not to prepare a smile or lie for her. She didn't get to feel better. I was finally starting to feel okay, and her arrival *now* was not going to bring me back to that bad place.

Mom sat on my bed and handed me my phone. "Okay, we don't have to talk about your love life." She bumped into my shoulder. "Can I at least ask how you're doing? Or is that also off-limits?"

I frowned.

She bumped into me again.

"How's your novel?" I asked, monotone.

She looked at me with a falling smile. "The enthusiasm in your voice is barely there."

"I don't know what you want from me."

"You're so serious," she said. "I almost don't know what to do with you." Mom tapped my hand. "Well, okay, I'll share my exciting news then." She drummed her hands on the counter. "My novel is complete! Leonard died and Clean became the queen and king of the realm." She squealed and kicked out her legs. "I can live again. What do you want to do to celebrate? We can take a drive to the Gulf and visit some of those cute Louisiana towns before climate change wipes them out, or we can go to the Audubon Zoo and the Aquarium of the Americas!"

She wanted to do all that now? When all I asked for a few weeks ago was a walk?

I stood up, taking some much-needed space.

Her smile fell. "Wait. Are you leaving? I just got home. I wanted to spend time with you."

"I've been home. *I've been here*," I said, trying not to get upset. "We can catch up later, okay? Maybe we can go to the Fly or this place I heard about in the Bywater called the Edge of the World. I just need a little space right now, Mom."

"*Or*, we can go to Magazine Street and raid the antique stores . . . with the pretty girl you won't talk to me about."

Did she hear anything that I just said? I needed space.

My phone lit up on the bed. Mom handed it to me without looking at the screen. I was hoping that the text message would be from Jessamine, but Saint was a very close second.

Saint asked me to meet him at the Treme house. I said yes because I was eager to see how his night with Joel went.

‧‧‧‧‧✑‧‧‧‧‧

I arrived at Saint's house two hours later. He was sitting out in the back when I arrived. Giant eucalyptus and lavender candles were set up on concrete end tables surrounding the beige patio furniture. I took a seat beside Saint on the striped blue-and-white patio cushion. His first question was "What do you want to drink?"

A bright green drink was sitting on the patio table in front of him. I pointed at it. "What's that?"

"Vitality," Saint answered, batting at the air with a handheld fan that said *YAAAASSS*.

I teasingly rolled my eyes at my friend. "What is in vitality? Is it alcoholic?"

"Of course not!" Saint said, snapping his fan shut and swatting my arm with it. "It is lime juice, a dash of lemon, sugar, and green tea."

"I'm okay for now," I said, sinking back in the chair. It was another perfect morning. There was a slight breeze and the temperature was comfortably sitting in the low sixties. I listened to the sound of palm tree and magnolia leaves brushing together.

Saint stared off into space, waving his fan back and forth. Something was clearly on his mind. I wondered if it was best to ask him what was going on, or if I should ask him what he was thinking about. Sometimes he wanted to talk about whatever was bothering him—and sometimes he didn't.

"You seem thoughtful." I said, testing the waters.

Saint nodded slowly. "You sure you don't want some vitality, Nashville?"

"Positive. If I want one later, I'll lct you know."

He sighed. It was a deep sigh. "Why does love have to be so hard?"

There was a sadness in Saint's voice that I wasn't used to hearing. He glanced at me, his eyes lingering. I scooted closer to Saint and bumped my knee against his. "What happened?"

He sighed. "Nothing. That's the problem. Nothing ever happens with Joel. The second it feels like we're getting close—scratch that, the second I feel close to him, he pulls back. He ghosts me. I don't understand him."

Joel and Jessamine sounded a lot alike. She did the same to me. But I couldn't say that I ever truly felt close to her. I *wanted* to feel that way. But it was mostly a want and not a reality. "Have you told him that?"

"I've told him lots of things," Saint said, voice cracking a little. "Sometimes he makes changes for a few days and sometimes he just says that he has a lot going on and he can't deal with me."

I wrapped an arm around Saint's shoulder. I didn't know what to say. This relationship seemed to be hurting him. And if something or someone hurts you, you should just let them go, right? Cut out the source of your pain, deal with the heartache, and move on, right?

But that didn't feel right to say. I knew Joel. I knew that he wasn't malicious and he didn't want to hurt Saint. I saw how he looked at Saint. If they were in a room together full of people, Joel always found Saint. He watched him. He seemed to really like him. But for whatever reason, that didn't translate in a way that made Saint feel loved.

Saint adjusted his fan. I couldn't see his face anymore. "This vibe is too heavy. Let's find another vibe. My heterosexually challenged friend, what is going on in your love life?"

I laughed. "I thought we were trying to get away from heavy vibes." My eyes wandered over to the satsuma tree in his backyard. It made me smile and feel anxious at the same time. *What is she doing right now?*

Saint stood up. "Let's have a change of scenery! I am bored with the courtyard and these birds. I want art. Let's go to NOMA. Do you want to drive or do you want me to call the driver?"

"I'll drive," I said.

⁘❧⁘

City Park was about fifteen minutes from Saint's house. It was a massive park that had live oaks that were hundreds of years old, several lakes, playgrounds, and even a sculpture garden. Another perk of City Park was the New Orleans Museum of Art.

Saint and I went to the museum first. He walked through the large space. I followed after him. Saint stopped in front of a painting by Claude Monet.

"Maybe one day the twins who drive us mad will have paintings here as well," he said.

We'd been in NOMA for twenty minutes, and he had been quiet until that point. I didn't know what to do with Saint's silence. It was so was unlike him.

After talking to his mama, it got me thinking. How much did Saint bullshit? He threw a ball for his nearest and dearest, but his nearest and dearest were his parents' friends? And where were his other friends? Now that I was thinking about it, Saint never invited anyone else to study with us or watch old movies. He said that Magnolia Prep was inbred. Full of "silver spoons" whose families had been in New Orleans for generations. My classmates grew up with Saint, but none of them were close to him. They admired him, but no one knew him.

Saint wrapped his black cape—at least that what it looked like—around his shoulders. "Let's sit down. Truly appreciating each masterpiece requires frequent breaks." Saint sat down on a bench positioned between two columns. I sat down beside him.

"Mona said she saw you last night."

"She did." I rested my balled fist against my cheek, still thinking about why Saint had so few people close to him. It had to be by choice because everyone wanted to be near him. The rare days that he ate lunch at Magnolia Prep, our classmates sat at our table and tried to have conversations with him. He was literally the most popular person at school.

"What lies did Mona tell you about me?"

"She said you were like her."

"How?" he asked, steepling his hands. "I don't have her straight layered pixie haircut or artistic talent."

He was going fishing. Saint mimicked serving a tennis ball to drive the point home. "Ball's in your court, Williams."

"She said y'all both show out, but it's not really who y'all are."

"What else did she say?" Saint asked.

"She said that you told her about me."

"Yeah, so?"

"Nothing, it's just what she said. I missed you last night, bud."

"You need to dial down the buds, bros, and dudes. Who is that? Does this Versace read *bro* to you?"

My cheeks got hot. "I don't bro you."

He stared into the room across from our bench. We had

yet to venture in there. I wondered what he was thinking. That annoying part of me worried that he was mad at me for calling him bud. It was stupid to get worked up over that. But he was my friend and I really cared about what he thought.

"You're so quiet, Batman?" I said, tapping my knee against his.

"Batman! The nerve, this is Versace!" He flapped the cape.

I shrugged and pointed to my flannel. "This is Dick's Sporting Goods."

My friend clutched his chest. "The straight tragedy of it all."

A family walked past—a gay couple with one kid in a stroller and a kid who looked to be about seven leading the way and asking tons of questions.

"Will New Orleans sink one day? Will this building also be underwater? Can we move here? I like New Orleans much better than Cleveland!"

I beamed at the family.

"That'll be you one day, Nashville," Saint chuckled. "You'll have two point five children, and you'll be taking them on a ton of trips between your writing tours."

I wrinkled my nose. "I doubt that I'll be a writer."

"What? Why not? I already selected outfits for your book tours. You know I'm going to them all, bestie."

"Would you love me if I abandon the writing path?" I asked.

"Um, yeah. I love you when you wear Dick's Sporting Goods. So you're totally stuck with me."

"Promise?"

Saint held out his pinkie. We did a pinkie swear. "Promise!"

For a few minutes we sat in silence. Conversations to fill the space popped into my head. I should tell him that Mom was home. I didn't want to talk about her though. "So . . . how did last night go with Joel?"

"Last night, I sat at home alone and listened to Adele and Beyoncé. Joel had some last-minute excuse about needing to help someone with trig homework."

I sighed. "I'm sorry, Saint."

"Don't be sorry. This is just a side-effect of being romantically attached to J-Squared. They like to build walls between them and whoever gets too close."

"Did you just say J-Squared?" I asked.

"Yeah," he said.

"I love that." I chuckled. "Why do you think they build walls?"

"To keep people out. I get so tired of the whiplash with Joel. But I don't want to quit him. He's pretty great when he allows his light to shine. When he goes dim though, it hurts."

I knew a lot about the hurt that came when Jessamine went dim.

"Are you wearing cowboy boots?"

I looked down at my jeans over my boots. That was a swift change of subject. "Yes. What do you have to say about them?"

"Nothing. I just noticed. That's all."

He was staring off into the distance, looking sad. I wrapped an arm around him again.

"What are you doing?"

"I'm chilling with my friend. You got a problem with that?"

He smiled at me, still sad. "How was your night with Legs? Did the ball set the mood for magic?"

"Kinda."

"Kinda? I want details."

"I'll give them to you in a bit." I giggled—it was all nerves bubbling up. "Would it be okay if we didn't talk about J-Squared right now?"

Saint laid his head down on my shoulder. "I guess we do spend a lot of time talking about them. What about us?"

"What about us?"

"A few weeks ago, I told Joel that I wanted to take a cross-country adventure with him. I thought it would be cool to rough it. Sketchy motels. Fast food restaurants. Tourist attractions. Making out under new moons and fighting over who would DJ. Love across state lines."

"That sounds like magic," I said.

"It did. But I'm not sure that I could depend on him." Saint flashed me a plotting grin. "You're the most constant friend I ever had. Would you consider being my travel companion? Can't you see it? Tennessee and Saint, the great American road trip before college."

"Saint Olivier Baptiste, I would love that!"

30
JESSAMINE

I OVERSLEPT. Usually on Sundays when I overslept, Joel woke me up. This Sunday he did not.

I stumbled to the bathroom. I was highly disappointed that I did not have to work today. Sundays when I didn't work were devoted to church. Mama was already feeling the Holy Ghost. Jesus filled every inch of our shotgun house. Her voice carried louder than the person singing on the recording.

The bathroom door was cracked open. I pushed it all the way open with my shoulder.

Joel was standing at the sink. His face twisted up in frustration as he struggled with a bowtie. Judging by his face, he was about to give up.

"Need help, JoJo?"

"No," he muttered.

I arched an eyebrow. Could've fooled me. I leaned against the door and crossed my arms, watching him continue to stubbornly struggle with the bowtie.

He sighed and dropped his hands to his sides. "I give up. How do you know how to tie a bowtie?"

"Mama used to tie Daddy's before church." I walked over and popped Joel's collar. "You look very handsome. Are you going to put on some cologne?"

Joel twisted up his face. "I don't know."

"You constipated?"

"*No.*" He rolled his eyes. "You're so extra. I'm just anxious."

"About?"

"Nunya."

He's so disrespectful. Typical Joel. "It's just like tying your shoes."

"That doesn't help me at all."

I sighed. "Bruh, a little bit of patience and a lot of practice would do you a world of good."

He balled his fist. I looked down. "What's up?"

"Nothin'."

I hopped up on the edge of the sink and kicked the door shut. "If you don't want to go out with him, tell him."

Joel started fussing with his cuffs next. He was wearing a lightning enamel pin that I made for him a few years back. "I don't know what I'm doing. Sometimes I feel like I'm doing all right. And other days all I want to do is lay in bed with the covers over my head."

"Let's talk it out."

Joel closed his eyes. "Talking it out isn't going to do any good. That's all I've been doing. I've talked to everyone and I'm still here, right where I started. The person I need to talk to is Mama. That's the problem."

"You don't have to tell her anything if you don't want to. It's your business."

"She'll find out. She's already asking questions. You know I'm not a good liar."

Poor JoJo. I couldn't imagine the pressure he was feeling. Mama put so much on him. He was her only son, the man of the house, a Black man, and a smart Black man at that. She expected him to go an Ivy League and be a doctor or a lawyer. Her expectations for him were so high, and Joel *always* met her expectations.

I squeezed his shoulder. "It's *your* life."

"Yeah."

"You told me that you liked Saint. If you still like him, stop letting everything else, all this outside noise, ruin your good thing."

He chewed on his lip. "I like spending time with him. He's different than me, and like I told you a while back, that's good. But his parents are celebrities. He attracts attention everywhere we go. His idea of a perfect Friday night is throwing huge parties full of people he doesn't know, while I just want to sit in and watch a movie. Saint wears what he wants. He does what he wants. It doesn't matter who is with him. Our worlds are too different. I like order and he likes whatever works for him in the moment.

"I *do* like him, though." Joel looked into my eyes and shook his head. "I don't know how to balance all this stuff, Jess. I don't know how to be true to who I am and balance what everyone else needs me to be."

I squeezed Joel's shoulders. I wished that I could wave a wand and take away his confusion. I wished so badly that I could. Seeing my twin brother in pain hurt. Joel made everything look easy. *Everything*.

Meanwhile, I had to lie to get through the day.

Joel brought his hands to his face. When he dropped his hands, they were wet. *He never cries. Ever.* I hopped off the counter and peered out the door to make sure Mama wasn't lurking in the hallway, then shut the door again.

"I don't know how to do this," he whispered, tears falling down his cheeks.

JoJo.

"Mama is just like Daddy. Men should be men. Gay is a choice. She would never understand," Joel said.

Joel's recollections surprised me. My memories of Daddy were tender and filled with music. He always took us to the corner store to buy candy. Candy that we had to eat before Mama came home from school. We liked sugar and Mama wouldn't let us indulge on her watch. Daddy always spoiled us.

Also, it was Daddy that made us fall in love with painting. I didn't want to imagine another side to him. A side that enforced that Black boys couldn't be boys, but they had to learn how to be Black men right away.

"Don't worry about her, JoJo," I repeated firmly.

"I have to worry about her, Jess. She's our mom. What she thinks matters. If she hates me, that matters!"

"Hey, hey, hey." I placed my hand to his heart and patted it. "Breathe. She does not hate you. She could never hate you." _You are her favorite._ I almost said the last part out loud. Thank God, the filter kicked in.

Joel started to tug at his bowtie.

"Hey! Don't mess that up or we'll have to start all over!" I swatted at his hands.

His shoulders slumped and his hands dropped down to his sides.

"Don't be ashamed of who you are."

"I'm not ashamed," Joel mumbled. "I just . . . I feel scared. I feel scared every day."

I took his hands in mine. "I'm sorry that you're scared."

He squeezed his eyes shut.

"You know that I take my role as your big sister very seriously."

"You're the same age as me."

"Don't knock my three minutes. I am your big sister even if you treat me like I'm twelve."

His lip trembled. He bit down on it.

"We will be okay, okay?"

He nodded.

"Say *okay.*"

"Okay."

I brought my hands to his face and curled my fingers on his beard. "Scratchy."

He smiled. "Did you clean the tub like Mama asked you?"

It was part of my never-ending punishment for dragging my feet on college applications and checking in with Ms. Nadia. "Yes, why?"

Joel got into the tub. He sunk down and crossed his arms over his chest. He closed his eyes. When we were kids, we used to pretend that the tub was a submarine. We would take turns getting inside, and we would close our eyes. In the tub, that was the real magic. Our tub was the only tub in New Orleans where you could see the coral reef and humpback whales.

I sat down on the edge of the tub and crossed my legs. I looked down at the wetness on his dark brown face and in his beard, the waves of his fade, and the left piercing in his ear. When we were younger, Uncle James told us that "real men" didn't pierce their ears, and if they did, they were only supposed to pierce their left one. Uncle James also told Joel that boys didn't hug each other. They shook hands like men.

That's why I hugged Joel. I hugged him all the time. Because my brother was a person. A human who breathed. A human who hurt. He wasn't a manufactured robot.

Toxic masculinity.

It hurt so many people I cared about . . . Joel, Solange, and I think it hurt Tennessee. His daddy seemed toxic.

"I'm going to protect you," I promised.

Joel brought his hand over his eyes.

I placed my hand over his and linked my fingers inside. *I won't let you go. Ever. You and me. Jess and JoJo. Always.* "Here I come to slay the dragons and the things that go bump in the night."

He cracked a smile. *There's my JoJo.*

"I know this is hard right now. It won't always be that way. It will get better."

"You talk like it's so easy, Jess. You don't have to worry about people figuring out that you're gay. You don't have to worry about that with Tennessee if he kisses you in public."

"It's not that easy for me. White people and Black people look at us. I pretend not to notice, but I do."

"It's *different.* He's a boy and you're a girl. One time, Saint kissed me in public and I spent several days worrying about who saw us, and who was going to tell Mama. It's exhausting. I hate it. I just wish . . ."

"Don't say it. You better not, Joel Xavier."

"I just wish I could fast forward to the point where it doesn't hurt anymore." His face crumpled up like a paper bag. "Because it hurts all the time and it hurts so much. I just want a break. I'm so tired. And I don't know how to be what Mama needs me to be, and what Saint needs me to be, and what you need me to be."

"All I need you to be is JoJo. You're doing the best you can every day and that's enough."

Joel opened his eyes. "Part of the reason I keep running from Saint is—half the time I feel fake, like I'm trying to be everything but what I am. Do you ever feel that way, fake?"

"Absolutely, with every breath I take!" I squeezed his hand three times.

The door opened.

"What's going on in here?" Mama asked.

Joel sat up.

"What's wrong?" She looked at Joel and then at me. "What happened?"

I wanted to protect Joel. Protecting Joel meant lying. Lying like that time Mama found gay porn on the computer—because she suspiciously knew how to check the history and Joel didn't think to clear it. I had lied in a heartbeat and said that it was Solange. It was bad. But at least Solange was out. I would lie again, too. All day, every day.

Mama set down the toilet seat and sat down. She braced her elbows against her thighs. Mama watched us with detective mode eyes. You couldn't even shift your body without her noticing. "What's going on in here? Why are you both crying?"

I'm not crying. Only when she pointed it out did I realize that my face was wet.

"I'm just confused, Mama," he said quietly.

"About?" she asked.

"Everything."

Mama glanced at me, her eyebrow arched and her lips tight. He sighed. "I don't want to lie to you . . . not anymore."

She shifted her body away from us, turning her legs to the

left toward the door. Her head was also facing the door. "We can talk about all this after church. We're already running behind. Jessamine, why are you not dressed? You may be late for everything else, but you will not be late for church today."

"Mama, JoJo's talking to you," I said.

"*I know.*" She raised her hands. "We'll have to continue this conversation when we get back. Your Auntie Myrtle has taken a turn for the worse. I was just coming to tell y'all that we have to go before she—"

"*I'm gay.*"

Mama closed her mouth. She looked at Joel with wide, silent eyes. Neither of them said anything. "What?"

"He said that he's . . ."

Before I could finish Mama pointed at me. "What did you say, *Joel.* Not Jessamine. *Joel.*"

"I'm gay," he repeated quietly.

Mama stood up and moved slowly toward the door. I watched her back.

"I'm sorry," he whispered.

"Don't apologize," I said.

"Jessamine!" Mama screamed and whirled back around. "*Get out!*"

I turned to her baffled. "What?"

"You encouraged this!" She pointed at me. "You did it with Darin and now you're trying to do it with Joel!" She smacked her hands loudly. "I will not stand for it, young lady. I won't stand for it. Stop trying to put these crazy ideas in his head. Stop trying to confuse him!"

She was screaming at me. Yelling her head off at me—and what did I do? Love my brother? Support him? Where was the crime in unconditional love? Hot tears sprung to my eyes. "What do you mean that *I* put ideas in his head?"

"What I mean, young lady, is that you—you—I don't have to explain myself to you. You're a child. A little girl. A child. Just get out of my sight! Leave! *Go!*"

Joel spoke up. "This isn't about Jess, it's about me."

"Stop!" she screamed at Joel. "I've heard enough from you. *Just stop.*" She narrowed her wet eyes at me, looking at me like she used to do when we were little when Joel disappointed her. When he disappointed her and I could be blamed for having a part in that disappointment.

She always blamed me. Always.

"Go," she said in the quietest scream I'd ever heard.

"He is still JoJo," I said through my teeth. "Nothing has changed."

Mama rushed toward me. I had an urge to run because I thought she might smack me for talking back. She grabbed me by the arm and jerked me up so hard it felt like my arm dislocated from the socket. I screamed.

She dragged me out of the bathroom, screaming and crying. I fell and hit my knee hard on the floor. She kept dragging me. She dragged me to the front door like I was trash that needed to be taken outside.

"Why don't you just do what I tell you to do? Why do you always go against me! This is your fault! This is *your* fault!"

Mama dropped to her knees and broke down in the middle of the floor, sobbing like she used to do right after Katrina. In the morning, she'd cried. In the afternoon, she'd cried. In the night, she'd cried.

"This is all *my* fault!" she sobbed into her hands.

I backed away from her, feeling the punch of sobs coming up. I reached behind me for the doorknob.

I opened the door.

Pushed the screen door open.

And crawled outside onto the stoop.

Before the tears came, I forced myself up and ran.

31
TENNESSEE

"A SHOOTING ON BOURBON STREET, THREE KILLED. A stabbing in Mid-City, one killed. Five armed robberies across the city, no arrests." Dad looked over the newspaper at me. "This city is full of animals."

I frowned at Dad.

"When you say *animals*, who are you referring to?" Mom challenged.

Now it was my turn to frown at her. She knew exactly who he was talking about.

Dad closed the newspaper and tossed it onto the table. "The animals are the people who are shooting, robbing, raping, and stabbing. Lauralee, how'd you manage to find the only city in the US worse than Memphis?"

He had been back in New Orleans for all of two hours and already they were fighting. Typical. I had no plans for today, but I needed to find some, fast.

"Memphis, like New Orleans, is predominately African American. Are you implying that African Americans are animals?" Mom challenged again. "And I read nothing in that paper about anyone being raped. Where did you get that from?"

This is why I will never take them to meet Saint's family. They will ruin my good thing.

"I am not a racist. I would never group a whole race of people together just because of a few bad seeds."

"Race isn't a real thing. We're all from Africa," she said.

Dad snorted, "Yeah, says the blue-eyed, blonde-haired WASP. Sorry to break it to you, baby, but you're whiter than cotton."

Here we go.

"Well." Her lips tightened as she cut into her sausage. "These days you sound more and more like Hitler."

Dad's face turned red. Before he exploded and flipped a table or punched a wall, I needed to leave. I pushed out my chair and grabbed my plate. Dad was done with his food. I grabbed his plate, too, and took it to the sink.

"How dare you say to that me!"

"I call it as I see it. You are part of the problem with America."

They went back and forth while I loaded the dishwasher. He was yelling and she was smirking. I wished that he would go back to Oxford, and that she would go back to Key West. Even if this house was a museum of loud echoes, at least it had been mine. No matter how big this house was, when they were both home, there wasn't enough room to hide.

"Tennessee!" Dad yelled.

I paused. I was almost out of the kitchen. *So* close. "Yes, Daddy?"

"Turn around, I refuse to talk to your back," he said.

I wanted to scream, but I couldn't scream. He'd never let me live it down. I did what he said, following the orders he barked. Why was he yelling at me? His battle was with Mom.

"I told your . . ." He paused and tilted his head toward Mom.

She threw her head back and laughed. "His mother, Richard. I am his mother."

"I told *her*—"

Mom laughed again.

Dad kept speaking. "That I'm spending Thanksgiving in New Orleans. We got a few months before you go off to the Ole Miss, so we can spend Thanksgiving up there next year."

"Over my dead body," Mom muttered.

I glanced at her.

"Let's review the Ole Miss application while I'm here," he said.

"University of Mississippi," Mom corrected.

"Politically correct bullshit."

After she said, "Do not curse at me," he immediately started to curse, but not at her. That was my opportunity to leave.

I went into my room. Shut the door.

I sat down on my bed.

I wasn't going to get angry. It wasn't worth it.

I balled my fist.

I hate them!

I winced at the thought. It was too much. They were my parents. I did not hate them. I just . . . strongly disliked them, and that was really messed up.

I raised my fist over my knee. No. It wasn't worth it. I didn't want to get upset. I didn't want to cry. I didn't want to scream. I didn't want to break—something.

That was too much.

I stuffed my fist in my mouth. Don't scream. Don't do it.

I could hear them yelling downstairs. He was being racist and she was being self-righteous. They were both wrong!

It's okay. Calm down.

Tears stung my eyes.

I wanted to scream.

Calm down.

My fists were shaking like they had a mind of their own. I had to take my fist out of my mouth because I was biting down on it too hard.

They didn't care about me. They didn't.

I jumped up. I told myself over and over again to calm down. But I was eaten up with anger. It was inside me.

I lunged forward and ripped the fitted sheet off my bed. That felt good and wrong at the same time. My pillows fell to the floor, and I punched my fist into one. I kept punching and punching.

Stop it.

What if they saw me?

I don't care!

I kept punching and punching until there were feathers everywhere.

I balled my fists into my eyes to dam up the tears.

They came anyway.

I lost control.

I wasn't supposed to do that—I was supposed to not let it get to me.

I wrapped my arms around my body. *Look what you did.* It wasn't okay. It wasn't okay. My pillows were destroyed and I wasn't sure how I was supposed to explain that to them.

They were going to be mad. He would yell at me and she would be concerned.

Why did I put myself on their radar?

Why?

I was so stupid.

⁓

When I woke up, it was quiet. I sat up. My room was a mess. The bed was hanging off the frame. My sheets were ripped to shreds, and feathers were still everywhere.

It made me sick. I did that.

I brought my knees to my chest and held them.

What if Jessamine or Saint saw this side of me?

My lip trembled.

They'd leave for sure. Mom and Dad wouldn't be the ones to scare them off. It would be me.

The real me.

⁓

I ventured out of my room to see if they were gone. The TV was on in Mom's room.

The door was cracked open. I peeked inside.

Mom was naked and so was Dad.

They were doing what they always did after she got self-righteous and he got extra-racist. They were having sex.

I closed their door and walked back to my room. I shut my door and locked it.

32
JESSAMINE

"HEY, AUNTIE MYRTLE, I brought some irises for you." I set the flowers down on the dresser and kissed her on the forehead. I glanced around Auntie Myrtle's room. It wasn't immaculately clean like it used to be. When we were kids, Joel and I used to dare each other to move a chair or turn the dresser to the wrong angle to see if Auntie Myrtle would notice. She always did. Her room also used to smell like baby powder. It didn't smell like that anymore.

Auntie Myrtle's eyes cracked open. "Who is this here? A sight for sore eyes. I was wondering what I had to do to get you to come around. I guess I had to be on my deathbed." She cackled.

It had been a while since Auntie Myrtle cracked a joke with me. I sat down and took her hand. Solange was on the other side, wearing a St. Aug sweater and jeans, brushing Auntie Myrtle's hair. "I'm sorry that I haven't been around much. I'm here now though."

"That's all that matters, sweet girl." She squeezed my hand. "I didn't want you coming 'round too much anyways. I like you remembering how I was, all of y'all." She coughed again. "This cancer took about all I had left, except for my winning personality."

"Too bad it didn't take that first," Solange said with a snort.

"If you're gonna be ugly, you might as well leave," Auntie Myrtle said.

"Why would I do that? I gotta change the will over while you're still breathing." Solange winked at me. "Thanks for coming, cuz. Is Auntie Jo and JoJo on their way?"

I closed my eyes. Now wasn't the right time to tell Solange and Auntie Myrtle about Joel coming out. Thinking about it got me all choked me up. "Mama should be here soon," I said, clearing my throat.

"Good," Solange said. "Mama has been asking about her."

"Death is hard on Josephine," Auntie Myrtle said, trying to sit up.

"Mama, no, don't do that."

"Why not, Darin? I can't get any worse!" She reached out and took my hand. "Your mama don't like death. The second I told her that I was sick, she started planning my funeral. Planning a funeral kept her busy. It kept her from having to stop and see the big picture. She doesn't know how to say good-bye. Which is why she holds on so tight—like me. We hold on so tight because we're scared of losin', but we end up losin' anyways." Auntie Myrtle coughed.

Solange jumped up. "What's going on, Mama? Do you need me to get the nurse?"

"No nurse can fix this, only the Lord in heaven." Auntie Myrtle squeezed my hand again. Every time she squeezed my hand, I felt bones breaking. Every breath coming from her mouth sounded so sharp.

Auntie Myrtle was dying.

She was . . .

I rubbed my lips together and looked down at her hand in mine. She was my auntie, but I never got too close to her. I used to think that she was mean. She'd beat you for stealing a bite of pie. She'd beat you for a disrespectful tone. She'd beat you if she felt in the mood to beat someone. She had been so mean. But now she was dying and she looked . . . she looked just like Mama.

Tears filled my eyes, and I looked away because I didn't want her to see me crying. I didn't want Solange to see me. This was her mama. Her mama was dying. And even though they always fought, that was her mama. I wouldn't wish it on anyone, losing a parent.

It was a hurt that I couldn't describe.

It was a thief that stole and stripped.

Auntie Myrtle coughed again—this time her entire body trembled. This time it sounded like her ribs were cracking.

She tried again to sit up.

"Lay down, Mama!" Solange insisted. "We can see you just fine whether you're laying or sitting. There's no point in you being uncomfortable."

"Fine," Auntie Myrtle sighed.

"Can I get you anything? Another pillow? A blanket?" Solange asked.

Solange loved her mama. It was obvious with the way she fought with her mama, took care of her mama, and stayed with her mama.

Auntie Myrtle looked up at Solange.

"What you need, Mama?"

Auntie Myrtle closed her eyes.

"Mama, what you need?" Solange asked.

Auntie Myrtle opened her eyes. "You been so good to me, baby."

Solange looked at me, her eyes getting big. She turned back to her mama. "What choice do I have? You put clothes on my back. Fed me that watery soup you called gumbo! That's what happens when a woman from Shreveport tries to make gumbo!"

Auntie Myrtle laughed and coughed again. "Oh, you complainin' now? When you were a youngin' you sucked that gumbo down like it *was* water."

"That's cause it was water, Mama. And all you ever had in the fridge was that ol' nasty gumbo!"

"I never had anything in the fridge 'cause you ate it the second I made groceries."

"Big boys got to eat!" Solange said, grinning down at her Mama.

I saw tears spring in Solange's eyes. She said *big boys*, not *big girls*.

"I wasn't good to you, Darin. I wasn't good," Aunt Myrtle said.

"What you mean, Mama?"

"I didn't understand you . . . I didn't understand a lot about you, but I always loved you."

I looked down at my lap.

Auntie Myrtle let go of my hand and reached out to her daughter. "I can't make up for lost time. I can't apologize for the damage I done did to ya. All I can do is try to make it right. Baby, go on. You don't have to hide from me anymore." Auntie Myrtle's lips trembled. "Put on all that get-up you put on."

Solange shook her head. "That's not important. What's important right now is you and making sure you're comfortable."

"I am, I am," she insisted. "I'm about as comfortable as I can be. Go on."

I watched as Auntie Myrtle, the woman who had gotten into many screaming matches with Solange about the way she was "choosing" to live her life, encouraged Solange to be herself.

"Don't make me beat you with the sharpest switch in the yard!" She swatted her daughter. "Go on now, before God takes me. Go on!"

Solange looked at me. "If that mean old woman starts to die, you better holler."

"Okay," I whispered.

"Why? So you can make sure you finish me off yourself?" Auntie Myrtle asked.

"Yep." Solange fluffed a pillow beside Auntie Myrtle's head.

I bit down on my lip. "I'll holler," I promised.

Once we were alone, Auntie Myrtle turned back to me.

"Promise me something, baby."

"Anything, Auntie Myrtle."

"Come here."

I leaned in closer.

"He's tough. Darin will fight anyone who gets too close. He's always been that way. But he won't tell you when he's hurting. He'll just lick those wounds and keep going."

"I know, she and JoJo are both built the same way."

"You too, it's the Blanchard way." Air dragged in and out of her lungs, sharp shards of cutting glass. "Promise me that you'll check on him. Swing by when he's not answering his phone. Have dinner with him even when he insists on eating alone—especially then. And tell him for me . . . tell him that I love him . . . something I never said to him while I was . . . ." She blinked and tears filled her eyes. "While I was alive. I never told him I loved him. I have so much regret. So many things that I wished I'd done differently."

"Auntie Myrtle." I wiped at her tears. "None of that matters right now."

"I wish I'd done better." She squeezed my wrist. "I wish I'd been better for him."

"What's all that boo-hooing about?" Solange said, coming back into the room.

She looked so beautiful. She wore a purple tulle dress with black gloves that came up past her elbow, a blonde bob lace front, and a crown on her head—full Solange regality.

Auntie Myrtle looked on, her eyes bulging at first, and then settling into dark marbles.

"Here I am," Solange announced. "By popular demand."

Auntie Myrtle coughed. Wet sounds and breaking ribs again.

Solange stood at the door, holding a pageant smile, grabbing fistfuls of her dress and glancing down. I turned to Auntie Myrtle. She stared back at Solange and pulled back her blankets.

"Mama, what you doin'? Nope, get back in that bed." Solange started fussing.

Auntie Myrtle held out her arms. "I will. Just do this for your mama."

"What, Mama, what?" Solange asked impatiently.

"When you were little we used to dance."

I hung my head as I felt another emotional overload advisory.

"We did," Solange said.

"Clifton Chenier, 'I'm Coming Home (To See My Mother).'" Aunt Myrtle pointed at me. "Play it on your phone, Jess."

"You ain't in the shape to two-step," Solange argued.

"Please, Solange," Auntie Myrtle begged.

I found the song on my phone. I put the volume up and nodded in Solange's direction.

Solange's shoulders slumped. "Okay. One dance." She bent down and scooped Auntie Myrtle up into her arms. Auntie Myrtle's lavender nightgown fanned out underneath Solange's gloves. The two danced. Solange turning her mother around and around slowly, and Auntie Myrtle hugging onto Solange's neck.

It was a moment—a memory that I would never forget.

How could I ever forget the last dance Solange shared with her mother?

······୨୧·······

When Mama arrived, I left to ride the streetcars. She didn't speak to me, and I didn't say a word to her.

I was on the streetcar when I got the news. Auntie Myrtle passed.

I sucked in a breath. I sucked in another breath. I kept sucking in breaths to hold off tears. But nothing worked. I fell apart.

She was there one minute, dead the next. Like Daddy.

Her casket would be open, though. Solange would make sure her makeup looked good. We would celebrate her life. We would look past all the times she hurt Solange. We would look past how she put Solange's clothes in garbage bags and threw her out of the house when she first came out. We would look past the damage she'd done.

Solange had had to crash with her friends because she'd had nowhere to stay.

When I looked up, I saw a face I needed to see. He was

running on the neutral ground between the tracks. It was pouring down rain, but he seemed oblivious to it. I placed my hands against the window and watched him go in the opposite direction.

I reached up. I needed to stop. I needed to get off this streetcar. I needed . . .

The next thing I knew I was running after him.

"Tennessee!" I screamed.

He kept running.

"Tennessee!" I screamed, racing through the puddles and the mud.

He didn't hear me. I could not stop running. He kept running and so did I. The devil was biting at my heels, and I was so tired of giving her my blood. I was tired. And like Joel, I didn't feel safe. I was afraid.

Auntie Myrtle looked so much like Mama.

What if she died . . .

Oh god.

The light blinked red, and traffic started down First Street.

When I reached him, I crashed into him, locking my arms around his waist. He stumbled forward. I locked my arms tighter around him. When I let go, Tennessee turned around.

"Jessamine?" He bear-hugged me like I was someone he knew, someone he missed. Someone who was consistent with him. "You're drenched."

"So are you."

"Let's get you outta this rain." He loosened his bear hug and took my hand. Tennessee started leading me somewhere, I don't know where, shelter maybe? I didn't want shelter. What I needed was to get rained on.

Rain hid tears. I needed that.

"I'm sorry I haven't called you."

"Don't be sorry," he said.

I closed my eyes. "Can you stay with me?"

"Of course," he whispered. "I'll stay with you as long as you need me to."

"Do you have somewhere to be, though?" I asked him.

"Yeah, right here with you. Seriously, let's get you out of the rain."

He was still talking about me. What about him? I wasn't the only one getting wet. Why was he out here in the first place? Once we were on the sidewalk under an awning, I stood on my tippy toes and kissed him. He tasted like rain and spearmint. I don't know why I kissed him. Maybe being radioactive was better than being sad.

Tennessee wrapped his arms around me. He felt safe.

For the first time, ever . . . I didn't want to run from him.

33
JESSAMINE

THE RAIN POUNDED against the hood of Tennessee's truck. I watched as the windshield wipers swished back and forth, leaving a rainbow reflection on the glass. Even though it was pouring down, the sun was still out. I glanced at the clock on the dashboard. Three P.M.

Tennessee had the heat on full blast. I was still cold though.

"Did you want to come inside?" he asked.

"Inside?"

"Yeah." Tennessee pointed to a mansion. "That's my house."

"Are your parents home?"

He got silent.

"If they are, I don't want to meet them."

"Yeah, I don't want you to meet them either."

"Because I'm Black?"

"No. That's not it at all. My parents are . . . a lot."

I sniffed and wiped underneath my nose. The one time I saw them at Commander's Palace they had seemed like a lot. After that, I had never asked about them and he never offered.

Tennessee took my hand and rubbed it between his.

"What are you doing?"

"You're still cold. You're shivering, Jess."

"The heat is working just fine."

"I don't want you to get sick," he said.

He was looking at me with this expression—this expression

that told me he needed me to feel better. It made me want to cry. "I'm okay. I promise," I lied instead.

"I'll be right back." He jumped out of the truck and ran inside his mansion. A few minutes later, he returned with an afghan. "Sorry about that." He wrapped the afghan around me, making sure that I was completely covered.

"Thanks? Now I'm going to burn up."

"You can take it off if it gets too hot. Or I can turn off the heater."

I rested my head against the seat. I watched him, sitting up straight with both hands on the wheel. He was the kind of boy that took care of people. I think that's what I liked the most about him.

"Did you want me to take you home?" he asked.

"No. Please."

"Did you want to keep sitting here?" he asked softly.

"Can we drive?"

"Of course, Jess. Where do you want to go?"

I closed my eyes. "The moon, the stars, Six Flags when it was still Six Flags."

"We'll drive then," he said. "Sound like a plan?"

I nodded.

⁂

Tennessee drove for a while. This was how much I trusted him. With anyone else, the second we crossed the twin span heading to the Northshore I would've dialed 911. I *never* went there.

But with him, I sat back. I let him kidnap me.

He drove with one hand on the wheel and one hand in mine. It was how Mama and Daddy used to drive. I rolled down the window and stared out at Lake Ponchartrain. The rain had stopped about ten minutes after we started driving, but the smell of it was still in the air mixed with the crispness of a New Orleans fall.

I texted Joel and asked if he was okay. He wasn't texting me back. I sighed and watched the sun make golden lights over the calm water, which seemed to stretch forever.

We ended up at Fontainebleau State Park. "Why here?" I asked when he parked his car underneath a huge live oak.

Tennessee turned off the engine. "We both wanted to get out of New Orleans. And I've wanted to come here for a while—but I . . ." He didn't finish.

"You what?"

"You're going to make me say it?"

"Yes. What?" I asked, poking his arm.

"I didn't have anyone to come with me." His cheeks reddened. He looked down as if he was embarrassed.

"Thanks for taking me. C'mon, before it starts raining again. Let's see what's going on out here in the country."

"Are you dry yet?" he asked.

"Yes. Between the heat and the blanket and you rubbing my hands, I'm about well done."

He chuckled.

"My hair is a mess though."

"No, it's not."

I wasn't about to argue with him on the dynamics of Black hair when it got wet. I opened the door and hopped out of his truck. He met me on my side and together we walked to a pier jutting out into Lake Ponchartrain.

I kept the afghan tight around me. "This is pretty,

Tennessee," I said, even though all the water made me feel like I was standing in a watery grave.

"Ain't it?" he asked.

I pulled my windswept curls out of my face. "Why'd you want to get out of NOLA?"

He stretched out his arms. The wind whipped around him. It almost looked like he was about to take off and fly into the sunset. I ducked behind him, using his tall frame to block the wind. I latched onto his flannel shirt and rested my head against his back.

"My daddy came home."

"Were they fighting?" I asked.

"I don't want to talk about me, Jess."

"I do."

"Why were you crying?" he asked.

I kept my mouth shut. He kept walking and I clung to him. Eventually, he stopped at the end of the pier.

"How 'bout you come around to the front?" he said.

"It's cold," I whined.

"It's hard to talk to you when I can't see your face."

Why did he need to see my face? I let go of his waist and stepped beside him. The sunset reflected on the watery grave that was Lake Ponchartrain. I wrapped the afghan around him as well. If he was cold, he probably wouldn't tell me. He was also the kind of guy to die of hypothermia because he didn't want to put me out by asking me to share the blanket.

"The sunsets don't look like this in New Orleans," I said, peering up at Tennessee's chin and nose.

"Not at all. This kind of reminds me of Oxford. The quiet and all the trees."

"What do you love most about a sunset?" I asked.

"How uncomplicated it is. The sun is always setting some-where."

"And rising somewhere else," I added.

"That's right."

I closed my eyes and leaned into his warmth. The wind was ice cold off the lake, but he was like a heater, thawing me.

We walked along the beach to a section where cypress knees were poking from the water. The cypress knees looked like miniature mountain ranges sticking up from the lake, like a maze of tangles. Tennessee sat down on a beached cypress log. I sat down beside him. For a while, we watched the sunset over the twin span, the bridge that led from the Northshore back to New Orleans.

"My auntie died today," I said.

"I'm sorry, Jess."

I couldn't look at him. "It's okay. People die. It happens."

"It's okay to be sad," he said.

"What does being sad do? It won't bring her back to life."

"No. But if you don't let yourself be sad, you'll self-destruct. Trust me, I know."

I wiped at my eyes. "And Joel came out to our mama right before that."

Tennessee, who always knew the right thing to say, was silent.

I huddled my arms around my body.

Tennessee broke the silence. "I'm happy for Joel."

"Me too, but it's going to be hard for him. He lives at home with her," I said. Our shotgun was only so big. Unless Mama was at work, she couldn't be avoided.

"He has you, though. That's something. . . . It's a lot. And if he ever needs a space to crash, he can crash with me for a while."

I leaned against his shoulder and closed my eyes. That was so sweet that he offered his house for Joel to crash at. Joel wouldn't, knowing Joel, but the thought was still sweet. I listened to the sound of the waves washing across the beach and the whistle of the wind. Louisiana had been home all my life, but not until I saw a sunset like this did I realize how truly beautiful it was.

"What do you think about spending Thanksgiving in Oxford?" he asked.

"Like England?"

"No, like Oxford, Mississippi."

I gazed up at him.

"With everything going on here, it might be nice to get away? You can invite Joel, Iz, Solange, and whoever else wants to come. I'll ask Saint—I doubt he'll want to come, but I'm gonna invite him anyway."

"If I say no and Saint says no, will you go to Oxford anyway?"

"Probably. I don't want to spend Thanksgiving with my parents."

"You'd be alone then?"

He nodded. "Alone wouldn't be anything new for me. Even when my parents are home, we don't spend much time together. I've gotten pretty good at enjoying my own company." He made air quotes around "enjoying."

"Yes," I said. "I'll go with you to Oxford."

34
TENNESSEE

"Tenn, are you sure you wanna spend Thanksgiving in Oxford?" Mom asked, looking down at her watch. She stepped onto the sidewalk as a huge truck made its way down St. Charles. "It's one P.M. With Daylight Saving Time ended, you won't get to Oxford until after dark."

"Yep." I tossed my duffel bag into the backseat.

"You got enough money?" Mom asked.

I hugged her neck. "Between the two hundred dollars you gave me and the three hundred Daddy gave me, I'd say that I have more than I need."

"Your daddy gave you three hundred dollars?" Mom reached in her pocket and pulled out a fifty-dollar bill. "Here, take this."

It isn't a competition. I raised my hands. "I have more than enough."

She stuffed the fifty in my pocket anyway. "You know that your friends can come over here. I'll talk to your daddy and ask him to act right."

"That's not going to work." *My friends are African American and gay.* "I'm leaving. I'll call when we reach Jackson."

"You sure you don't want to stay here?" she asked for the fifteenth time in the last fifteen minutes.

"Yes. I'm positive."

"I thought you left, Reb," Dad said, pushing open the gate and meeting us on the sidewalk.

"He's on his way," Mom said.

"More like he's tryin' to be on his way, but you're talkin' his ear off." Dad hugged me. "Did you check the air pressure in your tires, and have you changed your oil since you moved here?"

Before I could say anything, Mom spoke up. "The treading on his tires is a little low, but he should be fine to get to and back from Oxford. And Tenn rarely drives outside the city, so I doubt he's due for an oil change."

Dad scowled at me. "Reb, how come your mama knows more about your truck than you do?"

"Richard, he's been busy with school. He's a senior."

"That's not an excuse. His truck doesn't care if he's a senior or not. I told you, Rebel, when I got you that truck, *you* gotta take care of it. It'll give you what you put into it. Change the oil." He smacked the back of his hand against his palm. "Check the treading on your tires. Check the air pressure in your tires."

"Richard!" Mom pushed him back and stood in front of him. "It'll take him five hours to get to Oxford. Leave him alone so he can pick up his friends and get there while there's still daylight left."

"Who are these friend's he's going with?" Dad asked. "Do you know, Lauralee?"

I sighed. Why was he suddenly concerned about my friends? I had lived in New Orleans by myself. I could've had parties every night with drugs and strippers—they wouldn't have known.

"You should know who his friends are," Dad said to Mom. "They're going to be staying in our house."

"You don't trust my judgment?" I asked him.

"No, I don't," Dad said. "You're still a kid, even though your mama treats you like you're not. He shouldn't be on the road by himself. And he definitely shouldn't be spending Thanksgiving away from us. We're a family. We should all be together, even if it's here."

"I can take care of myself," I said.

"You what?" Dad said, his eyes daring me to repeat it.

Mom pushed Dad again. "Richard, don't make me fight you on this street in front of all these people." Mom gestured toward the people standing at the streetcar stop. "If he wants to go to Oxford, let him go. I trust our son. And whether you like it or not, he's going off to college next year. You better get used to him leaving."

Dad frowned as if the thought hadn't crossed his mind. "He's not leaving. He's going to Ole Miss. We'll keep the house in Oxford so he can live there while going to school."

"He doesn't want to go to the University of Mississippi," Mom said.

Dad looked at me, his eyes asking me if that was true. It was. I didn't know how Mom knew that, but I guessed she'd also be shocked when I told her that I wasn't going to LSU (unless Saint or Jessamine decided to go there). I'd already completed my applications for UC Berkeley and Stanford. Neither of them knew about that.

"I should go," I said.

"Wait," Dad said, "before you leave, I'll change your oil and check your tires. You don't want a blow-out, bud. I shouldn't have to do this for you. . . ."

"You don't have to."

His eyebrows dropped and he looked at me like I just stabbed him. "I do. Even though you didn't do what you're supposed to do, you're still my kid. I'm not trying to spend the next couple of hours worrying about the car breaking down in the wrong part of Jackson."

"I'll change the oil and stuff when I get to Oxford."

Dad grabbed my keys from my hand. "No, let me do it."

·····ço·····

Dad made me run thirty minutes behind. After making me late, he tried to convince me to stay again. Mom and Dad fought about it. I took that as my opportunity to leave.

Jessamine told me to text her when I was close and to wait around the corner. Her excuse was that she didn't want her mama to see her getting in the truck with a strange white boy. At least, that's what she told me. Whenever I asked her how things were going with her mama since her aunt passed and Joel came out, she changed the subject.

It was weird talking to Jessamine. She was super selective about what she wanted to talk about. When she didn't want to talk about something, she didn't talk about it at all. I hoped that she would treat me like more of a friend than a stranger in Oxford.

Jessamine tapped on the passenger door. I unlocked the doors and hopped out of the truck.

She looked around stealth-like. "You weren't supposed to get out of the car! Someone might see you!"

"You're going to have to claim me some time," I said, trying to joke around.

"Hey, Tennessee! Long time no see." Iz tossed her bag into the backseat and hugged me.

I hugged her back, "Hey, Iz! So glad you could come."

"Me too, thanks for inviting me." She grabbed onto Jessamine's arm and my arm and pulled us together. "Picture time."

"Iz, we got to go," Jessamine said.

I looked down at Jessamine. She was watching every car and every door as if she was scared someone would see us. Was she ashamed of me?

"Y'all, scooch," Iz said, signaling for us to get closer. Her eyes widened at Jessamine. "Chica, you're driving me loca."

"Fine." Jessamine tugged on my shirt and brought me closer.

"We could take a picture in Oxford if you want," I suggested.

"No, we'll do it here. She will make us stand out here until Christmas if we don't."

"New Year's!" Iz added.

Jessamine rolled her eyes. "She's so oppressive. Smile, too. She'll make you take a million reshoots."

I didn't know what to do with my arms. Jessamine solved that for me. She took my arm and wrapped it around her shoulder. She grabbed onto my shirt and placed her other arm around my waist.

Iz took at least twenty pictures, no joke. From every angle known to man.

"Okay, enough! We need to get to Oxford sometime this year," Jessamine said.

Iz rolled her eyes. "I think at least one of these pictures is good. There will be more photoshoots in Mississippi." She got into the back seat of my truck.

I picked up Jessamine's suitcase. It felt like it was full of rocks. "Jess, what's in here?"

"Satsumas," she said with a wink.

I smiled.

"I like this plaid on you," she said patting my black-and-blue plaid shirt. "PS, I made us a road trip playlist."

"Oh, I did, too."

"What's on it?" she asked.

"The songs that make me think of you."

"I think I'll like my mix more."

"Then we can listen to your mix." I gave in.

She looked down and then back at me. "Or we can listen to yours. It's not a big deal."

"I don't care."

"Okay." Jessamine went to the passenger's side.

I looked after her. The thing about Jessamine, the thing that I hadn't realized until then, was that she was like the tides. Like Mom and Dad, what she did, what she said, it affected me. I was the earth. She was the moon.

If she wanted me, I was hers.

If she didn't, I hadn't thought that far yet.

I slid into the driver's seat. "Seatbelts, y'all."

Jessamine leaned over and put on mine. She shook her head at me and tsked. "When you ride an airplane, they tell you to put on your oxygen mask first." She pointed at me and closed her left eye. "*Your* oxygen mask first."

"So cute," Iz said, leaning forward. "Tennessee, if it was me sitting up front, she wouldn't be checking my seatbelt. Precious-cargo bae." She cackled.

Precious-cargo bae?

"Do we have to bring her?" Jessamine asked me.

"Yes, chica, you have to bring me. Your mama thinks that

you're spending Thanksgiving with my abuela in Memphis. Which reminds me, at some point, Tennessee, we'll need to find some old Latina lady to let us take a picture with her."

I chuckled. "Okay, will do. Are we picking up anyone else?"

"No," Jessamine said. "Joel is spending Thanksgiving with Solange."

"What about your mom?" I asked her.

Jessamine shrugged. "I don't know. She made it clear that she doesn't want to do Thanksgiving this year. I don't want to talk about that. Where's your road trip mix?"

"Hey!" Iz swatted Jessamine's shoulder. "Be nice to him."

"I am being nice to him!" Jessamine exclaimed.

"Mhmm, I apologize for my BF, sometimes she talks to you crazy just 'cause she feels like it."

I didn't know what to say. All I could do was smile . . . awkwardly. That was how Jessamine always talked to me.

"Road trip mix," Jessamine repeated.

I wasn't sure if I wanted to share my road trip mix with her at that moment. Iz was in the backseat and she'd also be listening. And Jess did seem like she was feeling bothered about something. I didn't know if it was me, or the things she didn't tell me about. A playlist of the songs that made me think about her might turn her off. I should've thought through this.

"Tennessee?" she said.

"Yeah?"

"I want to hear your road trip mix."

"Are you sure?" My head felt like it was in a pot of boiling water.

"Where is it? Is it on your phone?"

"Naw, it's on a CD, in there." I pointed to the glove compartment.

She snorted. "A CD? When were you born? 1982?"

"They had cassette tapes in 1982," I said, completely missing the joke.

She reached out and took my hand. "Sorry."

"What are you apologizing for? You didn't do anything," I said.

"I was mean. I'm sorry for being mean. Sometimes I get mean when I have to wait around for a while. I got up extra early to make sure I was ready for this trip." She opened the glove compartment and pulled out the CD I made. I didn't tell her that I made a CD because I wanted to draw the cover artwork and write the songs on the back. There was also a letter in the sleeve.

"Can I see?" Iz asked.

"Get some business." Jessamine turned to Iz and smiled. "I'm kidding. Yes. You can see."

"Aww." Iz pointed. "Satsumas."

I had named the collection of songs "Satsumas," and I'd drawn a satsuma tree on the cover.

"Why a satsuma tree, though? It's so adorable but random," Iz asked.

I started to tell her what the satsuma meant. Jessamine cut me off. "He's my satsuma," she said.

I shifted my eyes to Jessamine. My heart slowed. I gripped tighter to the steering wheel.

She looked at the CD, that one curl falling in her big brown eyes. She turned over the CD, smiled, and nodded as if she remembered a song. And then her smile fell.

"Something wrong?" I asked immediately. The second I asked, I regretted it.

She placed the CD back in the glove compartment. "No,

nothing's wrong. Bourbon Street Parade was one of my daddy's favorite songs."

Was lingered loudly in the air.

⚬⚬

"Ladies, we're here."

Iz was still asleep in the backseat. Jessamine's eyes popped open. That was a light sleep. She sat up and looked around. "This is Oxford?"

"Yep. My home sweet home." I stared at my house. The house that I had called home for seventeen years sat on top of a hill. It was white with hunter-green shutters, a wrap-around porch, and wooden rocking chairs on all sides of the porch. Tall loblolly pines surrounded it.

Jessamine stretched out her arms. "It's kinda desolate out here." Jessamine tapped the window. "Where are your neighbors? Where is the closest store? Where do people go if they want to dance and listen to music?"

I chuckled. "Don't knock it just yet. Oxford has lots of charm and lots of heart."

"Maybe," she said, rolling her eyes at me.

I hoped that we got a chance to talk while we were there. She was sitting right beside me, but it felt like she wasn't there. I don't know. It was hard to explain.

"It's beautiful out here. This is big-sky and big-tree country. I live way out in the county. There's more going on in town."

Jessamine stared out the window. "I won't hold you to that, Tennessee Williams. It's looking a little *Deliverance* out here."

"What's that?"

"A movie full of rednecks from the hills of Georgia."

That didn't seem like a movie that she would ever watch. It sounded like a horror movie.

She cackled. "The only reason I watched that is because Joel lost a bet. I googled a movie that I knew would freak him out. It was between *Silence of the Lambs* and *Deliverance*. The squealing pigs beat the screaming lambs."

I tilted my head in Jessamine's direction. "What does squealing pigs and screaming lambs have to do with Oxford? Jess, look at the farmland. I mean, I know it's kind of dark, but it's peaceful out here. Rolling hills, the leaves actually change color, and do you smell the firewood? We can make a fire and sit out on the porch."

She reached over the back seat and patted Iz's leg. "Iz, Tennessee brought us out into the woods to turn our bones into wind chimes."

I winced. "Jess, you didn't hear a word I just said."

Iz started to wake up in the back.

I glanced at my house. Seeing it after a few months in New Orleans made me feel . . . uneasy. I shook my head, chasing away the thought.

Jessamine rested her hand on my wrist. I jumped a little.

"What are you thinking about? You seem a little . . . off?"

I seemed off?

"I'm fine," I said, believing it to be true.

She slid her hand down to mine. "I have to say a thing."

"Okay." I felt more uneasy. What was she going to say? Did she not want to spend Thanksgiving in Oxford anymore? Did she want me to drive them back?

"I don't want you to let me run you over with a tractor-trailer anymore or beat you up with satsuma trees. If I hurt you, if I'm not nice to you—you have to tell me. I don't always know when I'm being mean." Jessamine sighed and opened the door. She hopped out of the truck and shut the door behind her.

I sat in the silence, thinking about her words.

She wasn't mean. She was never mean. She just didn't know how to handle me. I think.

Iz leaned forward. "Tennessee, Jessamine likes you, BTW."

"Iz!" Jessamine opened Iz's door.

"What?" Iz yelled.

"Check out this view!"

"I'm coming!" Iz said. "What view can you even see? It's so dark."

Iz squeezed my shoulder and hopped out of the truck. She ran with Jessamine.

Across the county road, there was a downward slope of hills. The hills sloped in overlapping mounds down to the bottom where a large man-made pond sat. On the hills, there were cattle grazing. Oxford had a lot of hidden treasures like that.

I stepped out of my truck and stretched. I watched as Iz and Jessamine ran across the county road hand-in-hand. They crawled underneath the fence and started running down the hills toward the pond.

I leaned against the fence and watched as they reached the bottom. When they came back up, I'd have to give them a quick lesson on the ways of country folk, since they were city girls. Out in the country, you couldn't just run onto property that wasn't yours without risking being shot at or having some dogs sicced on you. Especially when it was dark.

Jessamine and Iz sat down near the pond. They were now

completely blended in with the darkness. I would've joined them, but I figured they might want some time to themselves. And I needed some time, too.

To check myself.

To prepare myself.

I thought that I was ready to go back inside my house, but maybe not.

It had been a few months since I'd been in there. I didn't know what landmines were waiting. I was a different person now.

On that porch, Mom and Dad had some of their worst fights.

Not *the* worst fight, but at least five of the top ten.

Six years ago, Mom told Dad that she was leaving him. And that she wasn't just leaving him—she was leaving with me. She told him that he wouldn't see us again. That day, it got really bad. She threatened him and he threatened her. The cops showed up.

Remember how she screamed?

Remember how he grabbed me by the arm?

Remember how he screamed?

"Let go of him! He's my child!" That's what she said.

He said that that I was his, too.

They tugged me like I was a wishbone. I cried because I thought they were going to break me. Physically, they didn't. I was still me. One Tennessee. But mentally, sometimes I felt like I was a bunch of pieces with missing parts.

35
JESSAMINE

I wish someone could teach me how to be a robot. I wish they could cut the wires. Turn off the feelings. Make it so parts of my brain didn't light up when I saw him. This game was getting dangerous. The plan wasn't to buy the book. I repeat, the plan wasn't to buy the book! I was supposed to read him for one night and return him to other boys and girls to read, but something happened.

Ronnie died.

Claudia died.

Joel fell in love.

Joel fell out of love—or at least he claims that he did.

And Auntie Myrtle died.

All these things happened so suddenly, which made it harder to turn off feelings. The tap was tapped and the emotions wouldn't stop flowing.

I really wished someone could teach me how to be a robot.

Because 30 percent like became 50 percent like.

And now that I was in the house where he was raised, like has become . . . it's become something worse. I tried to robot around his house with objectivity. I giggled with Iz at his childhood haircuts. All severe and bad. I giggled with Iz at the middle-school pictures of him with his first-caught fish. That picture was labeled "Daddy's boy caught his first catfish!"

In his pictures, the older he got, the less he smiled. When Iz wasn't looking, I inched closer to a picture of his family on the mantle. His daddy was smiling. His mama looked pissed, and Tennessee was looking down at his shoes, like he wanted to be anywhere but there.

"How'd you sleep?"

I jumped. He's got jokes. Okay, so what if I did pass out for several hours?

Tennessee's eyes searched mine. "You okay?"

I laughed it off. "Yes, sorry. There is a deer head on the wall."

Tennessee shoved his hands in his pockets. "You should make a point to get used to that. My dad has a thing for trophies. He hunted and stuffed all the dead things in this house."

I frowned.

"I can show you around?" he offered.

I didn't want to notice this, but I couldn't help it. There was something in his eyes that wasn't usually there. It was a quiet fear. A loud sadness. "Want to sit down for a second? You've been driving for five hours."

He blinked a few times.

I took that as my answer. We were going to sit down for a bit. I held Tennessee's hand and led him to the couch. He sank, spreading his legs out and burying his face in his hands.

Something was wrong with him. I leaned forward and placed my hand on his back. "Where are you, satsuma boy?"

"What?" he whispered.

"Where are you? You seem like you're ten thousand miles away. Like you're up with the Northern Lights." I crossed my legs toward him and rested my chin on his shoulder. I whispered into his ear, "I'm here, I'm here, you can talk to me, I'm here."

Even though he was playing hide-and-seek with his face, I caught a glimpse of smile lines. They were in his cheeks and imprinted on his forehead. I offered him the widest smile I could to hopefully lull him to okay.

Tennessee dropped his hands and showed his full smile. Then he took my hand and linked his fingers inside mine.

Lying was easier when a smile or a touch didn't hold me accountable. What if I liked when Tennessee held my hand? What if I liked talking to him? What if I liked him more than I ever wanted or planned to? What if that was the reason he was so terrifying? Senior year was already full of good-byes. He didn't need to be another good-bye added to an already long list.

He raised my fingers and kissed my knuckles one by one.

How could I be fake when he made me fall in love with him by doing things like that?

Tennessee took our entwined fingers, and he traced them across his cheek, across his eyes, across his lips, and he kissed my knuckles again.

If I was a robot, I wouldn't love him. I would make those wires go away. Cut the wires and replace them. I didn't want to light up when he was near. I didn't want to have to go out of my way to act like I didn't care.

"What's wrong?" I asked. I really wanted to take my hand back. He was confusing enough already.

"I'm just . . ." He shook his head like he didn't want to finish.

"You're just what?" I crossed my leg over his.

"Scared," he finished.

"Of what?" I whispered, resting my head on his shoulder.

Tennessee swallowed hard, his Adam's apple bobbing up and down. "I wasn't happy in this house. I was very sad. And that's too much, I'm sorry I'm saying too much. . . ."

I touched his face with my free hand and turned his face back to me. He looked down. He looked back at me. I grinned like he had a Polaroid camera ready to take a picture. "You're my friend, okay?"

"You're my friend," he said softly.

"And because you're my friend you are never ever too much."

"You say that now."

"I mean it, always." That was a lie. I didn't mean it always. When he was too much, I ran. When I was too much, I ran.

Tennessee closed his eyes and breathed in.

How can I return this library book?

He opened his eyes and pulled me to him. He hugged me, wrapping his arms tightly around me. He hugged me for a while, holding onto me like . . . like he loved me, too.

·····∽····

The next morning, we started the day with the trampoline in Tennessee's backyard.

The sky was deep blue.

The trees were full of burnt orange, cinnamon, golden, and brown leaves.

Iz was wearing yellow tights.

I was wearing purple tights.

Tennessee was wearing red gym shorts.

We spent a solid hour on the trampoline.

Iz did the splits in the air.

Tennessee did a backflip.

And I pretended like I could fly. It felt so nice, throwing my arms up and tasting the fall air. We were miles away from New Orleans and all of its watery graves.

⸱⸱⸱⸱⸱❦⸱⸱⸱⸱⸱

Later that evening, Iz and I sat on the porch with mugs of cider. Being out in the woods was weird. It was so quiet—the kind of quiet where I could hear animals moving in the woods and dogs barking from far off places. We'd been sitting on the porch for an hour, and I was starting to get restless.

"He said that we could look around the house."

Iz looked up from the book she was reading.

"Let's go." I jumped up.

"But . . . but . . . reading." Iz pointed down at her book.

"You can read inside where the light is better. These porch lights are too dim!" I grabbed her hand and dragged her inside.

We ran up the stairs.

I had no idea where Tennessee was. Maybe he was in the shower or taking a nap somewhere?

All the rooms were closed on the second floor. For a second, I considered waiting for Tennessee and clarifying that it was okay for us to see his house without him. It was only for a second. The first room I opened was his. I could tell because TRW was on the door. Tennessee Rebel Williams.

"Jess, don't go in there," Iz said, grabbing my hand.

"Why not?"

"Because you like him."

"So?"

"The door was closed."

"He said we could see the house, Iz. He volunteered."

"Did he volunteer closed-room doors?"

"Not per se, but we're here and the door is open now."

Iz shook her head and threw her hands up in the air. "I'm not going in."

I am.

Ignoring my BF, I stepped into Tennessee's room. He had left behind a lot in Oxford. There were trophies on the wall. I eyed the trophies and traced my hand along a writing desk. Who knew that he played football and soccer? Since when? He never talked about sports.

I skipped over his dresser.

I sat down on his bed and jumped up and down, testing it for firmness. Iz took that as her opportunity to go back downstairs. On Tennessee's bed was a box. It was open, so I curiously peered inside.

"What do we have here?" I pulled out a book made out of loose-leaf pages taped together with scotch tape. The cover bore a sketch of three people. A boy was in the middle with his arms around two people—a girl wearing a tank top and a boy with a skateboard and a hoodie wrapped around his waist. They were all smiling.

Was this his story?

I turned the page.

Tennessee told his best friend, Kevin, some things that Tennessee wished he hadn't. Tennessee told him about the silence in the middle of the night. The loud static that ripped through his ears after his parents stop fighting. He told Kevin about the anger. The anger that he couldn't control. The anger that terrified him. Made him worry that something was wrong about him. A wrong thing that would keep people away, if they saw it or even heard about it. They would run. Tennessee told his best friend that it wasn't true. He wasn't wrong and all messed up. He was okay. And he had to keep going. He had to get through the hard stuff . . .

"What are you doing?" Tennessee asked.

I looked up.

Tennessee's eyes widened, and he backed away from the door. The next thing I knew he was running. He was running, and I didn't know why.

"Tennessee!" I screamed, throwing the book down, and running after him.

What happened?

ONE MILLION PIECES OF TENNESSEE

"At her peak, Lauralee Sonnier-Williams was a visionary who breathed life into old tropes and made readers around the world fall in love with New Orleans over and over again. Her attention to detail was spot on, whether we were dropped into 1800 New Orleans or 1996 New Orleans. Her sequel, *View from the Edge of the World*, unfortunately, captures none of the elements that made its predecessor stand out. What was new and revolutionary is now outdated and unimaginative. Ms. Sonnier-Williams should have left a once-great story alone!" Mom read loudly over the rushing sound of traffic. She was basically screaming.

Mom had told me she was going to run ahead of me to clear her mind. I let her because I didn't expect her to do this. Mom pulled stunts. It's what she did whenever she was stressed or frustrated. Most of the stunts were harmless, or at least that was what I told myself—locking herself in her room for two days and not talking to anyone. Not eating for a day or drinking water. Hitting Dad when he said something she didn't like. Nearly burning the house down because she needed to "rid the world" of her manuscript. That kind of stuff.

This was the worst thing she'd ever done out of a long list of bad things.

I was too far away to stop her. And even when she started climbing up the railings of the Ravenel Bridge, I couldn't make my brain react fast enough. I watched her, frozen and dumbfounded as she climbed the railing of the bridge. Car horns went off and brake lights flashed. She pulled out her phone. Still frozen and in disbelief, I convinced myself that she was trying to get the perfect selfie. It was dangerous and reckless to stand on the guard rail of a bridge, but she did lots of things that I wouldn't do.

I broke out into a run when I realized that she wasn't taking a selfie. She was reading something out loud and teetering on the edge—like she was about to fall, or jump? "Mom!"

She acted like she didn't hear me. She kept reading.

"Get down from there." I held out my hand.

More car horns blasted and some people that had been running along the path with us stopped. A few people took out their phones and an older woman asked Mom to come down.

"Is that that writer?"

"Yeah, that's her."

"Take a picture."

"Mom! Stop this! Get down."

She kept reading. As I inched closer to her it became clear what she was reading—her reviews. She was reading the reviews of her book. Standing on the guardrail, she was reading her reviews. Suddenly, I got scared.

"WOODEN WRITING. TWO-DIMENSIONAL CHARAC-TERS."

She had been bad during her Charleston book tour, which was why I came with her. I had dedicated myself to being her personal assistant, which meant cheering her up when she was down. Bringing her food when she didn't want to eat. Forcing her to go on local tours after her book signing, which only fourteen people showed up to. I didn't expect that I would have to talk her off a bridge!

I kept asking her to get down. The older woman was right underneath her. Her hand was out, and she was telling Mom to take her hand. I was scared to get too close. It was really windy, and the fall from the bridge into the Charleston Harbor was too high.

What was I supposed to do?

"LACKLUSTER SENTIMENTAL DRIVEL."

For a second I got an idea. It was crazy and I don't know why I thought of it. I thought that maybe if I got up there, too, she would stop this. She'd see me, on the bridge with her, and I wouldn't get down until she did. I thought about it. But I couldn't. And I was also worried that me getting on the bridge might make it worse—I didn't want to die trying to save her. I also didn't want her to die.

Frantically, I called Dad. He picked up on the third ring.

"What, Reb. I'm working."

"Daddy, Mom is on the bridge, and I don't know what to do. What should I do?"

"What are you talking about, Rebel?"

I raked my hands through my hair with shaking hands. "She crawled up onto the guardrails, and she's reading her reviews."

"What?"

"Daddy, I think she might jump. What should I do?"

He went silent.

I needed him to speak. "Daddy, what should I do?"

"Put me on speaker."

Okay. Okay. I put him on speaker and inched closer to Mom, watching terrified as she wobbled. More people were trying to talk her down while others kept taking videos of her.

"Lauralee, did you take your medication?" he asked.

My jaw dropped. *Mom doesn't take any medication.* "Dad? That's not going to help."

She kept reading her bad reviews, louder than ever.

"I shouldn't be getting a call from our son telling me about how you're trying to jump off a bridge in South Carolina because of a few bad reviews."

"Dad!" My voice shook. A few camera phones turned to me. "I called you to help me."

"She's not going to jump."

"Yes, I am, Richard!"

My heart stopped.

"No, you're not," he snapped. "This is a publicity stunt. She's trying to find a way to sell more books. It's business. If she was going to jump, she would've jumped already."

She hurled her phone into the Charleston Bay and positioned herself like she was about to jump.

"Mom!" I yelled, running over to her.

"Jump!" Dad said. "If you're going to jump, just do it!"

I was speechless. Stupidly speechless. Dad was telling her to jump. And she was acting like she was about to do it.

I'm not sure what happened to me—I think I blacked out, because all I remember is trying to pull her off the bridge, and then ending up on the bridge myself.

And I don't know why that happened. I don't know why I did that.

⸺◦§◦⸺

When we got back to the hotel room, Mom asked me questions.

She asked me why I tried to jump.

I told her that I wasn't trying to jump. I didn't want to die. I was saving her.

And she looked at me, her eyes wide and worried. "I wasn't going to jump," she said, placing her hand over mine.

"But . . . you were hanging over the bridge."

"I wasn't going to jump," she insisted. "I was purging those reviews. Saying good-bye to writing. That's why I threw my phone into the harbor."

I searched her eyes, confused, because she was looking at me like I was the crazy one. Like I ran ahead of her and started reading reviews and almost caused several accidents on the bridge. She did that. *I was trying to stop her.*

Shaking her head, Mom pulled me into her arms and she hugged me tightly. "I'm sorry that you were confused. I'm sorry that you thought I was trying to hurt myself."

I stared at the wall blankly.

⟶⟀⟵

The next morning Mom was in high spirits. She went to her next book signing, which had significantly more people. And she didn't bring up the bridge incident again, at least not until we got back to Mississippi.

36
JESSAMINE

I DIDN'T HAVE TO GO FAR TO FIND HIM. Tennessee was up in a deer stand.

"Hey! You ran?"

He kept his hands to his face. I felt guilty—the kind of guilty that I couldn't talk my way out of. I bit down on my cheek, thinking carefully before I spoke. "I'm sorry."

He shook his head. "What'd you read?"

I should've listened to Iz. "It was just a paragraph."

"Those are personal."

"I'm sorry, I thought they were your stories. You told me that you'd let me read them."

"Not those."

I swallowed. I didn't know what else to say other than sorry? A part of me wanted to step back from the damage. Give him space and talk to him more about it when he came back to the house. But that part was very small. The biggest part of me wanted to talk to him until he came down from that deer stand.

He was more than the guy I 65 percent liked.

He was also my friend.

And reading his stories hurt him. I didn't know why it hurt him. But it did. And I had to own that. I cracked my knuckles. From the ground, it looked like the deer stand had room for two. *I'm going in.*

I climbed the ladder.

Tennessee didn't look up. Even when I sat down beside him, he didn't look up.

"Whew, this is higher than I thought."

He turned away from me.

I frowned. What I did—reading his stories—was that bad enough to make him hate me? Maybe that was the line. That was the one thing I couldn't get away with. He let me disappear. He let me kiss him one second and give him the cold shoulder the next. He let me make myself available only when I wanted to be available, and he always made himself available. But this . . . this was maybe the thing he couldn't forgive.

It was probably for the best.

If I made him hate me, that would close this chapter. End this thing. End us.

End the memory of our dance on Frenchmen. The stank faces we made to each other. The kisses on eyes and lips when the world got too loud, and we both needed it to be quiet. For a second it felt like hands were around my neck choking me and punching me in the stomach. I studied him.

"Tennessee, I'm really sorry."

"Jessamine, why'd you do that?" He asked it into his hands.

I placed my hands to my heart. "I wouldn't have . . . if I knew how much it would hurt you. I'm so sorry. I'm so, so sorry."

His face scrunched up like he was in so much pain.

I reached out to touch him. To hold him in my arms. To comfort him. Fix what I messed up. But I was scared. I was scared that what I did had changed things forever. And I don't know why it mattered, but it did.

"How can I make this right?"

"You can't make it right."

I bit down hard on my lip.

Tennessee dropped his hands and he sighed, deeply. I watched as stared out into the autumn-colored trees. His eyes were still and lost. I wasn't used to his eyes looking so hopeless. The thought that I did this really hurt me. I'd stop playing games with him. I'd be honest. I'd be open if that could bring him back to me.

"I thought it would feel good to be back here, but it doesn't feel good."

I reached out and took his hand. His fingers were ice cold—hypothermia cold. If he touched my hands and felt that they were cold, he would ask me to go inside. He would build me a fire or bring me a blanket. I wished that I could take over and do that for him. Take care of him like he took care of me, even when I didn't ask him to.

I couldn't.

I couldn't take care of him.

"You don't really know who I am. I um . . . I showed you what I wanted you to see," Tennessee said.

His comment took me off guard. What did he mean by that? I saw him. I was pretty sure that I saw him too clearly. I saw how much he cared about me, and that was what scared me the most. I opened my mouth to tell him that I knew him with absolute certainty. But my mouth and words wouldn't cooperate.

Tennessee pulled his hand out of mine. I brought my cold hands back into my lap and held them.

"Even if you didn't read some of the worst scenes in that book . . ."

My eyebrows dropped. "Worst scenes?"

He shook his head, his eyes looking from the autumn woods to the ground scattered with leaves. "To be honest, I don't really like writing. I never feel good after I do it." He rubbed the back of his neck. "Every time I write, it's for the wrong reasons. I started writing to connect with my mom. I thought that if I wrote stories like her, we would have something in common. We could share that and talk about our worlds.

"That didn't work. Because she was always critical of my writing. She picked it apart. It was too simple or my vocabulary wasn't big enough. And my dad always read my books. At first he did it to support me and encourage me, and then he started doing it to try and figure me out.

"So I started tricking him. I made up a version of myself that was like him. A good ol' all-American boy who played sports and dated cheerleaders. My only rebellion was changing my middle name to David and making that Tennessee go to Stanford.

"I left those books here for Dad. I knew he would read them all and try to figure out what's wrong with me. He read my books, Jess. So, when I saw you reading them . . ." Tennessee frowned and looked at me with wet eyes. "It took me back to sitting on my porch with Dad and him reading my stories out loud, making me feel like . . . like I was nothing."

I didn't know what to say. He'd just said so much. If Iz was here she would know the right thing to say.

Tennessee tilted his head to the side. "I don't know why I brought you and Iz here. That's my fault."

I closed my eyes and I said the only thing that I could, "I'm not your dad."

"No you're not, you're something worse than him. You're you."

I shook my head. "I'm not anyone."

"That's not true. You're the most important person."

I reached for his hand again. Tennessee's hand was shaking. I inched closer to him. I took both of his ice-cold hands in mine and rubbed them together. I even blew into them like he had done to mine when we drove to Mandeville after Auntie Myrtle passed.

"I'm not mad at you," he said distantly.

"It's okay. You can be mad at me. You get to be mad at me. I shouldn't have read your stories, unless you *chose* to share them with me."

Tennessee twitched his nose.

"Can we go inside? Iz and I can build you a fire."

"I don't want to go inside, but you should. Your hands are cold."

"*Your* hands are cold."

Tennessee looked down at our entwined hands. His eyebrows knitted. "I love you."

I raised my chin. That was the last thing I was expecting him to say. I panicked and considered taking my hand back and climbing back down the ladder.

What?

No, saying *what* would make him repeat it.

Why?

No, I didn't want to hear the reasons why.

I looked down at the deer stand.

"You don't have to say it back."

I couldn't. And it wasn't because I didn't feel the same. I just couldn't.

"Why are you telling me that?"

"Because . . ." He eased his hands from mine and crossed his arms. "I don't want to lie to you to keep you. I feel like . . . like I have to lie to everyone except for Saint to . . . to keep them around."

"What do you mean?"

He chewed on his lip. "I'm messed up, Jessamine. My brain is all messed up."

"What do you mean?" I repeated.

His lips turned down at the edges. "Sometimes . . . sometimes I get really down and I . . ." His lips tightened and he looked at me. "Before I moved to New Orleans, my parents made me go to a hospital. They checked me into this . . . um . . . program because they were worried about me. They thought I was, um . . . I guess, a danger to myself."

"Why did they do that?"

His cheeks flushed a dark shade of red. "Because . . . I got really sad and did things. I don't know. That's why."

"What *things?*"

Tears filled up in his eyes. It felt like I should stop asking him questions. Give him space. Give him a break. But a light went off in my head. A light that flashed red. It said, *Death!* Even more reason to let him go.

But there was also this fear that was grabbing onto him. Clawing at him. Snatching him up. Holding onto him tight.

He was supposed to be okay! He wasn't supposed to need me. I was supposed to be able to run. And trust that he was okay. That's how it was supposed to be!

"What things?" I repeated.

Tennessee hugged his knees. "There's a video. It went around my first day of school. I, um . . . can't remember doing what I did. But I did it. I guess I thought she was trying to jump and I was trying to save her, but she told me she wasn't trying to jump. And I just remember being sad and confused, because I was just trying to be a good son to her. I was just trying totakecareofherbecauseIwasreallyworriedandIdidn'tknowwhat elsetodo."

I immediately pulled him into my arms.

"I'm sorry, I'm sorry, I'm sorry."

"Shh." I hugged him so tightly. He kept speaking, stringing together words that I didn't understand. "Shh, it's okay, it's okay, it's okay."

37

JESSAMINE

"Are we okay?" Iz asked.

She was sitting at the kitchen table with a mug cradled in her hands.

"I think we are . . . now?" I sank down in the chair beside her. "I wish that I'd listened to you."

She stood up. "Do you think he wants some tea or coffee?"

"I don't know. He went upstairs."

She opened a cabinet like this was her house. "Let's see what they got." Iz grabbed a box of apple cider mix and another mug. She ripped open both packets of apple cider and poured one into each mug.

I stood and went to the stove. I filled the kettle with water and turned on the stove. Iz hopped onto the kitchen counter beside me.

I didn't say anything and neither did she for a while. I listened to the sound of the clock ticking, and I replayed the conversation with Tennessee in the deer stand. I found myself trying to push him away. I tried to convince myself that it was for the best. He had baggage. And I had baggage. And our combined baggage would crush us.

His parents had had him committed.

There was a whole case built against him. Yet fear and the urge to run didn't consume me like I thought it would.

He had been vulnerable with me. He told me the truth. And

he expected me to run. He told me that I mattered the most to him. That what I thought mattered. And he told me that he loved me.

When he said it, it wasn't like the admissions of love that I saw on TV. It wasn't Olivia and Fitz. It wasn't Whitley and Dwayne.

I smiled at the thought of watching *A Different World* with Solange on her computer. Those were the good days.

It was Jessamine and Tennessee. And that didn't scare me.

He didn't scare me. He made me want to stop and hold him to me, stay with him until he fell asleep, and help him be okay. Because how okay could someone be with parents like his?

Mama wasn't perfect, but I knew that she loved me. I knew that she also loved Joel. Even if they weren't speaking right now, I knew she loved us.

I looked at Iz, who was doing her best to act like she wasn't staring dead in my face trying to read my emotions like she was a bootleg counselor. "Guess what," she said as I poured the hot water into our mugs. We both went to sit at the table.

"What?"

"They have a whole gun room in their house."

"Of course they do."

"You know what that means?"

"What?"

She giggled. "If the zombie apocalypse breaks out, we are gonna be some badass chicks. *The Walking Dead: Mississippi Edition*!"

I laughed. "The only problem is that neither of us knows how to shoot a gun." I had a fear of guns. Guns and water. They both did too much damage.

"I'm sure Tennessee knows how to shoot one. He could teach us."

I reached for my mug and took a sip. I got a dark thought and worried that Tennessee might try to hurt himself that way. That really scared me. Too many people I knew had died and I just . . .

I stood.

"Where are you going, Jess?"

"To the bathroom," I lied.

Iz tilted her head to the side. "You should give him a little space."

"I'm not checking on him. I'm checking on . . ."

"The bathroom?"

"Damn." She caught me. Reluctantly, I sank back down.

Iz and I sat in silence for a while, drinking hot cider.

......ᘒᕀ......

I gave him space because I knew Iz was right. In the morning, Iz and I took a walk outside. When we got home, Tennessee had emerged from his room. He had a fire going in the fireplace and breakfast was waiting in the kitchen.

I exhaled when I saw him, not realizing how tight my chest had been since our conversation in the deer stand.

"Did y'all sleep okay?" he asked.

"Out like a light." Iz hugged him. "How'd you sleep?"

He hugged her back. "I slept okay."

I gave him a small smile.

He walked over to me. His cheeks were red and his eyes were lined with bags.

There were questions that I wanted to ask him.

"I'm sorry about yesterday," he said.

"No."

"What do you mean, no?"

I took his hands. "Don't apologize for that."

He glanced down, looking like he was ashamed. I looked to the fire. "That's a sexy fire."

Tennessee looked up, his eyes still sad.

"Let's sit by it for a sec."

He nodded. Holding hands, we walked to the fire. I sat down by the fireplace, and he also sat down. The fire crackled and popped in my ears.

He leaned forward and clasped his hands. I also leaned forward. "How did we get to be this way?" he asked, turning to face me.

"You." I shook my head. "You're the damn cat that's supposed to stay named Cat. You weren't supposed to have a name."

His eyebrows knitted together. "I'm confused."

I sighed. "*Breakfast at Tiffany's*. The cat was named Cat. She had to give it a name at the end because she kept it."

"You're comparing me to a cat?" He scratched his head.

"Ugh!" I grabbed his hand and squeezed it tightly. I forced myself to stay, feet glued to the ground. When I looked at him in Oxford, Mississippi, his eyes didn't glitter. They were hazel marbles. They were tired marbles. And when he blushed in Oxford, Mississippi, the blush wasn't triple strawberry. It was just red.

"You make me weak," I repeated.

He looked down at our hands and turned to me. "And you make me honest. I didn't want to tell you about South Carolina. But you make me honest."

I searched his eyes.

I hate you.

No, that wasn't true.

I didn't hate him.

I loved him.

And that . . . was what made me weak.

Tennessee started to pull away from me, but I kept his hands. I linked my fingers in his. Staying. Staying. Staying. Because running was the only thing that I knew how to do.

And I was tired of running.

"What's wrong, Jess?" he whispered.

"You."

He nodded.

"Why'd you do that to me? You radioactive"—I searched for the right words—"zombie!"

Tennessee looked confused, but he touched my face and pulled my hair off my shoulder. He trailed his hands through my curls. I opened my mouth.

The fire beside us popped and crackled.

I closed my mouth.

He looked back at me.

And I went out on a limb. I said the thing. The horrendous thing that had teeth and claws. The thing that wasn't like it was in the movies. Our thing was kind of heavy and a little sad, but it was ours. Our imperfect love.

When I said the thing, he took his hands out of mine and cradled my face with both his hands. He kissed me. This kiss was different than the other ones. It was soft. His eyes were open. I knew, because mine were, too.

38
TENNESSEE

THANKSGIVING ALWAYS MADE ME ANXIOUS. Any holiday, for that matter.

Unlike normal families that celebrated the holidays with board games and family dinners, Mom and Dad used holidays to declare war. I couldn't remember one holiday that didn't end in a fight.

Their track record of holiday wars was just one of the many reasons I fled New Orleans. I still couldn't believe that I was in my childhood home with Jessamine and Iz. *This is so nice.*

For the first time in seventeen years, I was having a normal Thanksgiving. The Macy's parade was on in the background. And Iz and Jessamine were standing near the stove laughing about something. I'm not sure what.

Yesterday had been a little rough—being back home stirred up things inside of me. Jessamine reading my writing hadn't helped. But we seemed okay now. Maybe she needed to read my old writings, because that way I couldn't hide anymore.

Jessamine was now sliding across the floor in her red tights and Iz was begging for her to put the knife down. Iz threatened to demote Jessamine from her duties of celery chopper.

"We don't want to have to take you to the ER, Jessamine! Ay, dios mío, can you imagine how far away the hospital is?" Iz turned to me. "Tenn, how far away is the nearest hospital?"

"Not that far," I said.

Jessamine slid back over to the counter and set down the knife. "Does *not that far* mean that it's in Tennessee, Tennessee?" After saying that she burst out laughing.

"Jess, I'm seriously this close to demoting you. Cut my celery!" Iz cried.

Jessamine theatrically bowed down to Iz and returned to her only task, chopping.

"The nearest hospital is about twenty minutes away, give or take," I pointed out

"You see"—Iz pointed a wooden spoon at Jessamine—"he just said that if you get cut your ass is grass."

"I didn't say that, Iz."

Iz winked at me. "Just agree. She's had three cups of coffee, which means that we have to be the adults."

"My hands are getting tired," Jessamine complained.

"I can tap in," I offered, pushing back the stool I was sitting on.

"Nope. I can't give up. I got this. I just needed to complain." Jessamine beamed over her shoulder at me. She was still actively cutting the celery and not looking.

Jessamine was such a hazard in the kitchen. That was a fact that I just realized now. There was still so much to learn about each other.

"You're done." Iz deserted the bowl of shrimp that she was deveining. She wiggled her fingers in Jessamine's direction. "If you don't step away from the celery, then I'm going to hug you with these ol' nasty shrimp hands."

Jessamine childishly crouched and held up her hands in a fighting motion. "Stay back or I'll unleash my one year of tae-kwondo on you!"

I stood and lingered by the kitchen island. Jessamine was in a giddy mood. I wasn't sure if it was the three cups of coffee, Thanksgiving, or Iz.

Iz playfully lunged in Jessamine's direction.

Jessamine screamed and ran around the island. She hid behind me. Iz still playfully approached, wiggling her fingers. Jessamine used my body as a shield to protect her.

"Tenn, please keep her out of my kitchen."

"I do what I want," Jessamine said, circling her arms around me and sticking her tongue out at Iz.

"Try me, boo, just try me." Iz went back to the sink and washed her hands. "Jess, stop touching Tennessee's sweater with those celery hands."

Jessamine rested her head against my back. "My hands are fine. I barely touched the celery."

I wasn't sure what to do with my body. Should I stand there? Should I turn to her? Should I move? Jessamine answered my internal questions by pulling away.

"Iz, after taking a small siesta I will be happy to return to my duties."

"No need, you have been relieved. Tennessee, what do you think about making her wash the dishes?"

Jessamine made a gasping sound. She stepped from behind me. "There are like a thousand pots! How much grease will I have to scrub off that pan of cornbread dressing?"

I didn't think cornbread dressing had a lot of grease. At least not how Dad made it.

"I'm immune to your tactics." Iz collected some seasonings and brought them over to her shrimp. "Tennessee, soon you'll see. Jessamine is such a princess. She never has to cook. Basically, Ms. Josephine, JoJo, and I wait on her hand and foot."

"Is that true, Jess?" I asked, feeding into the lightness in the kitchen.

She rolled her eyes. "I have no problem cooking. If you're gonna tell some truth, you might as well tell it all."

Iz walked over to the sink and washed her hands. "Fine, I was trying to save your reputation just in case Tennessee wanted to try your cooking one day. But since you asked me to tell the truth, I will. Tenn, her cooking is so bad that twice Joel has gotten food poisoning from her meals."

I winced. "It's that bad, Jess?"

Jessamine hid her mouth behind her shoulder, watching me with eyes that didn't look repentant. *Wow. Okay. That bad.* Note to self: No matter how beautiful and stunning and perfect she is, do not ever eat her cooking. "What did you make?"

"Eggs," she said, shrugging.

"Eggs!" I exclaimed.

"I know!" Iz slapped her hand on the counter. "Literally all she has to do is fry them, scramble them, or flip them, and she can't even be trusted with that."

Jessamine leaned against me. "I could be a good cook. I just need someone to be patient with me. Tennessee, I can observe while you make the sweet potato casserole and macaroni and cheese. I could even sprinkle the cheese!"

I grinned. "Bet."

"I foresee food poisoning in your future, Williams," Iz said dryly.

"He has faith in me. A little bit of faith will do a lot of good!" Jessamine said, grabbing my arm and playfully tugging on it.

Jessamine was joking and laughing, but something seemed a

little off. I could've been reading too much into nothing because of yesterday. But the Jessamine who sat with me on the deer stand and the Jessamine standing beside me now were night and day. That worried me.

Suddenly, the doorbell rang.

Jessamine gazed at me. "Are you expecting anyone else?"

I shrugged and walked out of the kitchen. Last night, I had texted Joel, Solange, and Saint and invited them all again up to spend Thanksgiving in Oxford. Joel was the only person that responded to the text. He'd said that he would try to make it.

I opened the front door and was pleasantly surprised to see Joel and Solange.

"Happy Thanksgiving!" Solange screamed and wrapped her arms tight around me. She was wearing a puffy red jacket and jeans with camo boots.

"Happy Thanksgiving!" I gushed, hugging her so tight. "I wasn't sure if you were going to make it!"

"I wasn't sure if I was going to make it! I thought Oxford was right around the corner, not in damn near Canada!" Solange laughed. "Do you like my outfit? This look is called gone hunting for a country man!"

I laughed.

"Let me edit that—a country Black man!" she said, squeezing my shoulder and laughing jovially. It was so great seeing her laugh.

I hugged Joel next. Usually, I was more reserved about hugging him. Joel had this unspoken rule about being touched, at least how I perceived it. Whenever I got too much in his space, he often pulled a disappearing act. Joel hugged me back.

"I don't smell no food cooking," he said.

"That's probably because Jessamine is pretending like she knows how to cook. Remember the time that little girl tried to feed us different types of cereal for Thanksgiving?" Solange snorted. "I almost threw her and her Fruit U-Turns out the daggone window!"

Before I could properly invite them in, take their coats and bags, and show them around, Jessamine appeared. She pushed me out of the way, literally pushed me, and hugged Solange and Joel at the same time.

"My Favorite Number Two and Favorite Number Three," she said.

Who is Favorite Number One?

I stepped aside as Jessamine took on the role of host. She grabbed Solange's and Joel's coats and hung them in the closet by the door.

"Y'all, the Williams' house is what we call rustic and country wood cabin. Over there we have a crackling fire, our very own lumberjack—Tenn flex those muscles . . ." She waited for me to flex, and like a cardboard cut-out version of myself, I did. Jessamine continued after I gave her the "gun show," taking her cousin and twin on a tour around the house.

I thought about following them and offering little details about the house, but it didn't feel like I was invited.

I still felt great about Jessamine and Iz being here. There was laughter. There would be an actual meal prepared. Last Thanksgiving, Dad had burned the turkey because he drank too much whiskey, and Mom had dragged him outside and let him sleep it off . . . in the cold. So, this was definitely a major upgrade. But still, Jessamine felt so far away.

That made me nervous. It made me worry that we weren't

okay. That she had time to reflect on our conversation yesterday and she decided that it wasn't worth it. I wasn't worth it.

The thought made my stomach churn.

What if we went back to New Orleans and she . . . she ghosted me for good this time?

"Hey." Iz's arm looped around my waist before I saw her.

"Hey, sorry," I said.

"Whatcha sorry for, boo?" Iz had this easy-going smirk on her face.

"Nothing, I guess."

"I heard Solange and Joel, which means that the kitchen is about to turn into a wrestling arena. Those two literally compete for best dish. We do not want to get in their way. Wanna start on your mac and cheese and other goodies and hang out with me?" Iz batted her eyelashes. "I come with funny Jessamine stories."

"Sold!" I exclaimed, trying to shake off the worry.

⋯⋯෧ஃ෧⋯⋯

"Jessamine, since you didn't chop so much as a carrot, why don't you bless the food?" Solange said.

Jessamine threw her hands up in the air, "Ha-ha, the joke is old now."

She was sitting to the right of me, and Joel was to the left. Directly across from me was Iz, and there was an empty chair between her and Solange. Saint should've been sitting in that empty chair. I had texted him again. He didn't respond.

Jessamine took my hand, bringing me back to the moment. Joel also took my hand.

"Amen," everyone said. I was a few beats late.

The table was bountiful. We had turkey, gumbo, and stuffed bell peppers prepared by Iz. Deviled eggs and red beans and rice prepared by Solange. Collard greens and pecan pie courtesy of Joel. And I made Daddy's cornbread dressing, sweet potato casserole, and butternut squash. Jessamine had been sentenced three times over, by everyone but me, to wash the dishes. I had already volunteered to help her. There were too many dishes!

We ate like a real family, passing dishes down the line. Iz served as the official turkey carver, and Jessamine was vocal about her role as the sugar dispenser, also known as the person who sliced and distributed the pecan pie . . . that Joel made.

I ate until I was so full that I had to unbuckle my jeans.

⚬⚭

Although Jessamine was sentenced to dishwasher, it turned out that I wasn't the only one who couldn't say no. Iz and Joel cleared the table and put the leftovers in Tupperware. Solange cleaned the counters and table. And we all took turns washing the dishes, but I washed most of them.

After we were finished cleaning, we went into the living room. A good fire was going in the fireplace. I pulled out all the board games we had, games we seldom actually played as a family.

Later that night, I facetimed Saint. I was surprised when he picked up.

"Happy Thanksgiving, Nashville!" he said.

"Happy Thanksgiving! Why aren't you here?" I fluffed the pillow behind my head.

Saint was also laying on his bed. "I have a good excuse. My

parents are both in town and they wanted to have a Baptiste Thanksgiving. We were all in the kitchen. It was a mess, but I have plenty of leftovers for when you come over next."

"Awesome!"

I almost told Saint that Joel, Solange, and Iz were down-stairs playing games. I also almost said that was why I wished he was here. They had a history that didn't include me. A history that they had to frequently fill me in on.

"Nashville, I went old-school and plotted out our route for the post-Magnolia Prep American road trip."

"Where is the first stop?"

"Right up the street, this doughnut place in Lafayette—ya heard me."

I snickered. "I love it. Food as the destination."

Saint got silent for a bit. I waited for him to ask me about Joel. He didn't. "So, um . . . every Thanksgiving that my family is in New Orleans we watch a Black Thanksgiving movie. Usually one from the archive. Mona and Claude had too much wine and they're passed out. Do you want to watch a movie with me?"

I looked around for my computer. An enamel pin sitting on my nightstand caught my eye. I picked it up and a wave of hap-piness filled me. The enamel pin was of a satsuma. I closed my fist around it. *Thanks, Jessamine.*

"Tennessee, I was just kidding."

I focused back on Saint. "No, I think that's a great idea. Let me tell everyone that I'm going to watch a movie with you—"

My door creaked open. It was everyone.

"We wanted to check on you, bro," Joel said.

"I'm good. Just talking to Saint." I glanced at my screen. Saint looked like a deer in headlights. "We're about to watch a movie."

I saw Jessamine look at my nightstand. I opened my fist to show her the satsuma in my hand, mouthing, "Thank you."

She made the shape of a heart with her hands. "Can we watch a movie with y'all?" Jessamine asked.

Joel sighed. "Jess, you're so rude. We weren't invited."

"Can they watch with us?" I asked Saint.

His FaceTime showed his ceiling.

"Saint?" I said.

"Sorry, I was muted." He returned on my screen wearing green eyeshadow. "Yeah, we're watching a Black classic, *Soul Food*. Who has seen it? Tennessee, turn the phone to the Black people and Iz because I know that you haven't."

I chuckled and turned my phone to Jessamine, Solange, Joel, and Iz. They were all raising their hands.

We spent the rest of Thanksgiving night watching the movie.

39
TENNESSEE

"HELLO, MY LOVES." Solange walked into Chicory and Grind dressed like an elf. She was wearing a green dress with huge gold buttons, red tights, black shoes curled up at the end. Solange had two gift bags in her hands, one pink and the other blue. "For Tenn-Tenn." She handed me the pink bag and blew me a kiss. "And for JoJo." She blew him a kiss. "Thank you for being the hardest-working employees ever."

"Aww, thanks, Solange," I said.

"Of course."

Joel looked in his bag, "Ah, you got me that PS4 game I've been talking about." Joel went around the counter to hug Solange.

I peeked inside the bag, and the first thing I saw was a picture frame. The picture was taken at the skating rink some time ago. In the picture, my arm was slung around Jessamine and she was leaning into me, holding onto my Chicory and Grind T-shirt and smiling. I'd completely forgotten that we took a picture that day. I went around the corner and hugged her.

Solange jingled her bracelet, which had bells on it. "I'm not staying because I have a date."

I drummed my hands on the counter. "That's exciting."

Joel scowled. "I thought you were taking a break from guys?"

She playfully snatched Joel's gift back and handed it to me.

"You have a PS4?" Laughing, Solange took the bag back and tossed it at Joel. "For your information, I have a date with a financial advisor. Thanks to that mean ol' hag, I got some coins that I didn't have before. And I'm doing some adult shit and figuring out how to invest in my future."

"Wow," Joel said.

"Wow, what?" Solange the elf asked, placing her hands on her hips.

Joel walked over to me and leaned against the counter. I glanced at him. He was smiling and looking at Solange kind of like a proud parent. She was also watching Joel, hands still on her hips.

"Who is this person?" He elbowed me. "She used to pay her rent on credit cards."

"Don't be putting my business out there."

"I'm not putting your business out there, and *Tenn-Tenn*, as you call him, is fam."

She looked at me and nodded. That made me smile, a ridiculous big smile. *I belong somewhere. I belong with them.*

"Cuz, you've come a long way from financing your life with credit cards. I'm proud of you."

"I'm proud of me, too." Solange raised her chin high in the air. She was smiling again more than ever.

Solange the elf waved at us, jingling again. "Call me if y'all need anything."

"Are you going to your financial appointment dressed like that?" Joel asked.

She jingled her bracelet with bells one last time. "Maybe. I wear what I want. I do what I want. What are they going to do? Turn me away?"

"I think you should wear that," I spoke up.

Joel looked at me crazy.

"It's exhausting spending all your time caring about what other people think. It can be like a statement."

"Where's *your* elf costume?" Joel asked with a laugh. "Since you like statements and all."

I elbowed him back. "If Solange tells me where she got it from, I'll wear one."

Solange said good-bye one last time and left.

I expected Joel to go back to his sketchbook because that's what he did. This time he didn't. Joel lingered beside me, leaning against the counter and watching the door.

"How's Saint?" he asked.

"Y'all haven't hung out?"

His head turned to me; he was frowning. "Not much since we got back from Oxford."

"Ah, I see."

"Have you spoken to Jess?" Joel said.

I chewed on my lip. "A few texts. We don't talk all the time like that."

Joel grinned. "If you like my sister, why don't you just ask her out?"

My mouth dropped. Joel laughed. I attempted to regain my composure. "You'd be okay with me asking Jessamine out?"

"I don't see why I wouldn't be?" Joel arched an eyebrow at me. "Saint likes you, Solange likes you, Jessamine likes you, Iz likes you, and I like you."

"Thanks, Joel."

"You don't have to thank me. I'm just giving you facts."

I leaned forward. Christmas lights twinkled around the

coffee shop. A tree was adorned with silver and gold balls and stars. Joel had been responsible for that.

"You don't have to answer this," I prefaced. "But what about you and Saint? Have you thought about taking things to the next level?" It was way out of line to ask that question. But I knew how crazy Saint was about Joel.

Joel balled his fist and tapped it on the counter to the rhythm of "All I Want for Christmas Is You" by Mariah Carey, which was playing on the sound system. "Honestly, Tenn, I have. I've thought about it a lot. But I don't think that it would be fair to Saint."

"What do you mean?" I asked.

Joel stopped tapping his fist against the counter. "Liking Saint has made me realize some things. Telling my mama that I'm gay has made me realize more things. I'm still trying to figure out who I am. Where I fit in this world. Saint already knows where he fits. And all of my unknowns make him uneasy. I gotta figure out who *I* am and what I want, before I can figure out *us*."

Joel's words sank in. *I gotta figure out who I am and what I want—before I can figure out us.*

Who was I? And what did I want?

What do I want?

⌁⌁⌁⌁⌁⊰⊱⌁⌁⌁⌁⌁

After my shift, I asked Jessamine to meet me at the Audubon Park Hyam Gardens. She had told me a while ago that she always wanted to have a picnic, so I put one together.

Last night after I finished my homework, I called Iz. I asked her what foods I should make (or buy) for a picnic for Jessamine. I asked Iz what Jessamine's favorite flowers were. They were daisies. And I asked her what I should get Jessamine for Christmas.

It was cheating, I know. But I wanted everything to be perfect.

Jessamine was a little late. By the time I saw her walking toward me, the line of lampposts leading up to the fountain had already turned on. Smiling, I stood and gave her the daisies.

"Bruh."

"What are you bruhing me for?"

"A picnic!" Jessamine smelled the flowers, even though they didn't have a smell. She tapped me lightly on the shoulder with the daisies. "You're the worst. And by the worst, I mean, damn you for being the best."

40
JESSAMINE

Tennessee got me daisies.

A part of me wanted to throw them away.

Daisies were scary. They were real.

If I kept those daisies, I would have to look at them.

They were like a symbol.

A symbol of that time in Oxford, when I hurt him, and he opened up to me. That time in Oxford when I gave the cat a name. And told the cat that I loved him.

Not 25 percent.

Not 30 percent.

Not 65 percent.

But 100 percent.

I couldn't throw away his flowers. When I got home, I put them in a vase. Set them on the table. And went upstairs.

·······⚬ℓ⚬·······

When we were on the deer stand and Tennessee was talking about his parents, I kept seeing the closet. So now, I turned on the light. There was my favorite dress shirt, the one with the peacock feather.

It used to smell like him.

I eased it off the hanger, surprisingly not afraid of Mama or

Joel catching me. I unbuttoned the buttons carefully and slid the shirt onto my shoulders. I closed my eyes and wrapped my arms around my body.

Daddy, I'm scared.

I opened my eyes, sinking a bit more. The sound of rushing water was in my ears.

It had been more than a decade since She came and took everything. She took our house. She took our dreams. She took our hopes. She took Daddy.

The only reason we still had these clothes was because Daddy had left them in his office at work. He was always prepared. Mama always used to joke that Daddy had a shirt, pants, and jacket with him at all times, because he never knew who he would meet.

I reached for his shoes and slipped them on my feet. The size elevens were way too big. I held my breath as I swam in his shirt and his shoes.

It didn't seem right that there was a closet half full of Daddy's clothes and shoes. A closet that no one touched or visited.

Water seeped in underneath the crack in the door. I took a step back. Closed my eyes. Counted to five. When I opened my eyes, the water was still there.

DÍAS DE LOS MUERTOS
PART 1

"Baby, we gotta stay," Daddy said.

Mama turned away from the car she was loading up. "Stay where? If you're talkin' about staying here, you are out of your mind."

"We got to," Daddy said. "My mama ain't going. She won't leave."

"She'll leave if we tell her she's got to." Mama turned to me and Joel. We were sitting on the porch eating our haul from the Candy Lady. "Y'all better stop eating all that candy. Do as I told you. Go inside and bring the suitcases out. We got to get on the road 'fore that storm comes."

I looked up at the sky, "But it don't look like it's comin' a storm to me."

"Jessamine. Go," Mama bossed.

Okay. Okay. I patted Joel on the back. He got up, and together we headed inside to the living room, where everything was packed.

Joel sat down on the couch.

"You better get up before she gets you. Mama in a mean mood."

He shrugged. "It sounds like Daddy doesn't want to go."

"It doesn't matter what he wants. If Mama wants us to go, we're going." The second I heard footsteps, I picked up a suitcase and a bag of snacks.

Daddy and Mama joined us in the living room. She looked mad.

"Babies, we decided that we're going to be staying in town." Daddy sat down on the couch beside Joel and wrapped an arm around him. "Does anyone have any questions or concerns?"

Joel hunched his shoulders and looked down at his hands.

"If we stay . . . will we die?" I asked.

Mama crossed her arms and looked to Daddy.

"No baby, we won't," he said.

"They said on TV that New Orleans is already underwater. And that it's shaped like a bowl."

Daddy looked to Mama, but she pointed at me. "Address her concerns. It's your mama that wants to stay, and you are entertaining it."

"Josephine, even if we did leave, Ninety is backed up. Everyone is trying to get out of the city. Who knows when we'll get to Shreveport?" Daddy reasoned.

"Answer your daughter," she said firmly.

Daddy reached out and took my hand. He pulled me onto his knee. "Do you remember the stories Nana told you about Hurricane Betsy?"

I nodded slowly.

"Nana and Granddaddy stayed for Hurricane Betsy. There was some flooding, but they made it through. You know what I say about New Orleans—this city is like a resurrection fern. Even when it's looking bad, New Orleans is never down for the count and that's 'cause of the people. We're going to stay with our girl, ride out the storm, and we'll be okay."

"It's a Category Three now," Mama said.

Daddy looked at the TV. For a second it looked like his eyes got heavy as he watched the TV. I also watched the white angry giant spinning in the water. That huge scary thing looked like it was coming straight for us. I swallowed.

Daddy said, "Is that all she got? She'll die down to a Two, and then a One before she gets here. Any other questions for me, kids?"

I shook my head.

"Okay. Who wants to ride with me to get Nana?"

"Emmett, we don't even have enough food in this house," Mama said.

"Josephine," Daddy said, softly. "You just have to trust me on this one, okay?"

"How can I trust you? Can you make that storm turn around?"

"I can't," he said, standing up. Then he took Mama's hand. "But I can promise that we will get through this together . . . as we've gotten through everything together."

⌘

Mama ran a brush through my hair with extra force.

I winced. "That's too hard, Mama."

With a sigh, she set down the brush and started to braid my hair into plaits.

"I'm sorry, baby. Just got a lot on my mind, that's all."

"Daddy said that he thinks we'll be okay. Do you not believe him?"

She was silent for a few moments. "I don't know what to believe, except that I wasn't trying to stay here. Your daddy is from here. He loves this city. He'll stay with his mama and weather all the storms, but I got a feeling about this one." Mama tied bright blue balls at the end of one finished braid. "I don't know, it's just in my gut, and it's making me uneasy. That storm went from a One to a Three . . . If it gets worse . . ." She focused on the next braid, working a comb through my hair and braiding with her other free hand. "You think we're going to die?"

Mama set the comb down on my shoulder. "Baby, you asked your daddy that question earlier and he said no."

"Do *you* think we gonna die?"

Mama looked up and turned my head back to the mirror. "Your daddy got the house all boarded up. We got what we could from the corner store. We filled up the tub with water. We got a tank full of gas. We have some snacks. Given the short notice, I think we're going to be okay."

I kept my eyes on Mama's, watching as the lines in her forehead creased and got deeper.

······⚬⟊⚬······

I couldn't sleep last night.

Nana was in my room. And when Nana slept in my room, she snored and talked in her sleep.

I crawled out of bed and walked in my white nightgown to the den. I stood in the entryway. Mama's hand was balled against her cheek, her nightcap was on, and she was reading her Bible. Daddy was fiddling with his harmonica. When I stepped into the room, his eyes met mine.

"Whatcha doing up, baby?" he asked in his soft, comforting voice, rich and velvety.

Mama's eyes flashed to me. "Back to bed."

"I can't. Nana is snoring. And she keeps talking in her sleep."

"Back to bed!" Mama said.

Just as I was about to turn to go, Daddy said, "Josephine,

c'mon, cut her a break just for tonight. She's probably up 'cause she's worried about the storm. Ain't that right, cher?"

"That's right, Daddy."

"Come on here." He patted his lap.

I skipped across the floor to Daddy. He pulled me into his lap and hugged me. "You ain't got nothing to worry about, baby."

"You sure, Daddy?"

"I'm sure."

"How do you know?" I asked, placing my hand on his cheek.

"I just know, pumpkin." He kissed me on the nose and then on each of my eyes. I smiled, my eyes closed. "I'm not going to let anything happen to you. Not a damn thing."

"Ohh, Daddy said the D-word."

"Guess I'll have to wash my mouth out with soap."

"Guess so!" I rested my head against his chest.

"Do you wanna tell me how a song sounds?" Daddy asked.

I opened my eyes and nodded.

Daddy placed his mouth against the mouthpiece.

"Emmett, Joel and Nana are sleeping," Mama said.

"Those are two people I don't have to worry about waking up. Both of 'em will sleep through a dynamite explosion."

I glanced at Mama to see if she would fuss anymore; she did not.

Daddy blew life into the harmonica and it came alive, vibrating through my chest and taking me up, taking me off, taking me away.

DÍAS DE LOS MUERTOS
PART II

The wind was howling outside. I flashed the light on Joel. It bounced off the fabric of our tent. Sometimes when it stormed, we asked Daddy to build a tent for us. Tents felt safe. "What are you doing?" I asked.

"Tryna sleep," he muttered.

"How can you sleep with all that noise? It sounds like the roof is about to come off."

Joel remained silent.

Because I couldn't sit still or sleep, I got out of the tent. Nana was sitting up and staring at the wall. I watched her shadow, wondering if I could slip past without her noticing. I took one step. She kept on staring. I took another, and she turned around to face me.

"Where are you going, girl?"

"To go and see what Mama and Daddy are doing."

She kept on staring. I sat on the bed next to her. She hadn't brushed her hair, so it was sticking up all over the place, and she kept rubbing her arms like she was cold.

"What are you doing, Nana?"

She wrapped an arm around me. "I'm just waiting for these winds to die on down so I can get on home and see what state my garden is in."

"You think you have a garden left? The water might wash it all away."

She sucked her teeth. "My garden better still be there. I planted that garden with your granddaddy fifty years ago."

"Didn't y'all get married fifty years ago?"

"You don't forget a thing do you, Jessamine Grace?"

I shook my head. "No."

Nana patted my shoulder. "That's right. Back when your Granddaddy and I got married, we didn't have money for a honeymoon. Shoot, we barely even had enough money to eat. So, we stayed right here in New Orleans and had a stay-moon. We made a garden. We made a baby. . . . That's probably too much information for your young ears."

The wind was screaming—so loud. I held my breath. It screamed and hollered. Whooshing and crashing.

Nana folded her hands and turned her ring over and over.

"Nana, why didn't you want to go up to Shreveport?"

In the darkness, her dark brown eyes were outlined with a ring of purple. They settled on the tent that Joel was still sleeping inside.

"I didn't want to go because my home is here and so is everything I own. That's your mama's people up there in Shreveport. And I don't want to impose myself on 'em. How I see it, I'm able-bodied. I can move around just fine. And if there isn't power for a few days, that'll be okay, too. It's not anywhere we haven't been before."

There was a loud crash. I jumped.

For a few moments, we sat in silence.

"Nana," I asked.

"Yes, baby?"

"Are you lonely?"

"What makes you ask a question like that?" she asked.

"Last night I heard Mama and Daddy say that they thought you were lonely. And that Daddy might need to come and check on you more."

She waved her hand. "They worry too much."

The wind howled and snapped more.

I couldn't wait for it to be over.

⸺⸱ஃ⸱⸺

"Mama, what was the book where the girl was in the attic for a long time?"

Mama patted the spot on the bed between her and Daddy.

"When did I read this book to you? Give me a clue," she said.

"I think you read it around my birthday."

"Was the girl's name Anne?" Mama asked.

"Yes. I think so."

"That book is called *The Diary of Anne Frank*. I was reading it to Darin. That book is a little too mature for you. Why do you ask?"

"'Cause I feel like her. We can't go outside. And I want to get out of this house. Because I'm going crazy." I felt back on the bed and kicked out my legs.

Mama smiled. "Is that right? *You're* going crazy."

"Yes." I stretched out my arms and my legs.

"There's an important difference between you and Anne. She couldn't just go outside after a hurricane passed. She had to hide because her survival was dependent on it. You don't know how lucky you have it. When you're a little older I'll read the book to you. You're still too young to understand all the themes."

I grinned up at Mama. I thought she was the smartest mama in the world. When I grew up, I wanted to be just like her, a teacher. "Can we talk about what we're gonna do when we get out?"

"Sure."

I crawled up to the top of the bed where Mama was. While Mama listened, I went down the list of all the things that I wanted to do. There were at least ten things on the list and it was growing. After Mama listened, she said, "Are you being a good girl and keeping your nana company?"

"I am," I said. "She seems lonely. She stares at the wall a lot. She talks to me, though."

"What'd y'all talk about?" Mama asked.

"Hmm let me see. . . . We talked about her garden, which she doesn't want to die, and we talked about Granddaddy."

Mama looked to Daddy. "She misses him. So does your daddy."

"He's in heaven now, and you don't feel any more pain in heaven."

"Yes." Mama smiled and she started to sing the song she always sang before church, "Jesus Loves Me." While she sang, I crawled into Mama's lap. She wrapped her arms around me and sang to me.

Daddy shifted in the bed beside her.

"Emmett, has that heartburn got any better?" Mama asked.

"Yes, *Mama*," he said, chuckling.

Mama sucked her teeth. "I'm just checking after you, 'cause lord knows you check after everyone but yourself. I done told you that you have to put on your oxygen mask first." She poked Daddy's arm. "You hear me, Emmett?"

"I'm fine," he insisted, kissing her on the cheek. "And who is this we got in the bed with us?" Daddy fixed his face crazy and lunged forward to grab me. I screamed out and kicked out my legs. "I got you! I got you!" He grabbed me and pulled me toward him. I screamed again.

Daddy tickled me and playfully nipped at my ear.

The wind outside was still screaming.

But we were safe inside.

⸺◦§◦⸺

There was a loud BOOM.

Daddy ran outside. I went running after him. Mama told me not to, but I ran out after Daddy anyway.

Coming down the street was an ocean of water. It was like when we were at the beach in Florida, but this wasn't the beach. The waves weren't supposed to crash at you fast on my street. The water wasn't supposed to be in the same place as cars and houses.

Someone standing on a porch started to scream.

And people walking in the streets started running.

Daddy picked me up in his arms. He ran back inside. He slammed the door behind him.

"What's going on?" Mama asked wide-eyed. "It sounded like an explosion?"

"Water is coming."

"What do you mean?" Mama asked, startled.

"Where's Joel? Where's Nana?" Daddy said in a big, booming voice.

"They're still in Jessamine's room," Mama said. "What water?"

"Get what you need, baby. There's water comin' this way . . ." Daddy set me down.

When my feet touched the ground, water started coming in through the doors.

I clung to Daddy.

Mama screamed.

Daddy ran to the back. I heard him holler at Nana and Joel. I had no idea what he was saying.

The brown water continued to pour underneath the door. Mama grabbed me by the arm and ran toward the attic.

The water was now at my ankles.

I latched onto Mama's shorts.

"Where's the ladder?" she screamed.

It kept pouring in. I watched it, shooting underneath the doors.

"Where's the ladder, Emmett?" Mama screamed.

Even though I was scared to let go, I knew that I had to help find the ladder.

I ran off through the house as the water kept rising. Mama screamed my name.

The rising water was up to my knees now.

41
JESSAMINE

Ms. Nadia asked me to meet her before winter break. She was expecting an update on scholarship and college applications. Once again, I was unprepared.

I walked over to the receptionist desk to greet Ms. Sherry. "Happy Holidays, Ms. Sherry!" I placed a baggie of freshly baked sugar cookies, baked by Iz and Joel, in front of her. Her face lit up like a Christmas tree.

"You didn't have to do that, baby!"

"Of course, I did, Ms. Sherry. You know you're my favorite." I winked at her.

She reached across the receptionist desk, her palm facing upward. The enamel cactus pin that I had made for her last year caught the light. I placed my hand inside hers. For some reason, I felt like I could cry. I didn't know why. I just knew that since I woke up, every little thing made me feel emotional.

Ms. Sherry gently stroked my hand. "Baby, whatever it is, whatever you got going on, just know that it's going to be okay."

"I'm fine! I'm just really tired. Senior year is like a roller coaster with nothing but dips and twists." I flashed her a toothy smile, wide and hopefully sincere.

"Ain't that the truth." She was still massaging my hand. I couldn't tell if she bought my story or not. "It has been a long time since I was in your shoes, but I remember never wanting it to end. The only advice I can give you, my baby, is to not get so buried in stress that you miss out on the good stuff. High school only comes once. You won't be able to get that time back."

Her eyes were a deep watery brown. I wished that I could be honest with Ms. Sherry. I didn't think that she would judge me. *Ms. Sherry, I can't do this. I'm so tired and all I want to do is sleep. I'm tired of thinking about college applications and saying good-bye to everyone. I'm tired.*

I didn't say it though. I kept on a Colgate smile and my ready for battle armor. There wasn't time to feel sad. So many people were counting on me—and I didn't want to let them down.

⁓

Before walking into Ms. Nadia's office, I adjusted my skirt. I'd run out of the house looking less than composed because I was running late. My skirt and blazer were wrinkled. My tights had a hole in them, which I of course just noticed, near my ankle. Ms. Nadia was going to read me for filth.

She wasn't alone in her office.

A Black girl who looked to be about my age in a purple skirt and black blouse, with a Chanel purse, was sitting across from her. I walked in on the tail-end of their conversation. Chanel Purse said that all her college applications were complete and that she expected to get a merit scholarship from Duke.

I lingered behind and eavesdropped. Ms. Nadia looked at Chanel Purse with a proud-Mama smile. She nodded to everything that girl said.

I wasn't jealous. I just hated that I had to follow Chanel purse and her Parisian bakery of achievements with my breadcrumbs.

"Jessamine, please join us," Ms. Nadia said.

It took a few moments to realize that Ms. Nadia and her flawless braided bun was talking to me. Chanel Purse turned pristinely in her chair and looked me up and down. Her eyes lingered on the tear in my tights. The way she looked at me made me feel small.

I straightened my back, relaxed my shoulders, and walked over to them with the kind of confidence only an Other could possess.

I didn't wait for Ms. Nadia to introduce me. I held out my hand. "Hi, I'm Jessamine Monet."

Chanel Purse gave me the kind of tight smile you gave someone you were just talking about. "Hi, I'm Brittany. I haven't seen you around before. What school do you go to?"

I told her. Brittany-Chanel-Stank-Attitude's smile got tighter. I didn't bother asking her what school she went to, because honestly, I didn't care. She told me anyway.

"I always love when my mentees meet," Ms. Nadia clasped her hands. She was unusually giddy. "Maybe y'all can grab coffee and discuss some of the schools and scholarships you're applying for?"

That sounded like a terrible idea!

"Maybe," Brittany said snootily. She cast one more scowl at my stockings.

I sat down and crossed my legs.

"Well, Britt." Ms. Nadia stood and walked over to Brittany. When Brittany stood, Ms. Nadia gave her a quick hug. "I'm proud of you."

After Brittany left, Ms. Nadia didn't go back to her Big Boss seat. Instead, she sat down next to me. Her sitting this close made me nervous. It was one thing to get professionally chewed out by her across the desk. But a get-your-act-together tail whooping from this distance . . . gave me instant shivers.

"I need a vacation," Ms. Nadia said.

My edges started to sweat. She never spoke about vacation with me. I was in for it.

Ms. Nadia exhaled. "I can't take a vacation, though, because I'm preparing for a big case. I'll probably be working through Christmas and New Year's. I know you're wondering why I'm telling you all this?"

"I think you're telling me this because you *really* need a vacation!" I giggled, selling a lemon that was dressed like okay lemonade.

Ms. Nadia stared for a while out the window directly behind her Big Boss chair. The window faced the New Orleans skyline. Beyond the skyscrapers the sky was a burdened gray, the kind of gray that promised a late-fall-almost-winter rainstorm.

A sad gray.

"I'm telling you this because I was digging in my drawer the other day and I came across . . ." She leaned forward and grabbed something off her desk. Ms. Nadia held up the water-color on loose-leaf paper. "When I can't physically go to the beach, I pull out this beautiful watercolor. I just stare at it for a while, and then I close my eyes. Can't you hear the waves and the seagulls?"

The tears that I had been successfully holding back were struggling to break free. No more pretending. No more being an Other. I almost reached out to touch the watercolor. Almost. I remembered making it for Ms. Nadia in May. Back then, the beach looked like a happy place. It didn't look happy anymore.

The white sand and crystal-clear water. The big sun in the sky. And the four rainbow-colored chairs meant for four, but would only seat three. Because the fourth person was long gone.

In May, that watercolor had been made for Ms. Nadia. But now I could see it clearly. The watercolor beach was not a dream. It was a life I wished I still had. A watercolor life where Daddy would always join us on the beach.

"What about SCAD?" Ms. Nadia said. "Your talent—"

I couldn't do this. Not right now. "I'm sorry, Ms. Nadia, but I have to . . ." I didn't know what I said. The words wouldn't translate correctly from my mind. All I knew was that I needed to go. I needed to run. So I ran.

⁓⊱⊰⁓

I didn't have an umbrella.

I could've called Joel, Solange, or Iz and asked them to pick me up. I didn't.

The rain pounded down on me. While other people took shelter underneath overhangs of hotels and in coffee shop windows, I defied the rain.

I let it seep into my scuffed ruby-red flats and my tweed blazer. There was a slight bite to the air, and the rain made it worse. That was okay. I raised my arms and skipped over disgusting brown puddles. I considered doing a twirl at the intersection of Poydras Street and St. Charles Avenue.

Like I didn't have a care in the world.

Rain couldn't keep me down.

Beaches couldn't keep me down.

Scholarships and colleges couldn't keep me down. *I banish thee!*

Saying good-bye. Ouch.

I dropped my arms. My soaked tweed jacket felt like its sleeves hung to the street. Even though the rain and my tears made it hard to see, I laughed as the streetlight turned red.

Someone honked and sped around me. "Get out of the street!" they yelled.

I wiped at my eyes and clicked my ruby-red shoes together. It didn't work. I was still in the street. Questioning everything and feeling more than an Other should.

⁓

Chicory and Grind usually played Christmas music after Thanksgiving. Today, what sounded like indie alternative rock was playing. It didn't fit with the Christmas decorations. I grabbed a seat near the window.

Solange wasn't there. I had no idea where she was.

When Joel saw me, he asked, "Why are you wet?"

"It's raining," I responded, not wanting to get into it with him.

"Don't you have an umbrella?" He grabbed my hand.

I jerked my hand free. "I don't like this music. Make it Christmas."

"You're being a brat."

I knew that I was being a brat. I'd rather be a brat than a Sad Girl. Being a brat or pretending like I was someone else always made life go down easier. A spoonful of fantasy always made the heartache go down.

"If you don't come to the breakroom where there is a heater and extra clothes, I'm calling Mom."

"You wouldn't dare."

"Try me. It's cold outside. You're gonna get sick."

I could've argued with Joel some more, but I wasn't at my best. And he never let me get away with pretending. He wasn't Tennessee. Joel called me out on my bullshit. Didn't he understand how much that hurt, to have to be real? I stood up; my whole body ached. Joel led me to the breakroom.

"Take off that thing," Joel said bossily, pointing to my jacket.

I shrugged it off. Water pitter-pattered onto the floor. Joel took the jacket and held it away from his body.

"Do y'all ever have any customers?" I asked.

"Yes."

I spotted an open notebook on the table. I wondered if it was Joel's notebook or Tennessee's.

Joel grabbed a heater from the closet and plugged it in. The red light flashed bright, and hot air warmed my damp tights. Joel was moving so fast. That made me want to cry, too. Joel always took care of me. He grabbed his gym bag and took out an oversize gray sweater and a pair of gray sweats.

Gray.

I was so tired of that color.

"Put this on," he ordered.

"It says Oxford." I stared down at the bold red letters. "Oxford, Mississippi, or Oxford, England?" I said *Oxford, England* with a British accent.

Joel didn't even bat an eyelash. "Mississippi. I borrowed this from Tennessee when we went to Oxford for Thanksgiving. Put it on."

"You should give it back."

"You can give it back," Joel said.

I started to fuss at him, but Tennessee took that moment to walk in with Saint. They were both wearing rain jackets. Tennessee's was classic yellow and Saint's was bright pink. They shook out their umbrellas.

"Jessamine, did you go swimming?" Saint asked.

I found a smile for Saint. "Not swimming, just dancing in the rain." I sang a little simple and light la-de-da song, raising my hands in the air and twirling around. *I'm okay, y'all! I'm fine. I'm so good.*

Joel, Tennessee, and Saint refused to buy my lemonade. They stared back at me with pinched faces. They poured my sour lemonade out at the stand. What was happening? I used to be so much better at throwing people off how I was actually feeling.

"Joel, why don't we pick up where we left off on Magazine Street an hour ago? I've always been a fan of public displays of affection," Saint suggested.

"I have homework," Joel said dryly.

"Public displays of affection!" I swiveled my head in Joel's direction. "I need all the details. What did I miss!"

"Nothing, nosy. You need to focus on getting out of those wet clothes," Joel complained.

I playfully pushed Joel away. "Saint? Details! Did y'all kiss in the rain?"

"I'm dry, unlike you. So obviously no." Joel groaned.

Saint kicked off his rainboots and set his umbrella by the back door. "Your twin kissed me in front of everyone and their mama. It was tres bon." Saint sauntered over to Joel and took his hand. I watched as Saint dragged Joel out of the break room. "I promise to spill all the tea once you're no longer sopping wet. Your teeth are chattering, love."

My teeth were not . . .

They were gone before I could say anything else

Tennessee stood across from me. It was so silent. The buzzing sound of the heater and the steady dripping of water from my clothes onto the floor filled the space.

"Jess, you should get changed or you'll catch a cold."

He sounded just like Joel. That was annoying . . . and sweet. "I know."

His eyes lingered, like he was 85 percent worried. I kicked off my ruby-red flats.

Tennessee walked over to me. His bright blue boots made squishy echo sounds on the floor. "How come I didn't know that you and Joel were born on Christmas?"

"I'm sure I told you."

Tennessee took off his rain jacket and draped it on a chair. "No, I would remember that. Saint said a while back that Joel was a Capricorn, but he didn't say when his birthday was until about thirty minutes ago. He mentioned needing to get a present for Joel's birthday and Christmas since it falls on the same day."

"Why didn't you run then?"

Tennessee opened his mouth and then closed it. The expression on his face was perplexed. "Why didn't you run?"

"I did run," I said.

"You came back."

I glanced at his sweater. He was wearing both the satsuma and book pins I made for him. The pins were near his heart.

It was raining so hard outside, pounding against the roof.

Tennessee didn't back down. I also didn't back down. I couldn't afford to answer his question. Not now, when it felt like I was drowning.

Tennessee inched closer.

I fought the urge to step back and press my hands against his chest. *Stay back. Don't come any closer. I can't love you. I don't want to even like you.* But I . . . I did love him and like him. That was the problem.

Tennessee pressed his hands, hidden behind the sleeves of his Polo Ralph Lauren sweater, which was strangely fashionable for him, against my cheeks. "Do you remember the deer stand? You were there for me."

I kept my eyes on his, saying nothing. He had a point.

Tennessee made this motion like windshield wipers on my cheeks. On a good day I would've teased him for being so Tennessee.

"I can be there for you, too. I want to be there for you, too."

You're not my boyfriend. The sharp cutting words almost flew out of my mouth like daggers. I flinched.

The lights dimmed.

I couldn't do this. I couldn't be the person Ms. Nadia needed me to be. I couldn't be the person Joel needed me to be. I couldn't be the daughter Mama wanted me to be. I didn't even know what *I* wanted to be.

I closed my eyes and touched Tennessee's sweater-covered hand. "You're going to make somebody really happy one day, Tennessee Williams. You got a heart of gold, kid. Don't let anyone tell you differently."

"All I want—" he started.

Because I knew where he was going, I stood on my tippy toes and kissed him. His soft lips tasted like a Christmas medley of chocolate and peppermint. In that kiss I silently whispered against his lips, *Forget me.*

When our lips parted, he said, "All I want is to make you happy."

42
JESSAMINE

"SO YOU AND SAINT ARE DATING?" Solange asked Joel a few days later. She stepped back to observe my Christmas tree decorating skills. The Christmas tree needed a lot of work. It was one of those fake trees, and it was missing several fake branches.

"I guess?" Joel shrugged.

Solange grabbed the ornament that I just placed. "Not there, this side is too busy." Rudely, she pushed me to the back of the tree. "That side needs some love. It's barren! And Joel, what do you mean you guess? I need details."

Solange was doing the most. With Joel, you couldn't ask too many questions. He shut down 100 percent of the time. But we all knew that one step in the right direction did not confirm that he and Saint were about to skip into the sunset.

She snapped her fingers at me. "Pass me that gold glitter ornament that Joel made in the second grade."

Why did I even bother helping her decorate! She micromanaged me and snapped her fingers at me like my name was Fido! Where was the love? Not in Auntie Myrtle's house, that was for sure!

Joel passed Solange the decoration. He paused and looked at it, confused. "I thought we lost all our ornaments in Katrina?"

"Not the ones my mama kept." Solange snatched the

ornament from Joel. "That woman was too cheap to buy her own Christmas ornaments, so she lifted them off other folks' trees. Yes, even kin. Just 'cause you're blood don't make you immune."

She flipped her hair off her shoulder and her burdened eyes fell on me. It was probably the fifth glance I got since arriving at Auntie Myrtle's house. "Jessamine is too good to help us do Christmas."

I rolled my eyes. "Not true! Every time I place down an ornament, you move it!" I narrowed my eyes at her hand, which was perched over an ornament placed by me. Exhibit A.

"Jessamine." Solange snatched up the ornament shamelessly and placed it elsewhere. "This 'tree,' if you can call it that, is threadbare. I think my mama got it from Wally World when we were living in Shreveport. There ain't much you can do to it."

"Wrong! I can always pimp out a tree. Even the saddest Charlie Brown ones. Who wants a refill on eggnog?" Neither of them responded fast enough, so I excused myself to refill my own already-full glass.

In the kitchen, I took a break. My mind was all over the place. After helping Solange decorate Auntie Myrtle's house for Christmas, Tennessee and I were going to go and see the Alvin Ailey American Dance Theater. Somehow, he found out that I always wanted to go to a show. I suspected Iz. That traitor.

We were in an okay place. The best place we had ever been. I enjoyed being around him. It was easy. Easy like slipping on my favorite sweater. He was easy. Yet . . . I was uneasy.

I had to run.

"Jessamine," Solange called. "We need a DJ."

I breathed in. With a nod, I joined my cousin and twin back in the den.

Solange tossed me her phone. "Play Mariah Carey or 'Santa Baby' first, and then you can DJ. Oh, also make sure to play 'Last Christmas' by WHAM. Oh and . . ."

"Girl, you are picking all the songs I slay in. I stay living on Christmas Tree Lane with Mariah and WHAM, don't play!"

Solange broke into a falsetto. "Trust me, I'm ready to play."

Even with all my talk, I wasn't. I put on "Santa Baby."

Solange lit up brighter than her sad Charlie Brown Christmas tree and started to sing, her voice dropping to a soft purr. She danced around the threadbare tree, rearranging the lights to cover up giant spaces where fake branches were missing. If you asked me, the tree needed more lights and more glitter.

She pointed to a reindeer ornament that I *knew* was mine because it had *Jessamine Monet, fourth grade* written on the back.

"Ah, that's where Boudreaux the reindeer went!" I exclaimed.

Solange tapped the ornament with an approving smile. "This is my favorite stolen one. I stole this one myself."

I gasped, "You stole from a child!"

Solange sucked her teeth. "A badass child."

"So that makes it better? Ornament thief!"

She winked and continued to sing "Santa Baby."

⸺⟡⸺

I looked down at Auntie Myrtle's obituary, which was still sitting on the table. "When are you going back to your room in Treme?"

"Mama left me this house," Solange said. "It's all paid off."

"I didn't know she did that. Do you still have your Treme spot?"

Solange nodded. "Yeah, but the lease is ending soon, so I'm thinkin' about staying here for a bit. I'll have to pay the property taxes. But at least I won't be throwing money down the drain anymore with expensive rent." She stared off just past my head. "It's a strange place to be—you know my mama left me some money? Did Joel tell you?"

"What?"

"She left me some serious coins."

"Two dollars and fifty cents?"

"No, sis. She left me some *real* coins."

"How?" Auntie Myrtle had always been cheap. She stole Christmas ornaments instead of buying her own. The only person she bought new clothes for was herself. Solange always had to go to school in used clothes. And it wasn't because Auntie Myrtle couldn't afford it. She was an accountant. Well . . . she used to be an accountant.

"It turns out my mom's penny pinching paid off. Every dime she wasn't using to buy me clothes was going toward my college fund and her retirement. She blew through her retirement with the cancer treatment, but she didn't touch my college fund."

I tilted my head. "You only went to Southern for one semester and dropped out."

"Rude!" Solange said, giving me the hand. "But true. Mama converted it into a savings account when I dropped out, with the hope that one day I'd go back to Southern or at least college, periodt."

My heart filled with joy at the thought of Auntie Myrtle saving up for Solange's education. Even when Solange chose to go her own way and Auntie Myrtle fussed her, Auntie Myrtle never stopped loving her. She could've done something else with Solange's college fund. She could've bought new cornucopia hats. She could've bought a roomful of mints to suck on ferociously when someone pissed her off. She didn't.

"What are you going to do with her house and money?"

Solange smiled down at a gingerbread house ornament. I was positive that one was also mine. *She is such a thief!*

"Well, just the other day I was making money moves and talking to financial advisors. New wig, who dis?"

"What!" I gave her a high-five with both hands and closed my fingers in hers.

"And I've been thinking about going back to college for a degree in business administration."

"Solange!"

She placed the gingerbread house on the tree. "Who knows, maybe God will have me sitting up in college the same time as y'all. Since I'm about to be finished with having to pay that Treme rent, your girl has options."

---·····๛·····---

Tennessee answered the door wearing a hunter-green polo and jeans. He hugged me and told me to come in.

"Are your parents here?" I asked him.

"No, they're in Destin."

I held onto him for a few moments longer, thinking about daisies, picnics, vulnerability, and good-byes. With his hand still on my lower back, he guided me inside. I looked around wide-eyed.

"Let me finish the steaks and then I'll give you a tour."

His mention of a tour made me freeze. *No room!* I didn't

think it would be a good idea to see his room here. Rooms had beds. And Tennessee was looking like a light snack and I was feeling peckish (ACT word of the day). Instead, I smiled and followed him into the kitchen and out to the back.

He was standing over the grill. "It needs a few more minutes and then we'll be in business."

Next, Tennessee took me on the promised tour.

He showed me the study. The dining room. The game room, which he said they never used because they were rarely in the same space at the same time. Probably for the best.

He didn't show me his room, though. Which was okay with me.

After dinner, we went to the Mahalia Jackson Theater. Our seats were in the front. As the show began, the lights dimmed and the dancers rushed out onto the stage.

I looked to Tennessee. He was splitting his attention between watching the dancers and watching me.

The water had been rising since we left Oxford. And I had been kicking my legs to stay above it. But it was rising so fast. And everywhere I swam, there he was, looking at me. Watching me. Touching me. Kissing me. And I didn't know what to do with any of that.

I did not know how to hand him the key and let him in.

My hands started to shake as I got to thinking about that day and night and endless series of days where the heat was clawing and the water was a stagnant, stinking, rising pool of bodies. Bloated starfish. Plump over-boiled dumplings. The strangest fruit of all. I brought my hands to my throat as the oxygen started to cut off.

I was suddenly back in the attic.

With the body, the stink, the death.

And I knew we were all going to die.

I swallowed hard and focused on the stage. There was a dancer up front. She was Black, her hair was naturally curly, her hands were over her eyes, hiding her face from the world. When she dropped her hands, she screamed. The other dancers rushed around her. They pulled. They pushed. She flipped and tumbled. She crawled and reached out. The dancers all collapsed into her, hiding her body. All that could be seen was her hand reaching out. She tumbled and crawled again. Horror was all over her face, and no one could see that she was dying.

I saw death.

I saw it when we got up to the attic.

The whites of Daddy's eyes still haunted me.

When I'm at school. When I'm with Iz. When I'm pretending. When I'm lying. When Tennessee is kissing me. When he's touching me. When he tells me he loves me . . . I still see the whites of Daddy's eyes. And I remember how this horrible thing that happened forever ago, this thing that I wasn't supposed to remember, still hurt.

"Are you okay?" Tennessee asked.

I stood up. "I need . . . I'm sorry . . ." I said excuse me to several people as I made my way through the aisle. I didn't even know if he was behind me, all I knew was that I needed to get out. And get away. Mahalia Jackson Theater was filling up with water and strange fruit was everywhere.

DÍAS DE LOS MUERTOS
PART III

The water. It was everywhere. It was in our house. It was in my mouth. It was in my ears.

"Breathe in. Breathe out."

My lungs were on fire. I tried to scream, but more water choked me.

"Again, baby."

I grabbed onto his hand and held so tight.

"Again, baby." Daddy's nostrils flared and then got smaller. "Again!"

I sucked as much air into my lungs as I could, but every time I tried to let it go, I choked.

Mama was crying in the corner, sandwiched between Nana and Joel. "We're going to die in this attic. We're going to die. Emmett, I told you! I told you!"

Daddy raised his hand. "Jessamine, listen to me. . . . Okay, baby."

My lungs were glued shut. The more I tried to breathe, the more it hurt. I clawed at my throat with wide eyes. I gasped for air. Why couldn't I breathe? *Where did all the air go?*

The water was now gurgling and bubbling up into the attic.

I gripped on tighter to Daddy's shoulders. We were going to die. *We were going to die.*

He pulled me into his arms. "Breathe, Jessamine!"

It was so hot. So hot.

I couldn't . . .

I couldn't . . .

As my head started to get heavy and the world fuzzy . . .

I saw Daddy.

Holding me so tight. Nostrils flaring. Nostrils falling.

And then I felt a hand in mine. A squeeze. Fingers inside mine.

In the fuzzy darkness, I turned to the right and I saw Mama.

"Breathe, Jess. You're okay, Jess. You're okay."

Tears fell down my cheeks and my lips trembled.

Breathe.

I sucked as much of the steaming hot air into my lungs as I could.

Breathe!

Water rushed around my ballet slippers.

Daddy kept me in his arms and Mama held onto my hand.

Even though it hurt and I was so afraid, I kept breathing. In. Out.

The water was now past my ankles.

I closed my eyes tight and focused on the feeling of Daddy's chest. He cradled my head above the water like he used to do when we went swimming.

Don't let me go, I used to tell him.

I won't, baby. I won't let you go.

And whenever his hand would pull away, I would tell him, *You promised that you wouldn't let go.* And he would say that he would only let me go once I was ready to swim on my own.

Baby, just pretend you're a mermaid. You can. You will. Swim on your own.

Through blurry eyes, I kicked my legs back and forth, pretending that it was a fin.

And my lungs started to get stronger, up until I felt the air whooshing in and out of my lungs again. I was breathing . . . and dying.

Even though the water was still rising, I kept kicking my legs back and forth. Swimming even though we were all drowning.

As I looked up at Daddy, I saw the smile on his face fall . . .

And his face twisted up.

I screamed.

Daddy's hands dropped from my head and went to his chest.

43
TENNESSEE

SHE WAS RUNNING.

It was flurrying outside. I didn't even realize that New Orleans could get cold enough. The wind snapped at palm trees and whipped Christmas lights from left to right. Through the blur of white, I followed Jessamine's red coat and her curly black hair. I jogged up to her. She had finally stopped.

I had no idea what was going on. I kept trying to find blame with myself. That I did something or said something. But deep down, I knew that I hadn't.

"Jess, what's going on?"

"I'm sorry, Tenn."

"Jess, wait!"

She stopped. "Please, Tennessee . . . just—just let me go."

I held onto her, my fingers wrapping around her arms. She'd found me in the deer stand in Mississippi. When I ran, she came after me. She didn't leave.

Jessamine's brown eyes filled with tears.

"What's wrong?" I whispered.

She tried to dart around me, but I blocked her, refusing to let go.

"Please, just tell me what I did. I thought everything was going okay."

"You didn't do anything." She shook her head and tried to move away from me again. Jessamine squeezed her eyes shut. It was almost like she didn't even want to look at me.

"We don't have to go back to the performance. I think there's is a coffee shop around here. We can go talk. Or we don't have to. I just want to make sure you're okay."

Jessamine backed away from me. "I'm sorry."

"You don't have to be sorry about anything."

"I do." Her lips trembled. "I do. You are so amazing."

My fingers loosened around her arms.

"I can't . . ." She bit down on her lip.

"Jessamine, don't do that. Don't . . ."

Jessamine shook her head. "This isn't fair to you. I shouldn't have let this go this far. It's my fault. You deserve someone who can love you back."

"Jess, don't do this."

"You deserve that, Tennessee. I can't give you that."

"There isn't a perfect way to love someone. I told you about my parents."

"I don't know how to do this."

"I don't know how to do it either, but we can figure it out together. I thought that was what we were doing."

"I'll hurt you."

"You're the best thing that's ever happened to me!"

"*Tennessee.*"

"It's true!" I was doing too much, saying too much, I could feel it in my bones and hear it in my voice, but I couldn't make myself stop.

"Even if it's true . . ." She pulled away from me. "Even if it's true, we can't do this anymore. I can't keep treating you like this. I see what my brother does to Saint. And I know it's what I do to you."

"It's not. It's different. I know you love me, you told me that."

"I'm not good for you," she said with hard eyes, frustrated eyes.

"You can't tell me what's good for me and what's not good for me. You can't tell me that."

She looked away, her jaw set, and tears in her eyes.

"Do you love me?" I asked in a small voice.

She closed her mouth, flecks of snow settled in her eyelashes and in her hair, but she didn't seem to see it.

"You told me you loved me in Oxford. Were you lying?"

She turned away.

"Were you lying to me?"

"No," she muttered. "I was not."

I wanted to take her hands again. Force her to understand that I loved her. And I loved her in a way that wasn't fickle. She didn't understand. When I showed my ugliest side to her, she didn't run. She stayed. She held me. She kissed me. She checked on me. She loved me—even when I was in a space where I didn't have much love for myself.

Why wouldn't she let me do the same?

If you love me, you'll stay.

If you love me, you'll trust me.

If you love me, you will let me do for you, like you do for me.

I took her hands again and I rubbed my thumbs in a circular motion, warming up her cold fingers.

Jessamine stared into my eyes. "When I said I loved you . . . I meant that. I do love you, as much as I can love anyone . . .

and because I love you . . . because you make me feel like—like it's Friday all the time, even on the worst days, I know that I have to let you go."

Please don't do this.

Please, don't.

"I don't want to hurt you."

"Then don't hurt me."

"I don't want to hurt you. But I end up hurting you anyway."

"Don't leave me, please don't."

She touched my face with cold hands and took a step back.

Jessamine left.

⁂

After she left, I wandered around the Quarter.

Musicians were playing Christmas songs on strings and fiddles.

Tourists were snapping pictures.

A man was walking up to people jingling a tin can and motioning for food to be dropped into his mouth.

The palm trees on Canal were all lit up.

I made another loop, walking along the river, and pausing on the banks to stare out at the dark, turbulent waves. The last ferry of the night was pulling away toward Algiers, and the *Steamboat Natchez* was whistling "What a Wonderful World."

For the last couple of months, I hadn't written a thing. I gave up on one destructive coping mechanism to chase another. Living gave me a purpose. Jessamine made me feel like someone, somebody loved. That was new for me.

Jessamine had helped me find confidence. The confidence

to speak. And the confidence to bet on me. She also showed me what it felt like to feel so much all at once. Fear. Love. Heartache. Hurt. Power. Strength. Weakness. Honesty.

She also showed me how to love. And now . . .

All I felt was this stabbing in my chest.

How could she be gone?

How?

When only weeks ago, we were sitting by the fireplace having a hard, honest conversation.

She took me to Wonderland.

And Wonderland ended here, on the banks of the Mississippi.

44
TENNESSEE

On Christmas, Dad came home.

He didn't give me the same space that Mom gave me.

"Rebel, come on downstairs and eat breakfast with me and your mama."

When I didn't respond, Dad walked over to the bed and sat down. He pulled back the covers.

"I'll be down in a minute," I mumbled.

"How long is this going to go on for?" he asked, tight-lipped.

"How long is what going to go on for?"

"You moping around the house. Staying in bed for days. Have you even showered, son?"

"Yeah, Daddy."

He sighed. A deep sigh like my existence annoyed him. "Your mom is worried about you, Reb."

For some reason that made me laugh. She was worried about me? How come she got to be worried after I had a few bad days, but I was supposed to ignore several bad *months* from her?

"What's so funny?"

"Nothing," I muttered.

"I don't like your attitude. Get up. Take a shower. Put on some clothes and eat breakfast with us." Dad turned away from me.

I watched his back and wondered if he ever felt human emotions. Did he ever hurt? Did he feel sad? Could his tear ducts produce actual tears or did he cry testosterone?

"After we eat, you can open your presents." Dad reached behind him and he ruffled my hair. "I missed you, Reb."

That sounded sincere. In the past I would've told Dad that I missed him, too. This time I didn't.

⸙

Later that day, I headed over to Saint's house. His gift was tucked underneath my arm. It was meticulously wrapped and topped with a bow. After a few months of being Saint's friend, I understood that presentation was everything to him.

He answered the door wearing a red onesie with antlers. I did a double take.

"Don't laugh!"

"I won't." I leaned in to give him a one-armed hug. "But what is this?"

"This, Nashville, is called Christmas joy." Saint did a spin. "Don't worry, you have some Christmas joy in your stocking, too. Come in!"

I stepped into the Baptiste palace. On a regular day it was stunning. During the holidays—red bows were everywhere, garlands and mistletoes, too. Even the replica of the David statue in the corner was festive with multi-colored blinking lights. I kicked off my boots by the door.

Instrumental Christmas classics were playing on low— "Carol of the Bells" currently. A waiter wearing a black tux and a red bowtie was standing near the stairs with flutes of what looked like eggnog.

"Saint, do you want to open your gift now?"

He paused at the foot of the stairs. "Let's open our gifts later." He flicked his wrist toward the towering Christmas tree at the far corner of the foyer. "Set that down next to your gifts."

Gifts. Plural.

"Do you want eggnog?" he asked, starting up the stairs.

"I dislike eggnog," I said, walking across the polished marble floor to the gigantic tree. It was so big that it had to have taken an army of people to decorate it. I set Saint's gift down. My eyes scanned the gifts underneath the tree. There were several for me. Several for Joel. And he also had a gift for Jessamine and Iz. Saint had such a huge heart.

"Follow me, Nashville!" he called from the top of the steps.

I jogged back to the winding stairs. Once on the second floor, Saint gave me a whirlwind tour. Like the first floor, the second was full of art, sculpture, books, and various artifacts from around the world.

The last stop on the second-floor tour was Saint's room. His room was surprisingly plain. Cream walls—I'm sure the color wasn't really cream, it was probably some color with a French name. He had a California king-size bed in the middle. Floor-to-ceiling windows showcased a balcony and a view of other Garden District mansions.

Saint picked up a camo onesie on his bed. "This is yours."

"Camo!" I probably owned three camo items, tops—a camo jacket, camo boots, and a camo shirt that Dad got me last spring. I rarely wore any of them.

Saint snickered. "Yeah, buddy. I can't twin with you. You done glowed up since August and I'm not about to be out-glowed by you. Even if I love ya, it ain't happening!"

Saint said that I'd glowed up. I wondered how, but I didn't ask. "Fine." I motioned for him to give me the camo onesie. "For you, I'll wear this egregious outfit."

"Hey! Don't knock the Christmas joy, and ACT words are banned in this house! We are done with standardized tests."

"What a relief." I walked over to a chair facing Second Street. I pulled off my sweater and then pulled down my jeans. Jessamine suddenly popped into my mind. I remembered that time she danced on Second Street. I closed my eyes and went back to that night. That night when it felt like we had more time.

That was the first time I fell in love with her.

I opened my eyes. The lampposts, the old live oaks, and Jessamine dancing disappeared. There was just the street now and the century-old houses bathed in sunlight.

I slipped on the camo onesie and pulled the hood with reindeer antlers over my head. "What now, boss?"

Saint snapped his fingers and did a twirl. "We dance. Open all the windows. And the doors just in case we want to tear it up on the balcony, too."

"Yessir." I felt good. Great, actually. I pulled up all the windows and opened the doors leading to the balcony.

Saint went to his computer, and seconds later "Jingle Bell Rock" filled the room. Saint started to dance first. Surprisingly, his dancing was worse than mine! But I guess I had no business judging anyone's dancing skills.

Saint did a cartwheel.

I jumped up and down, throwing my hands up in the air. I shook my hips like I was balancing a hula-hoop on them, and Saint did the same.

We were both so off rhythm to the song, but it was okay. My best friend and I were dancing uncoordinated and totally free to the rhythm of our own beat.

45
JESSAMINE

BIRTHDAYS ALWAYS MADE ME SAD.

I never showed it, though. Birthdays were when I really became an Other.

I took my sadness and I mixed it with a shot of pep, a teaspoon of energy, and skipped through the day like I didn't have a care in the world. I had to—because I knew how much our birthday meant to Mama.

On birthdays she went all out. She made her world-famous vanilla cake with homemade buttercream frosting for me, and her carrot cake with homemade buttercream frosting for Joel. Mama also went all out on gifts. She often took on additional shifts between Thanksgiving and Christmas just to sprinkle extra cheer underneath the Christmas tree.

I stared into the mirror in my room, practicing a smile. Practicing a laugh. Throwing my head back. I did a twirl and a spin. Still, the sadness stayed. I would need a little extra makeup to make the sadness go away.

I treated my face like a canvas. I painted my lips a bold shade of red and applied a striking glittery green eyeshadow to my eyes. I didn't stay in the lines. I painted green glitter underneath my eyes, I painted past my eyebrows, I painted to the creases. It almost looked like I was wearing a mask. I loved it.

When I went downstairs, I found Iz, Solange, Joel, and Mama already waiting in the kitchen.

"Finally!" Joel cried. "We've only been waiting for an hour."

He was so dramatic. It had only been forty-five minutes, tops!

"What's that rash on your face?" Solange asked disrespectfully.

"It's not a rash! Rude. It's called makeup." I hurried over to the table and took my spot between Joel and Iz.

Mama held out blue and pink lighters. I quickly took the blue one and started to light my delicious vanilla cake, while Joel took the pink lighter to light the foul carrot cake.

After our cakes were lit, Iz, Solange, and Mama sang "Happy Birthday" in perfect harmony.

"Make a wish!" Mama said.

I closed my eyes.

I wished to be a bird

　　　so I could fly free.

I opened my eyes and blew out the candles.

⸻⸻

An hour later, Solange, Joel, Iz, and I gathered in the living room on an old blanket. Two cups of water sat between us and various trays of watercolors.

Because I was in the Christmas spirit, I painted a town square with a huge Christmas tree in the middle. After the paint dried, I would go back and add specks of white for snow. This painting would be called "A Christmas Square in Rhode Island."

"How's the painting that I'm going to be hanging in my dorm coming?" Iz asked, leaning over to observe and claim my Rhode Island square.

"How much are you paying me for it?" I asked, pointing my paintbrush at her.

"Eternal love?"

"Ding, ding, ding, sold to the highest bidder!"

She giggled. "My hands are getting tired. Do you wanna go to your room for a little bit?"

I said yes, even though I knew that Iz only pulled people to the side when she was worried. Maybe my dramatic makeup gave me away? Once we got to my room, I shut the door. I sank down on my bed, and Iz took the spot beside me.

Tennessee's Oxford sweater was spread out on my bed. It was there because I planned on asking Joel to give it back to him. Iz casually glanced at the sweater. She was probably reading too much into its placement.

"Jess, you have two options. The first option—we can consult our library for a book of your choice." She pointed her gingerbread-socked foot in the direction of a pile of books by my bed. "Or we can go with the second option and you can talk to me about whatever."

Sitting there with Iz reminded me that in the very near future we might not be able to do this. What was I going to do without impromptu therapy sessions that involved a little crying, a little reading, and a lot of laughing? What was I going to do without her?

"Option two."

"Yay!" She clapped her hands and rocked from side-to-side. "Hug first?"

Iz opened her arms wide. Like the tides on the beach, I crashed into her. I gripped onto the fabric of her cropped pullover sweater that had an alligator wearing a Christmas hat on it. For a while we just held each other.

For that while, I felt safe, and my mind was quiet.

"I think that I've been a fantastic liar."

"Hmm?" she asked, leaning away from me.

"I thought that I was so brave. But I realized that I've just been scared, Iz. Senior year scared me. It forced me to think about change. All of these changes came so quick, and I guess I did everything that I could to resist them."

"Change sucks, one hundred," she said.

I broke our embrace and brought my knees up to my chest, hugging my tights.

There was a small Christmas tree with a paper birthday hat on it sitting on my desk. The lights on the tree twinkled white, red, blue, and green.

Twinkle,

    Twinkle,

        Little

            Star.

"I have to accept it. Change is coming. It doesn't matter what I do. It's coming."

"Is it just change that you're fearing?" Iz asked, resting her hand on my back.

My lips trembled. I didn't want to cry.

"Let it out, Jess." Iz rubbed my back in a soothing circular motion.

Tears streamed down my cheeks. A river of tears that I had been holding in since the start of senior year. As I cried, I allowed my mind to roam free.

All my life, my friends and family had been my security blanket. When Daddy passed and we had to move to Shreveport, I realized just how quickly the world could feel unsafe. I went from having everything—so much love, so much joy—to realizing that everything could be snatched away in an instant.

Shreveport was not the fairy tale that Daddy sold me in New

Orleans. Shreveport came with family members I didn't know, a new school, no Iz, and no more music from Daddy.

When we moved back to New Orleans, I did everything that I could to recreate the dream that Daddy sold me. When it didn't work, I pretended to be someone else. An Other. And on the occasions when it didn't work and I couldn't be someone else, I had my friends and family to lean on. Now, they were scattering like marbles.

I licked my trembling lips; they tasted like salt.

The scattering of marbles and the fear of good-byes was what caused me to push Tennessee away. I didn't know it when I was with him, but in the weeks without him, I'd time to reflect. It sunk in. Tennessee was just another person to leave me behind.

That was why I fought his watercolors and all the light he shined in my life. New boys were supposed to bring gray clouds and forgettable moments. They were supposed to remain library books that could be returned guilt-free. But he became a boy that colored my dreams.

He made me love him.

And because I loved him, that made him someone I would always miss.

⋯⋯⋯∽ℓ∘⋯⋯

The day after Christmas, the Monets had a family tradition. We went to the cemetery where Daddy was buried. Nana, who had passed away shortly after we moved back to New Orleans from Shreveport, and Grandaddy were also buried in the family plot.

Solange joined us this time because she wanted to visit Auntie Myrtle.

It was a cool and sunny day. The kind of day that made me feel like Daddy, Nana, Grandaddy, and Auntie Myrtle were all smiling down on us.

Mama sat down a vase of roses in front of the aboveground tomb. MONET was etched on front. I felt an ache in the pit of my stomach as I looked at Mama's name right underneath Daddy's. She closed her eyes and whispered something that only Daddy and our ancestors were meant to hear.

I bumped my shoulder into Joel, who was standing solemnly beside me. "You're quiet."

"I was just thinking," he said. "I was wondering if Daddy would be proud of me. I'd like to think that he would be—even if we didn't see eye to eye on everything."

I started to tell Joel that Daddy would be proud of him. But Mama beat me to it.

"He would be proud of you. He'd be proud of both of you." Mama stood up and she joined me and Joel. She used her hips to make room in the middle between us. "You know how I know?"

"How, Mama?" Joel asked.

"I know he'd be proud because I am proud."

The sun, which had disappeared behind a cloud, made a radiant appearance. It cast a golden glow on the rows of tombs.

Solange sauntered over. She was dressed dramatically in a body-hugging black dress that showed off all her curves and a Parisian-looking hat with netting. This look read widowed femme fatale. "Who wants Café du Monde?" she said.

"Me!" I said.

"That sounds perfect," Mama said.

"Who has cash?" Joel asked the group.

Solange raised her hand. "The one that made the Café du

Monde suggestion." She opened her Bendi-not-a-Fendi purse and flashed some bills. "Your girl doesn't have to worry about making that Treme rent no more, so she stays in the green. Let's go. Café du Monde on me!"

Solange led the way, swishing her hips from side to side down the avenue of aboveground tombs.

Mama, Joel, and I walked after Solange. I glanced over my shoulder at the Monet tomb. The sun was still shining bright. I smiled. Daddy was definitely here. I felt him in the sun, in the air, and in the trees. "I love you, Daddy," I whispered.

46
TENNESSEE
February

"RICHARD, DO YOU HAVE A PROBLEM?" Mom narrowed her eyes at Dad.

I looked up from my boudin-stuffed quail. We were sitting in a courtyard at a fancy old dame restaurant in the French Quarter. It was cold enough for our waitress to turn the heater on for us. With the way Mom and Dad were acting, taking turns blowing hot air, the waitress might need to turn off the heater.

Even though she was talking to him, Dad was looking at me, as if I had mutated.

"I do," he said.

I returned to my boudin, which was probably the best boudin I'd had since moving to Louisiana.

"Rebel, you know that person?" he asked, setting his fork and knife down.

"Yep, we're friends." I stuffed a forkful of boudin into my mouth and motioned my fork in Dad's direction. "Daddy, you're not eatin' your food."

"I don't have an appetite." Dad pushed away his plate.

Mom was still glaring at him as if she was daring him to say something, anything. He looked at her once and his attention was back on me. "Son, who is that person to you?"

At the beginning of January, Solange told Joel and me that she was scaling back on her jobs. I had been disappointed to find out that one of the jobs that didn't make the cut was manager at Chicory and Grind. But I understood.

Since we didn't hang out outside of work, I hadn't seen her in a couple of weeks. It was the best surprise to go to a Mardi Gras–themed brunch with Mom and Dad only to find out that Solange was our waitress.

"Who is that person to you, Reb?" Dad repeated. I wasn't sure how many whiskey sours he'd had at this point.

"Does that matter?" Mom snapped.

Dad clenched his jaw. "Lauralee, we are not getting into a fight." He balled his fist and set it down on the table. "I'm just asking Rebel a question."

"I don't like the question you're asking, Richard," she said.

I waited for Mom to do something dramatic, like flip the table herself or call our waitress, Solange, back to the table. She did neither.

"Y'all. We're here to celebrate Mama getting positive feedback from her agent on her latest book. And Daddy, you moving to New Orleans. Let's keep the mood light." I said it without feeling the usual pinch of nerves. There was a small part of me that delighted in this. I felt untouchable. Like he could flip a table or she could do something unpredictable and I would just ignore them and continue to enjoy my boudin.

Solange returned to the table. "How is everything?" she asked Mom and Dad, but placed her hand on my shoulder.

Dad zeroed in on her hand.

Mom also zeroed in on her hand and she smiled. Mom set down her napkin, and she stood up to shake Solange's hand.

"I didn't want to embarrass Tenn, but I can't sit still anymore and act like I don't know you. I've heard so much about you and thank you so much for hiring him at the coffee shop."

"I haven't met your *friend*," Dad said with a sharp tone.

Before I could say anything, Solange flashed a warning look in Dad's direction. "Look, man. This is my last shift. Which means that today is not the day and I am not the one."

Oh, so this place didn't make the cut either.

"Are you getting an attitude with me?" Dad said, standing up and puffing out his chest. "I'm the customer. I'm dining in this restaurant. You are serving me."

Mom also stood, as did I.

"Aww, hell no." Solange took a deep breath. "I warned you once. Don't make me go Calliope on your white ass."

"I wish you would lay a hand on me. You'd be limping back to wherever you came from," he said.

"Where I came from?"

Mom grabbed Dad by the arm. "We're leaving. Now."

"No," he snarled. "If this *transvestite* wants to pick a fight with me . . . then I'm going to finish it."

Solange took a step toward Dad.

"He's not worth it!" I said, getting in front of her.

"Move outta my way Tennessee. I got a thing or two to show him about a *transvestite*."

"We'll leave," I said.

I saw Dad reach for his holster.

"I told you to leave that at home! Especially when you've been drinking!" Mom yelled.

Solange threw her head back. "I got one of those, too. Are you going to shoot me? Is that what you're going to do?"

"I don't want you around my son. Whatever you are . . . I don't want you around him."

"Shut the *fuck* up, you idiot!" I hissed.

Dad's entire face went purple. For a long while, he was dumb-stricken, staring at me open-mouthed. "What'd you say to me, boy?"

I was tired of being scared of him.

Tired of trying to fit into a box to please him.

"I said to shut the *fuck* up. You're ignorant and small-minded. And I'm not going to sit back while you insult my friend. She *should* kick your ass. And I bet she could, too, because you're just scared and pathetic without your gun. But you're not worth it."

He took a step back, looking at me like a wounded dog.

Mom smirked.

I turned to Solange. "I'm sorry about him. He's drunk."

Mom pulled out her checkbook. "How much will excuse my asshole of a husband?"

"I don't need your money, white lady," Solange said. "I got my own now."

I touched Solange's arm. "Writing checks is the only way she knows how to say sorry. You would offend her if you don't take it."

Solange eyed Mom suspiciously. "Really?"

"Yeah."

"Well, then, shit, you don't have to twist my arm."

Dad stormed off.

"Bye, Richard!" Mom sang after him as she kept writing her check.

Mom ripped the check out of her checkbook, folded it, and

handed it to Solânge. "You're a beautiful girl." And with that she left, every eye in the restaurant following her.

Solange opened the check and her eyes widened. "What in the . . . *five hundred dollars?*" She snickered. "I need to get in more fights with your redneck daddy, no offense."

"None taken, he's terrible." I smiled at Solange and gave her a quick hug.

⸻

I really pissed Dad off this time because he got in his truck and went right back to Oxford. I wasn't sure when he was coming back, and to be honest, I didn't care.

Now it was a new year. A new year where I had space and time to realize what I wanted and needed. It was finally time to choose myself.

"Mom?"

She was sitting on her bed with her typewriter.

"Hey, baby." Mom looked down at the bag in my hand. Her eyebrows dropped and she sat up. "Are you going somewhere?"

"Yeah . . . I'm going to stay with my friend Saint for a while."

"*What?* Sit down, talk to me. What happened? Why do you feel like you need to leave? Is it your daddy?"

"No. It's not him." I set down my bag. "Well, it is him . . . and it's you too."

"*Me?*" Mom latched onto my arm and pulled me closer to her. "I don't understand. Ever since I finished the story, I've been right here; we've been spending time together. And I thought it was a good time."

"I know, and it's been great." I smiled half-heartedly at her.

"It's been great, but it's only a matter of time before you leave again. When your agent gets back your edits, you'll go into another mode. And you'll be gone again."

"I won't."

"You will. It's what you do. And I'm not blaming you for it. When he returns, he'll hate me. . . ."

"He won't hate you."

"He will," I said, staring into her eyes. "I've never back-talked him before. I've never treated him that way. And I know he'll think I'm disrespectful."

"He was disrespectful! He almost took his gun out on that girl."

"I don't regret being disrespectful," I clarified. "I have let Dad get away with a lot, and to be honest, I let you get away with a lot, too."

She blinked.

I stood up. There were other things that I wanted to talk to her about. I wanted to talk about South Carolina. And ask her why she never visited me in the hospital. I wanted to talk about her leaving. I wanted to talk about all the times she caused a mess and left me to clean it up.

I don't think that I ever did anything my parents didn't do. But when I was too much, I got sent away. Put on medication. Fixed by someone else, because I was too much. And I finally realized I resented that.

"I'm my own person. I'm not you. I'm not Dad."

"We know," she said.

"Bye, Mom." For now, I would leave it at that. I stood up and walked toward the door.

"Tennessee," Mom said.

I paused but didn't turn to face Mom.

"You're seventeen. You can't just go off on your own."

"I don't see why not. I've been on my own since I got to New Orleans." I didn't mean to sound so harsh, but it was true. "I'll text you later. Bye, Mom."

"This is your room," Saint flipped on the light switch.

"Whoa . . ." I dropped my suitcase. The room was about the size of a street *block*. It was so big that it had multiple entrances to the balcony. This room appeared to be bigger than his room. "Saint, this is huge. I can't. When I asked you for a room, I meant like a closet or something."

"A *closet?*" He scoffed. "My best friend doesn't sleep in a closet! How long are you staying?" Saint asked.

"A couple of days, if that's okay with you?"

"Just a couple of days?" He wrinkled his nose. "I was hoping that you'd stay through Carnival season. I have an extravaganza every weekend up to Mardi Gras and there are all the balls. We can sit right here on the balcony and watch the parade come down."

"Woof, sounds like a lot."

"Darling, if it wasn't a lot, I wouldn't be in the business of doing it."

I walked over to the bed and sat down. I couldn't imagine staying away from my parents for that long. Despite their faults, I did love them. And I hoped this space would allow me to see things a little more clearly, and for them to also see things clearly.

At our best, we were a family who spent an entire day

building a train together. We stuck with it. We made it go. We laid down on pillows, while Mom spoke about her stories and Dad played with toy firetrucks with me on the floor. Ten years later, that was still one of my favorite days.

A greatest hit.

Saint joined me on the bed. "Have you heard from Jessamine, Tenn?"

"No, and I don't expect to, honestly." I smiled at him.

He scowled and wrapped an arm around me. "That sucks, 'cause I was rooting for y'all."

"At least you got your man, right?"

Saint removed his arm from around me. "Did I, though?"

"You see him still."

"I do, but seeing someone doesn't make them available. I'm about to dive into a me-me-me session, so if you got something else to say, you better speak now or forever hold your peace."

I laid down on the bed and kicked off my boots. I should've done that the second I entered. He had other things on his mind because he didn't say a word. "Holding my peace."

"Joel Xavier Monet." Saint sang his name. "He was never mine. When we're together, he's with me up until he isn't. At first, I thought it was internalized homophobia 'cause most of the Black men I date—and I use that term very loosely—struggle with it. But I don't think that is the *main* problem with us. I come from here and he comes from somewhere else. He doesn't want to be a part of this world. And because I'm a part of this world . . . he doesn't want me."

"Has he said that?" I asked.

"He's never had to, it's just something I've always known."

I reached for a pillow and rested my head; it felt heavier

than usual. "But he kissed you on Magazine. A notoriously private guy kissed you on one of the most public streets in New Orleans. That means something, right?"

He shrugged. "Everything means something if you're determined to find meaning in everything. Anyways, I want to talk about us for a second."

"Us?"

"Yeah." He smiled to himself. "I was talking to Mona the other day and she reminded me that you went to my ball. I didn't even show up for it, because I was chasing after Joel. But you were there. You've been the one consistent person. Through loneliness or boredom or whatever you want to call it."

"You've been consistent, too. You know I love you Saint, right?"

He cleared his throat. "The search is over. I am tired of trying to make people fit into my life. I got people who accept me how I am. People who always pick up when I call. People who just get me. Tennessee Williams, will you do me the honor of being the archduke to my Louis XVI forever and ever?"

I smiled. "What are my duties?"

"I'm so glad you asked. As the archduke, your only duty is to be you. My best friend through the boys *and girls*, the soirees and balls, the for better and the bestest. What do you say?"

"I say yes, Louis. Forever and always. Hey, where's that map? Let's do some more planning on our great American road trip."

47

JESSAMINE
A Few Days Before Mardi Gras

How can you be honest with someone else if you're not in a place to be honest with yourself?

In the movies, they wore glasses and jotted down notes while you spoke.

She was not a movie psychologist. She wore big hair. Natural and curly. Like mine. Minimal makeup. Her brown skin was flawless. And she dressed boho chic. Every garment flowed. Every bracelet jangled. And her pumps or tennis shoes (dependent on the day) were always a welcome surprise—because the color never matched what she was wearing.

"Whenever you're ready," she said.

I anxiously glanced toward the door. Iz was waiting for me. I knew that she was right outside. And that always made me want to run out to her, like a child who didn't want to go to school alone. Because this was new. This monumental scary thing. With scary people. And unknown discoveries about the world. Four sessions in, and I still wanted to run.

Ms. Berry watched me. Her eyes were not quite analyzing, but observant. She asked me about Katrina, what I remembered.

It took over four sessions to get there. We touched on her briefly in the first three sessions. But Ms. Berry stuck close to the corner I felt comfortable hugging. She asked me about Mama and Joel. Sometimes we spoke about Daddy. One of her icebreakers had been what colleges I got into (Arizona and LSU).

She said I still had time to decide which to accept, but she didn't understand that there were so many other factors involved. I never mentioned Tennessee. Ever. And I was convinced that I had done a good job keeping that part of my life sealed up.

"Katrina," I repeated as if she was a distant enemy I ran into a few times every now and then.

Ms. Berry nodded and repeated, "When you're ready."

I crossed my legs and uncrossed them. Ms. Berry looked down, noticing that shift. It was another observation and seemingly not an analyzation. "I don't remember much." I shrugged. "When the storm hit I was . . . I was five."

She tilted her head to the side. "It must have been hard."

I looked down.

"Do you remember how *she* felt?"

I looked up.

"That little girl who went through a hard thing? A thing that changed so many people's lives and took so much?" Ms. Berry leaned forward and crossed her legs. "Tell me about her, tell me about that girl."

I sighed, filling the room up with air. "I was afraid."

She nodded.

"I . . ." My chest got tight as I dug deeper to reach for that part of me. That part that used to only come up during nightmares, but then started to appear everywhere. "I guess what I remember the most is all the dying." I hitched my breath. It felt like I should cry. I had cried about it so many times before.

In class.

In the shower.

Most days after meeting Ms. Nadia, because she reminded me that college and scholarship applications meant saying good-bye to my security blanket.

Katrina was an old ghost. An unnamed thing that disguised herself as other sharp edges of knives. I swallowed.

"I didn't know what it meant for someone to die until . . . until Katrina. How still . . . the body goes. And I remember the eyes. They stare. No one closed them. Because there were too many eyes to close." I wrinkled my nose as I felt the heavy cloud, finally bringing the storm.

Daddy died in the attic.

It wasn't the water.

It wasn't the heat.

It wasn't the hurricane.

It was a heart attack.

And all my life, I needed to blame something, and that something was Katrina.

She took so much from me. My house. All the pictures of my family. My clothes.

Ms. Berry handed me a box of tissues.

I shook my head because I needed for once not to run. I needed to face this head on, and remember what it felt like when my daddy held my head above water as I paddled, trying to break me free of a panic attack. And that punch to the gut when I saw his heart give out on him.

There had been signs. His chest hurt. And he was sweating. All the textbook signs were there, but Mama and Daddy were too busy preparing for the storm, so maybe I could still blame her.

She blindfolded us.

Prevented us from seeing . . .

That we only had limited time to make memories.

48
JESSAMINE
Mardi Gras

THIS YEAR, I wasn't in the mood to see the floats. But Mama was, even though things had been tense since Joel told her the truth. She put down her swords for one day and drove down to St. Charles Avenue with us.

Solange, Joel, Iz, Mama, and I were all piled into one car. It was a hot mess. And to make matters worse, *Solange* was behind the wheel.

We camped out for Rex in the Central Business District, right by Gallier Hall. The spot was unfortunate, because every time I passed by Gallier, I thought about him. The writer who challenged me. The writer who loved me. My satsuma.

As the floats came down St. Charles, my family got into it. Even Mama. She yelled. "Hey! Hey! Throw me something, mister. Give me one of those glowing beads. Yes. That one."

And she got it.

I watched them, jumping up and down with their hands in the air. Beads by the dozen roped around their necks. They looked good. My people. Happy and healthy. *And together.*

Iz took a rope of beads from around her neck and handed it to me. "Your neck was looking a little sad."

"Gimmie that glow-up one you got," I told her.

Her eyes widened. "I fought off five people to get this one!"

"Show 'em what y'all can do, babies!" Mama said to the St. Aug band.

"They'll throw more like that," I told Iz.

"Not like this," she complained, but she gave it to me anyway.

I hugged her and gave her a kiss on the cheek.

Coming down St. Charles, I recognized a few familiar faces. Saint was on a float with his daddy, Claude Baptiste, and some other retired Saints players. They were throwing beads from the side of the float. People were cheering and screaming out their name.

But . . .

There was another person on the float.

A face I knew very well.

I held my breath.

Tennessee.

He was standing by Saint, throwing beads. Glowing like the sun. He reached into bags and threw plastic beads. Saint was throwing what looked like golden lottery tickets.

As the float drew nearer, I thought about running.

But I didn't. I glued my feet down to St. Charles Avenue.

He saw me. Tennessee paused, mid–football stance, his arm held behind his head, other arm positioned in front of him like he was going in for a tackle or a touchdown, whatever football play that would be. He dropped the beads he was holding. A group of people scrambled to get it, and he leaned over the float, smiling at me.

Smiling at me like I didn't run from him.

Like I didn't shoot myself in the foot.

"Ahhhh!" Iz screamed. "Romeo, Romeo, wherefore art thou Romeo?"

I ribbed her. She was right. Why did Tennessee have to be

Romeo? I refused to be Juliet! "I'm not drinking no poison for him."

"You don't have to drink poison, y'all are older and much wiser than Romeo and Juliet," Iz said.

There he was. After two whole months. Two long months.

Tennessee moved away from his position on the float, and he ran down to the door.

Saint yelled, "Stop the float, tell that driver to stop the tractor!"

The tractor stopped, and the next thing I knew, Tennessee had me by the hand.

"Bring all your people," he said, red-faced. "Iz, Solange! Is that your mama?"

"Yes," I said, flustered.

"Mama, you can come, too," he said.

"It's not even your float. You can't just be inviting people onto it," I stammered.

"Yes, he can!" Saint said from above.

Breathlessly, I looked to Joel, and his inconsistent ass about knocked us all down to get to Saint.

"What are y'all doing?" Mama asked, confused.

"We're riding in these folks' float," I said.

She told us to go on, and sure enough, Iz, Joel, and Solange went on. I saw Joel pull Saint into a hug. A hug that lingered way longer than I expected. When he pulled away from Saint, I could see that they were both smiling. Joel then leaned forward and kissed Saint right on the lips, in front of everyone. *Go, Joel!*

Once Mama and I were on the float, Tennessee reached in the bag and handed me beads. He also handed some to Mama.

She thanked him with a gracious smile and questioning eyes reserved for me.

"All you got to do is throw beads and watch out for the drunk people. Their coordination is all thrown off. I hit this one guy in the head and he was pissed!" he said.

I smiled. "That's typically what one does during Mardi Gras. Throw beads." He looked good. And he was wearing a smile that seemed so easy. "I'm sorry . . ." I started.

"Don't be." Tennessee assumed the position to throw a fistful of beads.

I did the same, and knocked an old lady in the head. The old lady dived down, basically toppling a child to get the beads that almost knocked her head off. "Sorry!" I hollered.

Tennessee chuckled. "Jess, you have to watch where you're throwing."

"Sorry!" I apologized again. The old woman didn't hear me. She was already on the hunt for more beads. She was probably a tourist.

He took the beads from my hand and said, "Like this, watch me."

I watched him rear back, square his feet, and throw, releasing the beads with ease. "I like to get the back. The underdogs who got here later or don't like to be in the thick of it deserve beads, too."

I exhaled. Now wasn't the time or place to say it. But I needed him to know, just in case we never got the opportunity to be this close again. "I missed that smile." That was probably the wrong thing to say.

Tennessee turned to me. "Hey."

"What?"

He gave me his hand. "It's nice to meet you."

"Huh?"

"I'm satsuma boy."

I grinned, big. And I took his hand. "Hi, Satsuma, I'm, um . . . *Jasmine*—no, today I'm feeling a little wild. So I'm Gertrude."

He laughed.

I stood on my tippy toes and hugged him tightly. "I know this is asking too much, and it's the last thing I probably deserve. Because I wasn't ready for you then and maybe I'm still not ready for you . . . but not having you in my life is harder than I thought I—"

He kissed me once.

I breathed in.

He kissed me twice.

I exhaled.

"Count to five," Tennessee said, cradling my face.

I circled my hands around his wrists. "One—"

"Look at me while you do it."

I looked at him. At the heart shape of his eyes. The warmth of his smile. The deep circles of his dimples. His red lips. And my heart felt so full when I realized that he was wearing the satsuma enamel pin. "One . . . two . . . three . . . four . . . five."

"I *still* love you," he said.

And there . . .

Right there . . .

I decided that it was time . . . time, to finally stay. Arizona wasn't home. New Orleans was home. And I was staying.

"I love you, too . . . my satsuma."